Praise For

Boy With Wings

"*Boy with Wings* is a brilliant fever dream of a novel, a haunting coming-of-age story reminiscent of both Franz Kafka and Charles Dickens. Depression-era America and the carnival life is rendered vividly, but so is the beauty and courage of, yes, a boy with wings."

—Chris Bohjalian, author of *The Jackal's Mistress*

"A weird and wonderful tale, full of mystics, magic, and deep tenderness. *Boy with Wings* is vibrant and alive, the kind of book where the blood pumps mightily, truly all heart. It's fabulous."

—Kristen Arnett, author of *Stop Me If You've Heard This One* and *Mostly Dead Things*

"The human spirit is hard to break. Mark Mustian's *Boy with Wings* demonstrates the possibility of love and hope in the face of unimaginable hardships. A rich and powerful novel. Highly recommended."

—Jeff VanderMeer, author of *Annihilation* and *Absolution*

"Mark Mustian writes with the crisp, sharp, hard-hitting economy of a seasoned fighter. And combine that with the desperation, the gnawing, the fierce and loyal love of a great tale, and *Boy with Wings* delivers a knockout."

—Michael Farris Smith, author of *Salvage This World* and *Desperation Road*

"In this propulsive tale of the magic lurking inside our mortality, Mark Mustian has conjured a surreal hero. Here is a translucent rendering of boyhood and aberration, of the fault lines of race and the frailty of religion. In sentences that are equally primal and poetic, Mustian transports us through the shacks, camps, circuses, and back alleys of the Depression-era South, asking a still-resonant question: What's the price of belonging in a society that's already broken?"

—Katy Simpson Smith, author of *The Everlasting*

"A magical, highly imaginative tour de force. . . . Boldly original and unexpectedly profound."

—Readers' Favorite Reviews

"Mustian's story is a study in acceptance, diversity, kindness, and the possibility of marvels in life. . . . Vibrant with discovery, *Boy with Wings* is a winner."

—*Midwest Book Review*

"Riveting. . . . An evocative historical novel that celebrates distinctive individuals in the Depression-era South."

—Foreword Reviews

"In this imaginative novel filled with magical realism, religion and morality are turned inside out and upside down."

—Southern Literary Review

Praise For

The Gendarme

"Novelist Mustian writes relentlessly, telling [Ahmet's] haunting story in brief bursts of luminous yet entirely unsentimental prose and reminding us that, when life gets bloody, we had better watch out for our own humanity."

—*Library Journal* starred review

"Every decade or so, I find a novel that I sense, just by reading the basic description, will become unforgettable; after reading only twenty pages of *The Gendarme*, my impression was confirmed with great force. For this decade, and this reader, *The Gendarme* is that extraordinary, unforgettable novel."

—BookPage

Boy With Wings
by Mark Mustian

© Copyright 2025 Mark Mustian

979-8-88824-427-2

All rights reserved. No part of this publication may be reproduced, stored in a retrieval system, or transmitted in any form or by any means—electronic, mechanical, photocopy, recording, or any other—except for brief quotations in printed reviews, without the prior written permission of the author.

This is a work of fiction. All the characters in this book are fictitious, and any resemblance to actual persons, living or dead, is purely coincidental. The names, incidents, dialogue, and opinions expressed are products of the author's imagination and are not to be construed as real.

Cover design by Suzanne Bradshaw.

Published by

köehlerbooks™

3705 Shore Drive
Virginia Beach, VA 23455
800-435-4811
www.koehlerbooks.com

BOY
WITH
WINGS

Mark Mustian

VIRGINIA BEACH
CAPE CHARLES

For Eva K.

And, in the isolation of the sky,
At evening, casual flocks of pigeons make
Ambiguous undulations as they sink,
Downward to darkness, on extended wings.

From "Sunday Morning"
Wallace Stevens

PART I: 1926

CHAPTER ONE

Dark, and some close things. The smell of cut boards and dirt. His hands meet walls, his arms and head and knees, his feet. It's a box more than walls, pinning and cramping him so that he can't turn or stretch. He bucks and squirms—though she hates his squirming—his back twitching and sweat running, and when he yells his voice springs like a twig slapping at his face and neck. A blankety thing wraps his legs.

He pushes out and up, down, kicks his feet. She warned him, he remembers: to be still and quiet, to sleep and to hide. Wasn't he a smart boy, a good son, the best hider? He lies flat—is he hiding? He lifts again and bumps his head. It'd take time, she said, again and again, before. Her voice was curvy. "You must wait, wait for me to come back and the men to help then." He hates to wait, though, and his cries settle down on him, bouncing off the wood like beneath her old bed, the hardness below him, the darkness so deep. He wants his things now. He wants her back! He wants to hear laughing or barking or anything else. But he's stuck in this cramped and strange quiet. Alone.

At night at home, he can see things around him, shapes made of the floor and of the covered bed, but here he can't seem to. Did he lose his eyes? Goose bumps—that's what she calls them—swell up, something hard in his throat, too, and though he tries to hold it, he pees. The awful warmth comes and the smell soon behind it, and he hears things now or thinks them, whispered things like songs or words.

She held him and rocked him before the cloth wrapped his face, and when he slept, he dreamed bird dreams, of darting and pecking and flapping and swooping, feathers up, feet down, claws out. Sparks flash when his eyes shut. "Be brave," she whispered. "Be calm when you wake. I will come and get you, release you. Stay quiet and still."

Still. "Why?" This was shushed, finger to lips. Grown-ups do this. He is six. He makes lists of the things he knows: that he lives in Florida, before that in Alabama. That the car they rode in once was a Model Z. Or was it P? (He mixes his letters up.) That butterflies are first bugs. That the sun comes up and stars come out and men can touch wires on a box and make it sing. He knows that eggs are laid and will break, that in the sky there is heaven. He knows of mothers and fathers. He doesn't know why he can't move or see.

He cries or he thinks he does, his face and neck wet with it, and her crying comes too, from before: the sound past the doorway, the talk coming through that he knew was of him. A new voice—Mr. Paul, who owns the house, or maybe Mr. Tom—his words of noses or hoses, of being able to breathe, of how this trick would be made to work. (Necessity. What is necessity? Maybe a secret or a made-up word.) They talked about him this way, whispers that jumped like winged beetles or rabbits, and there was the time the man stared down at his back.

"Devil." The word whistled.

"It's just a mark. Lots of people have them. It's nothing." Her voice with bright lines. He's looked at his back in the mirror or tried to, the purple splotch forming a hill or a springy knife. It doesn't hurt and he can't touch or reach it, and he thought that everyone had one until he found out they don't. He asked his mother about it.

"Don't worry." Her face frowny-small.

Mr. Tom spoke some more, his yellow hair shining, not white like the boy's but close. "You'll have to do something, Lena. You'll have to go. Them people down at the church, they ain't gonna . . . The word's out. It's, well, it's just they *believe* this is . . . ! I even heard it at the jook joint when I took things out that way. You know—"

"I'm sick just now, Tom." Her low voice, the one that's like clouds or mud. "I can't run just yet. It ain't nothing with Johnny, nothing bad! People gotta accept it. And you, telling me this. You're believin' it too, are ya?"

"I'm just sayin' what I heard. Pastor Mills called it—said that mark could cast a pall, that the whole . . . Kids have died. Why, they'll burn . . ."

Voices rise, high ones like children, and he listens but they go away. They could be near or far, and maybe he knows them, though he knows almost no one. They've moved a lot, and at his few times at school, the others laughed or turned away from him. Or called him names: "Ogre!" "Freak!" He had to ask her what these meant. Some wanted to touch his hair, even one of the teachers, Mrs. Wickham, rubbing her hand through it, brushing and lifting his shirt. "I've never seen anything like . . . Your eyes are like emeralds. Are you an albino?" A rhino? He shook his head.

Others asked of his powers—other children, some adults. "We heard you have powers," they would say, their faces scrunched. He fell from a cupboard the one time he tried to fly. He's not strong like the soldiers in the picture books she brings home. He can't spit far or whistle or jump high or even swim. So he asked her. She answered calmly, in her softest voice: "You are yourself only. Don't worry on what others think. You'll do more when you're older." But if he were older, he'd break the box, lift the boards off like his toys, and toss them up and far away, and he'd have powers then, like a bird that gets bigger and flies. Maybe. Sometime, when he's older. Or after a while, or maybe not. He doesn't know.

He cries again, loudly. She won't like him crying. He has friends, pretend friends, Robert and Buster, and for a time they talk. He asks what they are doing (Buster: listening to the radio; Robert: playing with his toys) and tells them of the darkness, his hiding, and the box, at least until he grows tired. They don't care that he peed.

He won't be . . .

He won't let . . .

He won't stay . . .

He tries to hear more but he can't, his breath loud, and he screams some, gasping for air until his throat feels raw and red, banging his arms and feet till they're numb. It's as if he's under the water in the tin soaking tub, everything pressed around him and squeezing, making things blurry, the sound soft then gone, and how could she leave him, alone here in this cage?

He was cold before but is hot and things stink, and maybe he sleeps or dreams. He knows that things die and maybe now he'll die too, and he bangs on the box again, pushing each side of it. A spray of dirt washes in that he flicks his tongue at and breathes. His coughs rise the way hers do, a crumpled tail to them, and when he closes his eyes this time the dots fade, smoothed to thin ribbons, black and forgotten like something from long before. From far off a clink comes, voices again in the dirt and the dark, and he trusts and believes none of it, calmed now by the darkness, the closeness, until something heavy strikes the box. There's a tilting and scraping, the low sound of grunts and the hiss of breath blown. He stays still as she told him, waiting and not waiting, and when the top is ripped open in a flash of light, he is quiet still, cooled, saved. Seen.

Revealed.

CHAPTER TWO

Lena

Run, stumble, scurry. Stagger, skid, plunge and fall. What day of my life have I not spent in running, in dodging and hiding, seeking my own selfish, mean escape? First from my father and his fury and drinking, the madness that followed of my bland, burdened ma, the city and heartache and finally to this battered house. Running: from sickness but also from myself, from landlords and lawyers, innocence and prayers, from weather and hunger and anger and the blinding dark. From the people who want to find J and kill him, to take him from me forever, my reason to live gone. My only son.

I've tried telling J and explaining, offering up my glum regrets, and it could be that I'm muddled or loony. Maybe flat insane. I've sought to hide and to guard him, to assure him of my love up and through my life's end, but does he understand this? With him it can be hard to gauge. From the day he was born he's been tricky. Even the old midwife gave a "huh" when he dropped, spurting out of me in a rush of skin and blood. It wasn't just the birthmark or the shock of white hair but the way he looked at things when his eyes finally opened, the way he smelled like wet grass, iron, and clay. He never cried or cooed much, never nursed. His eyes were blue before they became green as leaves. He talked and ran when it appeared that he ought to, and he wasn't creepy or spooky, just distant and dreamy, distinctive. Unique. All mothers may claim this, but I had no one to relay these things to, no one to question or match up with or compare. J grew and was happy—isn't he happy still? We've survived. We are a team formed and shaped, joined and merged and still living. Life is a strangeness we struggle through every day.

The midwife must have said something. How else could the word have spread? People coming to watch him and touch him, coworkers and neighbors I had never seen or met. At this point I lived in Eastpoint farther down the coast, shucking at an oyster house after I left Tallahassee pregnant. Shucking was a brutal and nasty job. All the heat and salt and stink of those creatures, all day on my feet, but it was work and money we needed to buy food. I'd cleaned houses in Tally, which is where I met Doyle, where I first let my fantasies get in the way of any normal life. Who would have thought it—a junior high grad tied to a lawyer with a wife and kids? I suppose I was pretty then, still am in a wretched way, still prone to get looks if not approaches from crazy men. I thought to tell him I was pregnant but then never did so, and when he found out it went as poorly as I figured it would. The last time I saw him he wanted me to drink some vile something, and when I wouldn't, he forced me. Thank the Lord it didn't take. I went to Tennessee, to Charleston, and back to north Florida, never asking for nothing, wanting to make it for me and J on my own.

The thought of Doyle's face now sets my head near-on flaming, my breath rushing in and out. He's running for council or office; I saw a sign with his name big when I rode down Highway 12. I want to ask or to warn people, to tell of his slyness and lies, but I don't talk much now to no one. I don't seek out trouble, dig in the past, or even read the weeklies for the death notes there and news.

Staring at J now, I touch his stubbled head. I've cut his hair short to hide its strangeness in case anyone sees him, which they shouldn't, as he's dead. He stays in the cupboard we've built and holed out for him, and I play the grieving mother, which ain't hard to do. I sigh and cough so much that I can barely stand up straight, to where they've threatened to fire me at the bait store where I work, though I think Mr. Williams feels pity or something smutty toward me. I keep the stock tidy and balance mixed-up receipts, at least when I'm not chasing off thieves, bums, and giant rats. At night J and I go over his letters and numbers, and he writes things, he spells and reads. As soon as I'm well, we're gonna leave this sad place, go north and start over—run and do sidesteps and hide out somewhere else. I know about starting over.

"I have dreams, Momma."

This worry plagues me—of what the death ploy could have done, of the odds that existed then of his being truly harmed. How could a mother put her child through such strain? It was so mad and so risky, though they swore it was a parlor trick and the whole thing completely safe. I'd felt like a mouse in a trap, what with word getting around and people talking about him, seeking him out. Asking and threatening. Wanting me to show them his back, which I wouldn't.

"Everybody has dreams, son," I say, and it's true. Mine are mostly of searching and running, of hiding and capture. Grief building to collapse. I rarely sleep.

"Will you die?" he asks, his face jumpy and squinty.

"I will. You will too. Everyone, one day."

He pauses. "When?"

I smile-shrug and cup my hand around my eyes, as if peering far into the murk of the advancing wet fog. The house sits on a pond that stinks all year except in winter, and I wonder if my coughs make him fret. I wonder what it is that children know and truly feel. I've got to get healthy, or at least well enough to run, as the days will soon shorten here into rain and cold, the shack damp inside and never quite warm enough, wind sneaking in like a thief. J stares out too, into the trees that stand like soldiers, the pines waiting on orders to charge forth or retreat. I try to see into his thinking but can't, his mind as he grows so much more his own. As for myself, I fear that I'm sinking backward, to girlhood and childhood and on to my birth and the darkness before. Like a prophet or child, I feel danger creeping: a fox searching and skulking as we sit blind as to what will come.

His head tilts and wags. He's used to folk wanting to see him, to the dodging and hiding and moving and claims, the lack of any fixed home, and blame for this falls to me: a guilt I could push further back but I won't. I have dreams where he's taken, where he's killed by plan or neglect or merely chance, where he leaves me mistakenly or of his own furious accord. Awake, I see him grown: a banker or lawyer or some government boss like his pa, and he senses this somehow and puts a hand to his head, frowns in a clown face and asks:

"Who is he, my papa?"

I snort out my laugh. I want to say that if his pa even knew of him, there'd be pain—that if he knew of his . . . difference, there'd be worse. "He's a man."

"Is he alive?" So many questions, so few truths and signs. Mosquitoes buzz, constant.

"I think so."

"Can I see him?"

"I don't think that'd be wise. Let's talk of other things." I touch his back without planning to, jolting and tensing him, his head lifted up and about like a bird's. His eyes are his father's then, accusing and ravenous, and have I supplied him my rage in return? A single lasting, draining gift? When the preacher ripped his shirt off and pronounced him a devil, J only stared up in wonderment. The tantrums and tempers came later, over days and many stormy months. I seethed for us both when others warned me that they'd kill him, that when a little girl down the road got sick, he'd be blamed, and he was. We never discussed this; he never asked, but it could be that he heard it, hard as it is to keep secrets in tiny burrows and two-room shacks. The word came, more than once, that their plan was to burn us.

The death-faking scheme wasn't mine. They claimed there was no choice, that it was for the boy's sake, that nothing else could stave off this harm. Only two people know of it: Tom, who built the box and dug the rigged grave, and Paul, my sometimes lover. They're brothers: the Rowans. Tom had done this in a show. I don't imagine they'll snitch, but as I think on it now, do I wholly know this? It brings forth the terror from when the deed was finally done, the worry then of whether the ruse and lie after would work, the faith required in it, the fear and crippling shame. It should have been me in that box! I say this over and over and over to myself, a hymn sung or promise. I prayed enough to hurt my head. The relief on its opening brought me sobbing to my knees—him sweat- and piss-stained, big-eyed and silent—and I swore to myself after that we would never part for long again. J has been quiet and mopey ever since, stuck in his closet and indoors all the time, unable to run around and play in fresh air. It's unnatural, I know it; I hate it, but he's alive. But for what we did, I don't know that I could make that claim.

A car purrs outside, its tires swishing like insects. Paul? I motion J to his cupboard, which he enters with a duck and frown. I think to freshen myself or at least brush my hair, but steps come with a knock that strikes a coldness inside me. Paul or Tom wouldn't stop and knock. I cough my way to the door, the floor tilting so that I must hang on to the wall to stay upright, the grooves worn there, the rot and stains. There's a space between boards we've stuffed with socks to block snakes. I peer out at a tall man, a stranger. I crack the door.

"What is it?"

The man holds a hat in one hand. The other hand, and his arm up to the shoulder, is gone, the light falling strangely around him, slanted somehow and made shiny, bright. He's taller than me by at least a foot, thin-mouthed and staring like a bird looking past its beak. I think of the preacher, but this isn't a preacher, no collar or cross or speck of kindness to be seen. The preacher put his hands on me at the burial, my tears drained away then, my questions boiling up unasked: *What is God to be more than this love? Is a miracle to you one to me? Who is it that gauges sin?* I hate preachers, you see—hate them every one.

"You Lena?"

I squint. I haven't seen him before, and I'd remember a man with no arm. He isn't one of the neighbors. I don't open the door.

"May I come in?"

"What do you want?" The chill works to my spine, across to my chest. I draw back.

"I'm from Tallahassee." He smiles or tries to, but it comes off as hurtful. His eyes are as gray as a cat's. "I'm a friend of your friend." He nods at the door again. "Please."

I make no move to open it. "Friend?"

He pushes past, not rough but quick enough to get by me, creaking the floorboards in the pitched and beaten shack. He spins around. "I hear you got a son. Johnny."

I'm unable to speak. Then: "I did." I swallow. Sniff. "He's dead now."

The man turns back, eyebrow raised. "Hhmm. That so?"

I'm struck dumb, unable to blink or to breathe. What if J makes a sound? He's done that before, and the walls here are so thin—he's only six years old. Seven.

"When did that happen?"

I sigh. "A month back." My legs bend and I sway with it.

"What did he die of?"

"Same thing I got." I cough to show him, long and with hills and bumps. He takes a step back then.

"He buried here?"

I nod. Tears form and fall in plops. I hear scuffling from the cupboard or twitching or breathing, and surely the man hears this too. I sniff the tears back.

"Where?"

"Back of the church down the road. The graveyard."

"I'll stop by." His eyes take in the walls, the small room, the scuffed and bulging cupboard. He pushes the room's only door, his body slanted without the one arm, looks at the bed there, the clothes scattered. "I'm sorry," he says. But he doesn't sound it.

Another coughing spree spirals, long and with color. I notice a toy, a tiny train, left on the floor as if spun off its rails, misplaced there and glinting.

The man seems to stare at it. "You take care, now, okay?"

"I will." I shift and murmur, cough. I want to dance and wave my hands at him, distract from the rest.

"You know," he says, turning, "we heard he was . . . special. That so?"

I look up at this man who wants to take something from me, something vital and heavy and much more than his missing arm. The thought comes to hurl punches or insults or slit his throat. "Course he was. Special as the moon and stars." I should shout this up at him, flinging my anger through his nose and to his brain, but instead my voice is soft, still and emptied, cold. I would give up my life. "He was my son."

The car door slams, the motor snorts like a dragon, the tires swish again in the grass.

My back heaves and tears slide down my throat. I cough brownish clots into a crumpled and gritty rag.

CHAPTER THREE

They leave the house on a Saturday. Her coughs have grown worse, but she says that they have to go now. She tells him to pack his things up in a box, his color crayons and books, and he does, though he hates boxes. She puts other stuff in the crate she calls a valise, warning him to keep his head low till they're past the town. Mr. Paul gives them a ride, the three of them up front and their things behind them, and they board a boat to cross the big river—he can barely see the other side! Then an automobile; it's the boy's second time traveling in a motor car. The weeds and sticks on the roadside flash and blur as they pass, and he waves at a girl walking, but she doesn't wave back.

The car's engine sounds like the wind pulled through the house, sometimes louder or softer or chuggier, the air cooled and pulling at his head. He doesn't know where they're going or how long they'll be gone, but he wants to go faster, to smear things and dizzy them, to reach out and touch the sky, the sand, the trees, the sun.

He sits between the two of them, but it's her touch he feels the most. She has grown thin, white lines scattered now in her hair, and when she coughs her neck can become red and splotchy afterward. Sometimes she can't seem to gulp in any breath. Mr. Tom asked her before they left: "Lena, what'll you do?" but she didn't answer, saying only that they must leave and soon. He can smell her, if he thinks on it, and smell Mr. Paul sometimes too: his being more of an oily-type odor, his breath blackish, salty, and sour-sharp. Mr. Paul smokes cigarettes he rolls up with one hand, and often the tobacco gets caught in his mouth, little skins hanging there that he spits out in a rush. The boy likes to watch him smoke, his breath making the end red and the straight cloud from his mouth, and it smells good unless the wind blows it back on them. His mother once yelled when she saw Johnny pretending to smoke.

"How much ya got?" Mr. Paul asks, looking down the car seat. They're nearer to the ocean, the salt smell crisp and strong. The boy looks for waves but can't see them. The sun has gone high and hot.

"Not enough. But we'll manage."

He reaches into a pocket, causing the car to swerve. Holds some bills out. "Take 'em."

She waits but then does so. Another cough splurts, one of her bad ones, her eyes watering and face pinched like she needs to spit something awful out.

"Jeez, Lena."

"I know, I know. It'll get better."

The boy has heard this. He hears more than she thinks he does, even from before the dirt box—but he tries not to go back to it: the warning of others coming and threats made in turn, the claim that this danger was due only to *him*. Then the man with one arm, looking and wanting to know all these things. Who was the "friend"? He wanted to ask her but knew she wouldn't say. She'd say that boys should be quiet, listen up good, and not ask fool questions. He always has lots of questions. He bites his lip some to keep from asking more. He reaches out now and takes hold of her knobby hand.

The car hits a bump, and his back rubs on the seat. He twists at this bouncing, an itch there with a burn to it, but she has warned against scratching, and he makes himself still. If he rubs it on something, he feels a squishy lump, and when he asked her, she sighed and said he was born with this thing, that it was okay, that he shouldn't worry much. Then would say nothing more. He's not to mention it to anyone or to pick at or scrape it, as that could make it hurt or get bigger or spawn something somehow worse. Instead, he sits up and starts on his counting, as he likes to group and count out different things. He likes to read, too, and hopes there'll be lots of books where they're going. He's read the ones he has now and knows all their words. She's told him of libraries—buildings holding nothing but hundreds and thousands of books—and he hopes they will see one; maybe they'll see one! Things could be different now, better. They're going on to somewhere new.

"What's your plan?" Mr. Paul taps the steering wheel.

She shrugs. "We'll figure things out."

"We gon' meet again?"

A pause. "I don't know, Paul. I . . . I don't know what'll happen. I got to watch out for the boy here, okay?"

The man squeezes him once on his knee. Mr. Paul reminds him of a preacher—like the one who had stared at him, his voice ringing out and loud—maybe due to his size or shape or his firmness about things, or the way he uses his words. His mother said Mr. Paul was in a circus once, that he had done things like magic tricks, but Mr. Paul looked away when the boy asked him to do one.

Johnny knows about preachers, about Jesus and God and angels and the Word, despite having never been taught this and never going to any church. He had a storybook once—about Noah and the ark, David and Goliath, Daniel with the lions—that he liked to look through, though at some point not long back the book disappeared. He asked his ma about this, even cried over it more than once, but she said she didn't know where it might have gotten off to. When he asked her about devils, she told him to forget he ever heard that word, to never mention it to her or to anybody else again. Which he hasn't, though he hasn't forgotten it. The preacher's voice had shaken like a branch when he said it, like somebody had pushed him and the words bubbled and broke or leaked.

They see the water now, bright like a bluer sky, and the boy cranes his neck to look, still with his hand in hers. The white gull-birds dive and screech, the smell of the salt grown even stronger, like trainloads of the stuff have been dumped out into the air. At spots the sand piles up high, shaped by the wind or by some giant's hand, and he sees himself running and jumping upon these, landing in softness and springing back up again. The sand covers the road in places, the car swerving and tipping them about like a top as it steers around it, and he wants to do this forever, to ride and sway with the sun beaming and wind rushing, but when he looks up at her he sees that her lips are white and firm. She stares not at the water or sand but instead straight ahead of them, at the road twisting and entering the shade of stretching trees, its curves like a big squiggly snake. She brings a cloth to her face and turns almost away from him, as if she doesn't want to be seen, like she wants to become small and masked and invisible. He ducks his head then, as he knows this and thinks this. He wants sometimes to hide like a spooked turtle in its shell.

They cross a long bridge of a type he has never seen. He tries to count the things it stands on—gray posts like poles or blocks—but the car is moving too fast. A cloud forms above them, white and fluffy and sometimes covering the sun, so that they seem to drive through big clumps and dots of cloud-shadow down below it. More cars are out now, slowing them and passing by, and occasionally people will look or wave. Buildings take shape: a filling station; a diner; another building that has no door or sign. A few houses as well, farther back with sand driveways, their roofs stained orange and chocolate brown. Then more woods, more houses. They're away now from the beach. An old truck pulls in front of them, hauling what might be pillows or chickens, white feathers spreading behind it like dust. Mr. Paul slows, then goes around this, the boy watching the man's feet work, the one hand on the lever, the car groaning and humming as he shifts the gears.

"Lena, what if I was to come with—"

"No, Paul." Her voice is firm. "We'll be okay. I'll write to you when we get there."

"Write . . ."

"Well, I will."

"And from where?"

A pause. "I got kin in Tennessee. We've been through this, haven't we? After the boy and I get set up, why, you can pay us a call!"

Her words end on a fibbing high note. Nobody says much after, not until the man pulls into a dusty lot and the boy sees the train tracks, the train behind a building with people standing and walking before it, parts of the cars black and parts painted red. His heart catches and breath lifts—the motor car first and a train ride yet to come? She hadn't told him, he hadn't imagined it, and this must be the happiest, very best day of his life! His joy is a thing so real he can touch it, like a cake or a book or a furry dog. He looks for the engine and caboose but sees neither, the train stretching away in a long, narrow, magic curve. The air is so thick that it becomes dark and hard to see, and she holds the cloth to her mouth again but this time doesn't cough. A man wearing a straw hat scratches his head underneath it. A horn toot-toots somewhere, a woman straightens a man's shiny tie. Another man cries out, his voice high, "Well, I'll be!"

"Lena."

"Hush." She loops an arm up and kisses Mr. Paul's gray mouth, their faces turned into one for a moment, and the boy looks away from this quick and mucky joining. He wants to run around, to see the train up close and study it, to touch things and hear things and know them and find out more. She takes his hand back, though. Her hand is warm. Plucking a cloth cap from her bag, she places it on his head with a pull and tug, back to front, pressing it down against his hair.

"So you look like a fine young traveler," she says, a little smile on her lips. Mr. Paul grabs their things. The boy sees no children, no one to play with and share in this thing of wonder, only men in suits and women in dresses and one lady with an umbrella and what looks like a tiny dog. His friends Robert and Buster—he's the round one—don't have much to say, only "Wow!" and "Great!" and "Will it go now very fast?" He pulls at the cap as they walk up to the building, straining at his mother's arm, wanting to get there quicker, to run and *see*, and at this she turns and offers up a tiny laugh. Dents form in her cheeks, something he's never seen or maybe has seen and forgotten, and could he have forgotten this? It's another question.

She holds his hand yet as she stands in line before a window, behind a man in a hat who talks loudly to someone else. It's hot now and the boy sweats, stains forming under the arms of her dress too, and even Mr. Paul wipes once at his dark and bristly face. The boy takes the cap off to scratch at his head, but she pulls it back, her face hard now, and he sighs. "Sorry." He puffs his cheeks. The train blows and he jumps—is it moving and leaving them? Her hand pulls his up, her lips and voice near, her easy and steamy breath on him. "It's okay. We'll be on it and we'll have our things. It won't leave without us. Don't you worry yourself about it none."

She speaks to the window man but the boy isn't listening, as he's spotted another youth, maybe a year or two older, also wearing a tilted cap. This boy eyes him as well, their gazes locked as if in some plan or understanding, an exploring or game or contest or target, until something in his mother's voice pulls him back.

"Well, I didn't think . . ."

The man behind the window nods, talking through a small hole above another space at its bottom. The man is explaining something that the boy doesn't understand.

"But isn't it—"

"Here." Mr. Paul pushes some money up, and in a rush, she takes it, snaking it under the window. The man behind smiles and she quickly smiles back, turning to Mr. Paul but with something long in her face. The boy can't quite be sure of it. Money and pieces of paper return under the window, and she gives the money to Mr. Paul, who clears his throat and says softly, "Keep it."

"Paul, I can't . . ." She pulls her hand away, and at his release the boy makes for the train. It's not as shiny as he thought but much bigger and louder, with people standing inside of one part and a smell strong of smoke and sawdust and something else. A man in a uniform brushes some stairs with a little broom. His skin is dark—a Negro, the boy knows. He wants to reach out and touch the man's cap and hair.

"Hey."

It's the other youth calling. Red hair peeks from the cap's front edge, his face covered in freckles, some stretched into brownish lines.

"How far you goin'?"

Johnny turns and shrugs.

"We're going to Chicago. We change in Birmingham." The other youth's eyebrows bend, as if this change will be long and difficult. "You got any candy?"

The boy shakes his head.

"What's your name? Mine's Jeremy."

The boy goes unheard as a heavy woman with a cross at her neck calls out to Jeremy in a thunderous, disapproving voice. His own mother grabs his hand.

"Don't run off from me, hear? You have to stay with me, stay right by my side."

The boy looks for Mr. Paul, but he's nowhere to be seen. They sit on a bench with some other travelers, waiting for something—a whistle? a sign? The air smells of dust and sweat and perfume. Twirling his feet, he tries to watch it all: the sky, the people, Jeremy and his mother, the lady with the dog, the cars parked, the trees in the distance, and, of course, the train. It stretches past the building like a chained and waiting monster, two cars with windows and then others with different shapes, the engine beyond them blowing smoke from its top. The wheels are too small, he thinks, too much like toys—they look as if they could come off if someone kicked them hard. The cars with the windows are the ones painted red, some of it faded and peeling. A moth lands on the dog's head and he spins and bats at it.

Finally, a man's voice tells them to board. Some people go one way, some another, and the boy is unsure which car to move to, but she knows and he follows. The first car has curtains hung in its windows, and some of the men and the lady with the dog enter here. His mother leads him to the second car, climbing worn steps inside, where hard seats set in rows are faced one way, the windows open. They enter a row and sit, staring at the door at the end in front of them, the boy turning to look behind him too. His back burns and itches. Jeremy and his mother take seats in front of them.

A man sits near, takes his hat off and wipes his face, his hair with a dark ring on it. The boy's mother coughs, and the man looks behind him, puts his hat on, sighs. At her second cough he switches seats. Jeremy looks and smirks, whispering something to his mother, and she turns to look too but neither smiles nor nods. One of the men with a uniform walks past, hands in his pockets, and the train lurches and hisses but does nothing more. Smoke blows in through a window, its smell somehow different from the fire at home, curling blue around them even as Johnny waves it off. The man who switched seats lights a cigar with a red-tipped match. A whistle comes at last and again the train shudders, something below them groaning and popping with several clicks. With a jolt they move forward.

He wants to move too. Can he sit by the window? His mother shrugs and they change their seats. Outside there is little to see yet, another train sitting alongside them, a door clanging somewhere, the crying sound of metal scrapes. People laughing and talking and the clink-clink of glass and plate. They pass the other train to find trees grouped beyond it, a burst of cooler air, and a sweet smell that seems familiar—he can't decide why or from what. His mother sighs beside him as if she recalls something as well, but her sigh is broken by a cough that becomes several, and she dips her head as if to bury these in the seat beneath. Her entire body shakes, her head and neck, legs, and again people look: Jeremy and his mother, the man who switched seats, an older man and woman sitting a few rows farther up.

After a time, a soft boredom settles; he tries counting the trees but this makes him dizzy. He drinks the air in as if water and whispers to her of his thirst, but she shakes her head back at him, saying they will get something soon, that there's another car behind them—her words cut off by a long clearing of her throat. An older man in a uniform enters the car and begins asking for something. Passengers reach for purses or billfolds and produce paper of some sort. Several of the passengers speak and glance back at the two of them, the uniformed man turning and looking quietly on. Jeremy's mother almost points in their direction. The man's face is crinkly, a white mustache making his lips seem extra thick. He looks neither friendly nor mean. The boy looks for a holster or a gun at his waist.

When he reaches their seat, his mother holds out a paper, but the man waves it away. She coughs quickly, shortly.

"Honey, you're sick, aren't you?"

She doesn't respond at first. "I'm . . . I'm fine. It's just a cold."

"You got the consumption, don't you?" The mustache lifts up and down. "You can't ride. You'll have to get off at the next stop."

Her voice rises. "I'm fine! I paid for this ticket—"

"Talk to the stationmaster there. You can't endanger the other passengers."

The others look or try not to, necks bowed and listening. He keeps his head down too.

"I can't believe . . ." his mother says, but this is cut off in coughing, the cloth produced like a shield or a wand or flag. She begins a soft crying.

"I'm sorry," the man says. "I truly am. Next stop is Wewa." He moves past.

The boy whispers to her but she waves her free hand, her face splotched and breath fast. Jeremy's mother nudges him back forward, the hair beneath his cap like straw stuck there by birds. Sounds fall like rocks thrown or crow calls, like claps or rings or fuzzy hums. When the train stops a few minutes later, the old man comes back, this time accompanied by one of the Negroes. They nod without speaking, faces heavy, lips held in line, and the boy and his mother stand to leave as if prisoners. She scoops their things up. He scuffs his shoes.

No one looks as they follow the men to the exit, with the exception of Jeremy, who flashes what the boy's mother would call a spiteful little grin. Johnny manages to pause and break wind as they pass him.

CHAPTER FOUR

The platform is small here, boards near the tracks and a short building next to them, the word "Wewahitchka" painted in white letters across its top. He tries to sound this word out, the letters bent on his tongue, his voice high and odd-sounding. There is only the one structure, pine trees and the rail lines running past it like a belt. A lizard glances up at them in the sun, quivers and blinks, puffs its neck out in a purple fan. The heat prompts a look for shade but there's none. His mother strides to the building and pulls open the wooden door.

He waits outside, the wood with a sweet smell and warm to his touch, the lizard gone now into hiding. Crickets screech despite it still being morning, maybe noon now of the same cloudy, lengthy day. A dragonfly buzzes until it lands near the tracks, buzzes again when it lifts at his slow approach. Pine needles hang like brooms upside down, one tree leaning into another's long and waiting limbs. His thirst has grown and become hunger too, and maybe there's food in her bag that he tries not to think of. Chewing his lip, he makes marks with his shoes.

The sun brightens the tracks so that he almost can't look at them, their long swerve away in either direction captured and swallowed by the tall watching trees. He wonders at the tracks' sharpness, how hot they would be if he reached out to touch them, what would happen if he placed a stick atop one and left it there. His mother's voice rings through from the building, high-pitched and angry, a long silence following, and he hears nothing else. At last, she walks out, her face so red that he thinks someone has slapped her, but he realizes the color extends to her neck and arms. He twists and stands.

"Can you carry this?" she asks, bowing toward the valise.

He grins and nods, pleased to be asked, to do something or anything. He wants to help. "Where are we going?"

"Back." The word snaps. "They won't let us stay on the train due to my coughing—can you believe it?" She draws a breath. "Won't give me my money back either, the fiends. We'll have to find us a ride."

He looks around, seeing no one they might ask. No cars nor wagons, no buildings, people, or anything much at all. Only sky and trees.

"I think the town's this way." She points and they leave, following a dirt track that after a time becomes pavement, a few houses along it, one pink-mouthed dog. He shifts the bag—heavy and big and awkward to walk with—from one side to the other, noting the marks left on his hands. He falls behind, shuffling several times to catch up to her swishing dress, sweat running and stinging. When they reach a small store with a few cars in front of it, her coughs become blasts and breath escapes her for a moment, finally arriving in a great twisting, croaking gulp. Her face fades to white with it. She bends over, then straightens up. "Wait for me here."

She enters a door. He finds shade and sits, staring up at trees shaped like great pencils, some straight but a few curved and twisting, then at the cars, imagining himself driving and shifting their different gears. He copies the thrusts made by Mr. Paul's feet, positions his hands like he's holding the wheel, and for a moment he stands and reaches out, thinking to enter a car or just touch it, to make it all seem more real. A man exits the store and looks up, confused, and the boy pulls his hands back, thinks to turn away. The man's mouth opens to say something but he never does, one hand on suspenders made of rope, his jaw working like a fish in air. He opens the door to one of the cars and slams it. After a moment, there's a click and its engine growls.

Finally, she leaves the store. Her head shakes without speaking and she hands him a sack. Inside is an apple, a bit of cheese, and a bottle of cola, open. He takes a bite of the apple as she swigs from the cola, but when he offers her some, she refuses, handing the bottle to him instead. The cola makes him burp but it's cool and sweet-sparkled, and he opens his throat so that it fizzes and he nearly chokes. She is glancing off down the road, tapping a finger as if to a hushed drumbeat, the other hand a fist curled, her jaw shifting back and forth. The little hairs over her lips quiver as she speaks.

". . . want me to go to a hospital. What hospital? Ain't no hospital here. And pay with what?" She talks to herself more than to him. "Ain't gonna do it; we'll survive on our own. We're . . ." And with this she turns, her eyes wide and red-streaked. "We're staying together, you hear? They ain't putting me somewhere and you somewhere else."

He chews and swallows, so pleased to hear this that he wants to cry or to hug her. Instead, he heaves a burp up, loud and with taste to it, and this makes her head lift, her smile return and then disappear. He hadn't thought of them being split—why would they ever be parted or split? He wants to be with her always. He wants her to be with him. Even the thought of their parting makes his stomach grow stiff and cold.

After a time, they rise and continue, marching on in the same direction. They pass more houses, where people crane to look: an old man in a dark hat, a woman fanning herself on a little porch. A small boy starts to run to them, but someone unseen calls him back as if they've jerked a rope. A dog jumps and barks, teeth shown, spit flying, its tongue a red thing like candy gone long and soft. The boy wipes at his sweat, shifting the bag and hurrying to catch up again, and she offers to take it but he shakes his head no at this. He must bear and carry it, even if he bounces or drags it along the road. Soon they are past the houses, with only the dirt track left before them, their shoes making flapping sounds on the road like soft punches. The trees are so close that their path looks like a tunnel.

They stop to rest twice in the heat, his legs hurting so that they shake even when he sits. She stares down the road as she crouches beside him, her face red and hair wet and curled past her ears. She has let him remove his cloth cap, and when he wipes at his head his hand comes back wet. All he can think of is their shack back by the pond, how cool it is under the roof and with plenty of water there too, and his thirst is so great now that his lips stick with a gumminess. She snaps at then ignores him when he asks how much farther they have to go.

A wagon appears behind them, its presence heard before sight of it, hooves striking and wheels turning with even, steady draws and clinks. They wait for this by the roadside, his mother coughing and trying to make herself stop, her body closed in and shaking with a wobbly, muffled sound. When the wagon grows closer, they see that a black man is its driver, a single mule hitched in front, dust blowing behind and spreading out past its sides. She nudges the boy to put his cap back on his head.

The man stops as she moves onto the road. He holds a switch in one hand, long like a bug's feeler.

"Can we catch a ride? We're heading to Port St. Joe."

The man doesn't respond. Then: "Ain't going that far." A pause, a scratch at his head. "You got a ways."

"Can we ride as far as you're going?"

Another pause. "I suppose." He examines the switch as if something is written there, the trees making shadows like grasping dark fingers. He motions them into the back with his other hand.

The boy clambers in. The back of the wagon is a jumble of hay and odds and ends: three jugs, a rake, some piece of iron or equipment that he cannot name. He clears space for himself and for her, and she struggles in pulling herself up, coughing a little, but with a mutter and flash of skirts, she tumbles in. The man says nothing, hissing and flicking about with his switch, his head tipped back. The mule starts, sways a bit, pulls on. There's a creaking of board and wheel, a jerk and stop, swinging. The wagon begins rolling forward.

Shadows grow soon to dullness, the blanket of late afternoon. An hour passes or more—the boy dozes and starts. Her arm rests on his, and when he opens his eyes he finds hers are closed, the mule's clops firm and steady, the man's seat pitched and groaning as he shifts up front. Something about this is disturbing, as she's not coughing through her sleep, and he runs his hand on her neck and the small hairs there and wakes her, but when her eyes open she's not sad or upset. She looks around them and smiles, takes his hand and clutches it, her palm warm and soft, holding on to and squeezing him. He squeezes back, his breath released and swirling her thin hair, something washing over him that he accepts and knows the name for, that he's experienced to an extent before, a warmth after coldness or a dryness after rain: relief. He shuts his eyes again.

The man brings the wagon to a halt moments later, at a narrow lane's entrance between oak trees on their left. She coughs again as he turns to look at them.

"You ain't gon' make it 'fore dark." His eyes hide in the shadows. His fingernails are like flowers, thin and whitish pink.

She doesn't respond.

"Where you gon' sleep?"

A shrug, a turn. The boy puts an arm out, half rises, sits.

The man turns with a shaking head. "Come on with me then." He takes a long look down the roadway. His breath holds, then blows. "I'll take you partway in the morning. This road ain't too safe."

She coughs and pats her dress. The boy settles in again.

"You sick?"

She shakes her head. "I'm okay. Thank you." Her voice is papery, whispery.

They continue down the narrow lane. The trees are so tall they block the remaining sunlight, crickets screeching and cicadas buzzing, cooler now that they're cloaked in full shade. Twice they stumble through mudholes—mule first, wagon following—things jostling and cracking and tilting, the water as brown as old shoes. The trees smell like syrup, long scrapes down their sides like someone has marked space or time there, and he looks to her for agreement but her eyes have swung shut again. The man sways and hums, and the boy takes his time studying him: the hair on his head like a moss, the skin on his neck as marked as old tree bark, the tiny hairs on his arms that look like crosses, or hooks or chains. The smell of a fire comes, clenching the boy in a new thirst and hunger, and he searches the wagon for something to eat or to drink but finds nothing there. A snake crosses the path, wriggling straight to the other side with a rustle and final flick of its tail. The mule doesn't shy or even slow down for it.

They enter a clearing with several huts grouped around a fire. The structures are tilted, slouched in different directions, flimsier even than their own broken shack and made of odd objects: wood and pieces of metal, logs, and even a few spread palm fronds. They look like a wind's puff could blow them all down, flinging pieces like arrows. People are about—Negroes—and the fire spouts a grayish smoke, its smell different from the train and the fires he has known before this. A small boy yells and points at the wagon, and this causes others to pause, to stop what they're doing and watch. The wagon proceeds to some shacks beyond the first group—larger but no more substantial—and halts. There's silence then as the harness quits creaking, the mule sighs and makes a humphing, whisking sound. The man turns to them, his eyes gleaming white and brown.

"Gonna take you to see Mama Lo."

He swings down rather quickly, no effort made to tie the mule, and disappears into a house. No other people stand before these stick shacks, only some chickens cackling and pecking, more smoke snaking from somewhere, clothes hung out on a line. An old dog raises its head, sniffs and rises with difficulty, sits back down. The boy's mother, awake now, makes no move to stir from her spot deep in the wagon, her head up and looking, her hands spread out wide. Johnny wants to get down, to explore things, discover, but he sits and waits. She begins a new coughing, pulling the rag out and up around her face, things rattling in her throat like wet stones. A woman comes out of the house where the man disappeared, gray-headed, her hair in strange knots and her lips shaped like rock. She takes a long look at them and goes back inside.

Her words carry from the shack's interior. "... bringing in another stray... Why you doin'...?"

The man's voice isn't heard.

"... Josephus, and her sick too? You think you can't catch that, or I can't? You gonna kill us all!"

Again, they hear no reply. His mother shifts, the coughing spell finally ended, tears or sweat at her eyes that she wipes back with her hands. A moon has risen, eyeing them through the rails of trees. A boy emerges from one of the other shacks and looks up at them, light flickering behind him like a smile. The mule swishes its tail at some flies. From somewhere distant comes the sound of a woman singing.

The man comes back out. "You gon' stay in the barn." He gives a shrug, inclining his head past the mule and behind them and back. He's older than the boy thought, though Johnny's not sure how much, given that he's not good at picking ages, even among kids and white folks. The structure the man points to is set back in the trees, so dark that he hadn't noticed it. Another mule waits there, ears up by a wooden fence. His mother makes long, slow turning motions. Even in the fading light, he can see that her face is pale and her eyes dim and glass-colored. He leans in and whispers to her.

"I gotta go."

She nods and he jumps down, runs into the woods, and in a rush undoes his pants. His pee crackles on the leaves and straw, and he keeps looking around him, thinking that he shouldn't be here, shouldn't be gone from her, bared now like a baby and maybe lost, maybe newly seen. When he turns to go back, he finds the boy from before just behind him, so close that Johnny nearly jumps. He makes to flee.

"What's your name?" says this black boy. His words are hard to make sense of.

He stops. "Johnny. What's yourn?"

"Elias. Your mama sick?"

He makes a shrug, slow.

"How long you stayin'?"

"I don't know." A tiredness weighs on him, the long day and walk, and he needs to get back to her. "You got any water?"

The other boy darts away, back before Johnny can button up and leave the woods. A tin cup is held forth, filled. Johnny slurps from it.

"Thanks."

"You stayin' in the barn?"

"I guess so."

"It ain't so bad. Stinks though. Sometimes they send me there."

He returns to his mother and helps her down from the wagon. It's almost as if she can't walk, she moves so stiffly and slowly, like her bones have gone soft or maybe the rest of her is wrapped up tighter. The old lady watches them, others looking on now too. Whispering, frowning. Elias returns to his shack. The barn's one side lies open, with space for the mules and a little loft stretched above it, a ladder tacked on the wall. The old man motions toward this and the boy scurries up it, the area at the top low and not tall enough for him to stand, covered in mounds of brown hay. A blanket lies crossways.

"Can you climb?" he asks his mother, but she doesn't speak or nod. She drifts to the ladder as if caught in a dream, grasps the first rung but makes no try at climbing. He looks to the man but can't see his face well, as this place has grown shadows and is now almost fully dark. Johnny climbs back down, thinking that perhaps they can sleep with the mules, but his mother's head shakes as if she hears his thoughts. With a long sigh she straightens, reaches and pulls herself one board up, sways and hangs for a moment like a bird caught in a breeze. The man takes a step forward but stops. Behind them a chicken squawks, a mule blows in protest, the singing from far off returns like a taunting wind. Again, another arm out, a step, a new tremble. By the time she reaches the top, her body is shaking, and he wants to help her and push her up and into the straw, grabbing for the bottom rung even as she hangs there above him. She falls across the top more than reaches it, her legs dangling past the edge, and at this he climbs and pushes against her, but she lies still and doesn't move anymore. The man says, "Hey, now," and she shifts, crawling painfully to the point the boy can't help but sniffle and cry. She brings her knees to her chest and coughs, loud and long and with a watery sound to it. Afterward she spits. By then the man is gone.

Enough light comes in for the boy to make shapes out. He touches her and they hug, arms around one another, and he's surprised at how fevered and warm her body feels. Her skin is soft and rubbery, sweat wetting his arms and face, and she rocks back and forth with him. She lies on her back in the straw after this, her chest heaving up and down as if being pushed.

"Are you tired?" she asks, her voice low and rough-sounding. "I'm so tired."

"Yeah," he responds. "Hungry, too." The water he drank seems long ago now. "You think they'll bring us some food?"

At first she says nothing. Then, stirring, groaning: "Where are we?"

"Up in the loft with the black folks, remember? The Negroes."

"Uh-hmm." She rolls to one side, looking up and across at him, her eyes glassy as they were before, horselike and large in the darkness. "We're gonna be okay, J. I think we're gonna be okay. Don't you lose your shirt now, boy." Her teeth gleam and shine then, like they have their own light behind them.

The wave comes again, the relief as he calls it, but not as sharp or strong as it was before. He touches her face and feels the heat and the wetness. "What can I do?" he asks, but she's fallen into new silence. Her eyes flutter and waver and shut. She waves in the quick of exhaustion, but also laughs, a chuckle that turns his head and brings his own smile. Then she stills again.

He closes his eyes too but he can't sleep yet. If they can make it back to their shack, make it out of the darkness, she'll be better and they'll go on as before, maybe try again soon for Tennessee. He reaches out to the low roof, counting his numbers to try to calm his mind, telling himself that there's plenty of space here, room for them to stretch and move about and breathe. Things shift around him—stirrings and scratchings from beneath the damp straw, rats or mice prowling—the mules chewing and whining and farting down below. Farther, the singing stops and snatches of voices rise behind it, words he can't catch or grasp, as if they arrive in a different order or language. He's staring at birds fluttering, maybe bats, when a light shines below that pulls him to the loft's edge to peer down at it.

A candle or torch looms, a boy's voice behind it. Elias, his face hidden. The odor of food past the hay and the smell of animals.

"Hey, your dinner here. Come down now and get it. They don't want me up there."

The boy climbs down the ladder, his throat juicing as he goes. "You got water?"

"Yeah."

He can see now, two plates and a jug before Elias. He grabs them. "How come you can't come up?"

The other boy shrugs. "They worried I'd catch her sickness. Yours too."

"She's gon' be fine." His voice rings high and strange.

"What's wrong with your hair?"

"My hair?"

"It ain't right. Ain't like nothing I've seen, even for white folks. Them neither." He jerks his head.

The boy reaches out and touches Elias's dark hair. It's less mossy than stiff, like dried mold or a bristle sponge. He pulls his hand back, ducks his head to allow the same feel of his own.

"Hmm."

"I'll take this up." Johnny points at the food. "Where we . . ." He pauses. Coughs. "You got an outhouse?"

"Yeah. Back of that main shack there. One for men's is missing the door."

He turns to look, tries to gather the food, but realizes he'll need to bring some up and come down again.

"She get bad, you call me," Elias says like he's grown, like he can offer some lesson or bring help.

The boy dips his head. "Can you stay with that light just a bit?"

"Yeah."

He gets the food and jug up in two trips. The light forms dim spikes above him and below, showing long cobwebs and sparkly clouds of dust. When Elias leaves it is dark again and still, hot, and mostly quiet. The boy digs at the food with his fingers—he's not sure what it is, or whether there's a fork somewhere provided, but it's warm and he eats it fast, saving some. He guzzles the water without spilling it.

"Mama, there's food." He tries to wake her but she coughs and turns. "Can I get you some water?" She feels hotter now, and he's sure she must have a fever. Maybe if he can get her to drink some it will cool her down. He holds the jug to her lips but manages only to splash her, as he can't see what he's doing and she isn't offering any help. Even this bath doesn't stir or wake her. He calls her name and shakes her arm hard, but all he gets in response is a turn back and a sickly moan. His heart winds up, his breath so fast that he's barking and snorting, and it's as if he's back in the box, caged and pleading and all alone. He grabs her body and wraps himself up around her, feeling her sweat and her heat, her smell now like something spoiled. Should he call someone or do something? He starts to cry but stops himself in this, telling the wall that he's strong, that she had said they would make it and things would be right. They just need to reach morning, the night driven off and things again brighter, like the box being reopened, and they'll climb down the ladder and take their quick leave. She will be ready, as she was ready before! He nestles in closer, her heartbeat meshed up with his, engulfed in the odor of her halting and trembling, tart and ragged breath. Her hand strokes his hair. A dog or wolf howls, the sounds still of the mules and people talking far off, the smells also of hay and dung and old smoke.

For a time he drifts off, then wakes again, fearful and shaking her, but she moans and hums. Things are quieter now, the moon higher in the sky, and he sits for a moment, wet in his clothing, takes his shirt and his pants off and lies back down beside her. A bird cries and something rustles below them, stirring the mules, but this doesn't much worry him.

He talks to Robert: "Hey, what you doing?"

"Nothing. Getting ready to eat. Buster's in trouble."

"What'd he do?"

"Smarted off to a lady. She told his ma."

He clutches his own ma and falls to restless sleep, where he dreams he is a fish in the ocean, plenty of water around, and finds he can breathe it as fish do, point himself by twitching his body. Crabs are below him, ripples above, and he can taste the salt and the ocean weeds. His tail is a whip's crack, freeing him to glide or dive.

He wakes to a light and a man's voice.

"Get up, son." For a moment he's not sure where he is or what he's done. The old man kneels beside him. The boy reaches for his mother, and she's there but she doesn't move. Her body is cool, and silent.

"You got to get up, now." The voice is low and kind, like a turning stone. The man takes a breath, deep. "She done gone."

CHAPTER FIVE

Mama Lo

That child. Showed up with his mama sick. I asked Joe what he was thinking to bring 'em, what he had gone and done that for, and he said he hadn't no choice, that he couldn't just up and leave 'em out there on the road. I suppose that is mostly true. He brought it all on, though, showing up with his mule and these strange guests behind him. Smiling and shrugging, his hands out by his sides, looking off in the trees like he does when he breaks things. There's a part of me that treasures and loves him for this, and a part of me that blames him still.

I worried about sickness. The whole camp could get diseased! The workers and families and children exposed, and what would we do then? There's no doctor for miles, none that would journey out to see us even if there was. Josephus just won't think—won't think about nothing past his nature, his next meal, and sleep—and his kindness will soon enough ruin or kill us. Others came to me when he rolled these two in, these two dusty white people, and him wanting 'em to stay in our house! I told him no, the others saying much the same, and after the ruckus he put 'em up in the barn. I didn't want even this, but later I fretted on it—her sick and that boy maybe only seven, lying up there with the mice and what else, and I sent 'em food, then sent Joe later to check on 'em. He came back with what I feared he would, what I saw on his face before words or much else—the sorrowful news that the sick white woman was dead.

How could the boy not have caught what she had? Joe said he stuck to her close like an eel, that he had to pry him a-loose, the boy shrieking and wailing and so odd-looking, too, his stubbly head like a fuzzy peach. The group met in the night about what to do—with the body still up there and him just a-clinging! Some said call the sheriff, but that plan was squelched. Others said tell Boss Jim, but that fell down too. What would he do if he knew Joe had done this? Better to hide this quick and pretend it didn't happen, that it was somebody else's sad and shifting dream. Hester saying the boy was evil and such. Bert and Joe tried to talk to him some, asking 'bout other relations but getting nothing there, him sobbing and screeching and telling them he had no one. He was a runt of a thing, in addition to his being odd. The questions and whispering went on for some time and kept everyone up near about until dawn.

In the morning it was decided to dump her in the swamp. There just wasn't much else to do. Gator would get her then—it's best not to think on it—but we had to do something, and a fire would have sent too much smoke. The body needed to go, and so the men saw to it: Josephus and Bert and Big Mike. I made 'em wear gloves and wash in kerosene afterward. They put the woman in the wagon and Josephus hauled her off. The boy fought and screamed and tried to crawl in there with her, saying that she wasn't dead and other such rolling nonsense, so that several of the men had to step in and hold him back. Josephus was gone 'bout all day but claimed no one had stopped him or said anything worrying. I wanted to slap him, for bringing all this onto us, when I should have been more tender, more understanding and extra Jesus-kind. His face when he got back seemed older than usual, his skin pinched and dry-looking, his normal color gone dull and gray.

We talked more of the boy—none of us then knew his name. I tried talking to him, too, at least from a distance, but I couldn't get nothing more than what the others could. He was a pitiful thing, and my mother-blood felt for him, losing his mama like that with him so young, but he needed to go somewhere. Josephus had said they were headed for Port St. Joe, and it was decided that he would take him there the next day. Cat and me talked on it.

"How could he not have no one?"

"I guess some people just don't."

"Too bad we can't ask that mama. What was she doing here, anyhow? All sick like that out in the middle of the woods here with us." Cat is Bert's wife and has some nip of sense to her. Most of the other women here are near babies, and don't.

"Says he don't want to go. Says that they'll kill him there."

"Pshaw. Who'd kill a boy?"

"I don't know. It's strange, Cat. I got me a feelin' on it." And I did. My stupid heart is near 'bout big as Joe's. I was thinking that maybe the boy could stay on—that we could hide him till we figured things out, find someplace good or better for him to go. I didn't say this, but in the end I didn't have to.

"Lo, it won't work. You'll get you and Josephus and the rest of us kicked out. You know most camps only take men to begin with. How you gon' explain this little white boy here just showed up?"

She was right. There'd be risk then to all of us, and that was if he wasn't sick. Better to have Josephus take him on as we'd planned, drop him even if he didn't want to be dropped. Let some white folks deal with this problem. We got enough problems of our own.

I tried talking with him one more time. Elias went with me, and he seemed to have some take with a boy close to his own age. Elias knew his name: Johnny. I had him come down from the loft, watching him close for any sickness or coughing, but there wasn't any that I could tell. His face was red still, and there were splotches and stains on his clothes, his hair all strange and shiny. He smelled like a worked-up skunk. I wondered if he was albino, like those white squirrels you see sometimes. I once saw a white gator. Ain't nothing wrong with 'em—they're just missing some something that gives 'em a color. I told him that we'd take him to Port St. Joe, try to find some of his family, but he frowned and shook his head at this. Elias asked,

"Where's your pa?" but the boy said he hadn't one, or if he did, he didn't know of him.

"Where's your ma from?" I asked, but he said he didn't know this either.

"You been to school?"

He shook his head.

"What did your mama do?"

"She worked for an oyster house." His voice was low, childlike.

"Well, that's something. Maybe we can take you by there and see if someone can't help."

Again, he shook his head.

"I know it's hard, 'bout your ma. My mama died when I was young too." I paused to see if he'd look up, and he did, for a spell. "You go on. That's what you do. After a time you just accept it." I had my nanny to care for me, though, then my aunts. This boy didn't have nothing—at least that's what he said. It caused things to boil up inside me, like steam looking for a place to go. I felt my heart swell on up to where I could near grind my teeth on it.

The next morning, he was gone. The boys tracked him through the woods, found him a mile or so off, bug-bit and filthy. Brought him back and cleaned him up some, Elias talking to him and asking him didn't he want to go to town, as there'd be things to eat there and places to go, maybe white people to help, and the boy seemed to listen some. By then it was midday, still time to make it down the road, and he climbed into the wagon and sat behind Joe like a calf being carted. He was calm then, at least until someone tried to put a blanket on him. Then he screamed like the Devil's kin, said he couldn't stand to be under no covering. They finally set out with the sun still high up.

I cried when he left—I couldn't help myself in it. Big ole silly me, sillier even than crazy Joe. He was just a *child!* I spat in my knowing that I couldn't do anything more. Cat came and hugged me, whispering that it was alright, that this was for the best—for him and for all of us—and I couldn't bring up the strength to argue. Me, born a slave, trying to teach what was taught me, learning being the only way to escape this life near-on to slavery, worrying about some lost white boy? Things just seemed kind of reduced, muffled and lifeless, with him and his mama turning up and gone so quick.

The episode made me look around myself a bit, judge and think hard on our camp life and our living. We're here because the men learned the trees, starting with Josephus way back in Caroline, where my mama knew his mama and one thing led on. We worked a farm, worked for the same man who had owned us, Mister Owen, and I carry his name now—Roberts—though I don't ever say it much. In this day people need two names, need a means to be listed, and I guess that's for the better, or at least it seems so now. I was ready to leave that old life and farm, to go anywhere and do anything more, to make something work—me and Joe both. To be free. He got a job working trees, and we moved, to Georgia for a while, then to Florida near Jacksonville. Sometimes the trees tapped out, one time the landowner died, another time Joe got in a fight with a man, and we had to go.

My boys Sam and Junior started up in this place and stayed, till Junior went to the city. My girls left soon as they could. Ain't I raised 'em all up with my best? All of us working and working, out here in the trees rather than up and into town, but that's been alright, I say. Out here you can breathe. Still, it ain't easy. It ain't all that much. We owe still at the commissary, no matter how much we sweat and work. We ain't that much free. We don't often see white people—the woods riders, the overseer. Occasionally the landowner. But no little white boys—and nothing like him.

And then he was back. Josephus arrived about dark, and there in the back of his wagon was that buzzy head, white as a bucket of salt. I didn't get a chance to ask before Joe wheeled the story out, quick little word spurts like a fishline being thrown.

"He wouldn't hop off. I told him he had to, that I'd throw him out myself, but he just wouldn't budge. I tried pleading, I tried pushing him. I was afraid I was gon' get in trouble myself, shoving on some little white boy like that. I tried to trick him, but that didn't work neither. We rode out to where he said he thought his house was—tiny place way back in the swamp—but once he saw it, he said that he couldn't stay, that we had to go back then. So we did. I done gave up trying to sway him towards something else. He don't say much, anyway. He's a stubborn one, that boy—stubborn as a kicking mule. He just is."

I sighed but of course I was happy, my toes curled up tight. It's my born curse to care. I can hate myself for it. "He cough at all?"

"Nah."

"How you feel, boy?" I asked.

He turned, his face open. "Alright." His voice was low. "Thirsty."

"Elias, get him some water."

The others took to their grumbling, tossing the worries back that I had voiced myself: that we were taking on trouble, that he was well but we'd sicken, that something about it just weren't quite right. I beat 'em all down, my voice hard as rain: "We'll give it a chance for a week or so now, keep him up in the loft, check him then for the sickness, check everybody for sickness, see if anyone comes along to look." I was near to spitting, my nose leaking too. "It's what Jesus would want," I called out, a bit softer, and those that believe hung their heads and looked shameful.

"You need anything, Johnny?" I asked him before he went, for it was getting on dark. We gathered him up some food.

"I need my mama," he said. Everyone went quiet and stared.

"Your mama gone," I said softly, as sweetly as I could make it.

He seemed to study on this a minute and then went up in the loft.

ONE WEEK STRETCHED to two, then to three and on to several years. He became one of us, or at least part of us, playing with the other children, his skin browned by the sun. I thought about trying to find out more about him, to ask around as I could, but that seemed a mite foolish, and so I never did. We let his hair grow and it came out white as cotton, like he was some kind of a lambkin or angel. I never saw anything even close. It was near two months before I chanced to see his back. Elias had told me of it, though I couldn't figure out what he meant, as Johnny always had a shirt on. One day he didn't, and I saw the blotch—this mark near from his neck to his tailbone, purple and shaped just like a big hunting knife. It liked to take my breath from me, seeing it all stretched and curved, and when I looked close I could tell it had a raised part too. I asked him, "That thing on your back hurt?" but he shook his head, embarrassed about it, and began wearing his shirt again. Later he took it off like the other kids, and after a while everybody got used to it. He was Johnny, and that was that, and he couldn't be anything more or less than who and what he was. I saw myself in relation as some big-hearted mama dog, taking on a critter or castoff, a forsaken and helpless little pup.

He was smart, that child—not with much schooling, but he knew all his numbers and could read things right good. I give the children their lessons, and he was always quick with his. He liked studying things: trees, frogs, stars, ants, food, skin; any kind of machinery. He never asked questions like some children did. The others were curious about him at first, but I think they liked him, or grew to when his newness dropped. He and Elias were close, always huddled together and chatting, which was fine with me. They read their books, wrote their names and their letters out, did their maths all lined up and spread. I never worried about Elias like I did some of the other kids.

Johnny had a good humor and nature, but he could get angry too. One time he wouldn't come when I told him and I switched him as I would the others, but on his bottom. I took care about his back. He ran from me then so that I had to grab him and hold him, and he wouldn't submit like the rest when they've gone and done something bad. Another time I told him to quit telling other children what to do, him being all bossy-like, and you'd have thought I had slapped at his fluffy little head.

"You're not my mother!" His face red like some white folks.

"No, but I'm what you got now. Your mother woulda done this too." And I held him and switched him, though he scrapped and hissed like a coon caught, his gums back and teeth grinding loud and long.

After a while, Johnny and Elias became helpers, going with the men when they did runs in the trees. The men used the boys to hold the aprons or cups when they nailed them, to keep buckets steady and a few other things. In the days when they weren't working far from the camp, the boys would serve as runners if the men forgot something or needed to tell someone something else. The dip buckets were too heavy to help with, and the boys weren't tall enough to scrape, but sometimes they'd push a wheelbarrow or carry tools behind the men or bring the water. This made Johnny and Elias feel big, like they were real workers and truly part of the trade. They weren't allowed anywhere around the still shed—the fire and all made things too dangerous—or to use a yoyo or swing an axe, though. They also weren't allowed near the tunk, on account of the men that took to their drinking and the carrying on that happened there.

A story come out of that time that really tells something about Johnny. One day when he and Elias were out with the men, a bear came creeping up. There was a-shouting and a-hollering and the other men ran in, fanning out in a circle with the bear caught in between, them taunting and teasing it, running back if it charged or jumped. Said the bear was snarling and barking something fierce, teeth out like a wounded dog, that it climbed a tree and climbed down again, and one of the men swung his hack at it but missed.

Then this boy gets in the middle of things, yelling at the men to stop—this little white boy that ain't barely waist-high. The men laughed but let the bear run off, or they may just have tired of it. I asked Johnny on this when I heard, and at first he wouldn't talk about it. Finally said he felt something for the bear, being all alone and different from all the others, and I said I supposed this was rightly so. I was glad for him and the strength he had to do this. It showed spunk, a good heart, and his promise. I was glad too for the bear that I never saw scared or suffering.

It was this working, though, that likely caused what came to happen, that made Johnny more marked and more widely seen. I blame myself for it now, but what were we to do? The boy couldn't stay hidden like a bone buried by a dog. He never went down to the big camp with the commissary, but the men swept on through, and others new to the trees might have seen him or heard of him from someone saying something else. A boy with sun-white hair and a strange purple marking, out in the sticks there with a bunch of coloreds? Word was bound to get out at some point, and it did. I could kill when I think on it. Sometimes I can smell death in its lurking. I always worried that the woods rider would be the one to see him, but I think it was someone else—people running their mouths like people do: wondering about him and where he'd come from, how he looked like he did and came to be out in the woods. There had to be a story, and people love stories. It probably wasn't even something mean.

I knew from the moment I saw that boy that he would break my heart. It took a few years, but in the end it was as I feared. It wasn't his fault or mine or any of the others around us, but he swung and took a big ole hammer to it. Smushed it, Johnny did.

CHAPTER SIX

The smell is a thing he will always remember, the candy-like odor of the dark, sticky gum. Resin and dip, oil and flow—the men have their pet names for it. Blood from scraped trees that seeps down the gutters to pool in clay cups, hauled off then in buckets to the great and yellow, fiery still. A different smell waits there, related but different, and though he is told to stay away, he goes to watch: the men unloading big barrels of gum, the skid pole raised and great kettle with its heavy top, the other tubs. Things smell burnt at the fire but sweet, too, and strong, almost harmful. There's something about it that reaches out and calms him. He feels the heat even back in the trees.

Treading the pathways through the forest he's come to know, watching for snakes but knowing their patterns, he is shirtless and barefoot; the children rarely wear shoes. The men do, big boots that he covets, as he wants to be big like the workers, strong enough to swing a hack or hogal from tree to tree like they do. The fastest of them cover an acre of trees in a single hour, up and down and up, their hands waving and flapping like great wiggly birds. The trees in some places are lined up strangely in rows, and he understands why when he sees other, baby trees planted by hand. There are different jobs: manning the dip paddle, toting the barrels, keeping the fire right, recording the tallies, scraping the rosin—all for the purpose of producing "spirits," as they're called.

He asks Elias of this, how the big barrels exit and where they go when they leave, and the other boy explains that they are used to build boats. Johnny asks him how, asks one of the men this too, but neither replies to his question, and when he asks Buster and Robert they only shrug and shake their heads. He dreams sometimes of boats, huge ships like in wars and his storybooks, with smokestacks and anchors, motors and decks, shiny and polished with the spirits the men produce.

He learns about trees: how to cut them in a "cat face" so that the cuts don't wound or kill, how dangerous winds and a windthrow can be. How burning the floor clears the brush and makes for stronger trees. (That's another smell.) How there are different pines, some growing faster than others, some with big cones and some that are small; how there's a difference between sap and gum. How the trees have both boy and girl parts, and some can grow eighty feet high in the air.

He wants to know all about everything he sees and then touches, the sum of it counted and grouped in his mind: the system and structure of the camp and its branches, the fact that it's owned by one person—a Mr. Johns no one sees. The woods riders telling the others what to do and when. The names called to enter the tally, the wagons taking them deep into miles of trees. The workers are paid in something called scrip, shiny metal pieces that look like money but aren't and can only be used to buy things in the commissary, like beans or bread. He sees all manner of animals—raccoons and possums, deer and turtles, foxes, skunks—and learns not to rile or fear them. There are stinging nettles, lightning bugs, yellow jackets, prickly pears, skinks and chiggers, ferns and cypress knees. In the woods there are mishaps, too: men cut or burned. A tree fell on an older man named Smith and killed him. A mule went mad and tore up a wagon and driver before somebody felled him with an axe. He hears crying and moaning and once two men fighting. Another time a cracking whip.

He misses his mama. At first he couldn't sleep, and when he did sleep he dreamed of her, waking at times and reaching around for her body, listening for her breathing only to find her not there. How he would welcome a cough or a whisper, even a frown or scolding or an angry pinch! He looks for her smile and dented cheeks in the sky, in the birds and leaves rising or falling, but there is nothing left—only the animals and trees, the long days and warm nights, the people pressing around him like the walls of the dreaded box. He keeps watching and waiting for the thump of spades or shifts, signals or changes, but he is by himself. Even the birds seem to not look his way. A hole has returned to the center of his mind and heart.

They let him move from the loft after several weeks, away from the mules and mice and into the same shack as Elias. There they sleep side by side on pallets placed on the floor, a few boards below them to keep the wet and the bugs off, and at first the smell of the dirt made him sick. The sound of rain on the roof here is different and softer, as if water catches and stays rather than plopping on and rolling off. It's hot in and among the trees, the heat as solid, almost, as the ground, with no breeze like their shack had, and he finds that he is always sweating.

Elias's father—Sam—and the men mostly ignore him, although the woman Hester stares at him and shies away, making him eat after the others do, giving him orders or refusing his questions. At first, he's bothered by how everyone's skin but his is dark, and he thinks that he will darken in the sun like they do, which to a degree he does. He notes that there are different shades of colored, regardless, from coffee to night tint to something not far from sand. He keeps his shirt on, wary of his back and all the attention it spawned once, but after Elias teases him about this, he takes it off.

"What is that?" Elias asks him.

"What?"

"That thing on yo' back."

Johnny sighs and shrugs. "Birthmark. Lots of folks have 'em. Coloreds too." He's not sure if this is true or not.

"I ain't never seen one. All white people got 'em?"

"I . . . I don't think so. No."

Elias nods, and that's all the questions he has. Others are more curious.

Mama Lo: "Child." She stares and wants to examine it. Asks him if it hurts, if he can feel it. Even rubs her hand on it once, but he won't let others do this. He wears the shirt again.

The girl Bessie jumps on his back and pulls her dress up, riding him there until he bucks her off. He can feel her bare rump and hair. She runs off giggling and screeching, her dress browned by dirt and wear.

The woman called Cat: "That thing is some kinda sign."

Another woman, Mavis: "Can I see it?"

He refuses. Eventually he sheds his shirt again, the shame of it dwindling, the others having grown used to it and to him, and for a while no one says anything more or asks to see it or touch him. They wanted to run their hands through his hair, too, and he suffered through that drawn-out phase. He doesn't like to be touched by anyone, even by the other children.

There are eight kids here in all, ranging in age from fourteen down to two, four boys and four girls. He learns their names and the things they will do, how Sarah is prone to cry a lot and Bessie is like a mama, how Ralph can lift things twice as heavy as Johnny or Elias can, though he's younger and smaller. Johnny's age, since he doesn't know it, is pegged as eight, same as Elias. On occasion he sees the others unclothed, the little ones mostly, and he comes to understand more about boys and girls, a knowledge Elias passes on when things are dark and they're to sleep. Sometimes he hears what Elias calls "sparkings": men and women who sound like they're shoving about or fighting, calling each other names and laughing or crying out. Once Naomi, a girl of twelve, opened her shirt to show him her teats, rounded things with darker nipples like buttons, though Mama Lo switch-whipped her when she heard.

But it's Elias that the boy follows and talks to, shares things with and hounds with his many questions. They're like brothers, or friends, and he's never had a brother or anything near a friend, except for

Buster and Robert, and they're not new or even real. The boys spend most days as one, exploring and studying, talking and eating, and their nights lying face-to-face. Johnny comes to know Elias, his thinking and the way his body works, his face and his habits, almost as well as he does his own. Sometimes he can tell beforehand what Elias will say, and when, and how he will say it. He tells Elias things too. Secrets he's never told anyone—about his mother, about the little he knows of his father. About the place they lived in before and had to leave, and why.

He never tells him about being placed in the box. He thinks about doing so, even decides just what he'll say, but then finds that somehow he can't, at least not yet. Not just now. To speak of it aloud would make it somehow return, brought into light to happen once again.

For a while he has nightmares of the one-armed man, but these dim and fade. He thinks of his mother each day, though, still, crying and asking where she is buried; something tells him to save her as she once saved him, that she is out there waiting and he must find her and bring her back. Josephus and the others say she was put in a lake, deep in the swamp past the trees, and finally due to his pleading he is taken to the place and shown it. The lake is quiet, without ripples in the water or any sign that she was ever there, and he wonders if they are telling him a story just to shut him up.

He sneaks back regardless and drinks from it, wades in it, and if he knew how to swim, he would toss himself in and float. He likes sitting beside it—the fireflies flashing like sparks, the frogs sometimes so loud he can't hear himself cough or speak. One time he sees a gator up on the shore, its short legs thick and doglike, its snout lifting something caught in its jaws that slips out. Another time a hawk swoops down on a squirrel just before him, talons long and outstretched and the whole movement soundless, leaving his heart gripped and pounding, the bird gone with one great flap. He squats by the lake and listens to it, smells of it, touches the top of the water and feels like he is touching her. He tells her that he misses her, that he knows it was all his fault. Sometimes he cries into it so that he can hardly breathe.

The children have chores, and Johnny's main one is toting water, which is carried in pails from a spring not too far off. At first he can't lift the pail and is forced to half fill it, the water splashing cold and clear, but gradually he becomes stronger, muscles developing in his shoulders and around his neck. He also helps with the dishes, which are washed in water heated on the fire in a big black pot. In the afternoons and sometimes at night the children play, their favorite games being tag and something called hide-and-seek. He's not much good at hiding, his hair giving him away, but he becomes faster as his feet toughen, and he's used to the woods and trees so that he begins to look forward to the games rather than dread them. There are a handful of books in the camp, and he reads, sometimes to the younger children. Sometimes he makes up stories to entertain and to teach them, to pass the time or make him think more, or to charm and please.

It takes time to learn all the kinships within the camp. Mama Lo is married to Josephus, and Sam is their son, but Sam's wife, Hester, is not Elias's mother. The little girl Rebecca is his half sister, the others cousins. Occasionally more join the side camp, as it's called: a tall man named Rip who is somehow related; a man and his wife, James and Agnes, the others dislike. So much is new to the boy here—like cussing.

He asks Elias once, "What is shit?"

The other boy laughs. "That thing comes out yo' butt. But it's a bad word. Don't let Mama Lo hear you say it."

"A bad word? What's a bad word?"

"Word you ain't supposed to say. Like damn. She hears and she'll switch you."

"Why are they bad?"

"Boy, you know *nothin'*!"

There is more: how soup is good for most sickness, how men can go crazy from liquids they drink, how some words can mean one thing but also something else. Elias tells him of something called the Klan, men in white robes who kill coloreds, and for a time Johnny has nightmares, of hooded people approaching just as his mother once feared those nearby. He tells Elias of the things he knows best, particularly his rides in the car and on the train, stories which capture and enchant the other boy to no end. Elias asks of them so often that Johnny adds things to the trips: a plane swooping down upon them, robbers demanding that they stop. Sometimes the other children want to hear these too, but it makes him feel guilty to tell them. He makes up more: a great storm that drenched them, another train that jumped the tracks. After a time, he tires of stretching out things, and refuses to tell the stories or answer questions on them again. He doesn't speak often to Robert or Buster anymore, nor they him.

The others tease him at times. They point out his paleness and difference, and some of them call him names: "Whitey." "Fuzzy." For some reason "Splat." They jump on the things he doesn't know or gets confused about.

"Splat, you got a charge on?"

He thinks that they mean underpants. Mama Lo insists they wear them. "Yeah."

"Oh, really. Right now?" Their smiles widen. "How often you get 'em on?"

He shrugs. "Well, all the time."

"Can we see? Let us see, Splat! How big is that charge?"

"I'll need a bigger one soon 'cause I'm growing."

Even Elias is laughing. "Johnny . . ."

"Lordy!" There's more laughter, eye rolls, and some pointing. He is lost then, and heated, hating them and himself and the trees, birds, and sun. Even Hester, nearby, starts grinning and snorting. Elias finally takes pity and whispers to him what they mean.

They play tricks on him, also—losing him out in the woods, saying that they're dying or that they've seen his dead ma—but in time he plays tricks too. He tells them that Robert and Buster are camped out in the trees, and that when the wind blows you can hear them, to which the others say they can hear them as well. He convinces the girls there's a ghost in the privy, so that for a while they won't go, until he tells them that if they say "Eeba Mola" twice, they'll fool the ghost. He and Elias wait and listen for the Eeba Molas, including Hester's, before their giggles alert the others to their game and joke. He even tricks one of the little girls, Mary, into eating a beetle, caterpillar, and ant, until she gets stung and he feels bad and confesses this prank to Mama Lo.

He gets sick once after he's been there some time—a fever and chills—as do others, though nobody seems to blame this on him. He thought they would, recalling his mother's words and his fear that followed them, to where he tried to hide his brief sickness, though Elias knew. Elias tends to know a lot. He can see and find things and work out what they mean, whether they are said or intended or important or something else. He has lots of sayings, customs, and opinions too.

"You know that thing on your back growin'."

His head pulls when he speaks. One of the girls says that Johnny also does this.

"What?"

"You know."

And he does, or at least he fears this to be so. He feels it catching sometimes when he turns over in his sleep. When he reaches back to feel of it, there is a cord of hardened skin. "You think it's coming off?" he asks, his voice scratched-sounding and hopeful.

Elias peers around him. "I dunno. I'd say could be. You want me to cut it?"

"No." He shifts back.

"Maybe your pa was an eagle, or a buzzard. You think on that?"

"No."

One of the workers, Mister Jim, passes by, a hack balanced on his shoulder. The bulb at its end makes it look like a tree and root.

"You need us, Mister Jim?" Elias calls.

"Not now, boy." A white-toothed grin.

They only recently began helping the men. Mama Lo at first forbade it, but when they agreed to get their lessons done early, she gave in. Maybe Elias's father had something to do with this shifting. Sam is one of the working men, tall and strong. He doesn't talk much, not like Elias.

"Mama Lo wants us to grow up to be something else, to get out of these woods—that's what she says."

Johnny had heard her say this.

"But I'm gon' be working like them, strong and so fast, faster than you, Johnny. I'm gonna do six acres of trees in an hour, something that ain't never been seen or done before. Cutting and scraping and toting. Earn me enough scrip to buy the whole commissary."

"Me too. I'll be the tallyman. I'll keep track of all you do, counting up every bit."

"That'd be good. We'll be a team, then. Start us a business, maybe start our own tapping camp."

"Would there be girls in it?"

Elias thinks on this. "Well, sure, back in the camp. Children too."

"You gon' have children?"

"Well, I hope so. Ain't you?"

"I suppose." His thoughts on the matter don't proceed far. Children mean mothers and fathers. For a while Mama Lo and the others asked where he was from and the name of his papa, and didn't he want to try and find him? Of course he does, though he never says this. He imagines his father to be a guard or policeman, a soldier or judge.

"You all quiet. You thinking about your ma? Or your pa?"

Elias can read him too.

"Thinking who among them girls would be my wife."

"Ha! You can have 'em. I'd rather take an old mule. Besides, Rebecca's my sister and the others are cousins. Can't marry no cousin, so I won't do that. And you with that white skin. How would those babies turn out?"

He hasn't thought on this either. He's not seen a white person since he arrived those years back. He doesn't really think of himself anymore as white, or think about skin much at all, except his back. He does think of his father, and the dreams of going to find him have grown. Back when his ma was alive, he only wanted to know him—know who he was and find things out about him, to see where he lived and how. He wants now to talk and to ask things, to learn more and find his kin, to understand why his pa left them. He can ask Mama Lo questions, and even old Josephus, but it isn't the same and he's not sure the why of it. He sees himself sometimes like a leaf floating in his mother's lake.

"You want to stay here?" Elias asks.

"Stay here? Whadda you mean?"

"With us."

The boy's heart jumps. "Course I do. Where would I go?" He thinks of his mother still here. He can't leave her.

"Oh, I don't know. Back to your people."

Again, it's like Elias sees into him. "I ain't got no people."

"You got some somewhere."

"Nah. Just me."

"Good. I don't want you to leave. I want us to stay here forever."

Johnny relaxes because this is what he wants too. He sighs and begins stretching, the skin on his back pulling and itching so that he must shift to scratch. If he rolls his shoulders forward, he can feel things lift and spread, and he spends a moment wondering what it will be like when he's older, whether it'll be big enough then to bother him or to do things on its own.

A few days later he is down at the main camp, "spying" as Elias calls it, watching the workings of the firebox and the still. It continues to strike and awe him: the stiller and his assistant stoking the firebox just right, "'cause if it gets too hot, it can blow," or so one of the men told him. The fire orangey white like the sun, the men glowing dark with their sweat and in contrast, caps back on their heads, their arms long and dangling. The rosin trough and the strainers, and if he is close enough, he sees the black sludge in it, the sweet-burned smell made even darker and stronger. That syrupy, powerful, honey-like smoke and smell! The man up above pours gum into the copper kettle, the steam rising above this, the boilerman listening to the tailpipe to gauge the heat. The dip barrels and then the larger ones, the ones big enough to flatten a rushed or careless man. The pine needles above flash silvery in the shifting light.

Johnny is so intent on the process that he barely notices the man who is pointing, turning to someone and asking about the pale-skinned boy. He is a black man the boy has never seen, but that's not so peculiar, as men at the camp tend to come and go with speed. This man has a long beard, which is different, the heft of it making his face look extra large. The boy slips from his hiding place and returns to the side camp. It never occurs to him that he should worry or fear this—that danger might exist through the trees and past the glowing still.

CHAPTER SEVEN

Elias

Johnny and me are like brothers or more, maybe closer than brothers—kinda hard to say. For the most part it's good, an adding-on to myself in my living and thinking, even near-on to magic. At other times, though, it can bring down cold rain.

It's caused problems with Hester, for one thing, or made old problems swell like ticks. I knew Johnny was special the minute old Joe pulled the cart up, that white hair like it was mowed this and thataway and strange. I'd seen white people before but nothing close to like him—none of us had, not my daddy or Joe or Cat, or even Mama Lo. To Hester he was scary. Hester calls hexes and hoodoo and believes in all sorts of crazy stuff.

Hester's my stepmama. My real ma is dead just like Johnny's, and that might be why we're close. I cried over my mother too, though I was young when she died and don't remember too much.

Eloise was her name; they said she was the prettiest Negra in all of north Florida, maybe the whole of the blessed state! Course I can't see her face clear now. Sometimes I make up things so that I think I see or smell her—things I tell Johnny. I ask Daddy sometimes, but he won't talk much on her, and Hester don't want to hear about her none at all. My daddy told me he'd never find another like her, and he didn't; he found him Hester. She came on a year or so later, the sister of one of the men who worked then at the camp, and within a few days they were married. My daddy don't talk much, and he told me, "This your new mama," but she ain't never liked me none. She pure-on hates Johnny.

It took some doing to even allow Johnny in our house. Hester didn't want this, and Daddy didn't much either, but Mama Lo and I begged them, and eventually they gave in. Johnny wasn't much trouble, and he did chores and whatever they asked, but still Hester fussed on him. "He's just a mouth to feed," she said to my father. "Ain't we got enough of our own here to watch?" Rebecca was three when Johnny came on, and they've had no more children since then. I think Hester somehow blames this on Johnny too.

As close as we are, me and Johnny are different. There's his hair and skin, of course, and that thing growing on his back. Hester says it's the mark of the Devil and shies away when she sees him turn. Others want to examine and touch it. I've touched it a few times myself, but it ain't no big thing. For a while I wished I had me one too. I even said this to Daddy, but he laughed and knocked me on the head. "You got enough trouble, boy. You looking for more, now?"

We got other differences, me and Johnny do. He wants to know how things work, and he's good with maths and reading and writing but downright stupid about lots of other stuff. He don't know nothing about birds and critters. I've had to teach him this near from scratch. He called a coon a possum once, a hog a cow. He couldn't tell crows from jays or from bluebirds. He near about stepped in a snake den before I pulled him back. He also don't know about people, and it makes me wonder what white folks do. Are they not sparking like coloreds? They got childrens, so I guess they must, but Johnny didn't know nothing about that neither. The boy needs some schooling, and it's a lucky thing he got with me.

For a long time Johnny missed his ma. There's been several times he disappeared that I knew right where he'd be—down at Straw Pond where they put his ma's bones. He likes to sit there and talk to her, to imagine he sees her and feels her close by. I asked if she smiles much or talks back but he wouldn't say. He told me that sometimes he thinks she ain't dead, that she'll be coming back and he will be ready for her, expecting her, prepared and waiting up to go. For a time I pretended my ma was buried there too, and I'd sit with him and we'd dip our hands in the water, though I knew that she wasn't, as she died before the camp was there. Bessie told Johnny a gator got his ma, and Johnny's eyes got all red, and he liked to have gone and hit her, but he always looks now for gators. Sometimes we'll see them, noses out of the water and those knotty and bubbly old eyes looking like they know.

My teaching of Johnny has gone to other things, too: how to swing an axe; how to hold a snake; how to tell the caterpillars that sting from the ones that don't; how to catch fireflies—there was a lot he had to learn. He didn't know about newts, about sinkholes or titties or stink bugs or rum, about tornados or woodlice or mama bears with little cubs. The boy didn't even know much on God when I quizzed him. I had to explain how God made all the world and sent his son down to check on it, and the son didn't like what he saw. You got to pray to them both, to make sure they stay happy; they like for you to praise them, too, and sing them lots of songs. It's why Joe does those long prayers before we eat, so we'll all get more food.

Johnny knew a few things—some stories he liked to tell—but he didn't know none of these basics of how things really are. It makes me wonder all the more about what learning it is white folks get.

Johnny and me talk every day. Do we have secrets? He knows most of mine but not all, and I figure it's the same with him. He has these nightmares where he thrashes around and wakes me up, wakes up Hester and Daddy too, which ain't at all a happy thing. He won't ever talk of 'em, though—won't never say what caused him to holler out. I ask him if he remembers them later, as sometimes dreams can leave, and he says yes but won't say nothing more. My secrets are different, and maybe not all that hid. I take up some for Johnny. He don't know what others say, and I don't bother to tell him: both the children who claim that he's weird or not of us, and the older folks too.

'Specially Hester. Hester and all her witch tales and nonsense, talking about potions and spells and things you got to do or not do so that a haint don't get at you. She's got the other kids looking left before they pee and stirring their food first with a hickory branch, plus lots of other fool notions. And she jumps on Johnny—treats him real bad. Makes him do the worst chores, yells at him more than most, runs him down front of the others, particularly when Daddy or Mama Lo ain't near. He don't seem to mind much, but it sure grates some on me. I took her on once about it.

"Why you do him this way?" I asked her. She'd made Johnny scrape the black cook pot for hours, and he hadn't done one thing wrong to suffer that.

"What you mean?" She has this way of talking with half her mouth, where it looks like she's ignoring you. It's like one side of her face don't turn or bend.

"You're making him do all the bottom work, like he's an animal or a slave."

"What you know about being a slave, boy? You don't know nothin'."

"How you know what I know?"

"You gettin' sassy? I'll tell your daddy, and we'll see what he has to say."

"Tell him, then. I ain't afraid none of you, and Johnny ain't neither. You ain't my mama nor his. You're just an old skirt-flipper."

I didn't know quite what this meant, but it got a big comeback. She took a swing at me with a skillet and put a knot on my head. That night Daddy whipped me and didn't say much while he did, just told me to respect her or I'd be getting more. I near about bit through my lip in my pain and hate of her.

The other kids tease me. "Where's your pet?" they sing out. "Where's that Whitey?" That's what they call him. When I strike back, they call and coo. "You get him wipe yo' behind? Or you wiping his?" Yet they all want to take my place, to be the one friendliest and closest. He's like a honeycomb or a gum spill, the way he attracts things, and they stick. Bessie is always around him, talking and asking him things real sweet-like. The little ones follow him even when Hester and Cat tell 'em to quit. Even old Joe always seems to be about and near him.

Mama Lo notices this, and me, too, saying, "Now, Elias, others can spend time with Johnny. He's not yours. Don't be jealous. Do you know what jealous is?"

And I think I do, but he *is* mine, and I want them all to know it. We're not in love—that's for boys and girls, men and women—but it's something sort of kin to that. He's my friend, my best friend. There don't need to be nothing more to it.

The other thing I never tell Johnny is how curious I am about white people. How is it that they live in towns with streets and fences and lights and we live way out here? I've seen some of the houses from the wagon, from out front on the road—these thick monster things, and I asked Joe how many families live there, and he said he reckoned just one. In that huge old house? And he says yeah, they got the money, and when I ask him why, he says he don't know. Johnny says he never lived in no big house, just a shack not much more than ours.

It's all about money, Daddy says, but as usual he don't say much more. How do you get money? Work, and so I want to work, and Johnny and I make our plans in amongst the trees, cutting and tallying and making all sorts of scrip, which I think is the same thing as money. But when I ask Joe if that gets me a house, he won't say. I asked Mama Lo once if we're poor, as we were reading about poor children living way across the sea, and she sighed and said we were rich in some things and maybe poor in some others. She said we are rich in that we love each other and are healthy, but when I asked about the big houses she told me I need to get away, that people need an education to get a big house. So I'm gonna get me an education *and* cut more trees than anybody. I ain't told Johnny this part yet, as I'm still working it all out. But he can live in my house with me when I get it.

ONE MORNING, AFTER Daddy goes to work, Hester comes screeching out saying someone stole something from her. She says this to me and Bessie, like we were the ones who done it. Johnny is gone to the spring or the pond or somewhere—he's not around. Soon others are gathered, some adults watching too.

"He done stole it, he did!" She stomps her feet like a nervous chicken.

"What's that?" Cat comes walking up.

"My money saved. I had two dollars rolled up in my things, and it's gone! That white boy took it, I know! I seen him rootin' around."

"Rootin' around what?"

"In my stuff—what you think? This place ain't big enough to turn around in, and he's always poking his nose about where he shouldn't."

It occurs to me that maybe Johnny did steal it. He's been talking about wanting to run away. Or it could be that Hester's making the whole thing up, to try and get rid of him. I'm thinking hard, imagining Johnny returning, her loud and accusing, the others still gathered up . . .

"I took it," I say.

They all look surprised, even Hester.

"Why?" Bessie asks.

"Just borrowing," I manage. Lying can become so smooth and loose. "I was gonna put it back. I just wanted to show . . . just wanted to have . . ."

"Give it now," Hester says. Her hand stretches out flat. Her face is curled into something that ain't quite a smile or frown.

I glare and go to my own stuff. Beneath my books and inside a branch I scooped out I have coins and some things I keep—matches and a rock I found, a bit of a wasp nest for luck. I empty the coins into my hand and count them; they don't reach two dollars. I go and give them to her anyway, she still with her hand out, and look her in the face straight on. I know this isn't the mix of coins she's missing, if she's missing anything at all, and I almost dare her to say something.

But she doesn't, she just takes the money, then grins at me real sweet and pleased.

"I'll tell your daddy when he gets home," she says with her face turned, going back inside to stash my coins. The others gather behind her and ask, "Why'd you steal, Elias?" Even Mama Lo: "Child, that ain't like you." I keep my mouth shut like a trap. When Johnny gets back it's like nothing ever happened, no one saying things to him—or at least not that I hear. That night Daddy whips me so hard I can't hardly walk after. I'm sure everyone in the side camp hears it. I don't scream or try not to. I don't cry out much. Daddy talks to me just a bit, more than he usually does, lifting my face with one hand, his palm hard as tree bark.

"Why you done this, huh?"

But I won't say nothing. He whips me some more but I still don't. Again, he talks.

"You gon' be strong when you grow up, but you gotta be smart. You is smart, but it can't be in the way of thievin'. There ain't no shortcuts in life, or at least none that I know of. Do me and Hester and your mama proud. Don't be no damn thief."

I don't say nothing to Johnny about it, though he asks. A fire burns inside me like a torch when I think on it, and I wonder if hate makes you stronger, like a tree that's been cut but lives. I finger the welts on my back and even show them to him, but when he offers me salve to heal them, I tell him no.

CHAPTER EIGHT

He knows something is wrong when the children are made to go play, the adults called to meet up in Mama Lo's gray-brown shack. Clouds pack and block the sky, a slice of blue tucked behind them like a wound. The murmur of voices escapes from the shack, a few words up and floating: Lo's forceful ". . . don't tell me . . . !" Another, lower tone, maybe Sam. "It ain't us."

Elias and the others guess at reasons why. Are they closing the camp? Has someone gotten sick or died? The girls toss out wilder notions: that a big storm is coming and they all have to up and leave; that a pack of man-eating dogs is waiting just outside the camp. Johnny remains silent through all this talk, declining to join it, listening as the shack words come: "disaster," "buckra," "boss man"—"dangerous." Somehow he knows that the meeting is to do with him, and when it breaks and Mama Lo comes out with Josephus, approaching to tell him something, a wave rises to his heart and farther, streaming into his nose and mouth like something has burst within.

"Johnny, I don't think this is nothing bad, but it was bound to happen, now. I suppose it was." Mama Lo's eyes are red, raised, and wide as the advancing night. Josephus nods beside her but keeps his eyes down and doesn't speak. "You see, some white men came to the main camp and said they heard you were down here with us. Want to know what you're doing here, who you are. Why a white boy is here with us Negras." She lets a long breath out. Josephus only nods again. "There ain't nothing wrong with it, you being like one of us now, and

I don't even think of you like that . . ." She stops, coughing. Josephus pats her on the arm.

"It'll be alright, boy," he says. His voice is slow, like rosin caught in the slurry. "They just want to see you, ask you some questions. Maybe they let you stay here like you are."

At first the boy doesn't speak. He sees the preacher man who called him a devil, the man in the uniform who made them leave the train. He sees rows of other men, faces grim, skin stained and waxy.

"I don't want to go."

"I know you don't," says Josephus, "but we ain't got no say. You at least gotta go meet with 'em. They want you to come down to the commissary tomorrow."

"What if I don't?" His tone is whiny, with what Mama Lo calls "sass." She switches those spouting it.

A silence follows. "That could be bad for us all," she says finally.

He dips and turns, wanting to run now, to take his things and sprint far into the trees, to dive into the water that his mother lies beneath. They take his quiet as acceptance, or maybe surrender, or even fear, Josephus putting his hand on his head. "It'll be alright, boy. Just rest up. It'll be alright." Johnny steps back but doesn't say anything more to them, doesn't burp or cry yet or holler—all the things he thinks he could likely do.

The other children stare. The adults look up and away, eyes shifting, arms quick to chores, calling out to each other in voices overloud and brisk. Candles are lit, a fire smokes and crackles. Johnny goes into the shack with Elias and, though it's not fully dark, takes out his pallet.

"So you leavin'," says Elias. It's not a question.

He turns and doesn't say. He breathes deep and trembles before his voice leaks like a drain: "I don't wanna go nowhere. I want to stay here with you. Why would I go with white people I ain't never seen?"

"Maybe you ain't gotta go."

He considers this. He supposes it possible, though it doesn't seem likely. His breath winds so tight he can barely turn or breathe. "Why don't you come with me?"

"What white man gon' take me?"

"You could work for 'em."

"Doing strictly what?"

Johnny thinks. "We could run off on our own."

This time Elias is silent.

Only a few days before, Johnny had listened as Sam whipped Elias, worse than the switchings old Mama Lo gave, going after him with a leather belt. Hester whispered to Johnny then, "You gon' be next, Whitey. You the cause of this, you and yours," but it made no sense, neither the whipping nor the bite and meanness of her words. Elias showed him the marks later, on his bottom and across his back. "What'd you do?" Johnny asked him, but Elias wouldn't speak to it.

Now Elias asks, softly, "Where you wanna go?"

"Somewhere with lots of trees. That ain't here. Where they don't find us."

Elias pulls his own pallet out. "When?"

"When it's good and dark." He has read tales of youths escaping and running away, usually off to sea. He doesn't want to go to sea, though he needs to go somewhere, and he wants Elias with him when he goes.

"Okay."

"You'll do it?"

"Sure. Wake me up when you're ready."

It takes forever for the camp to go to sleep. Elias snores gently, head back and chest out, but Johnny is too jumpy to do anything but wait. He hears people shuffling back and forth to the outhouse, some sound that may be a sparking. From somewhere laughs rise up, a smoke odor drifting. Finally, he hears only insects and the night. He makes himself count to 100 twice. He reaches out and shakes Elias.

"Hey."

Elias pushes him off. He shakes harder.

"What?"

"We gon' go?"

Silence. Johnny's heart slips like a stone. Then: "Alright. Wait, now."

Elias stands in the dark, slips into his trousers. His stepmother and father sleep just past the boys' beds, so getting past them is tricky, but they can always claim an outhouse trip. The two adults remain still and silent, their breaths pushing out with a hum and a buzz. The boys creep past them into the swell of the clammy night, the moon out and painting things shiny like a silver sun. In the trees things are dark and hidden, secrets kept and held within. There's a night smell and tree dust and a shifting, fitful, patchy breeze.

Elias whispers, "Where we gon' go?" but Johnny shakes his head, pointing to the bright, moonlit trail, the narrow track leading back to the hard-packed road. They set off along this, silent in their hard, bare feet, and for a moment Johnny feels a lightness he's not known since the moving train, as if his body has become a shadow's slow, dancing wave. He touches his leg and wants to also touch Elias, not to have contact but just to make sure he's there. They're only a few steps down the roadway, though, when a figure steps out before them, sturdy and real enough, raising dark, treelike hands.

"Thought this might happen," mutters old Josephus. "Believe me, boys, that I sure do understand. You can't run from things, though. It's taken me a long time to learn this. There ain't no slipping past, just like there ain't nothing given free, except maybe in heaven. Now go back and get some sleep. If you make me do this again, you gon' be real sore for it."

The pain stretches down to Johnny's knees, the same rise of his breath as when they'd left the train, the dark of when his mother grew stiff and cold. Why is he always pulled from things and made alone?

———∞◇∞———

HE DOESN'T THINK he can sleep but he does, and when he wakes the birds are flitting and whistling already, running their songs up and around and in the trees. He rises but Elias is gone, and the hurt from the night before comes floating back. Have they all of them left him? He stumbles out into a normal day, the others going about their morning chores, the men preparing to go on to their work. Again, no one looks at him, not even the children, as if he is a ghost now, already gone and drifted off somewhere else.

Only Mama Lo walks over, the sun on her skin warm and silver brown, her voice soft and calm. "Hey, baby. Hey, baby." Offering him breakfast of a biscuit with syrup and corn mush he can barely eat. He needs to know where Elias has gone and where he will have to go himself. Is he still to leave? The side camp looks different, smells somehow changed and sharper and burned-like, turned into stale dust and ash. Shadows are like skin with hair stretched or fur matted. Mama Lo stays silent and near him as he eats.

"Go ahead, now. We gon' go in a little while. Don't you worry 'bout nothing. Okay now, Johnny boy?"

If he's to be alone, can't she leave? He doesn't want anyone else to talk to or see him. It's like he's been shamed, by his skin or his back or some other strange something, like he's done a thing wrong or hurtful, or even mean. He thinks his way back: to Elias and his beating, to Hester's spiteful words, and the thought stirs again that it really is all due to him. If he'd only been smarter! If he'd only tried or done more. Has Mama Lo learned that they tried to leave here in the night? Josephus must have told her or someone, but she smiles and says nothing regarding anything to do with this. Only: "Clean yourself up, now, hear? Wash your hands and your face. I got some clean clothes you can put on for today."

He can barely hear or see things; he can't seem to walk or think. Can he go to the lake one more time, just to see her? He could slip off and be back, no one would know or miss him or care, but when he sees Mama Lo watching, he discards even thought of this.

"You'll want to pack your things, too, hon," she says sweetly, her voice with some snags. "Just in case you need 'em. I'll hold on to 'em for you when it's time to go, then. That sound okay?"

He has so little: a few books he brought with him that he's long outgrown. The toy train he and Elias used to play with. Nothing of his mother except a metal bracelet; little of what came before. He shakes his head.

"I understand." Her voice is whistling, low. "Get your shirt on, now. I'll be with you, down to the main camp. Josephus too. We'll be right there."

But the knot in his belly remains, stretching and pinching. To bring something along makes it look like he's leaving, and he is not leaving: he's decided this. He plans to tell them—any white person, anybody there—right off when he meets them. He plans to be bold and firm. They will know and see.

It isn't until they start from the side camp that he sees Elias. Peeking from behind a tree, the other boy neither smiles nor waves, only looks on with his eyes large, his hands on the tree and staring. Mama Lo pretends not to see him, not to notice Johnny stiff and looking back that way. The boy thinks to do or say something, but what would he do or say? Birds call from the trees, mockingbirds, cardinals—he knows this now, has learned this. The stare stretches a minute, an hour or longer, and then it's gone.

"You ready?" she says, and they're off, trudging beneath the tall branches, Josephus following behind them by a step. No one speaks as new birds call, flapping to and away from them, as squirrels twist and make leaps. Fog hangs in streaked, rug-like layers, the sky like a resin the trees have spewed upward. Pings of metal on metal, the coarse scraping of tins, the tick-tick of axe and hogal and hack. Mama Lo hums something that trails off and stops, and for a second the boy knows it, a tie to some brighter place.

He's thinking on something from a few weeks back, when a cheery tree man named Roy had his finger chopped clean off. Roy had been preparing to hack at a tree and slipped in soft rain, and the hack cut right through his finger, a piece of it flying off and onto the ground below. Johnny and Elias were helping Roy and another man, Will, and saw it, the blood spraying from the cut hand in a red curve, then dripping, Roy holding one hand with the other. Will grabbed Roy and wrapped his hand up in a towel, and Elias ran for help, leaving Johnny to stare at the finger—small like a stick and bloody, with bone peeking from its end—and wonder then what would happen to it.

He pointed it out when the other men showed up, though nobody really looked at it, one man finally kicking dirt over it as if to hide this shameful thing. The boy assumed that Roy would soon die, that the finger would need to be buried along with him, and he marked the spot so they could find it again. But days later Roy and his laugh were back, his hand in a bulging cloth, and then he discarded this to reveal the stub of what once had been. Johnny thought to tell him of the finger's location, assuming the man would want to know this, but fear or something more kept this knowledge to himself.

He thinks that if Roy didn't die after he lost the finger and all that blood, maybe he can survive too, even if he leaves the side camp, and for a moment the thing in his belly lifts. He reminds himself that he's not leaving, regardless. He reaches for the firmness and boldness he had pledged.

Before they arrive at the commissary, Mama Lo stops and dips into her bag, pulling from it something soft and folded. It's the cap he wore when he arrived, wrinkled and crumpled but otherwise still the same. She hands it over to him.

"You wanna put this on?"

He does but it fits too tightly, his thick hair bunched beneath. He thinks to take it off, raises a hand to do this, but she shakes her head.

"Leave it on, just for now, huh?" Her voice is kind.

He has never entered the commissary or even been very close, only peering from outside under the protection of the flanking trees. The fire still is located some distance farther back. The commissary has a porch where he's seen people talking, stillers and scrapers and deckhands, and today some stand there, looking up now as the three slowly approach. One is a white man with a mustache and a broken beard, a large hat on his head that shields his face and brownish hair. His skin looks sandy next to the others, like he might have soap on it or have taken sick. He holds a paper in his hands as if studying it.

A black man with a beard stands next to him, a Negro also on the other side. The bearded one nods at the white man, like he has shown something true. The three approaching stop before them, a quiet following their footsteps, the sound only of the calling birds. The white man steps forward, down off the creaking porch.

"What's your name, son?" His voice is loose, like a snake before striking, his teeth the color of tree bark.

The boy says nothing back.

The man pauses, kneels so that his eyes are below Johnny's, looks back up. "Don't be afraid, now."

He still doesn't speak.

The man looks at Josephus, his voice harder. "He don't talk?"

Mama Lo nudges the boy. Silence still. "His name Johnny."

"I didn't ask you. Johnny, how'd you get here?"

Nothing. He looks up.

"Look at me!"

He looks down.

The man grunts and stands, directs himself back to Josephus. "How'd you get him?"

The old man steps forward. "He just showed up. We tried to find where he come from. Took him to St. Joe but he wouldn't get out the wagon. Came back, stayed with us ever since."

With a swing the man cuffs Josephus, sending the older man sprawling. Mama Lo sucks in air. The man, again: "Don't lie to me, now. How long?"

There's a long second of silence before the boy throws himself on the white man, battering the bearded face with both hands, snatching at his beard and ears until someone lifts him off. The man's hat is knocked to the ground during this charging, and after righting himself, he picks it up. The top of his head is balding, the sparse hair stringy and wet-looking, pulled. He touches a hand to one ear as if blood has spouted, his lips drawn to a whistle.

The two black men hold the boy as he pants and still lunges, legs kicking like a chicken's, a taste in his mouth like iron or soap. His mind has gone blank now. His teeth clench and grind; snot leaks and runs. He's never hit anyone before in his life, that he recalls.

"Well, as I was saying . . ." The white man turns to Mama Lo.

"I dunno, suh. Maybe a year on or longer." A part of her jaw twitches.

The man makes a hissing sound. "Boy, you ain't got kin?"

Neither Mama Lo nor Josephus have mentioned his mother. He shakes his head once.

"Talk, boy!" the bearded black man yells. The others turn at this. The white man snatches the cap off Johnny's head at the motion.

"I ain't leavin'," he says, quietly. His voice is high next to theirs.

"There you go," says the white man, suddenly friendlier-sounding. "Son, you can't stay out in the woods with these darkies. Looks like you 'bout gone half wild yourself." He looks to the man who spoke, the others. "He been here a year and ain't nobody said nothing?" His face is still red, his ears, jaw, neck, and chin.

The others look down, even the bearded one. "No, suh. Didn't know of it. Soon as I saw it, I said, 'What is this?'"

"I ain't leavin'," he says again, louder.

The white man frowns. "Yes, you is. We gon' talk to the sheriff, see about straightenin' this out. This ain't gon' do, you being out here like this. Just ain't gon' do, now."

Johnny bolts, three steps from the men and gone, or he would be but for Josephus grabbing his collar and holding on, pulling back.

"Nah, son, you got to do what the man says." His voice is low and soft. "It'll work itself out. I done told you now, didn't I?"

He struggles but stops. Mama Lo leans in and hugs him. "You be good, you hear," her whisper like a summer fog. She hands him her sack with his clothes, her palm firm and hard. Her eyes are his mother's lake, water-pooled and a kindness, but with a flame held beneath that surprises, an anger he can almost touch. He swallows. Stares.

He cries now, too, his breath fast and short, and he so wants to hurt them, to share this pain that has struck him like an axe. He takes a long breath, his feet lift, and he follows, behind the commissary to an old truck parked in an oak tree's purple shade. He looks around then, thinking he'll see Elias at another tree, coming to free or to save him, but there's no one besides the black men watching and guarding. He doesn't see Mama Lo and Josephus leave. The white man nods and motions, and the boy climbs in the truck's open front. Taking a piece of something from a pouch, the man pokes in his mouth with his fingers, pushes his lip out, wipes a hand and spits.

"You with a bunch of niggers, boy. You even talk like 'em. You might should be thankin' me." He slaps the cap on the boy, despite Johnny's pulling back. "If you swing at me again, I'll hurt you." The man whistles a little and snorts once, shakes his head.

Johnny hasn't seen a car or truck since before the train. That trip seems so distant, blurry as if he'd not lived it, as if he only passed through it in a long and hazy dream. The man is shifting and spitting again, the motor grumbling low and true beneath, and it's as it was before but then not. He is older. He has seen and knows now much more. When they reach the hard roadway, they gain greater speed, to where the movement makes him dizzy and his hair whips past the cap, and if he closes his eyes the air seems to push up and lift him. It's like running but faster than he has ever run, almost like flying, and he wants to tell Elias of it but Elias is far away.

He watches the buildings and puddles and mail drops, the dogs that bark as they pass, the horses and plows making rows and lines out in fields. He hasn't been out of the woods since he entered them with

Josephus. White people appear on the roadway, and again they look strange: so many clothes on their bodies, their faces narrow and red like they've been burned. He takes his cap off and tosses it from the car, and the man doesn't notice or maybe doesn't care. They slow when they near the town, the man turning and shifting the car behind a building with a grunt and twist. He turns as he shuts the motor, his breath raw, the engine murmuring some before dying. The boy gives a start and a shudder just then, making a noise that sounds broken and similar.

"We're gon' go inside now and talk to this man. Don't even think about trying to run or hit anybody else. If you do, it ain't gon' go good for you."

Johnny climbs down from the truck, follows the man as he opens the door to the building and enters. There's a small desk there and a room with bars that must be a jail cell, grooves worn deep before it in the wooden floor. A big man sits behind the desk, dressed in some kind of uniform, different from the train uniforms, a little electric fan making ticking noises on his desk. The man's hair is slicked back and his face shaved, his belly heavy on his belt. This must be the sheriff the grown-ups spoke of.

The man who brought him shakes the other's hand. "Clete, this is what I told you. Out there in the woods with them darkies down at the gum camp. They say he been there more'n a year. He don't talk much. 'Bout wild, too. Tried to clock me one earlier." He rubs his jaw briefly, points to the boy's bare feet. "Says he ain't got no kin."

The sheriff examines the boy. No one speaks. He shakes his head, stretches his neck around. "Ain't never seen hair quite like that." He looks up at the other and back. "Boy, you need a haircut!" He smiles, not unfriendly-like. "Sit down here and let's talk, okay? You got nothing to be scared of."

The other man continues standing. "You need anything else from me?"

The sheriff shakes his head. "Nah. Check with me later, or tomorrow, if you would."

"Yep." The man starts to leave. "The coons say he got some weird markings on his back."

The sheriff turns to the boy, smiles again. He's missing a tooth in a gap a pencil could fit through. He leans back. "I think I got some suckers here. Want one?" He pulls a lollipop out of the desk. The other man exits the door.

The boy hesitates, then accepts this. He's remembering his thirst from when he and his mother came off the train—the silent, slick heat then, the way she turned her head. He sticks the lollipop in his mouth, the sugar quick on his tongue.

"Now, how'd you end up way out there?"

He responds in bits. He doesn't know. No, they didn't treat him badly. He helps with the trees, he does his lessons. He wants to stay, he likes them very much. He is ten years old, he thinks. The sheriff shakes his head.

"Son, you just can't stay there. We got to find your relatives. Everybody's got some relatives. Those that don't's got the state. You say your mama's dead?"

He nods, slowly.

"How 'bout your pa?"

A shrug. "I don't know."

"What's your last name, anyway."

The boy tells him Cruel, what his mother said.

The man's head shakes again. "Ain't heard of none of them. You sure that's right? That ain't something the darkies give, is it?"

"No."

"'No, sir.' You lived in St. Joe?"

Shrugging, remembering. The smell of cut boards and dirt.

The sheriff frowns. "Man says you got marks on your back. Did they beat you?"

Again, "No. No, sir."

"Best let me see."

The boy pauses again, then turns, takes his shirt off. Waits.

The man whistles low. "Don't look like no beating, but I never seen nothing like this. Go on and put your shirt back on, now. You got other markings?"

"No."

The man's eyes now have a different look. It could be wonder or disgust that now sits there, maybe confusion. Or maybe it's eagerness—something the boy can't seem to share.

The sheriff wrinkles his lips and looks off. His face shines with sweating. Bugs circle a light bulb above: little black moving dots. "Tell you what, boy. I'm gon' have to ask around. I want you to stay in that cell there. You ain't in no trouble; it's just that there's nowhere to put you. And now that you're here, I can't have you running off. You just got to sit. Okay, pal?"

Johnny shrugs again and enters the caged area. There's a bench and a bucket and the smell of pee and old sweat but nothing more. He tries to keep his thoughts from the box and being trapped. His breath hurries and rises, his face hot but not too much. The man closes the door behind him, looks back in.

"I'm gon' lock this, okay? Just 'cause I can't have you runnin'. I got to step out a minute, and then I'll be back. You need something? Food?"

He shakes his head once. He'd like a book but won't ask. He'd like to be back at the side camp with the others.

"The bucket's there if you need to go."

He says okay.

The sheriff is gone a long time. He examines the cell, including the bench and its underside, where a few things are carved: someone's name, a rough picture of a woman with breasts and tears. There's a web in the corner but no sign of a spider. The bucket is crusty with dried half turds, and stinks. The lock is rusted, the bars smell like blood. From outside he hears wagons and the occasional motor car, people laughing and talking, but no one enters the building. He sticks his hand out through the bars until his face is pressed on them, metal on flesh, and he wants to bang his neck and head. A flying bug lands that he sneaks up on, its wings tucked and legs cocked, feelers waving like hair. The shield-like wings. After a while he lies down on the bench and falls asleep, and when he wakes the place has darkened and hunger gnaws at his stomach like a beast. The sheriff stands past the bars, rattling a set of keys.

"Boy, this here is Mr. Don and Mr. Slim."

At least the boy thinks that's what he says. He's still foggy from sleep.

"They gon' take you to hep find your kin. Run you up to Tallahassee and see if they can't figure something out."

The sheriff doesn't look at him as he says this. The two men have half beards like the man back at the camp. One is tall, the other short. Their clothes are wrinkled, the smaller one with a smudge darkening his coat.

"Hello, Johnny," the tall one says.

BUSTER: "There's no good in this. This is a trick, now."

ROBERT: "Run!"

His belly shakes. The sheriff's head remains down, papers strewn on his desk like he spread them there purposely. A ring gleams on a finger, flashing by the single light. Someone clears their throat. The boy wants to cry out, to call someone for help, and he thinks to pray as Josephus had at the side camp, to ask for protection, mercy or rescue, or for something else. Buster? Robert? Please, please, Elias.

He pauses a moment, then follows the men, feeling that he's up on a bridge with darkness stretched now below him, threatening him, pulling him, and he has leapt out into the night.

PART II: 1931

CHAPTER NINE

BUSTER: "The ants will be here in the morning—Dexter and Alford and Calvin. They sleep at night."
ROBERT: "Do they sleep? How do you know this?"
BUSTER: "I just know it. I watch them."
ROBERT: "And William, and Edward?"
BUSTER: "The roaches. They like the dark."

THE VOICE COMES first, high-pitched and quick-paced and like nothing he's ever heard. His head tilts and eyes close, the sores on his ankle red and angry under the chain. Stilled, he listens: the men talking elsewhere, the crickets outside, his heart's thumping loud in his ears. The chain groans in moving, its length such that he can walk to the bucket to pee or squat; they take the chain off for him to take the pail out and dump it. Eleven steps. A sleeping pad drapes a corner, but for the most part the room is bare. He sits on his haunches, the slam of a car door familiar, the crunching treads to the house, as people are always entering or leaving. He flattens his back as he looks up. He no longer mopes or cares.

The front door opens, words dribble and flow. Again the voice, squeezed like the person—a woman?—has suffered some injury.

Usually, it is only men. He hears the two laugh, but the voice is what holds him, even as he taps his feet not to listen, her coughs and their talk slicing through to him like an axe: ". . . I don't know . . ." "What, in the middle of this Depression?" "Ha! I never . . ." "Well, you tell me."

A scrape, heavy footsteps. His heart turns at the sound, his mind fixed in cautioning that it cannot be her—she is dead; they're all dead now. Only he remains, and the searcher, if there is a searcher. What is there to look for now? His shirt is scratchy as he pushes up off the floor, his face hot. Sometimes they give him spoon bread or candy. He looks about for the roaches and ants he calls his friends.

The tall man enters, strides over and unlocks the chain. Stares at him, coolly: "Play pretty, now." Lifts him by the arm and escorts him out to the large room with its dirty brown couch and chair, where the light is so sharp that for a moment it blinds him. His sight jerks and catches: first the man, black-haired and hard-looking, his hands so large that they look like great mitts, then the figure with arms crossed beside him, a strangeness. A doll woman, she is tiny, to where at first he thinks she's a child, the man's child, but it's her voice that he must have heard. Her chin hangs in a strange and grown-up manner, her face shiny with makeup, her thin lips streaked red. Bosoms protrude, eyebrows, a purse. Wrinkles and jewelry. A perfumy smell.

"Ah," she says, looking up at him, offering neither smile nor frown. He's been told not to look at faces, to remember no one and recall nothing, but how can he not stare in wonder? Blond hair is twisted tight into curls, her eyes black like pellets, feet crammed in small shoes. The purse weights a plump arm. She turns to the tall one, like she's used to all of the questions or bossing others around, or just to being surprising, able to shock and stun.

"What's his name?"

"Johnny."

"Johnny what?" she chirps.

There's a silence. "Johnny Cruel."

"Nah." A smile forms, her teeth gray and uneven.

The man standing next to her rocks back on his heels.

"You got any schooling, boy?"

He looks to the others, who nod. "Some." His voice is low after hers. "I can read."

She shows her teeth again. "Good. How old are you?"

He looks down. "Twelve." He's unsure.

She looks to the others, back to the boy. Sets her teeth. "Let's see your back."

He turns, watching the two now, the men who direct and punish and feed him. Again, he seeks their approval; they squint and nod, agree. He shrugs his shirt off with a twisting, snapping sound, holds it warm in his hands without squeezing. Looks at the wall with the crack like a spider running. Counts to ten, slowly. Waits. They make him wear too-large shoes.

A breath draws deep. He assumes it's the man's but it could be the woman's. Her voice when it comes is a whisper.

"Squat down."

He does without looking. It's hard not to fall, and he uses a hand to keep himself steady. He senses movement behind him and flinches, awaiting her, shifting, glancing up at the two before looking down again. For a time nothing happens; then her touch makes him twitch, as if she has poked him with a pin—they've said he should be used now to the handling, but he never is. Her finger traces his spine's top to rest on the small protrusions, the winglike things that have grown despite his attempts to erase them; he cut part with a knife once, his back aching and burning for weeks. Down, down. Some men have licked them. His hands grasp his knees, his eyes closed, his neck stiff. His mouth is as dry as the dust on the dented floor.

"Alright." She near squeaks it. "Stand up."

He turns as he does so. He thinks of sunsets, of clouds. She is facing the others, though. Her eyes sparkle as she speaks.

"You his relation?"

"Guardian."

"Uh-huh. How much, again?"

"Five hundred. Nothing less. Cash."

"Birth certificate?"

Heads shake.

"Papers at all?"

"No."

A pause. "Two hundred. That's it."

The tall one snorts, the short one quick in following. The tall one again: "This a joke, little lady? You must think we're some fools." He points a long finger that bounces up and down a bit. "Go on and get out of here."

The woman turns, the man with the big hands too, his face down. The boy wants to sigh or weep, though he doesn't cry much anymore, and what did he want from these callers—what did he look for or expect? Visits are common and he knows the men receive money, but have they offered him up for sale before? He's not known or considered this. He's not sure what to think. The last time he ran, they caught him down the road, chained him and flogged him, made him eat his own waste. Eleven steps to the bucket. Eleven steps is his world. He's learned to presume nothing, to ask nothing, to think of hope as the thinnest and slightest of filmy clouds.

The short one starts things, saying: "Maybe they should pay something, just for our trouble," sliding past the others to block the door to the sun behind. For seconds no one moves or speaks, until the dark man grabs Shorty in a blur of hair, clamping big hands on his scrubby neck, wresting a muffled "oof" from the other man's puckered lips. The boy wants to yell, "They got guns! The tall one . . ." but he needn't, the woman having produced her own, a fat white pistol that looks large in her hands. She points it at the tall man, whose face twists into lines. His laugh when it comes is tired and skittish-sounding.

Coins clink. Bills drop slow to the table, the gun staying balanced in the lady's tiny hand. "Two hundred fifty. That's plenty fair. We'll be taking him and getting on now, just like you said." She motions to Johnny.

Silence again. A cow lows somewhere far. "Honey, what are you thinking?" the tall one asks, his voice prickly as always. "Even if you leave now with this boy." The short one rubs his throat, slumped still near the door, the dark man standing beside him. "You set a bird free of its cage, it comes back." He turns and shrugs. "You'll find that he'll run. He's no good." A brief pause, a slow sniffing. "You got you a show or something? Or are you people just . . ." Another pause. A wipe at his nose. ". . . some sort of freaks?"

The woman makes no answer, still pointing her gun. She turns to the boy. "You got things?"

He looks for approval but then glances away. Stepping back in his room, he grabs the few books they gave him, her bracelet he hid, some clothes he can tote pressed to his chest with one hand. His breath comes so quick that he can't think or hear, can't see in the light, and the room's stink so strong, and they will beat him—he knows this. They will catch him. Did he sleep and dream . . . ?

The woman stands where she did, the others also remaining. The large-handed man beckons the boy to the open door, and as he trots there he thinks to turn, to search for rage or for shame, but he doesn't—he stares ahead. Above the door is the picture of Jesus, beside it the painting of a beach scene with birds, the sun's burn like a lantern or signal past the doorway. Shorty has vanished and Johnny whirls now to look, fearing to find him with pail and whip waiting, part of some game filled with more wicked, sweating men.

The tall one threatens the woman. She responds softly-sweet. "I've seen a man eat cut glass, now. Another put a nail near through his head." A cough, somehow loud. "I ain't being disrespectful." Then: "Do you like that kneecap?" The gunshot rings as if searching or circling the house, a high-pitched howl trailing like a child denied a promised treat. The boy begins twitching, but the dark man only shakes his head. They're out at a car now, an open-top truck of a type Johnny has never seen, and at the man's direction he climbs into the back with his things. Smells rise of fuel and mud, perfume again, iron, sawdust. A taste forms in his mouth of dirt or blood, or something strange.

When he turns the woman is walking toward them. She moves in a slow, twisting way without looking behind her, heavily, carefully, her purse held with two hands. Is she a child playing dress-up? A gnome dropped from a star? Climbing into the truck with some effort, she sits and pushes her purse aside. Glances toward him in the back.

"I'm Esmerelda. Some call me Tiny Tot, or Tot. This here's Carl."

She faces the front, and the man shifts and drives. Miles pass in silence, trees and farms with crops brown in the fields, patches of green splashed near ponds and dips. He hasn't left the house in what must be some months, and the scenery and movement make his head swirl and hurt. Railings and posts pass, houses and gates. A horse bent and grazing. A gray flock of birds. A smell—sassafras? Mint or something like it. He makes the world and his thoughts go away; his eyes closing, breath slowing. The tires hiss and whine, the wind. After a time, though, he finds that he wants to say something to them, to try to make sense of this change and his flight. Has he swapped one jail for another? He thinks of a balloon he once watched, swelled up and lifting off the ground in a breeze, shifting and floating with no weight left to fall, until it burst and dropped. A shudder rips through him, though the truck's moving thrills, the motion, the ride, the departure. He has left. He is going fast, somewhere. He has hoped for and wished for and dreamed of this.

Gritting his teeth, he leans forward, speaks. "Where we goin'?" He swallows. His voice sounds newborn.

She cocks an eye to look back at him. A mole he'd not noticed before dots her face. "Why, where the people are, Johnny." They pass an old plow that looks sucked up by the earth, a car with its tires off. Tall, reaching, swaying pines.

The man laughs and she joins him. The truck groans at a shift of gears. "Everybody's looking for something, Johnny." She nods and smiles. "It's what I've learned, over all these many years. People are funny. Different pulls them in. We're like a religion—something not of this world. Everybody just wants to know, and to find out. Everybody wants to see and be thrilled."

CHAPTER TEN

Tiny Tot

We picked up Johnny from a farm in Georgia—me and Carl. I'd heard about him from someone at the show, an old man with no teeth who asked for a dollar if it came to be. When it did, I looked to pay him the dollar—fair is fair—but couldn't find him. We moved on. That's the way things work in this shifting sideshow world.

Johnny was a freak just like the others, just like me, and I knew his promise from the moment I saw his back. Chained in that house, those men doing who knows what; he wouldn't speak to me about any of it, saying only that he was from Florida and that his ma was dead. He was twelve or thirteen, he said, but acted eight or seven. He was a scrawny thing—like he hadn't been eating or seen the sun all that much. It was like the whole world was new to him: the truck, the trees, even the air. He was nervous and ghostlike. I guess he'd been stuck in that house going on several years.

I've known many freaks in my day, but Johnny is one of the purest, right there with joined twins, pinheads, and the armless or legless, far past the merely strange. Just something nature slipped up and did. There's no wrong to it; in fact, it shows his uniqueness, an absolute difference from almost anyone else alive, and that's a blessing to my mind, and something I know well. People have misjudged me the whole of my life, and I think with Johnny they did the same, at least at first. He was wide-eyed and sweet, just a thin kid still growing, maturing, and green. With his hair and eyes alone, we could have made money, but with his back? Ah, he was a treasure, a fable, all aces.

We were set for gold.

He joined Alexander's Traveling Oddities right away. There's no Alexander. People can't believe that I run the thing, but it's true. I bought out McKenzie when his show failed in Minnesota, took the sword-swallower and a knife-throwing act, and kept on. That was two years back, and I've added to it: We've a minstrel act and a flats joint, and I'd like to add girls but haven't done so yet. I've got plans, ambitions. A big tent, maybe swings and cats. The stars of our show, though, are the freaks.

So much about shows is illusion or talent, but some is what nature bares. I've seen plenty of fake snake women painted prior to every act; bearded women with hair glued in place; he-shes who are hes; "wild men" that are crazy drunks. But the real stuff, the real freaks—well, there's nothing like it. I got my start on the Brant show at age ten; it's why I first took a shine, I think, to Johnny. My parents just let me go. I'm sure now they were paid for it. I was scared, I was with strangers, I didn't know what to do; I was three foot six. Old Mr. Brant was a lecherous beast, but I survived and even grew to enjoy the life. I liked to be looked at and fawned over. I liked the hype. By the age of thirteen, I was the talker for my own solo act.

I'd never seen anything, though, exactly like Johnny. He's got a ribbon of cartilage or skin along his spine, extending out from a purple birthmark, that is growing still and dividing. Expanding, to where you can pull each side down. We advertise him as "the Winged Boy," and it's true; it looks like as he grows he'll have appendages hung there, some kind of large and unused, dangling wings. I saw a human tail once, a man named Barton who was briefly part of our show, a plait of hair and skin off his rump like a rope, but it was nothing near as grand as this. There's a hierarchy among freaks, a respect for those with the larger flaws, if you will, above even the jealousy of the show workers. Johnny's oddness rivals the greatest, and I take credit for finding him. What could surpass this? A centaur? A dragon?

I should have shot both the brutes holding him as a public service, if for nothing else.

He was like a soldier back from war when he joined us, and I was careful with and about him, having been through this pain myself. I kept asking about relatives—didn't he have some blood or kin? He claimed he didn't. I figured given his age that he might not be long with us, that some relation would arrive and demand his return or want payment, but it was worth the risk. When I asked how he came to be with the men, he wouldn't answer; he wouldn't talk about them at all. I asked him about his back too.

"What do you think of it—your growth back there?"

He frowned and shrugged. At first I thought he might be an idiot, but clearly he is not. He can count and read, which is more than can be said for most of this loutish group. He wants to know more. He picks things up quick.

"You know that you're special, right? Just like me."

This seemed to intrigue him. "What do you mean?"

"We're freaks, quirks of nature. Oddities that most have never seen. One in a million; in your case maybe ten million. It's nothing bad, nothing to be ashamed of. It just is."

"What . . . what am I supposed to do?"

I wanted to hug him. "Nothing, to begin with. We'll set you up. People will pay to see you, to see your back. No one will touch you."

He jerked at this. "Are you sure?" His voice was high then.

"Yes, I'm sure. We're your family at this point, Johnny. Families protect each other, right? I'll protect you."

He looked so doubtful.

I laughed. "And it's not just me. You met Carl; he's my fixer. Some call him 'the patch.' He makes sure things go smoothly. You'll meet the others too. I have a daughter, and nobody's touching her either."

This seemed to calm him. "Where do I sleep?"

"I'm putting you with Sheila. She's the tattooed lady. You'll be safe with her. Come on, let's go meet her."

And we did. I introduced him to Robert the sword-swallower

and Alfred, who juggles and has a vent act; Otto the pinhead; Bud, who paints and sets it all up. Sheila was, as I expected, very happy to meet him. The others were curious or envious or cool. I didn't bother getting him with the minstrel folks. He'd meet the rest of our merry crew in due time. The flats group I kept him away from.

Sheila had come on with us a year back maybe, hopping off the Maddox show. Her father was a tattooed man she followed into the business, getting her first ink, she told me, at the age of eight. She's covered pretty much head to toe. Now in her forties, or so she says, she looks good still in her swimsuit when she shows her skin, which probably helps as much as the tattoos to sell her show. I've seen her take on stray animals, and recognizing motherly instincts, I thought she'd be good with Johnny. At first he seemed scared of her; what child wouldn't be of a gal with snakes painted on her arms? I told Sheila she was responsible for the boy, that she needed to protect him, and she didn't argue or fuss. She stays in a little tent that is part of our women's quarters, and he went on with her. I think he was so shocked by the whole of our group that he couldn't have said much or protested if he'd wanted.

Twenty-seven people make up our outfit. I learned early from Brant, and learned it again when I bought this, that all of this stops if we can't make our weekly nut. Without enough funding, even the greatest acts don't endure, the jumps can't be made, the people can't be attracted to provide the cash to keep us churning on. Rain on a show night is cash washed down the drain, and there's breakdowns and fees and charges. Squawkers, complainers. People quit. It's all just a great circling, and so many can't see it through. I'm focused on costs and funding, having survived years with Brant where we had little to eat and almost no one came to see us—when a show at any price was too costly to attend. The Depression has hurt workers, hurt everyone, even freaks. Things are a bit better now, though the audience is poor or poorer, and I keep a close and tighter hold. People think I'm not tough enough, but I am. Looks deceive. Perverts stare at my chest and get a thrill. That man holding Johnny wasn't the first one I've put a bullet to.

We set Johnny up as the blow-off. That's the act at the end that customers pay more to see—the special something, the super-odd. I did the talk myself. We didn't have any banners yet or do any other promotion, but my talk was effective, if I say so myself:

"Folks, he's only just made his way to our planet. We don't know where he's from—some say Mars, some Jupiter, but who could know?—only that he's just not like us. He's the strangest, the most unique; I promise you've never seen anything like it in your life. If you're not amazed, I'll give your money back before you can even ask!

"This event is for men only, as we believe it's too troubling for the feminine eyes and ears. And please, I have only a limited number of tickets, only a dime each. Usually, they're a quarter! You'll leave shaking, you'll leave wondering, you'll go to church for a solid month straight to set you free. He's the winged boy, folks. Some say he's an angel. You decide for yourself. Only a few tickets left, now! Hurry up! Everybody'll want to see."

Bud bought the first ticket, priming the money pump. A line formed as planned, the ticket taker slow to make sure the line was well seen, to build excitement and interest—all our normal tricks. I peered in on that first performance. The men were grouped behind a railing Bud had built, and we made them wait a few minutes, near the point of complaint, before Johnny came on out. He was wearing a cape Sheila had found for him, some tights loaned from one of the girls.

Even in the bad light his hair shone, his green eyes looking odd and alien. The men stopped their talk at once, stopped their shifting and rustling, only leaned forward, faces crumpled, mouths dropped, and stared. Johnny stood a few feet beyond them, far enough to be out of reach, and Carl was there to enforce this. The boy walked up and down like we'd told him, not smiling, not talking, looking above the audience like he truly was from somewhere else. After a few passes he turned, whipped the cape off, and exposed his back to them. An intake of breath followed, a few odd whistles, some sniffing and mumbling. Johnny walked backward, close again so the men could see, and there was pushing and jostling. None of the cries of fakery we sometimes hear, like with the fake fetus. No catcalls or grumbling or jeers.

One more pass and Johnny left the tent, pulling his cape back around him, his white hair the last thing seen. The men filed out, wide-eyed and silent. No one asked for their money back. It was a monstrous success.

CHAPTER ELEVEN

Sawdust and hammering, people and signs: "Alexander's Traveling Oddities Presents: The Amazing Zorat! Sword-Swallower, Fire Breather"; "Only at Alexander's: The Wooden Talking Boy!"; "See the World's Smallest Woman, Here!" It's like nothing he's known, something pulled from a dream or the fairy tales he once read, with dragons that swoop down and wizards, ogres and giants, princesses, sultans, and elves.

He doesn't know what to make now of any part of this. He doesn't know what to do or think. This is his *family*? The word forms without speech, without movement of his tongue or lips. New smells come, new sounds: movement and patterns, structures, people, banners, stares. He thinks of the escape again, and of the house, the chain and his steps, the men. His friends the bugs. The cloud of the life before that he has lived.

The woman Sheila is describing things, advising him, scheduling tasks and explaining. At first the sight of her made him shake, this woman with markings all over, or at least on the skin he can see: her arms, her neck, everywhere except her face and ears. Her hair is more orange than red, and she talks so fast that he has trouble following, even when he's listening, and he's not listening just now. She moves her arms when she speaks, up near her head or in lines as she's pointing, and more than once he wonders if she's wearing tight, strange-marked clothes. Every few seconds she stops and looks back, a great smile playing to him, eyes sharp and brightened, nose tilted to the air. Otherwise, she talks on.

"We'll get you set up here—it's not so bad. Tot's not cold or evil, just money mad: it's all about rent. Pay the rent! I guess we all have to. She's been through hard times, as have I, as I suppose you have too, though you're still so young. How old did she say you are—twelve? At twelve I was in a show with my father; we were big stars! We were just something else. By fifteen I had a wedding ring. Crowds were huge, and it was work but still fun. Animals, trains, clowns, all the oddness. You'll hear language from some—just close your ears! They're filthy men. Are you thirsty, or hungry?"

He only nods.

"Cookie will have something. Let's walk over there. It's slough night; we'll be tearing down later to jump, and with this crew if you don't eat when the food's out, you starve. I'll introduce you around—have you met folks already? There's Tot, of course, and me. Zorat the sword-swallower; he also does a little fire. Alfred with the vent act. Boris, who throws knives at Alfred and plays the accordion. You've met Carl the patch. And then the freaks: Wilma the bearded lady—she's quite nice, though she can do some grousing; Otto the pinhead—also nice, but with the brains of an infant; and Kenneth the dog-faced man—not so nice. And there's more. I forget how many of us are out here on the show." She pauses, turns to him. "When was the last time you *bathed*?"

They've reached a cook tent, its sides stained, the odor of food drifting. A bald man with big arms and a sad face sits peeling potatoes.

"Cookie, this is Johnny. Johnny, Cook. Ethan Cook, our cook." She laughs in a bright sound burst, higher than her normal voice.

"Hello." The man shows no interest.

"Johnny's just joining. You got anything he can eat?"

The man makes no movement. After a moment he gets up without smiling, rummages around in a black case behind him, produces a loaf of bread and a knife with which he hacks a slice, also a block of cheese. He neither looks up nor speaks while doing so.

"Cookie doesn't say much," Sheila whispers to Johnny, loud enough for the man to hear. "But he's an angel at heart, ya know.

Right? Stay on his good side. He'll get you hot water for a bath or a shower when you want."

The man hands him food, still without looking. His arms are as large as pink tires or tree trunks. Tattoos on his hands look like gloves or strange talons.

"Thank you." The boy's voice seems a squeak.

The man turns and grunts.

"There's a water barrel behind Cookie." Sheila bows, continues. "I've got an extra cup you can use. Everyone keeps their own cup, for dog soup! That means water. Let's go back to my place and I'll get it."

Her talk bounces on: her father the tattoo artist and the pain of first ink, how now she's so used to it that there's no sting. The midways, the freaks known. Again, he half listens, staring at others as they stare back at him, some of them head down, sighing and muttering, whispering mysterious somethings to themselves. He wonders what oddities lay concealed beneath their pants and shirts. His breath as he thinks this catches halfway up his nose.

"Hey, Zorat!" she calls but doesn't bother to introduce them. He met Zorat earlier, with Tot, but it's as if Johnny is Sheila's now, a hold she must wave and flaunt. They enter the tarp behind "SEE THE TATTOOED LADY!" into a compartment that is half tent, half wooden trailer. Inside is a mirror, a cot, a trunk, table, and chair. "Home!" she says, smiling.

Unsure of where he should sit, he starts to lower himself to the ground.

"Sit in the chair, honey! I'll sit on the bed."

She stares at him now, quiet after all her talking. He swallows and looks off, the bread and cheese glued in his throat. His head tilts back.

"It's gonna be fine," she says, softer now. "I know it can be a shock. You've never been on a show before, right?"

He shakes his head.

"It's not bad. It's actually kind of fun. No one will hurt you. I'll make very sure of that."

He shifts and squirms. "What . . ." He can't manage it. Another swallow, his face heavy, hot. "What do I do?"

She shrugs and laughs. "Just let people see you! That's the beauty of this show, of you just being you."

His gaze falls away.

She leans forward, her face serious. Her lips move before her words. "Johnny, can I see it?"

"What?" His head jerks.

"Your back. That's what they'll be looking at—what they'll be paying for. I just want to see what we've got."

He shifts again, slumping, then stands and shrugs off his shirt. He starts to take his pants off too, but she stops him.

"No, no. Turn around. It's okay."

He does this. Her breath rattles and snags some. She doesn't say anything, doesn't move much. Then: "Okay, you can turn back around." The smile has returned, her eyes bright and gleamy. "Well, you're going to be a star, hon. That's all I'll say. Tot has found her a banner act and a gem. A prime draw to sell."

He tugs his shirt on, and with a rush she pulls him to her, hugging him fast up against her face and chest. For a moment he fights this, twitching in grief and terror, thinking it's like before after all, until finally he sags and calms. She smells sweet, like perfume. Her body is soft and as such unfamiliar, her skin almost glistening, the whorls and lines pushed to strange new forms. For a moment he sees the boy Jeremy's freckles, stretched and now curving, forming a rose first, a donkey, a clown's face. She pulls back.

"Johnny, we'll do the best we can. Is there anything I can get you?"

He pauses, twisting his shirt straight. His tongue knocks against his teeth. "Do you have any books?"

THEY HAD ARRIVED in the morning after driving all night, and after the food and a cup of water, his eyes close on their own. He wakes wrapped in a blanket, lying on other blankets stretched out crossways on the ground, a pillow beneath him, one shoe in his hand. He feels for the chain but can't find it, can't judge for a moment where he might be. The woman—Sheila, he recalls now—stands above him, clad in a tight-fitting outfit that shows even more of her ink and skin. His eyes follow a ship's form, a face and several flowers, a name wrapping over her shoulder. It's like a tale is told there, across her. She sees him looking and smiles.

"Yeah, there's a hundred of 'em—more now, I think. Some tell a story and a few are just there. Some I still like and some I no longer do. But it's me." She laughs, again the high sound that's so different from her normal voice. "And you're you. You got to get up now. You're the blow-off tonight."

He struggles up, something caught in his belly. Rising now to his chest. "The what?"

"The blow-off. The last act. People pay more to see you."

He pauses, lifts his head. Bites his bottom lip. "I don't want to do it."

She smiles still. "It'll be alright." She touches his arm.

He pulls back.

"Hey, I'm sorry. Nobody touches you unless you want 'em to, including me. Is that fair?"

He nods. Sweat forms, an itch.

"They've come up with a little outfit for you, okay?" She holds out a shiny something.

"No!" He shrieks this out, his arms thrashing and flapping. He looks around for an escape. Now it's Sheila who is pulling back.

"What's the matter, Johnny? Don't scream. It's nothing bad!"

He can't form words. Memory hangs but he blocks it; he won't return there, won't bend himself upward or send himself back. For a time, there's a silence, the two of them breathing hard. Finally, he mumbles: "No dress."

Her laugh surprises him. "It's not a dress, Johnny. It's a cape. See?" She extends her arms, draping a blue-and-red square of material between them. "Everyone has a costume. But don't scream, okay? Somebody will think that I'm murdering you in here. Just take and hold it." She pushes the cape forward. "You just wrap yourself up in it. It doesn't make you a girl."

He takes it after pausing. The cloth is cool and smooth. He wants to vomit, to sleep more. "I don't want to do it."

"Johnny." She squats near, her marks again forming different shapes. "Let's do this one time, okay? It's what you're here for. I promise you that it won't be so terrible—it won't. Will you trust me?"

He looks down. A rustle follows, a swishing of tent flaps as Tiny Tot enters to join them. Johnny's hands clasp his shoulders. He takes in long, noisy, shaking breaths.

"What's going on?" Tot too is dressed up, fresh makeup applied and her hair styled and curled. He's surprised again by her shortness; she barely reaches Sheila's waist. She offers one look at him, the next up at Sheila. "He okay?" Her movements are sharp. Her voice rings high but with a firmness, force.

"Just opening-night jitters. He'll be fine. Right, John?" Sheila's lip juts up.

He picks up the cape, looks from one to the other. Quietly then: "Yes." Again. "I guess. Okay."

Tot smiles, her lips flashing red. "Well, let's get you cleaned up. You need to eat too! Come on, now. Toilet?"

It becomes a great swirling. The areas of the show that before had been calm spin now with new movement: men toting things, Boris hammering and sweeping, others in the cook tent talking, laughing, and eating. He is shown the "shower"—a hose hooked to a barrel placed on a truck (the "water wagon," he learns) and from which water flows—and the toilet, a hollowed-out wooden chair placed on a platform above a bucket. (Apparently a bathtub is filled for Tot and some of the ladies and brought inside a tent.) Music plays: an accordion, maybe a piano.

From afar he hears a voice, several voices, dipping and flowing in a honeyed song. A boundary has been erected, men taking up stations. There's an air of excitement, of promise, but also of purpose, as it was in the forest with the men waiting to scrape their trees. It dawns on him now that this is a job as well as performance. Beyond he sees wagons arriving and cars—the show's guests. A few oil lamps are lit, providing a silvery and snaky, smoky light.

Sheila hustles him to the cook tent, then the toilet (he can't go), back again for a drink of water, as he forgot his new cup. He splashes himself wet in the shower, glancing around for those who might be looking on. Back at her tent, he changes into clean clothing, or at least puts on shoes and pants that she gives him, wraps himself up in the cape. She asks if he wants a mirror, but he turns this down, his head hanging, hair flopped. His eyes pool and cloud with the fullness of hot tears.

"Listen, I have to go on now, but I'll be back in thirty minutes." Sheila bends and smiles. "Then I'll take you where you need to go. Okay? Do you wanna see my act?" She pauses. "Here, let's comb your hair."

He shakes his head, his back turned to hide his crying. Examining his legs and the scars still striped there, he half thinks on running, on blending in with the crowd and within hours being somewhere else, but where would that leave him? He's had thoughts of return to the side camp, to Joe and Elias and all the rest, but that dream has faded; he has no money, no family, no idea even of where to go. He thinks of boats, cars and airplanes, carts and wagons, trains. Could things have grown now into something worse? For the first time in a while, he thinks hard on his mother, inhaling in the hope of her smell coming, a memory he hasn't retrieved in so long, but nothing hits. He's still listening for her voice, trying to remember the things she once told him, of his birth and his father and the scattering of facts he holds, when Sheila's head pokes back inside the tent.

"Ready?"

His heart lurches. Is it time? He struggles up, a man led to his hanging, clad in this silly costume, an oddness and spectacle shown now to the crowd. A shocking freak. Sheila leads him back behind the tents, where the air is cooler and a grass smell clings, into another tent not unlike her own, in which a platform has been erected with a rail placed in front. Across from this sits a single chair. One side of the tent is open, perhaps to admit more light and air, though the tent remains shadowed and gloomy. A string of bulbs across its top shine like distant, tiny stars.

"Hear her?"

And he does—Tot's voice is beyond them, sailing and prodding and pitching and selling, calling him the greatest and oddest, the most splendid and the truly strange. He stares down at his shoes, his nose dripping, his tongue grown extra large. His heart thumps like a hammer's heavy fall. Sheila nudges him once, her face and arms even brighter than before, a tattoo behind her ear of a dog howling made clearer. She gives him a slow, hopeful wink.

"You got it, boy. All you do is walk in, stare at the men for a minute, sit down in the chair, and when Tot tells you, turn around and take the cape off. You stand there for a minute or two, walk up and down so that everyone can get a good view, and then it's done! Walk on off and we eat some candy. How's that sound?"

He shrugs and tries smiling. The sick feeling from before has found its way to his belly, and he's left with the idea of crapping now in his cape, of showing *that* to the audience, and the thought makes him laugh and shriek. Sheila frowns and claws his arm, attempting to put a stop to this.

"Hush now! They'll hear you! You don't want to spoil the show."

Her grip digs and hurts him, his giggling brought up short, and he spins himself to her in a twist that makes her slump and fall. She lands on her back, surprised, her own rage quick and dull in her face, her eyes sharp. Her teeth look like rocks. Tot is suddenly behind her.

"You ready? What are you doing?"

His breath is short, his fists balled and sweat running, and he's thinking of the time the men beat him so badly that he couldn't walk, after he snapped at a paying guest. Tot raps on his knee for attention.

"Get behind the curtain. They're coming in!"

And so they are, a shuffling line of rumpled men, three or six or ten of them before he is pulled back from their view. Again he is warm-faced, whirling once more when Tot's voice breaks and launches, amplified somehow like a god's: "And here he is, gentlemen, that oddity from another land, that one of a kind, one in ten million, born to an unknown mother, a gift straight from the clouds. Please welcome the one and only Johnny C—the boy with wings!"

Muttering and a few handclaps, and he finds himself suddenly inside the tent, the cape on his shoulders and falling down his back. Maybe Sheila pushed him or Tot has simply willed it, but he walks out as they told him, sitting and then striding from one end of the rail to the other, at first not looking but then looking at each of them, one after one after one. He flourishes his cape, then turns his back to them and sits again in the chair. A murmur rises, different in tone from only minutes before this, a few words breaking: ". . . where is . . . ?" ". . . some fraud . . ." ". . . back in Toledo . . ."

Again, Tot's voice squeaks. She's standing next to him somehow, peering and holding a small oil lamp. "Now, the moment you've waited for. Be prepared, as even grown men have been known to faint." She pauses. "Don't tell your wives about this. Don't tell your children. Don't tell anyone." Another pause. "He's a living, breathing monstrosity. Here he is—Johnny Cruel!"

He rises and, keeping his back to them, slowly drops the cape. Off his shoulders, exposing his side, over the hump on his back and with a rush the cape falls, lying then twisted and shapeless on the ground just below. A hiss sounds behind him, new grunts and shifts. A few cries: "What the . . . ?" ". . . can't be . . ." ". . . just putty, right?" ". . . sticking it on that boy . . ."

He stands there for a minute or two, tears dripping down his face, walks to one side and then the other before wrapping the cape back over his shoulders, turning and striding past them and out. Sheila is behind the tent's wall, her eyes alive with excitement, their near fight forgotten, and he sees others watching: Zorat, Kenneth, Alfred, a few others unknown. One blond-haired girl, a look of surprise or maybe confusion on her face, as if none of this makes even the slightest sense. He wipes at his eyes and walks on past them all.

"How'd it go?" Sheila asks him. She's almost jumping up and down.

His breath is calm. He squints up at the sky, the dried salt on his face cracking and his neck bent beneath this, fighting an impulse to laugh or to hug her. The stars form different shapes like white ink. He pulls the cape tight, feeling it catch on his wings—for isn't that what they are? Looking out at her now, he gestures outward and shrugs. Turns his palms up. Smiles. "It was fine, I think."

CHAPTER TWELVE

"That's not your real name, is it?"

"Johnny?" He's sitting with Sheila in the back of a truck. Zorat is there too, and a tall man named Lenny, another man with big arms they call Bud. All of them telling tales—jackpotting, they call it. They all seem to be sunburned, red-nosed and -eared and with lines stretched past eyebrows, each missing several teeth. Fingers stained muddy brown by their smokes.

"Johnny Cruel."

The boy stares. "What my ma told me."

"She's dead then, your mother?"

The others look on and listen.

"Yes."

"And you have no one else?"

Why is he always asked about this? He hates talk of mothers, of his mother. He's never seen his kin in Tennessee. When he was back with the men he dreamed of escaping and finding them, but how would he find them? He's thought of asking for people named Cruel. He's thought of going to Florida to look for his father, asking there for Cruels, as wouldn't they share that name? Something tells him, though, that this wouldn't work, that it's better to see himself as a stray and an orphan. To start anew and never think about looking backward. To turn things like this or try to, shift and guide all such talk away.

"Where are we going?"

No one seems to know. "It's just the next jump," responds Sheila. "North Carolina?" She lifts her hands. "It's all pretty much the same but for the weather."

"That ain't true," Lenny says, lifting his head. "Big cities make a difference. They bring on some separate crowds. We generally do the small stuff, though, as that's what Tot says she likes. Says it keeps us out of most trouble, spreads our name out and such."

"But the marks, now, they're the same."

"Mostly the same."

"Not always, but yeah. It's always some something. Had a woman last stop nursing a ten-year-old in her lap."

"Nah!"

"You're lyin'."

"I am not. Her teats looked like barn rope."

"Lord have . . ."

"Ha!"

"Man by her told me he'd been married thirteen times. That weren't countin' the tweeners. He looked near wrung out."

"Woman came to the show carrying her dead dog like a purse. Thing was all greasy and stinking, its fur on her clothes and hands."

"Haha."

"And they say we're the weird ones! You see it all here, Johnny, everything swirled and sunk. The public put on a proud, loud display! They're all just like rats, nosing around something they might can take or eat."

Johnny looks out and off, at the fields and forests and ponds and spread lawns, everything green except grass browned to straw colors, the curves the road makes against rocks and hills. Much of it is strange and new. A tree stands in a pasture's sparse middle, its branches stretched out like a man flinging up his arms, and he realizes he's near forgotten what trees could look and smell like, their bark and branches and needles, their roots and trunks and leaves. If he thinks hard, he tastes them, the sweetness and crunch clean and crumbling and ropy. For a time, he had nothing of trees but his memory, his stark and delicate, bright and passing dreams.

"The big shows—the circus, now—they go by train." Sheila shifts and continues. "That's the way, I can tell ya. That's comfort. With Mathers and Cole, that was how we went."

"That's the way most carnivals went. Tot says we're more nimble, more modern now, ain't that so? We can reach out to folks that ain't never been seen or met."

"Modern? Shit."

"At least you're not behind a horse like the Negras. By the time they get to one show, they got to leave on for the next. That's how it was in the twenties, and back before."

"Until a truck breaks down. Then a horse sounds mighty good."

"A Hoover wagon—a broken car pulled by mules." There's a laugh, several.

"What trouble?" the boy asks. He's behind in the conversation.

There's a pause. "People who don't like our shows. Say that they're evil. Like our Robert right here."

They turn and look at Zorat, who holds a book open in his hands. Johnny sees that it's a weathered Bible.

"The Devil abounds, whether we believe he exists or not," Zorat says. He smiles, as if to show that he means no harm by his saying so. "It's all here." He points at the book with a thumb curved like a bird's head. "I didn't just make it up."

"Robert, please." Sheila sighs. She looks over at Johnny. "Robert's been gripped by God."

"Gripped by freaks, too. You hear they're making a movie?" Bud rises and turns, round arm muscles twitching. "Motion picture with freaky folks?"

"Who told you this?"

"I've heard it twice. Johnny Eck's in it—you all know Johnny? Half boy walks on his hands? I used to work with him back at Ripley's."

"Robert thinks freaks are cursed." This comes from Lenny, twisting his head back like a rearing horse, as if he might snort of a sudden or throw down great hooves.

"I never said that." Zorat smiles again. "The freaks here are the ones who've managed somehow to survive. Unlike the dead babies, or at least the real ones in the jars: two-headed fetuses that didn't live, embryos connected back-to-back or leg-to-leg. With some animals it's more common. I've seen a live two-necked chicken, a cow with a big third eye. Our freaks are wonders, for sure. Amazements." He taps his Bible. "But I don't ever dismiss Satan."

"He's just jealous," Bud says. "He's got to work at his talent, keep at and sharpen it as a skill, while you just walk out there and *boom!* People give cold cash!"

The others grunt and chuckle. Zorat, or Robert, doesn't say anything in response, just shakes his head slowly, the smile still across his face. The boy thinks of the preacher who called him out as a devil, the one who started him down this long, twisted, painful road, and did he invent this man or imagine him? The memory has grown so dark and dim. Sometimes he thinks that his life before was a dream or this is—that he'll find himself back with the men or Elias or in a box underground. Josephus used to read some verses of scripture each Sunday, followed by a few prayers, but that was it. God and religion he knows little of past his storybook, and as with everything else, he wants to see and learn more. Maybe his face proclaims this, when he'd prefer more to keep it hidden, as for the rest of the ride Zorat pages through his Bible, stares out the window, or looks fiercely and closely at him.

HE LOVES THE acts. After a few weeks he's seen or sat in on most, sneaking a view under a tent or sitting in the audience with the patrons, his hair tucked beneath a cap. No one seems to notice him or says anything to him or about him that he hears. Most of the acts are "single O's," he is told, each with a single performer. Many of these appear several times each day. He's amazed by it all: how Zorat can expand his throat and chest to take the sword in; how he breathes out plumes of fire like a dragon's evil cough. How Alfred can make his wooden dummy Cletus talk, to where you would swear the words come straight from Cletus's painted mouth. (Alfred even lets him touch Cletus once, to feel of his eyelids, to listen to his hollow chest for any breath.) How Alfred stands still as Boris tosses knives into a board around him, the blades pinning a sheet tight to Alfred's frame. ("Balance, kid—it's all balance and follow-through," Boris tells him. "Your arm tracks your mind.")

He is fascinated by the "pickled punk": the jar supposedly containing an aborted fetus, really a "bouncer" that is pieces of twisted sponge. The freaks are different but also charming and thrilling, trotted out for people to gawk at, doubt, or mock, for mumbled phrases like "Oh, my" and "Can you believe it?" and prompting faints and shrieks. Their acts are their own: Otto rides a tricycle in loops and grins; Wilma the bearded lady arm-wrestles men and defeats them; Kenneth the dog-faced man recites poetry and sings a song. As the setup man, Bud paints the banners, erects and takes down the tents, goes into the nearby towns to drum up interest in the coming shows. He spreads sawdust and lime in the latrine hole to cut the smell, helps out at the rope lines, sets fire to the trash before the show departs. And Tot can be seen everywhere: supervising the tent setup, accompanying Bud to town, checking up on performances, talking the bally out before the several acts. Turning the tip, as the showpeople mark and call it—convincing people to pay and to take themselves inside.

Although several of them perform as the talker, Tot is by far the best. Given her own stature, she draws a crowd, and the force and enthusiasm of her words always drive men into tents. Men are the show's primary patrons, occasionally a few women, only rarely children. For a time Johnny scans faces for sign of the men he left, come now to find him and return him to their service, but he never sees anyone he thinks might be them. The guests look much alike: clad in work clothes and hats, maybe arrived straight from the factory or market or the farm, the smell and cloud of tobacco smoke always about their heads. Sometimes he sees them drink from the lips of glass jars. Sawdust and hay and boards are spread to fight the dust and mud. Sitting and waiting for his own performance, he imagines the men outside hearing Tot's call and being swayed—by curiosity or horror or boredom or something else—to part with their money, to take a chance then and enter, to watch for a few moments. He asked Tot after a week whether anyone ever demands their money back.

"People don't mind if they're duped, Johnny," she replied, "if there's some wit to it or a smile sent, if they're left just a bit *wondering*—it's all about the wonder, see? It's all casting magic spells. But you're the real thing, now; there's no gimmick or fakery. That makes it all the better. That's what makes things really sing."

Two parts of the show are kept shielded from the remainder: a small tent known as the flats, which he is forbidden to enter, and the minstrel tent located in the rear of the show's roped-off ring. He asks Sheila about the flats tent but doesn't receive much in answer, only that it involves men and gambling, and that if a problem occurs with the patrons, usually it's there. This whets his interest, and for days he lingers within sight of the tent itself, watching men enter and, later, make their exit. The flats workers don't say much and keep mostly to themselves, even when within the cook tent, and he knows only one by name: Wilton. He's unsure of how many work in the effort. He observes Tot enter and exit the tent almost every night.

The minstrel tent produces music, the singing he heard his first day at the show. He's not prohibited from going to it like he is to the flats tent, but Sheila warns him to "stay away from those Negras," which he doesn't really understand. On his first visit he is struck by the grace and force of their music, the voices uplifted and brown skin he knows well, and for a moment he feels like he has reached his home.

After the first act he speaks to one of the women, though she proves stiff and unfriendly, her advice to "go back where you come from" so unlike what he knew before. Does she assume he's a patron and not a part of the touring show? After a time, they acknowledge him, but a distance remains that he can't quite make sense of. When he speaks of the side camp, they shrug and shake their heads. The minstrels don't eat with the others in the larger group and as far as he knows don't even use the same toilet. They pile into their wagons and depart just after singing. As he thinks on it and looks around him, they are the only black or brown faces with any connection to the show. He never sees coloreds attending Alexander's Traveling Oddities.

During the days he can do mostly what he wants. He helps some with the setup or takedown when they jump, but on the days where they stay in the same place, he explores. He notices that the show is set up the same way each time, with a main entrance and ticket booth, a central aisle with trucks parked to form a funnel, banners strung on them and tents placed behind, flags stretched across their tops. This forms the "walk-through," the type of show they run. Some call it the midway, though Sheila says it's really not. Off at an angle is the flats tent; far in the back, the minstrel show. During the acts, the cook tent sells Amos and Andy dolls, peanuts and soft drinks, pretzels and block-shaped popcorn bricks, sometimes iced cream. Peanuts in waxed paper sacks. Without electric lights there are torches, which bring to things a different feel.

Only five artists merit trailers: Tot, Zorat, Kenneth, Sheila, and Otto (with Walter). Everybody helps raise and take down the tents, even some of the women. His show tent is shared with Zorat, and soon banners for both are unrolled outside it: "ZORAT THE MAGNIFICENT: SWALLOWER OF SWORDS AND FIRE!" next to "SEE THE ONE AND ONLY, NEVER BEFORE FOUND ON EARTH: THE WINGED BOY." His banner has a picture on it, and he must admit to its likeness: his eyes a grass green and his hair white as milk, but the wings they show are fully formed like a bird's, and this puzzles and bothers him. Another proclaims:

"$10,000 Reward if the Boy Is Not Alive!"

He likes to look at the banners and count them, noting the care with which they are removed, rolled and folded, unwrapped and hung, arranged, even scrubbed with rags. The smell of old canvas mixes with sawdust and popcorn, the combined odor of it as unique as that of the side camp's still. When his banner is first displayed, the others gather to look, praising Bud and his talent, a few of them kidding Johnny that the boy pictured is his twin. Only Zorat seems put off by it, sniffing and looking away when it is tacked up next to his. The boy hears his complaint to Tot that folks will think Johnny part of *his* act and feel shortchanged, but Tot brushes this off with a cackle: "We'll see, Robert. We'll just see."

Often during the day, and on the long truck rides during jumps, he reads. He scours the show for books, asking the performers and workers for written words as if starving, having been held for so long with so little to be found or had. His haul is mixed, from old newspapers to copies of the *Billboard* sheet to romance novels Sheila and Wilma keep to the Bible. He reads them all. He particularly likes newspapers, and after a show he sometimes prowls in the darkness, on the lookout for a paper some customer might have dropped. These are always engaging and produce lots of questions, both as to word meanings and to what a story might be about. He asks Sheila things like "What does 'conspicuously' mean?" and "Where does oil come from?" often, and she becomes vexed when she doesn't know. He determines that probably half the men in the show cannot read, and those who do read don't read fast like he does.

Surprisingly, Zorat is the one who doesn't tire of his questions, particularly if they are about the Bible, and long discussions are had about the Israelites and their suffering and what Jesus did or didn't do, particularly relating to the afflicted.

"Johnny, do you believe?" Zorat asks him.

"Believe what?"

"That Jesus is God's only son. That he died on a cross to save man."

"Sure, I think so."

This seems to offer some relief. Zorat rubs a square black jaw. "So many don't. So many souls going to hell that it saddens me, Johnny—it truly does. Everything is offered, but somehow, they just can't see. If you read the Bible, it's all put right there: love and punishment, the pathway and darkness. It really is a gift, in the purest sense, of the single, simple truth."

Zorat is more willing to discuss the Bible than he is his act. Johnny watches it often, almost every day, and he likes how it's the same but then sometimes it isn't. Clad in a turban and a long, flowing robe, Zorat makes a grand entrance, sweeping into the tent like an Egyptian god, music from Boris's accordion playing in time with his arrival. He recites a long history that even the boy knows is false, of how he came from Armenia and grew up at his father's forge, how his father and mother and sister all swallowed swords, and his father had even swallowed a long gun once. He then brings out his knives and presents these to the audience, allowing them to be touched and felt as to their hardness, a confirmation that they aren't made of rubber and don't fold in upon themselves.

After this display, Zorat returns to his spot before them and appears to go into a trance. The accordion plays once more, a long pause following in which the crowd begins shuffling and coughs. Finally, Zorat grasps the smaller of the swords with both hands as if to stab himself, places the point to his chest and turns his side to the audience, tilts his head back, and holds the sword high above him. Again, there's a pause, the music stopped now, the audience tense and waiting, until slowly the sword drops, the point entering Zorat's mouth, then extending, his throat on its sides bulging, the sword dropping in inches until only the hilt is left at Zorat's nose. He turns around then in a complete and measured circle. Sometimes his eyes remain open during this movement, large and pushed-out-looking; sometimes, they're flat and closed. It makes the boy's stomach curl up, his own throat stretch and thicken. Zorat remains in this position for what seems a long time—really less than a minute—then pulls the sword quickly out.

The entire process is repeated with the longer sword. At the end Zorat turns his back to the audience and someone, usually Bud, hands him a wand lit like a torch. With a rush he turns and breathes fire out toward the audience, flames spitting from his mouth in a fiery eruption, and the audience shrieks and steps back. He does this again and again, the accordion music swells, he bows low to the audience and exits. Sometimes he dips the wand in his mouth like the sword, but not always. Once, as the boy watched, the fire seemed to exit his nose. The audience generally loves it, and there is much hooting and hollering, a reaction so different than at the end of Johnny's show.

He asks: "How do you do it?"

Zorat shakes his head. "It takes much practice, John. You are teaching your body to do something odd. It's a matter of becoming accustomed."

"Is there a trick?"

"No, no trick. I must be very careful in that which I do. I must concentrate fully the entire time I'm performing. If I don't, I can hurt myself, and that would mean I must stop the act. Once I was forced to lay out for a month. If that happens again, she will fire me this quick"—his fingers snapping, his head tilted back and mouth open like a grave. "Look at this." His tongue and gums are crisscrossed by scars, the bubbled flesh in his throat, too, and around his teeth. "With fire you get burned." He shrugs, his arms up, more scars there. "You get used to it, over time. It's the price of my entertaining."

Johnny contemplates things that might liven his own act up, something more than simply showing himself and revealing the oddness of his back. He asks Sheila and Zorat for suggestions: He could read something, perhaps. He's not much on singing. He doesn't have other talent. Neither of them have much to offer, shrugging and suggesting things (dropping down from a wire, flapping his arms as if wings) that won't work.

"Don't you worry, Johnny," says Sheila. "Right now you're the biggest act. Just be yourself and enjoy it, relish all the attention. Tot saves the best for the blow-off, the thing that's like nothing else, that they'll pay more then to see. And that's you! You're the best."

ONE NIGHT IN Virginia, he has a dream of the one-armed man. He has dreamed of him off and on through the years, flutters of memory and dulled, cloudy scenes, but this is different and vivid, sharp-edged and made alive. Rather than advancing toward him, in the dream the man steps back, and the boy sees that in fact he has two arms hanging at his sides. Palming a knife with one hand, the man begins cutting his other arm at the shoulder, blood spurting and flowing until with a crack the bone breaks, the hand flops, and the arm is wrenched off like a jar lid unscrewed.

During this chopping he offers a sly grin and stare, his teeth clenching at points but without noise or any speaking. Only a hacking sound echoes, a ripe smell lifting up, meat and bone jutted oddly. Sliced tendons dangle like wet red snakes. The boy awakens gasping, sweat-drenched and almost sick, and for the rest of the night he remains up and guarding against something, trying to convince himself that this dwells only in his mind. Capable of removal with will, force, and restraint.

SHEILA HAS A mirror that she examines herself in often, another smaller mirror so that she can also see her back. Before each of her acts she surveys herself top to bottom, clad in her sequined outfit, while he tries not to watch or stare. He's become used to the tattoos but wishes she would wear more clothing. The mirror he has avoided, catching only glimpses of his own face in passing, but one day during her act he remains in the tent and picks it up, holds it out, frames and scans himself.

Peering back is a thin youth, white hair uncombed and short, his eyes a chilly, moldy green. Hesitating, he removes his shirt, examining the sparse hairs under his arms, looking closer at the down on his face, at his teeth. He positions the small mirror, his heart almost rippling, turning about as he's seen her do, holding the mirror up to view his neck and back. The tufts of hair he's found at his crotch are here too, spread down his spine and on the attachments now grown there, these ridgelike things that show signs of increased dividing, larger at the top than the bottom, smoothed and flexible-looking, wooly, pinkish growths. If he twists, they will flap and shake some, a swinging feel to this movement, each looking somehow like the sponge-formed pickled punk.

He puts down the mirror and fastens his shirt on, his hands sweating, flattening his back and standing straighter, his chest out and chin. Already it's hard to sit in a chair or lie flat on his back much. He considers for a moment never removing his shirt again.

He begins to notice things about his act: the size of the audience; the response of the crowd; the others sometimes watching. His events are packed, despite the payment required, sometimes with a crushing that pushes the audience up against the rail. Benches are constructed, bleachers. Ropes to form a single line. The other acts aren't like this— people wander in and out, sometimes only a handful to see Sheila or Zorat or even Wilma arm-wrestle, with no need to pay anything more just to come inside. They'll do their acts six or eight or ten times on a show day, while he does his only once or twice, and is there resentment that follows this? He can't be sure. He asks Alfred once: "How do you do it, over and over and over?" The answer: a shrug, a smile. "It's a job. It's what we do." A wink, his hands out. "We're professionals, Johnny.

Until we die, and maybe after, too."

Whereas for a time he hears only a dull hum at his acts, now words cut through like they did that first night: "... boy is a freak, I tell you," "This shouldn't even be allowed," "... can't believe my own eyes," "It's all fake, it's a fake! They're just pasted on there," and, with frequency, "Now drop them britches, boy!" Once a man calling, "I'm a doctor. Let me see. A doctor!" Another: "It's a demon! Fallen here now, I say!" After some weeks, Tot asks if she might touch his back during the performance, to disprove the complainers, and with some reluctance, he agrees. Her touch is light and respectful, and after a time he doesn't mind it much. Once someone leans past the rail and he feels a different, harder touch, but in an instant Carl is there, escorting the offender off as Tot continues talking. Another time the rail itself breaks from the pressure, and for a moment arms twist toward him like vines, but Tot swings her torch and again Carl is there, pushing the crowd back with a voice loud and rough. Grumbling, shuffling, the men—mostly soldiers at this show—shift and obey, retreat.

He takes note of the show members watching, once even Cookie the cook on his break. Their faces show different expressions, of awe or curiosity not unlike the paying audience, others pinched in disdain or something else. "Jealousy," sniffs Sheila when he mentions this new awareness. "You're the star, and they want to be. There'll be some that aren't nice—you mark my words, Johnny—and when they're not, you just tell me, and I'll go and check them up."

He keeps looking for the young girl he saw his first night, though he never sees her at his act or anywhere else in his searching, and he concludes that she wasn't part of the show, that perhaps she snuck in the back as a patron. Then one day he sees her or thinks he does, peering from a flapping corner as he makes his way to the tent. He's reluctant to ask of her; she could be an illusion, like Cletus the dummy or the preacher or even the one-armed man. Eventually, though, he stutters his question to Sheila, his heart beating in his mouth.

"Oh, that's Winifred," she responds. "She's Tot's daughter."

"Her daughter?" He recalls now Tot mentioning her. "Is she . . ."

"She's normal-sized."

"How can that be?"

"It's not that unusual. Something in the genes, I guess. I don't claim to understand it."

"Who is her father?"

"Some say it's Carl, though I tend to doubt that. It's not discussed."

"Why do I never see her?"

Sheila shrugs and smiles. "That you'd need to ask Tot, Johnny."

CHAPTER THIRTEEN

He meets Winifred at, of all places, the toilet. The custom, he has learned, is to wait at a distance if someone is clearly "on the seat," and sometimes a line forms. One afternoon the boy approaches and sees neither a line nor anyone's legs beneath the door, but as he mounts the steps a girlish voice calls out, "I'm here!" and he halts, skin prickling, and retreats. He's on the verge of running away when the door swings wide and the blond girl exits, smoothing her dress as she descends the few steps. She looks coldly at Johnny.

"I would think you would have more courtesy," she says as she passes. She is tall, taller than he is, with a slight swell of bosoms and hair curling down her back.

For a moment he cannot speak. Then, spluttering: "I'm . . . I'm sorry. I didn't see . . ."

There's silence as she halts before him. Blue eyes snap, a streak of brown in one iris, and he sees the resemblance to Tot, as if the tiny woman has grown bigger and younger, with longer hair. "Maybe you need spectacles." She hurries off.

He looks for her afterward, in the camp and around the tents. He takes to walking by Tot's "room"—a trailer that attaches to a truck, so that it looks like a small boxcar—hoping to see or hear her, to speak to her once again. How old is she? Does she like to read? What does she do all day? He snags a few glimpses: of her dress as she leaves the cook tent, of her walking once with Tot. How odd they looked together! It was as if Winifred escorted a thicker, younger child. He looks for her at his shows but doesn't see her again there, until one day he does: peeking from beneath the fold in the tent's smoke and near darkness, just as he turns from the men and drops his cape. For the several long moments, in which Tot holds the torch and runs her hand up and down his back, even as he is marched along the rail before the patrons, he stares at her, and she stares gravely back. When he is finished, escorted through the canvas folds and before he reaches Sheila's tent, he looks for her again, but she is gone. Telling Sheila that he needs the toilet, he scours the camp, passing Tot's room, circling the other tents and the trailers, even going outside the ropes in the dark, but he doesn't find her.

Just as he is giving up, a commotion interrupts, a chorus of yells rolling from the direction of the large flats tent. Johnny's act and the flats tent are the last things to close each day, as Carl and Bud and others start escorting the patrons from the show, beginning the teardown if they're making another jump. On this night there's a huddle of men in the darkness, lamps lit and feet thudding, Bud striding past with eyes fixed and jaw set, moving toward the growing throng. Johnny turns and follows, staying far on the hubbub's outskirts, watching as he once did the gum still from the shielding trees. The men shift like birds, some now arriving and others giving room, shouts echoing of "Stand back!" and ". . . needs air!" Calls for help and a doctor. Several men hurry off, a cry over their shoulders, "Swindler!" ". . . rigged, I told you . . ." "He deserved . . ." "Fucking thief!"

The boy pushes in closer. No one pays him attention, and he finds in the group's center the man Wilton on the ground, Bud kneeling over him. Wilton's shirt is stained dark, and a knife protrudes from the top of his stomach like a key. With a wrench Bud pulls this out, tossing it aside and yelling, "Give me a rag, a clean rag!" with his head back, his eyes sparked by the torchlight. Someone runs, someone else strips his shirt off and hands it to Bud, who turns and stuffs it into the wound with both hands. The men around him are blabbering, murmuring. Bud again: "Bring a car. Where's the car?" as if no one can hear him or understand anything. Carl arrives, whispers something to which Bud scowls, Tot behind them. Carl turns to the others.

"Alright, this is under control. Clear out. If you're a guest, you must leave now. Show workers, take your stations."

It reminds the boy of the tree worker's cut finger, the panic and stir then, his thinking the man would die soon. He recalls his surprise at how life could endure and withstand, still keep on. Would this man carry a hole in his belly?

Everyone steps back a few paces, though no one leaves. "I said move!" Carl yells, and this starts an exiting. Johnny finds himself suddenly next to the blond-haired girl.

"What happened?" she asks, her voice a half whisper.

"Someone was stabbed." His heartbeat lifts. He feels important in saying this.

"Who?"

"One of the flats men."

The girl sighs. "Mother says they're all crumbs."

He looks away and back. The lamplight flickers against half her face, her skin white on white, her curls squiggles on her head. He smells the bleach used on the tents, the mildew beneath this. "Do you know them?"

"Not really. I see them around just like you."

"Why are you always hiding?" His breath pushes this out fast. "I never see you much."

"Me?" She makes a face. "Mother doesn't like me out among the workers. Says they might get ideas. She says most of them are cranks or drunks."

He's not sure what to make of this; does that include him? "What do they do in the flats tent?"

"Gamble." She sniffs. Now she sounds important. "Men try to win at games, and often lose. I suppose someone lost and had his money taken, and maybe he didn't like it very much."

They watch as the groups disperse, as Tot stays behind to talk with

Carl. Bud is directing others to lift the injured man, who clutches and moans at the effort. The borrowed shirt juts from his belly like a growth. "How old are you?" he asks.

"Thirteen, same as you."

He turns his head.

"I know a lot about you," she continues. "Like where they got you. I've watched your shows. I've seen your back."

Again he's not sure what to say, how he might respond to this. His throat has closed now like a snare, and he thinks of Zorat opening his mouth, his throat, his body . . . She smells fresh as he turns to her, like soap or cut flowers. Her eyelashes curl like flags. He asks: "Do you like to read?"

"Winifred!" Tot blocks her response.

"I've got to go." She takes his hand and squeezes it, rushes to join her mother. Tot looks from her to the boy and back.

"Get on to your tent," she tells Johnny. "Everybody quick, quick. We'll be making the jump from here soon." Her voice is dagger-sharp. Already, ropes slap and boards creak. A tent puffs up and slackens, falls.

He leaves the two and finds Sheila outside her tent, searching for him. "Where've you been?"

"Nowhere." He glances off.

"What's going on?"

"A man was stabbed. One of the flats men."

"Jesus." Her hands rub her hair, her skin color shifting. "That could shut the whole show down."

"What do you mean?"

"Never mind. We gotta tear down and jump."

His gaze runs. "When?"

"I thought in the morning, but maybe now."

"How could it shut the show down?"

She waves her hands at him without answering.

The word comes soon to move. Typically, they pack the night of the last show (even during the last show) before a jump, preparing to leave early the next morning. Theirs is a caravan of cars and old trucks—nine, excluding the minstrels' wagons. Twice cars have broken down, delaying them or forcing them to leave people or things behind. Tonight, the word comes to prepare to go within the hour. Men bustle and hammers are swung, cars and trucks loaded, trailers hitched. Clamor and grunting and yelling and cursing. Sheila's tent is collapsed and pulled into its boxy state, and the boy has just boarded a truck with Sheila and others when lights stream through the dark. Two cars stop just beyond theirs. Moments later, word rushes past them like a wind: "Cops."

He makes to jump down from the truck, to find out what is happening, but Sheila halts him with an upraised arm. After a time, he tells her he needs to pee, and he does but then manages to get close enough to see and hear a little. Small Tot and big Carl are framed in the headlamps as on a stage, black on black and silky white. The glow skirts and wraps them, casting great shadows, Tot's the larger through some trick of the dark and light. He can't tell what they're saying, though he recognizes Tot's tone: pleading, explaining, promising, demanding. The discussion goes on, so long that he must return, and from the truck he can see only lines and shapes. He wishes he had light to read. Finally, the word comes voice to voice that they're moving. Men stir and grumble, motors shudder, bellow, fire. There's a clanging as something falls, a new round of cursing. Their truck vibrates and rocks and coughs.

"What do you think happened?" he whispers to Sheila once they start. He's so tired that his head droops.

"Oh, she paid them off," Sheila says. "Everybody has a price, or at least most seem to."

He's surprised. "The police? Has that happened before?"

"Sort of. It's happened on other shows I've been on. Not necessarily the show's fault, or anyone on it. Everybody tends to have a hand out for something."

Shadows pass in the blur of the highway, Johnny's head falling and knocking as sleep comes. At some point he wakes in the growing light of the sun, the truck still in motion, cars passing and his head jerking till he sleeps again. When he wakes anew they have stopped, the trucks positioned in a green, open field, the next setup starting, the men with the rigging, banners spread to be hung. The sound of grunting and hammering marks the morning, birds fluttering and a rich, burned coffee smell. A man's voice saying ". . . electricity and a toilet. Things are looking up!"

A dog appears and then Otto, chasing behind on all fours to the laughs of the others, headshakes and handclaps, the dog with a whine and a merry bark. Johnny clambers out into the brightness of daylight, the energy and gladness of beginning, the ordered chaos of layout, production, and plan. For the briefest of moments, he sees himself *part* of this, of something larger than he is, a pack or a band or group—shifting and strange as it may be. He stretches his back some, stares at the banners, listens for music, and offers his help to them once again.

THE FLATS TENT doesn't accompany them to this stop, the men with it apparently gone now from the show. The group as a result becomes tighter and smaller, as despite their remove the flats men were still present, helping with the setup, in line for the toilet, their truck part of every jump. Their tent's site is absorbed by other tents, but the circle has shrunk now, as have the crowds. Bud takes extra fliers and posters into each new town, but the advance work doesn't change things. Men drift and trickle in, whereas before they came in twisting lines and waves. An unease pierces and saturates the crew, a mumbling heard of finding other employment, of leaving the business or running out and switching shows. Tot is absent for several long spells, sparking more talk and rumor, even an outburst one night in the cook tent by

Wilma, until one morning a truck arrives after they've made a jump, tooting its horn as it enters their area. A woman hops out, several women, a whole troop of them clad in bright hues and skirts. A single skinny man. Sheila looks them over as they huddle with Tot.

"Oh, lordy."

"What is it?" he asks.

She puffs a cigarette. She seems to be smoking them more now. "I'm not certain, but I can guess. It looks like we've got us a girly act."

"A what?"

Sheila shakes her head, lips pressed together. "A cooch show." She pauses. "You'll see, Johnny. Just you wait."

A new tent is erected, but in the back, near the minstrels, not where the flats tent was before. He is curious, as are others; Zorat and Alfred join him in looking on. He glances around for Winifred but doesn't see her anywhere.

"How long do you think it lasts, Al?" Zorat asks.

The other man shakes his head. "'Bout as long as the flats, I reckon. Glad to see it though, huh? Without it we might be in a soup kitchen soon, eating Hoover stew."

Zorat laughs, a sound not heard often. His face forms a sneer or frown as he turns to Johnny. "Sodom and Gomorrah, son. We're reaching the bottom of depravity. The gambling tables weren't enough? Now we're selling enticement and baring sacred flesh. We've gone from the exotic to the indecent. It can't get much lower."

"What do they do?" He doesn't understand.

Alfred smiles. "Show a lot of leg, sometimes more." He clears his throat, his tongue placed between his teeth. "Come on, Johnny. Let's go and meet the girls."

He follows Alfred toward the new tent. A redheaded woman with curls emerges, talking to someone behind her. Zorat turns away and shakes his head.

"Hello," Alfred offers. "I'm Al, this is Johnny. Welcome to the show."

The woman smiles, some of her teeth missing. She is older than the boy thought, with a ring of fat like a collar. Her fingernails are painted red. "Hello, there," she says softly. "I'm Ruth. Glad to be with you. This here's Wanda and Gladys." She indicates two others behind her. There are seven in all, including the slender man.

"What's your show like?" Alfred asks. "I do a vent act. Johnny here is a freak—a boy with . . . a special something."

"Well, we've got the best revue east of the Rockies. We do some dancing and singing. Folks seem to like it real well."

"Where you coming from?"

"Oh, another show. Money's better here, or seems to be. We'll give it a run."

Alfred grins.

"You a freak, eh?" she asks Johnny.

He nods, his head down quick.

"What do they call you?"

He doesn't respond at first. Finally, "Boy with Wings."

"Well, that should be something. Come by the show later, and we'll give you a special viewing. You'll see how good we are when we perform."

A new banner is painted: "SEE THE ST. LOUIS REVUE! THE PRETTIEST GIRLS IN AMERICA!" Sketched out in charcoal, Bud inks it with black paint first, then with color. ("You have to use heavy canvas," he tells Johnny. "Otherwise, it'll rip and tear. The banner is as key as the talker.") It's placed in front of a new and splashy red tent. Their act takes place before his, and so Johnny catches only part of it before he has to leave. It starts with the girls standing in front of their tent, Zeke the slender man playing a trumpet beside them, several of the girls swaying and shaking tambourines. They're clad in short dresses and kick their legs up in a line, drawing aahs and claps from the crowd that soon draws close. At one point in another song they shake their behinds at the audience. Later, he is told, they offer paying folks a more private showing inside the tent. It's sort of a blow-off like his act, and he notices his crowd decline after their arrival, though he doesn't mind this much. He asks Zorat what happens in the girly act's special blow-off.

"More of the same," he responds. "Showing their bodies. It's blasphemous and vulgar. God's wrath can't be far."

HE KEEPS HIS search up for Winifred, peeping out of his eye corners, turning and hoping to catch a glimpse of blond hair. After one show he stalks the tents, circles the rope line, makes a pass by the toilet, and even peeks in the shower, all with no sign or success. He finally decides to present himself at Tot's trailer, so great is his desire—his desperation?—to see her, his formless and unshaped thought that she could leave. He still feels her touch, smells her hair and sweet skin, and did he invent this or dream it? He seems to think of her all the time. When he knocks on the door and it opens, he expects Tot's short form but instead finds a smiling Winifred, perched as if waiting, her teeth gleaming white and straight. The room inside is made up like a house, with rugs and paintings and a big, star-faced clock. At first, he doesn't know what to do or to say to her.

"Hello."

"Hello."

"Do you want to go out, to walk around?"

"Yes. Let's do."

"Do you have to ask, ask your . . . mother?"

"It's okay."

They head out into the growing darkness. The last of the customers are edging out past the tents, some of the performers milling about in their costumes. There's no jump tonight, and so the show folks will gather, meeting for food at the stained cook tent. Some will slip off then to town and its offerings, others to drink in the trucks or darkness or in their tents. He knows a little about drink but not much, from the side camp: the men who went to the tunk Mama Lo warned him of, becoming loudmouthed and crazy after their swigs and slurps. Elias told him that drinking was against the law, and maybe this explained the paper bags and sips he saw taken in shadows and off in corners around and about the show, people with heads down and eyes dropped.

"Have you heard of the new act?" he asks. He finds himself breathless. Would she take up his hand again, palm in palm? His fingers move toward hers but jerk back before contact. She smells of marshmallow or taffy—he can't decide which.

Winifred nods. "Mother told me they were coming."

"What did she say?"

"That she was glad to have them."

"What about the flats men?"

"She said that their time had come. I'm not sure what she meant by it."

They are silent so long that sounds heighten around them. Noise flows from the cook tent, the crackle and smell of warming food. Conversations, the chug-chug of laughter. Splashing and the scrape of plates. "Are you hungry?"

"Not much. Are you?"

"Nah." Again, silence. "Do you like being here?"

"Here?"

"I mean, with the show."

"Where else would I be?"

He considers this. "I don't know. In school, maybe?"

She sniffs and sighs. "Mother talks of that. She keeps saying she wants me to go to boarding school, that I need a real education and such. She always wanted to attend school, to learn, though she couldn't. But I don't want to do it."

He twists in the darkness. "Do you do schooling now?"

"Yes. Mother gives me lessons. I hate it."

"Do you like to read?"

"No."

"I do."

"Do you like numbers as well? Maybe you could teach me math. It so frustrates Mother."

"I'd be glad to try." There's a pause, a wavering. "Is she okay . . ." His voice falters. ". . . with you being with me?"

Winifred twists her hair. "She doesn't like me being around the men here, or even most of the women; I've told you this. And the freaks she treats like animals, or pets. Or maybe children—yes, children. But you're different from most, I think. She's so excited about you, about the draw and the uniqueness of your act. You're something special. She talks about you all the time."

"She does?" His stomach pulls. "What, uh, what does she say? About me, I mean."

"She wants to improve things, to hire a photographer to give folks your picture, or maybe buy a camera that someone here can use. They could take photographs of you then, and some of the other performers. She's heard that other shows do it. Someone wants her to sell miniature Bibles. She's talked about mind readers and exotic beasts. She's always planning and thinking, her mind turning like a top—always looking around for new acts or things to dip into. She lives for this show."

It's been so long since he's been around anyone his own age, anyone really to talk to. He sees children some at the show but never comes close to or speaks to them—it's like he's been placed off in a lit glass cage, remote. Winifred, though, is real and near him, and could they talk on forever? It's like it was with Elias but different, and maybe it's his fear that she will turn and leave, or that he will be forced to go, or that he'll do something to scare her. Maybe it's just that she's a girl.

A shape appears out of the darkness before them—another child—that instead becomes Tot.

"I'd better go," says Winifred. Her voice is low and tuneful.

He waits for the hand squeeze again, but it doesn't come. It's too dark to see Tot's expression when mother and daughter meet and turn away.

CHAPTER FOURTEEN

Sheila

Johnny became a part of us, part of me. It took some time but not that much, given all that went on and his state when he arrived. I figured he'd been through a lot, though he never spoke of it, and I couldn't get Tot to say much about him. Only that she found him in Georgia, that the place he lived in was horrid and bleak, that she had to fight some men to get him out. I questioned her several times, as I wanted to know everything about him and his life and background: where he grew up, the truth on his parents, his learning, habits, worries, and likes. She claimed not to know much of any of this. For the most part, even now, I believe what she told me then.

We got him going that first night at the show. Tot thought it important, and I didn't disagree: his need to understand that he was there to be watched and seen, to be on stage like the rest of us, to go out and do it and enjoy things as best he could. The first night was hard, him new and not knowing us, and we make him put on a costume and get out there and expose his back! He near went crazy, tussling with me, but then he marched on out, the light shining and men gathered close, and it went great. The crowd was caught—you can tell when they're hooked and when they're not—after Tot's talk brought them in. Johnny shook as he stood with his shirt off, skinny and strange-looking like a lean, homeless cat, and I felt so sad for him then! But once he had done it, he'd done it, things went okay from his end, and he became used to the show and this life and to us. I never regretted our doing any of this for him.

I've been around this business for years, and as such I've seen some freaks. On account of Tot being who she is, we've attracted some good ones, including Otto and Kenneth. (Wilma, though she has a beard, might be classified as more a working act.) You have to approach freaks in a certain manner, I've found, and accept them for what they are or aren't. Otto is practically brainless but sweet and is cared for by the setup man Walter, who works with Bud. They seem to get on well. Otto is liked by the other show members, though some of the men tend to tease him and such, and Walter sometimes steps in to set things right again. Apparently, Otto (for all his small brain size) has quite a lower apparatus; I have not seen this, nor do I wish to, but such has been brought forth for shock or jokes some among our crew.

Kenneth is a different thing, a true strangeness with hair coating all of his body (this I *have* seen) and a disposition somewhere between ticklish and fierce. Kenneth isn't slow or mean but seems to dislike people and wants to be left alone, a difficult hankering on a traveling show like this. Disagreements have grown to fights: one with Boris and one with Cookie, of all gents. Kenneth produces good crowds, though, so he's not likely to be left by the roadside or kicked off the show. I'm not sure what his money setup with Tot might be, but I'm willing to bet it's much better than mine. You learn to protect yourself in this business—and as such, I don't blame him—as if not, you can be exploited. I learned that from my pop early on.

Johnny is plenty smart, and with an engaging and pleasant nature. He likes to read, and I've combed the show for him in search of material; I've even given Bud money to buy books on his trips to town. We've worked out our living arrangement over the course of the last two years, as at first he slept on the floor near my cot, but eventually we procured a cot of his own, placed on the opposite side of my small tent and booth. It's rather tight quarters for any two folks, but he doesn't seem to mind it much, and we respect each other's privacy well. I'm sure he's seen me unclothed, and so I've seen him, but we're more like brother and sister, or maybe mother and only child. The men tease him, wanting to know what's going on or when he'll move on to their side, as housing at the show is imperfectly divided between men's and women's tents. Sometimes he cries out in his sleep.

Eventually he is bound to go, as he's grown so much that our tent can seem crowded, and I see signs of life changes—his voice and hair (his hair has grown darker, more normal) and size coming on. His back has developed too, though he doesn't like to speak of it or even for me to see it, despite his showing it almost nightly to the wider world. He must sit in a certain posture now for his back's growth to remain concealed, almost like he has breasts to be constrained and buttoned up. Some clothes not to be worn because they would reveal too much of that wonder tucked beneath.

He's developed a friendship, maybe a relationship, with Tot's daughter Winifred. This surprised me at first but probably should not have, as they're the only youngsters on the show. I was more shocked that Tot allowed it, as she has a strange connection with her acts and freaks and is sheltering and protective of Winifred. But Johnny is different, of course, and everyone seemed to accept this almost from the very first. Soon we all became used to seeing their dandelion-like heads together, and I even noticed them once walking and holding hands. I wondered if I should talk with Johnny about the birds and the bees and such, and I asked Tot once about this. In typical Tot fashion, her reply was snappish, blunt.

"I've already talked to him and to her. I told him that if he brings that thing out of hiding, I'll chop it off and cut his wings."

"Hmm. Sometimes, Tot, when you're young and excited—"

"I keep my eye on 'em, Sheila. You tend to your own affairs."

This, of course, stoked my ire. Johnny *is* my affair—she awarded me him, even urged this. It sparked another terse exchange between us.

"Tot, are you putting some of the money from Johnny's act back for him?"

There was the briefest of pauses. "What do you mean?"

She knew just what I meant. In most shows, performers the

audience pays special to see are on a piece-rate arrangement, where they get a portion of the cash that their acts produce. "He gets none of the blow-off?"

"He's a child. He's getting free food and board, just like you."

"That ain't fair, Tot, and you know it. You're using him. That seems clear to all." And it does, despite her providing him a home when he didn't have one before, despite the safety and food and his outward happiness. It's the wrong and injustice I see in it! I'm looking out for *him*.

A tirade came in response. "Who are you to be saying this? After I took you on from that rat show you were with? You're welcome to leave now if you don't like the way things are!" Her voice grew even chirpier. "The fucking nerve. Go ahead and walk out. You think someone will pay you half of what I do?"

I knew she would react so, but I couldn't help saying what I said. She *is* taking advantage, and it's by shrewd design. My own theory is that to her this justifies Johnny's involvement with Winifred, but I know better than to say this or to provoke her any further. Besides, my point and position have been made very clear. Maybe age has a way of bringing courage with it, strength and doggedness trailing a bit behind.

I worry about Johnny's future, and about my own path. How long can I keep showing my skin and have people pay to look? Soon enough I'll be old like my pop, as shows quit their hiring and he'd sit at my aunt's in Queens, a beer in one hand from his breakfast on. He died with no means left; I had to pay for his plain grave and burial. He started me in this when I was younger than Johnny. I wanted so to be like him and be with him always, to be on stage! My mother died early on. I'm not book-smart, but I know stuff: I read and think, I watch things and listen. I believe Daddy ended up being proud of what I've done. I've taken more care with my money and been more mindful of my fate, as I hide most of my pay in a cabinet's false bottom. I don't trust banks much after the crash and run. My appeal, though, is declining, as I've moved from big to smaller shows, and the money I make is a fraction of what it was before. I could run my own show, but I don't have the drive for it, don't think I'm as forceful or fearless as Tot. And with the world in this state?

I try to explain this to Johnny, but he's in a different place, his fame and worth rising, and if Tot were to dump him, others would take him on. I've tried to get him to see the patrons as more than rubes, to feel for and about them and to be unashamed of what he does. We offer interest and excitement to what are dull and brutal lives. Would he rather be taking his shirt off or spending days behind a plodding mule? Johnny can seem blue or down on it, shamed at times by his difference, at other times fierce and enraged. I figure it stems from his loss of real family and whatever happened to him before he joined our show. I try to offset this, to show calmness and patience, to give him support, loving care and protection. I tell him that sometimes you just continue on.

The show has changed as shows do, with new acts and performers as others are fired or leave. Within the last months Tot has brought on Myron the giant—this hulking man who says little and is supposedly seven foot five—and a monkey named Kip who, with his handler, Gordon, does some tricks. Wilma left. No one knows how or why, but one day she was just gone. There was talk for a while of us joining a bigger show, and this juiced folks up, visions of train cars and new gear and massive crowds following, talk of animals, ten-in-ones, plush museum shows. I've heard that some of the biggest now have mechanical rides for their customers. But this merger didn't go. Children now make up a greater part of our crowds, and although they were never excluded before (except from certain performances, like Johnny's and the girly act), now they run loose and wild, poking in the tents and rigging, peeking in places they shouldn't.

Johnny remains the star and principal attraction. One of our trucks now has his image painted on it, which I'm sure cost Tot a bundle: "S<small>EE THE</small> W<small>INGED</small> B<small>OY</small>!" She paid a man to take photos and had these printed up, cards glossed on one side and with his story I wrote on the other. The photo was shaded to make it look like he had giant wings:

"Johnny Cruel was born to a bird of prey and a human, the only known living offspring of such an unlikely pair. He likes to read and take walks, and to flex his great wings, which if fully extended reach six feet across. People ask if he can fly, but he's not fully formed yet. He's just fifteen! As one of the eight living wonders of the world, thousands have traveled to see him."

This was puffed up, of course, but not by much. After each performance, Johnny dutifully signs photographs for people who pay even more for this. Sometimes this can stretch for an hour past his act, and you can tell he grows restless and tired by its end, as the show is then closed or closing. Still, it helps get the word out and serves to broaden his growing fame. Now when we make a jump, the first question from our customers is about the winged boy. People still faint when they see him, an effect known as falling applause. After every act he receives gifts of some sort—food, underwear, toys—that he piles up in my tent. No one at the shows is asking for the middle-aged tattooed girl.

We're nearing the end of our tour now, preparing to winter in Florida once again. This is where most shows spend the offseason, and it provides an opportunity to recharge and connect with friends and other acts. To sleep in a regular bed, to use a flushing toilet. To go to a real beautician. To not be packing up again each few days. It affords me an opportunity, also, to get tattooed, as I have plans for another one. I mention this to Johnny one rainy night in Carolina.

"When we get to Tampa, I'm gonna get me a new tattoo, based on you and me."

He frowns. "Why?" He looks up. "I'm not sure what you mean."

"It's just something I want."

He rubs his hands.

I continue. "I don't have room for more, really, but I've decided I'm going to block out some others." I pause, my breath trembling. "I'm going to get a tattoo of some wings."

He looks even more confused. His head tilts as he concentrates, his mouth in a lovely line. "But why?"

I feel my face flush. "Well, it's something I want to express, in honor of you. I love you, Johnny."

It slips on out. I didn't mean it like that; I love him as I would my son that I've never had—the one big regret of my entire touring, working life. There have been men and conception before, hopes and intention and dread but no child. Now it's too late, or soon will be. Tot gave me a gift. But I know even as I say it that there will be damage from me declaring this.

Johnny says nothing. We go on about our days. I watch him closely—this is my pleasure, my duty and charge—without crowding him or butting in. He roams the grounds during the daytime, helping out if he's needed. I see him walking, watching the acts, eyeing the crowds as if he's a patron rather than part of the parade and show. He is friendly and smart and well liked by everyone. He spends time with Winifred and I think helps with her studies, walks with her, talks to her, each of them full of secrets and sunny smiles.

The relationship I question is the one he has with Robert, the sword-swallower who calls himself Zorat the Great. Robert is odd even by sideshow standards, given his saintly outbursts and the way he looks at folks, his habit of reading the Bible and keeping mostly off to himself. I'm guessing he's in his thirties, maybe forties; why no wife or girl? If there's been one around, I certainly have never seen her. Even on those Sunday nights (we do few shows on Sundays) when we get rooms at a small hotel, with baths and bathrooms and everyone ending up in one another's bed, I don't hear tell of him with someone else. He says he was married once, but I claim to be the daughter of Zeus in my act; I'm not sure there's much to this. And I don't care, as everyone can do what they want with their lives, except to the extent that it has an impact on Johnny.

The two of them talk a lot, mostly on faith and religion, and it appears that Robert is schooling Johnny in this: a cause for concern, given Robert's zeal and strangeness. I believe in God and Jesus and all that hocus-pocus, but this man is a holy fool, well past the point of godly and on to unglued. Sometimes when I observe them talking, Robert's eyes shining bright as stars, I see the depth of the man's greed and wanting, perhaps due to my own state of hope and need. I tell myself that I'm different, and I am, as my interest is that of a guardian angel or mother, and I've never wanted for Johnny more than the best of what he can be. I can't say the same for Robert. Yes, we're all misfits, some far off the edge and norm, but I worry about what lurks behind Robert's wolfish eyes. I vow to stay closer to Johnny, to ward off any peril: spiritual or physical or emotional, or something else.

Then Tot decides Johnny needs to leave my tent. Some say it was the men's teasing, or that the boy complained to Tot, or even that I'm too close to Johnny, but one day she comes by to see me, which is rare. She has on the wig that gives her a bigger, helmeted look. It's the afternoon before an evening show. My heart begins sinking the moment I see her. Tot has this cruel streak.

"I think it's time for Johnny to have his own space."

"What do you mean?"

"He's just getting older. You know how it is." She makes a vague twirl with her finger.

Speaking to Tot can feel like talking with a child, but this is illusion, I know. "Did he ask for this?"

She seems to regard me for an extra second. "No. It's just my idea."

"So he'll have his own tent?"

"I'm thinking of putting him near one of the men, to keep an eye on him."

"I think that is dangerous." My response is quick.

"Why?"

"Well, on account of what happened to him before."

Her eyebrows lift. "What happened to him?"

"Well, I don't know exactly."

"Then you don't know. He doesn't seem bothered by moving."

"So, you've talked to him?"

She nods, and the wig shifts.

"And who . . . whom are you putting him near?"

"I'm not sure yet. Maybe Alfred, or Robert."

"Not Robert." Sharpness.

"Why not?"

I pause. "I don't know." I'm half turning, ducking, not wanting her to see me fume or weep. "Robert is just so . . ." I want to say strange but halt myself.

Tot nods again. "Help Johnny get his things packed, okay? Make this work, Sheila. It'll turn out fine."

She leaves before I can move or speak again. I sulk and mope, sweeping clothes into random piles on top of Johnny's cot, gathering up the papers, magazines, and books. I cry then—I can't help it—sighing deep into my bosom, shrugging a bit and staring out. When the tent flap lifts my heart reels, but it's Otto, ducking his head in and calling, "See! See?" like he does, scratching his head before running off. The thought of Johnny in Robert's clutches gives me bitter shakes, and so I nip out of a bottle I keep stuffed with my dresses, a cure I seek only when confronting some crushing pain. Maybe if I bought him a Bible . . . Maybe if I begged Tot more . . .

In the meantime, where could he possibly be? At last I hear a rustle outside and shift, compose myself. I check my eyes and face once before I turn.

"Hi," he says, as if nothing has happened.

"Oh, Johnny." I want to rush to him madly but take a step or two back and forth.

He tilts his head.

My chin juts. "Tot tells me you'll be moving quarters."

"Yes. I've talked to her some on it. I think it's about time now, don't you?" He appears unconcerned but doesn't look at me, his face down and turned. I take in his back, his height, his hair that needs cutting. (Cookie does this for those who don't go to town. He also pulls teeth.) I think back on my avowal of love.

"Why is it about time?"

He shrugs. "I should leave at some point."

I add gaiety to my voice. "I don't understand it. Where will you go?"

"I'm not sure yet. I'm fine with anything." He pauses, then says, almost as an afterthought: "I won't be far."

Anything? Won't be far? "Oh, Johnny." This time I close the distance between us, taking him in my arms as I did that first night. Again, he resists before his body melts to me, and I'm so overcome that I weep. I don't even sense this, my hand slipping up his shirt in the back and rubbing him along his wings. It feels so natural, more so than touching a man's resting thing, so supple and folded and hairy, at least until Johnny screams and pulls back. With one arm raised he blocks space between us, and with the other he slaps me. Does he slap me? Maybe it's not quite like that.

"What are you doing?" he sputters. His face is a red, sinking sun.

"I . . . I'm so sorry." And I am. My face stings and I struggle to right myself from near falling. I don't know what happened. "I didn't mean—"

"You aren't to touch me. No one is to touch me. That was our agreement—you told me. You promised."

I did but am shocked still by his rage. It's near to what it was that first night, his frenzy when I offered him the cape. "Johnny, it's . . . it's all love. One day you'll understand it more. I'm not sure I fully do. It's just that I care for you. I care and worry so."

He's edging away from me, his back shielded from my gaze, and when he reaches the tent flap he whirls in a flurry and becomes tangled up, flailing and muttering before completing his hasty flight. I sit in my chair and stare then at my hands, the tattoos from long back that are fading, a clutch in my heart that makes my fingers do a dance, knowing that things are doubtless going to change.

Love. Motherhood. It's hard not to hold a bitterness. I think of a man, Vince, who would hit me when he drank. Life's door can close or open.

The next morning Carl arrives and escorts me from the show.

CHAPTER FIFTEEN

The move over to the men's quarters occurs without incident, other than Sheila's departure, and he now occupies a small side tent adjacent to Boris and Alfred's. Their tent is bigger than Sheila's (though not as big as the main tent, which houses six or eight men), and his space affords him seclusion, but he can't get Sheila off his mind, worrying that he caused her to go. Why did she leave, and without saying goodbye to him? He didn't speak to others about her and didn't know she had left, not until he went by the tent to find her things gone, the tent bare, no one around willing to answer his questions.

"Where is she?" he asks Zorat.

"I thought you'd know. I wake up this morning and she's gone. It can happen."

"But was it because of me? Because *I* left *her*?"

"You left her?"

"I moved into the side tent next to Alfred and Boris. Tot said it was time. She told Sheila too, and, I don't know . . . I think it upset her." He shakes his head.

"Maybe she was jealous and left. She seemed to me quite possessive. Did she touch you?"

He looks up. "She's been kind to me since I've been here." His memory of her rubbing his back brings a guilty chill. His outburst. She has helped him and been like a mother, he enjoyed their laughs and talks, and now she is gone. His stomach clenches, burns. People are always leaving. He asks Winifred.

"What happened to Sheila?"

She shrugs. "She left? I don't know." The brown splash in her eye—the left—is impossible, so lovely in contrast to the wider, greater blue.

"I don't want it to have been because of me." His belly tightens. Maybe Winifred will leave now too.

"Johnny, a lot of the show is because of you, at this point. I know you were close with her, but that wasn't going to be forever."

This much is true. Still, he keeps expecting her to appear with her smile and sequins, to laugh the high laugh that's so different from the way she speaks. Her absence makes him recall, too, his mother's death and the hole then: how he mourned her for a time but then seemed to forget her, folding himself into life in the woods. Would he now forget Sheila? She told him she was getting a tattoo in his honor, but he doesn't want anyone to honor him. He wants people to stay where they are. Perhaps he should ask Tot why Sheila left, confirm whether it was because of what he said and did. If only he'd not been so mean and sharp with her just before this! He should never have responded in the way he did. Something stops him from asking Tot, though—maybe fear of her answer. Maybe, he thinks, it's better not to know.

He works more now than before, helping in teardown and setup, rolling the banners, even pounding iron stakes. The show always seems to be tearing down or setting up, with things stored in a certain order, like a puzzle. Bale rings, leather cords. The heavy canvas. It all takes lots of time. He still spends days wandering, often with Winifred in tow, examining things, watching and puzzling and learning. He loves visiting the minstrel tent, and sometimes he'll go in and sit by himself, waiting for someone to appear and begin singing. Several are familiar now and smile or wave hello: Velma, the lead singer, and Sarah, a large woman; Maxwell, a big man with a voice like a ringing bell. They speak to him sometimes. Maxwell: "Music is heartbreak." Sarah: "What's inside that can't get out?" He considers theirs one of the prettiest sounds he has ever heard—the voices blended together, whether on gospel-type harmonies or more modern tunes—and he'd be pleased to sit for hours, eyes closed, and listen. Winifred has less interest in waiting and watching. She wants to go other places, see other sights and do more things.

"Have you smoked?" she asks him. A slim eyebrow hitches higher, its color a shade darker than her bouncy, curly hair.

"Smoke?"

"Yes, you ninny. Cigarette?"

"Nnn-no. Have you?"

"Of course. You can try one with me."

He thinks back to his pretending to smoke and his mother's scolding. Her talking-to voice. Mama Lo's, Sheila's. That of someone else.

"Okay."

They're behind a tent on the far side of the enclosure, near the ropes that mark the perimeter and boundary of the show. He glances around for anyone looking, but who would stop him? He is almost grown. Winifred produces two rolled cigarettes and a match she strikes after several tries, its flame with a sour smell. She lights the end of his and he sucks and quickly coughs, dropping the cigarette so that he must fall to the ground to find it. Winifred laughs so hard that she begins coughing too.

"What are you doing?" she asks when she can find her breath and straighten.

"I don't know," he responds, laughing now with her. When she lights his anew, he repeats the whole sequence, her laughs coming all the harder, arms clutched around her waist. When he picks up the cigarette, it burns him, making him drop it once more, masking the fact that the smoke has made him want to vomit. All of the coughing brings new memory of his mother, her choking and gasping, and for a moment, things dip and dim. He sits in the grass and remains sprawled there.

"Oh, Johnny," she breathes. "No one can make me laugh the way you do."

He smiles at her through his pain. He's so happy to be with her, happy to be here; the show hasn't been lonely. Was that due to Sheila? Or to the dark time in between, the time he refuses to name or call forth, the chain and hurt then. He reaches out for her hand, the warmth there and softness, the blood beating patiently through her open palm. It's like water somehow after the most savage of thirsts.

On another occasion she introduces him to drink.

"C'mon, Johnny—you've never tasted booze?"

He shakes his head. "Will this be like the cigarette?"

She laughs. "No, silly. Worse. This will get us in trouble if Tot should find out. She's strict about giggle juice."

"Where will you get some?"

She smiles. "Don't worry, John."

Some days later she produces a bottle, a brownish liquid sloshing about in its cloudy depths. He turns to her, brow raised. "This is it?"

She takes a swig, her neck back and grimacing, water wiped from her eyes. "Yes. Now your turn." Her voice has gone deep and hollow.

The drink is like medicine, only stronger, and it makes him want to spit it out or blow his nose. He breathes deep against a burn inside, a draw and an opening. He coughs a clumping cough. *"People like this?"*

"Only for what it does." Another swallow, another frown. She hands the bottle back. "One more, then that's enough."

He chokes it down. Afterward he is swimming, the sky somehow brighter, the tents blurred and shifting about in the breeze. Sounds bleed from the show area, music and talking and footsteps and laughter, but it's distant and muted, caught in blankets of air. He trips over the rigging, and she laughs once again, picking him up and holding him to her, her breath warm on his face, and when she kisses him he is surprised but not offended or disturbed by it. Her lips are wet and taste sweet from the liquor, her nose snug next to his, and he clutches her back just to hang on to something. Then pushes away, the memory on him of Sheila, her hand gripping his own back, the anger then, terror.

Winifred smiles still. "What's the matter? I assume that's your first kiss too? Your first honey cooler?"

"Is it yours?" Other memories intrude, of men and their bad teeth, their breath sharp and stinking.

"Maybe." She flips her hair, the light in it sparkling. "What will become of us, Johnny? What will arrive or could happen next? You and me and this show, this strange world—all these acts and freaks!" She twirls in a circle, stumbles and almost falls, her dip for a moment exposing the small orbs of her chest. "It's like nothing else." She laughs again, her voice high and echoing. Her hands grab his shoulders, his neck. "What other life could we lead?"

HE WATCHES BORIS with the knives, Zorat and his swords and fire, Alfred juggling and talking through his dummy.

"He learned that in prison," Boris says, indicating Alfred.

"Prison?"

"Yeah."

Johnny is quiet and wondering. Thinking. Then, "What'd he do?"

Boris looks up. "I can't recall, rightly. Something to do with money. Others spent time in the pen too—Lenny, Bud." He shrugs, his mouth even. "People make mistakes."

HE HAS A birthday, his sixteenth. They'd had a party for him once at the side camp, with the kids bringing small gifts, and he has vague memories of his mother before this with presents—maybe the train and its track? Tot bows and begs his pardon, saying she forgot on his fourteenth and they were mired in a storm the next year—three of the trucks stuck in a gluey mud, days to get it all moved—but on his sixteenth they have a big gathering.

Everyone arrives after the patrons have left, even the minstrel performers and Kenneth, and Cookie produces a big square cake. There are candles to blow, a game or two held, some presents offered, and even red balloons! Winifred sits by his side as he opens gifts: a writing tablet, some new books, a silver cross given by Zorat. A new banner is unveiled in his honor: "SEE IT NOW—ONE OF THE SEVEN WONDERS!" Motioning him over, Tot whispers in his ear, "Johnny, didn't I tell you that this would be family?" He ducks and grins. The minstrels lead the others in singing "Happy Birthday," and there's applause. No one asks or demands more of him, and his mind grants the push of his dark thoughts far away. People are smiling, and joyous and giving. He considers it one of the luckiest and happiest days of his life.

ONE DAY DURING his show, a man calls out: "Hey, I'm your father!" Johnny's back is to the crowd, so that he can't see who says this, but his hands shake at the sound, so much that he drops the cape twice and shortens his standard performance. Later, Bud tells him that someone—he assumes the same man—approached Tot with this charge but when questioned admitted his claim to be false.

"Trying to cheat her," Bud explains. "I'm surprised we ain't seen more."

For weeks and weeks after, he listens for this again, thinking despite everything that it could be true: that it could be his father, come at last to rejoin him, to make him complete now and call him his own. If only he had turned and identified the speaker! For a time his dreams trace a reunion with this faceless man, white-haired then dark, blue eyes turning greener, wings on his back too, burns and scars. But nothing comes of it.

After another show he's approached by a short man with a limp. Carl or Bud usually monitors things afterward, as often when he is signing people draw close and want to touch, and the men step in to stop this. For a moment he fears it is Slim, the shorter of the men he lived with in Georgia, and he recoils until he sees that the man is a simple freak, a grotesquely oversized eyebrow stretched across half his forehead. It makes his face look painted or pasted with hair.

"Can you get me on?" the man asks. "Please now, will you take me?" He places a hand out. "I need a job so. I need to eat. How can I hold a job when I look like this? How, huh? Can you help me? Can you get me on?"

Carl hustles the man off before Johnny can say a thing, but for days he thinks of the man and his eyebrow, the gleaming eyes beneath gray and maddened and desperate. Johnny looks for him in the shifting crowds, though the show keeps on moving, people come and go, miles pass and days drag, and he never sees further sign of him.

One day in the midway he sees a man with no neck—a solid slope made from his head to his shoulders, his body an upside-down *V*—and is the man just unshapely or a fellow freak? A new part of the show? Following him around, Johnny concludes that he's only a patron—odd-looking, yes, but watching the acts like all the rest. Some stares fall his way, a few comments made also, but the man doesn't seem to note these or care. It's almost as if he enjoys being their subject. Johnny's head turns in wonder, maybe resentment or envy, or even mild distress.

"JOHNNY, WHAT WILL you do with your wings?"

They're sitting cross-legged in a tent's shade. It's hot out. A mosquito buzzes.

Winifred tosses her curls like a cow calmly whipping its tail.

"I don't know. Why should I have to do anything with them at all? What will you do with your . . . arms?" He almost said breasts.

She laughs, knowing this. "Expose them. Let the whole world see their beauty, before they are thin and gone. *Use* them." She shakes her head. "Proclaim love and truth."

HE FINDS HIMSELF one day with Alfred, outside the girly tent.

"C'mon, let's go inside." Alfred has rust-colored hair and a smile as if he holds secrets.

"Are we allowed?"

"They'll tell us to scram if they need to."

"Okay. Sure."

The inside of the tent is much like the others, except for its odor—a perfumy smell. Plenty of sawdust coats the ground, more lights strung than in his tent, and in the middle a makeshift stage has been built. One of the girls, Madeline, stands upon it, hands on thick hips, peering out at them through the dust and gloom.

"Well, hello, boys. Come to see something?"

"What you got to show us, Maddie?"

She smiles and dips her head. Crooks a finger. "Come closer. I wanna get Johnny up on this stage."

"What for?" he asks. A half laugh escapes him.

"I think a proper initiation."

"A what?"

"We need to introduce you to a few of life's finest things."

"Like what?" They edge closer.

"Well, have you seen one of these?" She flings something out to them, small and black, hairy, and they each take steps back. An animal? He picks it up off the ground, this pad of fur shaped in a long triangle.

Alfred snickers. Johnny is puzzled. "What is it?" he whispers.

"Johnny." Madeline has her hands on her hips again. "Give it back."

He hands it to her.

"I didn't figure you'd seen one."

He still doesn't understand. Alfred is laughing, a series of chuck-chuck-chucks.

"You see, Johnny," Madeline continues, "sometimes we have to provide an *illusion* to our audience." She takes the piece of fur and holds it between her legs. His face flames now in a slow and sheepish understanding. "People don't mind being hoodwinked, at least sometimes. It's part of the game." She shrugs and smiles. "We call this a mi-muff."

"Oh."

"Is that all you have to say?" She bends over facing him, bosoms plump above her dress. "I could show you some other things." She straightens, twisting herself up. "You don't look like you're fooled too easy, Johnny."

"Now, Maddie." Alfred shakes a finger. "Don't go corrupting this boy. I'll be back later if you need to show anybody anything."

Madeline gives the greatest of sighs. "Well, okay, Alfred. I guess if you insist."

Afterward, the boy's skin tingles. He wants to tell someone, but whom would he tell? Not Winifred. Sheila is gone. Later, he speaks to Zorat.

"It's going to bring the show down, I tell you. The things I hear." Zorat's head waggles back and forth.

"What do you hear?"

"Nothing that you should know. You should study the Bible. Read Leviticus and tell me your reaction. Second Samuel. Judges. Kings."

Johnny frowns and nods. He's becoming familiar with some of it.

He even understands, to a degree, the source of Zorat's passion—how religion can be a guidebook to manage, shape, and run your life. There's so much to accept: repentance and love; doing good works; grace shown to the needy; faith in things you can't see. Did his mother know of this gospel? Did she believe? It's one of the things he'd like most to ask her.

So much is beginnings, he thinks, and what each person does with them, how bad things are turned back or don't need any twisting, pain shifted to places or shoved down different paths. For a time at the side camp, he thought his was the only mother who had ever died and left. Before he joined the show, he didn't know there were other freaks. He's beginning to understand the world and its vastness, see how much is different and how big everything can be. Entire states and countries! Different tribes and lives. Alfred offers advice that is broad and seems sensible: "You work with whatever life gives you. You just do your very best."

That night he's coming back from the toilet when a low grunting stops him, a wet, husky, slapping sound. At first he can't find or place it, thinking it the noise of an animal or wind through tents. Some beast creeping upon them, intent on destruction, disorder, or worse? Peering into the darkness, he makes out Carl, pants down and hips thrusting, the white of his bottom going back and forth. For a moment the boy stops, remembering, pressure and pain swelling as he sees that Carl is with one of the girly-show girls, curly hair down her back, her neck up like a turtle's. She lets a long sigh out, a sound like a cat makes or an owl in its moaning, and in seconds they both turn toward him as one.

Neither stops in their thrusting or seems in the least shamed or stunned, the sounds continuing like muted speech: the slapping, the grunting, the sighing, the whistled moans. He stares and gulps, thinking to wave or to say something, but he doesn't, as how stupid or bumbling would that be! He knows nothing, has learned nothing. He is an Otto-like, unformed babe. Stumbling, hurrying, he keeps on through near darkness, back to the silence and safety of his cot and tent. There his breath slows, his heart thumps; he tries to block things from his mind. He thinks to read from his Bible but doesn't want to turn or strike a match.

The next day there's a commotion just as his act is about to start. He is waiting outside, cape folded around him, listening to Tot's bally talk when she stops midway through. Shouts fall and follow, the rumble of feet and sounds of quick movement, long voices distant and fading, trailing away. He peers into his show tent but finds no one there. Again, the marching and shuffle sounds follow, echoing away from both him and his empty tent. Dropping the cape, he shrugs on a shirt and pokes his head out, still finding no one anywhere about. Has there been a bad accident? A new and fetching act? Finally, he circles the tent and enters the main aisle of the show, following people with heads turned, pointing and moving, a crowd massed before the girly girls' bright, striped tent.

A man with a collar and several policemen are there. Tot's voice rises above others, then Carl's, but it's the man with the collar who speaks the loudest, his words ringing in the air:

". . . not acceptable! Our community's standards don't allow such trash! And with children present! These women should be returned to wherever they're from, taken out of this shameful yoke, and these human oddities—they should be consoled rather than shown for profit! Not trotted out like this for demon greed."

More policemen arrive, maybe six or seven. He isn't sure what town might be closest—Knoxville? Maybe Asheville? The faces are blurry, the sawdust thick and the lime smell strong, lights flared and mud, the sounds of Carl and the girl echoing from the night before. He can hardly keep track of any of it. A large, uniformed man, red-faced and with sideburns, yells, "Who's in charge here? Who runs this show?" When Tot answers, he laughs. "Please! Who's in charge?"

Several women clad in black kneel before the girly tent, and he sees that their heads, covered in cloth, are angled downward in prayer. His attention sways to the preacher, the memory of the one from before in his head, and is their role to lay blame and clean and cast things out? He feels that he has been accused himself of some wrong. Several of the girly girls peer from behind their canvas, looks of confusion or dread—he can't be sure—cast on faces made bright with paint. After a time, the red-faced policeman demands that the girls come outside. They comply in a single file, some in their show outfits, others in coats and wraps. It's a clear and chilly day. The crowd is murmuring, one man shouting, "Take it off! Take it off!" even as others tell him to quiet and respect the clergy. It takes time to sort all the people and talking. Johnny joins Alfred and Boris in watching, asking, "What's going on? What is this? Where are they going? Does anybody know?"

Boris shrugs. Alfred says: "I expected it sooner or later. Some places don't like the girls showing skin. Every show I've been on with a girly act ended just like this."

"Are they being arrested?"

"It looks so." The girls, all out of the tent now, are escorted by the uniformed officers, to the sound of a few handclaps and a handful of muttered jeers. Children dart in and before them, mice scurrying before a herd of beasts. Tot and Carl are taken along too, or else demand to accompany the others, Tot a moving blank space in the crowd. The dark women remain kneeling, heads tilted like ravens, their dresses fluttering in the sudden and shifting breeze. A final policeman follows, holding a broom with a series of furry things dangling like animals captured and strung up on a line. The boy breathes to the others: "The mi-muffs." There's chuckling.

Zorat moves to join Johnny, Alfred, and Boris.

"Didn't I tell you?"

"Did you call them, Robert?"

"Only in my prayers. But I must say that it's deserved."

Alfred spits and plucks at a suspender. His usual smile has gone missing, his face as stiff as Cletus the dummy's. "Maybe so, maybe not. In my view they ain't done nothing wrong. A payment to the judge gets 'em out."

"Maybe."

"Maybe."

"It's all a business, this performance—it is. This whole show."

The others are silent. Boris then: "Everything's a business."

"And that's okay."

"Okay by me."

"Business doesn't know right from wrong." This from Zorat.

The kneeling women rise, faces weathered and gray.

"I'm not judging, just saying. Business exists to make money. It's neither good nor bad."

"There can't be bad business?"

"I didn't say that at all. Only that its purpose is amoral. It just is."

There's a pause. "And Johnny here, what of him?"

The boy starts. "Huh?"

"Were you praying on him, that the cops would haul him off too?"

"No, that is different."

"How so?"

"Never mind. Solomon warned against lewdness. Johnny, this is all in the Bible."

The boy shifts and frowns. It seems that most things are.

TOT AND CARL return a day later. The girly-act girls aren't seen again.

CHAPTER SIXTEEN

Zorat

The boy found Zorat. I found the boy.

In this place, of all places, this bastion of fanfare and oddness and sham. Each of us having arrived per God's plan but by different paths: he plucked as a child from even worse debasement; me per my will, my need to be valued, and my primal fear.

I grew up in New Jersey, the son of a millwright; my mother sewed and taught kids in a grammar school. I was the oldest of six, and the first part of my life was what passed then for normal—school, sports, family, work, sleep, eating, church. We were raised Catholic, congregants of a small parish, regular attendees at the twice-weekly dour mass. I was an altar boy, as were my brothers, and though I heard the stories about some of the boys and a naked priest, this was not then my realm of suffering. My grief was brought, as I think on it, by other things: my getting a girl, Rachel, pregnant; my brush with a certain wicked professor later on. Yes, I attended college; I'm certain I'm the only one on this show who did. But that was after the pregnancy and Rachel's move to end it—an act that nearly killed her—and my parents tossing me out of my childhood home at eighteen.

I worked different jobs for a year, first in New Jersey and then in New York, before I decided I wanted to earn a college degree. I had no idea how to do this, what I would study, or why I even wished to go, but I managed to gather enough money to apply to college in New York, and to my surprise I was accepted. There I found myself in a religion class, the Williams building, second floor, one autumn with a Professor McAlpin. This was 1926.

The professor was a large, ruddy man, an admitted atheist who taught religion. I've since learned this is not that rare. Why he took such an interest in me, I'll never know; maybe he sensed a weakness or freshman frailty, or maybe he simply liked my looks. It was midway through the semester, my Catholic dogma laid bare and thin; McAlpin was accomplished at making one self-question: why beliefs exist, the *illogic* that governs so much of our lives and every thought. I had completed a paper on St. Augustine, I remember, and he asked one day to speak to me after class. I assumed that I was in for a critique or some censure, bracing myself for the onslaught and attack, but he was flattering, friendly, and warm. "You're one of my best," he told me, whereas I would've sworn that he barely knew my name. He asked if we might have dinner sometime, to talk over the world and my future, and of course—given my doubt and confusion—I agreed.

Professor McAlpin's apartment on the Upper East Side was so handsomely furnished that even in my greenness I wondered how he kept it up. A cook served us our meal, and the professor plied me with sherry, the talk of Spinoza and Saint Jerome, Jezebel and the Buddha, and I suppose the sherry went to my head or maybe he put something in it. The next thing I remember was awakening naked below the professor, his breath blowing and groin straining, and I cried as I wrangled and managed to buck him off. There were breasts, somehow, and a wetness; I can offer no understanding. My head was fogged for days and weeks. I quit his class and dropped out of the university, went back a year later and finished my degree. Avoiding his other classes, I saw him only once—in a hallway where he ignored me, which in light of things was just as well.

I thought for some time about thrashing or killing him, but this is a product of the Devil's black urge. I graduated with a BS in religion, and perhaps my grip on the Bible is a mix of my childhood and this. I'm no longer a practicing Catholic, but I reach out daily to God, as there is so much to glean and to master. I know that I am a sinner and scarred but also saved, and that Satan is circulating still in the world. I tend to think about these things, look for and study them. That makes me a bit edgy, mistrusting, and maybe different from other folks.

One day, jobless in New York, I went with a friend to Coney Island. The carnival show was then a part of it, and while I was gazing at the banners and lurid signs, a small voice screeched up at me, "Well, you coming in?" I looked down to find a woman—a midget, we called them—waist-high beside Ralph and me. I couldn't help but start laughing.

"Sure. Are you a part of the show?"

"Of course I am. It'll be worth your while."

She had a forward way of speaking, even in her high-pitched voice, a brashness that we both respected. We paid our money and toured around, looking at the oddities, watching a vent act and fair magic performance. By the time we left, she was standing where she was before, hands on small hips, scanning the crowd for new marks or prospects.

"Hey, we never saw you there."

"Well, you didn't stay long enough."

"We can come back tomorrow."

"I think you should."

"Do you have any jobs?" This was posed as a lark, though I certainly needed something.

She narrowed her eyes. "Do you have a talent?"

"No, but I can learn. And I'll work harder than anyone you know."

Her tone was serious. I thought at the time that she was being polite or making fun. "Meet me at two tomorrow. I may have something for you then."

And she did. She worked on the McKenzie show, and I was hired on as a rigger—a roughy, a helper—my pay mostly in a bunk and food. I figured I would do it a few months until I could find something better, but it's lasted five years, the last two with Tot running the show herself. The sword-swallowing I picked up as time shuffled on, my training from an old carny who knew the methods and trusty ways. It's strange being a part of a show, traveling and setting up and entreating, *performing*, and I still see myself leaving, but for some reason I've stayed. I think maybe God had me do this, that I'm traveling the country charming the masses for Him, praying and studying, steering and waiting, poised for this malformed boy to drop in.

I first saw Johnny the night the kid arrived. As showpeople we're attuned to acts, especially the new ones, and there was a buzz when he came aboard. I heard it from Lenny and Wilma and others.

"Tot's got a new freak."

"New freak, a boy. Say his back has these humps like wings."

"A true strangeness."

I doubted this. There were and are other freaks on the show, real human oddities, but no horns or tails or talons or angel wings. The others are harmless, more or less, but they trouble me, as I find their display immoral, the shameless and eager profiting from human flaw. I acknowledge that some see the opposite—that Otto, for example, has a better life on the show than he'd have off—though I look for the hand of God in the question. Why are these few so claimed? Curious as were others, I peeked in on Johnny that first night. He was scared, poor young fellow, his skinny torso revealed to the crowd of roughnecks and laborers, but that he was special was clear. His back has distinct pinions, split and growing from between his shoulders in perfect form, rubbery-looking and solid but capable of flexing and pliable. I wanted to touch them, to put my hands and face to this amazing, dreamlike thing. It couldn't be real! It had to be otherworldly, a delivery from Satan or from God.

The surprising thing was, after I came to know him a little, that he seemed more or less like a normal boy, just a twelve-year-old kid with developing, stretching, sprouting wings. He won't talk about his past, which I assume contains hurt and sadness, and this shared darkness may be what brought us close. He was and is keen on learning, including the precepts of our God and religion, and as this is something I have knowledge of, I've been pleased to teach and share. I don't attempt to guide him, or to group things as right or wrong, but as he wants to know things, I tell him, though it's grown a bit dense and entangled as time goes on.

On his arrival Tot put him with Sheila, a sure mistake. Sheila is shallow and selfish, scheming and needy, and their pairing played out the way I thought it likely would. I had conversations with Tot at the beginning and end of this linkage.

"She's going to corrupt him. You know this."

"How do I know this? Educate me, Robert."

"You know Sheila better than I do. And I know her well enough."

"Corrupt him how?"

"Overwhelm him. Project all her need onto him. Tot, there'll be a crisis—I'm saying it now, and you know it's true."

"She's good for the boy, as a woman. We'll see how it goes."

"It'll come to bad ends."

"And he'd be better with you?"

She said this to tease, knowing I wished him with me, where he'd be welcome and safe and retain his own soul, but she insisted on something else. It could have been a jab, a nod to the debt I can't seem to repay her, a lording of her status as employer over me. I've pondered before what impulse drives her, my theory that due to her size she must always prove her worth, show that she's smarter and tougher than most. "No one gave me a chance," she will say, although she gave me one. Without her and this job and Christ, could I breathe? She says, "I take the world as it is, not as I want it. I give people what they wish." But not all, like those who depend on and work for her—a failing we've fought and argued over now for years. She can be sweet and decent and charming, and she does love her daughter, yet there's something at her core I see as dark and grim. Does it climb up to evil? I expect to be dismissed by her at any point without cause, as she threatens everyone on the show from time to time with their release.

Maybe she has to do this to survive with her business, but anything in her way is met with coldness and a rigid will. During my time here, I've seen this occur more than once. I've seen grown men melt in submission before her, repellant and awkward in their pleading.

In one of the only talks I had with Sheila about Johnny, she told me she thought Tot was using the boy to his harm.

"How so?" I asked, sensing division and conflict. I'm not so pure as to spurn a given edge.

"Money," she replied, sniffing as if at a child or dullard. "And power. Everything goes to her. He gets little or nothing."

This was true, although nothing Sheila or I could do was likely to change that. I thought it would drive a wedge between them, and it did. I never heard what event hastened Sheila's leaving, but I wasn't at all surprised that it occurred.

Johnny is enthralled with Tot's daughter, Winifred. In a way this is sweet, but it reminds me too much of my own history with Rachel and the unhappiness that union wrought. Sometimes I wonder where Rachel is now, maybe home with mean toddlers or all alone in a mountain hut, and try as I might, I can't summon much sense of her—neither her face nor her voice nor much of anything at all. I don't try to steer Johnny from Winifred or warn him of the pitfalls that trapped and plagued me; it isn't my place to leap into his heart's affairs. But I brood, for odd reasons, my thoughts drifting and circling. I don't see Tot allowing their relationship to continue.

There's always been guesswork on who Winifred's pa might be. Some will say Carl, which I don't think is true, or the prior boss McKenzie. (Jesus, I hope not.) I did hear Tot one night lament that she'd been in love once.

"Only once?" I responded.

"Once hurt." She paused. "And you, Robert?"

The shield I've built clangs and shakes as I mull this, maybe not unlike the thick armor surrounding Tot. They all assume I'm a fairy, which I say I'm not, as I've had relations—obviously, with Rachel, and a few others here and there. One former performer, Leo, wanted me to swallow his cock as I do the swords; I politely refused this, though I've sinned with others. Even Tot came to my tent a few times early on. What does that bowing and dabbling make me? I can be so weak. I'm careful in giving my heart out, as I assume Tot is, and maybe this is the glue that has held us this long. We're distrustful of all—jaded, doubtful, and leery in our quick march on to death. Breathing fire like a dragon! Keeping all else tight inside. At least until Johnny landed and shocked us, opening me up as if he'd taken a knife and hacked my heart.

It took time for us to know much of each other. There was Sheila, of course, cold and overwatchful, though I had my defenses up too. The resentment of freaks by working acts was a factor, combined with my view that these brutes are more spawn of Satan than fruit of God. Proximity, time, and his friendly nature wore me down, and I became convinced more and more that he was a gift straight from above. When Sheila left and Tot put him with Alfred, it hit me like a kick to the shins. How long would this last? I have nothing against Alfred, or Boris, per se; they work hard like I do and mostly leave me alone. I worry how they will impact the boy, given his interest in God and things blessed and religious. They harbor no such wonder, reverence, or tact. **Hear, O Our God.**

TOT BRINGS ON new acts: a giant named Myron and a man Gordon with a monkey, two banner-front shows. Myron appears quite the dimwit, having little to say other than "Hello" and "Nice day." (I thought this also of Otto, until he surprised me one day by whispering, "They're falling for it.") The act consists of Myron holding Tot's hand—to reach him she must mount a chair—before he lifts and parades her about on his shoulder as she waves. Tot seems to enjoy this, and Myron is gentle, neither frowning nor acting goofy or rash.

Not long after he arrives, Alfred and Boris announce a special "contest" on an off day, an exhibition of the nether parts of Myron versus those of Otto, for the measurement and amusement of the other workers at the show. Of course this is vile, and I won't attend or support it, though I worry for Johnny. Given that he lives with Alfred, can he not be coerced? Men are such pigs.

On the day of the event, I make my way to the shower with chagrin, where Otto is already stripped and jumping up and down, yelling, "See! See?" with his appendage flapping about like a hose. A crowd has formed of some dozen or so men and women—I see Tot's head past others' waists—money flashing and folding in quickened hands. There's no sign of the boy.

Myron is much more refined in his exhibition than Otto, and I catch only a glimpse of his great unveiling, his purplish banger that sags like a rotten eggplant. (Apparently Myron is declared the winner, after some dispute and measurement.) Instead, I circle the group, still looking for Johnny and finding him on the show's far side, not with Winifred as I suspected but sitting and reading by himself. I take a seat next to him.

"I see you missed the contest too."

"Yeah." He smiles. "It's not something I desired to see."

This relieves me, I think. "We agree. I find sometimes that I can't stand this place."

He keeps his head down in his book.

"How's it going, living with Alfred and Boris?" I try not to sound prying.

He shrugs. "It's okay."

"What are you reading?"

He holds up a torn copy of *The Life and Opinions of Tristram Shandy, Gentleman.*

I lift my gaze. "Do they read much?"

"Who?"

"Boris and Alfred."

"No, but it's okay. They're all right." He smiles again. "They're not luminous like you."

He mispronounces it—isn't that like a reader? "Loom-in-nus," I correct him. I keep my voice low to hide my bliss. "Where is Winifred?"

"She's back in her trailer. We had an argument."

"Oh, over what?" My envy may spread. I look away: His face is so perfect, his lips like the halves of cut, moist fruit.

"Tot has told her of change coming."

"Oh?" I'm thinking he means change in the world—the repealing of Prohibition, maybe civil war in Cuba. The dust storms swirling in the West. The boy reads lots of newspapers.

"Coloreds are going to be allowed in some shows."

"What?"

"That's what we argued over. Not that they should come at all—Winifred agrees that they should, as long as they have their own time. I think they should be allowed in with all the rest."

I roll back to take in the sky. His youth and goodness still stun and amaze me, though I've witnessed and noted them now many times. The honesty and sense of fairness, the reaching out; I could kiss the grass or pluck the air straight from his curvy mouth. The perfection of him makes me doubtful, in addition. I blow out a long, staggered breath.

"You're right, of course. It'll be hard for people. When will this start?"

It begins the next night, and it *is* hard for some, including Lenny, Gordon, and others. I overhear Alfred and Boris in their grumbling.

"Things must be getting desperate, her allowing the Negras in."

"Nobody knows anything that goes on here. Nobody tells us nothin'."

"Even with their own time we'll be marred. Won't nobody white come here after that."

"How will they know?" Boris is chewing on something.

"Oh, they'll know. Plus, it means extra shows for us. And do we get paid more? Of course not."

"You're right. You say something to her?"

"Why? Tot don't take requests. She'll tell me she'll find another vent act, easy-pie, and she will. I ain't happy. Thinking of cutting my act some, bringing things short instead."

"Aha!"

Then there's Gordon and his monkey, Kip. Their act consists of Kip sitting in a booth and "reading minds," assisted by Gordon, Kip walking on his hands afterward with a cup, seeking tips. He doesn't do much. The ruse is weak. While Gordon keeps up a banter in the act, as if he and the monkey are the best of all friends, when the show ends things are different. Kip is kept in a small, filthy cage, to which Gordon, tipping a drink back, hurls barbs and slurs.

"Shut the fuck up, you! Enough! Can't you keep it closed?"

The first time I heard him, I assumed he was speaking to me.

One day I find a group gathered around his cage, Gordon standing back, head up and watching. Money again appears to move hand to hand.

"C'mon now, Kip, you can do it!"

"Gordon, get him going!"

"We got any girly photos?"

"Whose mind is he reading now?"

I deduce, growing closer, that the men are urging on the chimp's masturbation, betting on some level of results in his toils. Doubtless signals from Gordon, here as always, tip the money scales.

"Have we sunk to this depth?" I can't stop myself saying. The men make no comment, intent on their subject. It's like the calm before a scrum or fight.

"C'mon, Gordon. There ain't nothing happening. I laid my money . . ."

Gordon reaches into the cage and pokes at the monkey. So much for signals. I can't see what he does, but a squeal and bark follow, a sound of real pain. The men mutter and nod. Gordon reaches in again and pokes.

"There you go."

"Don't be a monster!"

The men lift and turn at the interruption. Johnny has appeared among them, face bright, eyes glowing.

"What, boy?" someone calls.

"It's just a . . ."

"We only . . ."

"Why are you doing this?" Johnny squints as he shouts. "It's not right or real. It's all a mean trick. Do you not see and hear this?"

Gordon sneers. "Life's a trick, son." He steps forward, pushing the boy in the chest with both hands.

Staggering back, Johnny ducks, then flies into him, knocking him to the dirt with a slap and muffled "oof." A scuffling like footsteps follows, a rattle. Fists fly to the man's face and blood spurts, a sick thud and crunching. Bellows of rage and new pain. The men stare, then move in to stop this. The monkey screeches through all of it, mouth opened wide.

"Hey!"

"Easy now!"

Johnny keeps punching. Thwacks come and crackles, Gordon's head slamming to the ground. Three of the men pull the boy from on top of him.

"Jesus, kid!"

"What the hell?"

Gordon lies still before struggling to his knees and feet, his face wet and purpled, blood and spit dangling from his lips. "What . . ."

Alfred speaks. "We're just having some fun, Johnny."

"It's nothing but a monkey. An animal."

"It's just fun, don't you know?"

"Little bastard broke my nose!" Gordon is shaking, his belly pushing up and down. Blood from his face falls, splats on his shoes.

"Leave him be." The boy's voice rings firm and clear.

"Okay, okay. Easy now, Gordon. Johnny, nobody's hurting nobody."

Johnny steps before the cage, his back swiveled around to it. For a time, there's no sound, only the hissing and whimpering of the animal behind him, Gordon's low and quaking moans. It's as if some power or force holds things still.

"Alright, let it go." I'm not sure who says it.

"Another time, Gordon."

"All bets go home."

There's a shuffling of money, of hands and men. Gordon glares at the others, at Johnny and then at me. I try not to smile but I might, my lips pulled up close. It could be a small and mocking little grin.

I follow the boy as he walks off toward Tot's place. Clearing my throat, I trot and overtake him, thinking to say something weighty or stirring about this strength and act. This stunning *vehemence*. To offer my simple thanks.

"You did the right thing, son."

His face is disturbed-looking, his eyes gone teary red. "I don't know what happened." His hands have grown black with the blood, and he stares. "How could . . . ?" His head shakes and his shoulders, his arms flapping up and down. "It's so . . ." He calms and goes silent.

"Fierceness for good is demanded by God, Johnny. Living is violence. It's all okay."

His face remains still. "Before I came here," he says in slow cadence, as if telling this tale to a confessor or a crowd, "my friends were the ants and roaches in my room. I came to know them, to see and admire them. They were real. They were alive." He turns and stares at me, his hands clasped. "Do you understand?"

It's the only time he has spoken to me of his life before. I haven't pried and don't do so now, and he offers no more of it, but I understand him more than most. I know so much of shame. Later that night, I weigh this as I read my Bible, as I lash my back with the whip that leaves the scars no one sees. I had thought of the freaks as an ugliness, a blight wrought by Satan, but here is virtue revealed. My mouth dries as I think on it, this nod to the blessed, grand, and the divine, a reason to live, still! A vision; a portent. Isn't all love wrapped in fear? I kneel and cross myself, bow and burn and thank God for it.

CHAPTER SEVENTEEN

He's reading a newspaper, the *Jacksonville Journal*, when the past comes striding back. They're on their way to their winter quarters, the last few shows before a two-month break, and the entire crew can feel the finish, the talk loud of home-cooked meals (nothing against Cookie!) and walks, of beaches and bonfires and grapefruit and the like. The air is cool, the day sunny and cloudless and bright. Thwacks come from Boris's knife throwing, the sound like a car's knock or drum, and he likes to sit and to watch this: He could keep watching forever—the concentration and vigor, the control, strength, force and skill. Today, though, the sound stops and Boris's head pokes through the side tent—the space equipped with a cot and a trunk to hold his clothes and books and things.

"Hey, there's someone outside says he knows you." Boris's teeth flash as he speaks. They're like boulders or pillars, seeming too large for his head.

The boy puts down the paper. He's been reading of the nation's economy, of how 25 percent of its people are now unemployed. "Can you shoo him off? At least until showtime?" People who claim to know him have become much more common. It's only late morning. The show opens at three.

"I can, but he won't get in then."

Johnny gives a puzzled look.

"He's a Negra."

The shows to which they admit coloreds are hit or miss, maybe dependent on the day or place. No one seems to know whether they will occur or when. The grumbling about them continues. The crowds still aren't large.

Johnny stands, then sits. He should avoid this, regardless, or take someone—Boris or Carl—along as a shield. Tot has warned him not to venture too close to the patrons, as he is now so widely known. "People are drawn to fame," she said with her head shaking, her lips thin and set. "Sometimes that's good; it's what drives our shows forward. Sometimes, it's not." Something about this, though, intrigues him. He folds the paper, lays it sideways on the cot.

"Where?"

"I'll take you."

He follows Boris out to the camp's perimeter, where rope has been stretched between posts to mark it off. A single puff of fog hangs balloon-like in the air. The sun paints the tops of tall trees a yellow white. The boy has seen coloreds before at these lines, sometimes whites, those without funds or barred for other reasons. Lot lice, they call them. At showtime Bud and the men patrol this roped line, making sure crashers don't enter, and there are stories of breaches and of ducking schemes, of urchins assembled, fake disasters, and more. Johnny has seen men chased off. He bows up his shoulders now, standing straight behind Boris. He's wearing a cotton shirt that for the most part hides his wings.

Boris points to a black man standing near the rope. "There. He's been out here for hours, or so Lenny says." He pauses. "You want me to wait?"

Something about the black man is familiar. The boy halts. "No, you go on." Even on the rope line, he's only a shout from the other showpeople. "Just keep an eye out for me, if you will. I'll be fine."

Boris nods and walks off. The boy approaches, slowly.

"Hey," the man says, eyes open, mouth wide. "Remember me?"

It's Elias, grown now or almost, taller by at least a foot—taller than Johnny—and bigger. He sports a small mustache.

"I . . . I thought . . ." The boy can't get words out, can't grasp or take this in. It's like plunging deep into a gopher hole or gator den, or falling from an unseen cliff. He clears his throat, coughs, stamps his feet. Finally, "What are you doing?"

Elias laughs, the old laugh. He's missing a front tooth. His eyebrows are thicker. "I heard about you, word getting out even way down here. Thought I'd come out and see you for myself."

Goose bumps creep up, spreading along Johnny's back. "You're not at the side camp?"

Something flares in the other's eyes. "Nah, the side camp shut down. We had to move on. Leave and go somewhere else."

"You still working the trees, though? I remember we were gonna be partners, gonna start our own business, our firm."

A slow smile. "Nah. Got out like Mama Lo always said I should. Gum prices bottomed out, everything closed. I work at a hotel in Jacksonville." He sighs and smiles. "Making it on through, now. Yes I am."

There's silence. A duck flies above them, its wingbeats near unseen. "How's Mama Lo?"

A pause. "She died. A couple years back now. Josephus too." His eyes make rapid blinks. "It's been hard, Johnny." His voice lowers and falters, the boy's name slurred and tumbling out. "And my daddy's gone. But I got my own son now."

"What?"

He smiles again, the missing tooth making him different even as he's much the same. "Yeah, little boy named Arthur. A year old."

"Wow. So you're married?"

A shrug. "Yeah."

The boy cannot conceive of being married. It's a thing others do, those settled and older and wiser. He imagines Elias sleeping with this woman-girl, undressing and sparking with her. Tot's warning and his own fear have kept him from exploring much. He's done nothing with Winifred other than kiss her and touch her breasts.

Elias shifts. "You got a girl?"

A cough, a look off. "Yeah. Her name is Winifred." This seems so modest in comparison. She's not a wife. He is still a boy.

"So," continues Elias, "you famous now, I guess?"

Johnny shrugs, his face down and hot. "I don't know. I just do this." He motions back at the tents, the show.

"And you like it?"

Like it? Compared to before, it's certainly better—it's a better life. He thinks back on their dreams for a moment, their hazy, see-through child-plans.

"Sure, I guess."

"What do you do, exactly?"

He breathes out. "I show my back." There's a pause. "People pay to see it."

Elias frowns and looks off too. A train-like whistle comes from behind his lips. "I never saw it being this way. Did you, Johnny? I mean, if you're happy, that's great."

"Are you happy?"

Another smile. The boy notices a paper sack at Elias's feet, the neck of a bottle peeking out. The sweetness he has smelled on men before.

Elias catches the glance. "Sometimes," he responds. "I been through some stuff. I guess you have too, eh?" He laughs without joy in it. "You never were much good at hiding. But as smart as you are, I thought you'd be using that brain."

The boy's mouth sets. His nose leaks and he wipes it. "And you, are you using yours?"

"Hah! I wasn't meaning to taunt you. Life has dealt us some things to push back on—ain't that right?" He kicks at the sack and the bottle by his feet. "You push back, you go on. Here we are, both of us, being the things others would have us be."

Johnny is silent. The sun stripes the grass shades of gold. Then: "Hey, do you want to come see the show this afternoon? I can get you a ticket." He thinks to mention the minstrels but does not, realizing how this would sound. He wonders that he even thinks it.

Elias shakes his head. "Nah, I just came to see you, Johnny. I don't need to see nothing else."

A horn honks far away; dim notes sound from the accordion. The boy is gripped with the sudden urge to disrobe, to turn and show his back and wings to Elias, as doesn't the other want to look and see? Wouldn't he be impressed by their growth and their oddness, by the development of this *spectacle*? The desire to do this fades, though, replaced by a worry that he knows so well, the dread that someone near him is leaving. He shuffles his feet. "Will I see you again?"

"Sure. You come to Jacksonville, go to the Windsor Hotel. You'll see me there."

"And the others, Bessie and the girls. What happened to them? Where are they now?"

Elias half turns. "Scattered. Some I don't rightly know."

"And Sam"—Johnny wants to confirm—"Sam is dead."

A slow nod. A glance back. "Shot hisself, Johnny. Some things you can't push on past."

MAYBE IT'S THE visit with Elias. Maybe it's the nearness to the break. At the show's next (and last) stop, near Daytona, he decides he wants to go to town. The other performers go from time to time, but not the freaks; Otto and Kenneth and Myron remain at the show. Along with him, on account of his fame and the risks of conflict due to his strangeness. According to Tot, this had happened on another show, where a man known as the Alligator ventured into town and scared some children, so that the entire show had to be canceled at a loss. Even when their show is part of a fair—like the Illinois State Fair or the Fireman's in Pennsylvania (a rarity, since Tot says the animals and contests distract from her events)—Johnny and the freaks don't venture out. Yet Tot seems to go everywhere, and to take Winifred with her when she does.

"It's not that exciting, Johnny," Winifred says. "We walk around, look in a few shops. Sometimes we'll eat in a restaurant. Mother, of course, draws lots of stares, but she stares back or ignores them and says that all of it is good for business. She says she wants me to feel that I can lead a normal life."

"But not me, huh? Not someone who's a freak."

"Johnny, you're famous. You know that. You could cause a scene."

"I'm going to go."

"Please, just don't." She kisses him, long and with passion, and he responds but is tense and restless. He runs his hand up between her legs, feeling her underthings there, the smoothness and warmth of her. She releases and slaps him once across the face.

"What was *that*?" Her face is the pink of flowers, of sunsets.

He recalls his own slap at Sheila long before. His face is hot, his eyes down. Can she accept him? Forgive him? He fingers his flaming cheek. "Winifred, do you love me?"

"Of course I do. What is going on?"

"I . . . I don't know. I've been thinking."

"Do you love *me*?"

"Yes, yes I do. But what's the future here, Winifred, for either or both of us? Am I doing this when I'm sixty—still showing myself so that others stare, still an object to be seen and used?" The conversation with Elias joins the three of them in his mind: None now has a father. Winifred still has Tot.

She grips his arm, her other palm out to keep them apart and at a distance. Her look is caring, her tone tender, warm and soft. "Johnny, we'll make it work. We're not yet adults! We've got time, and wherever you are is where I want to be. It doesn't have to be here."

He sighs, his jaw loosening. "I saw someone I knew before."

"A black man."

He frowns. Everyone knows everything on the show—her response only proves it. For a moment he's beneath the ground again, the smell of the dirt strong, the heat and confinement. The closeness. "Yes, I knew him when I was small."

She hesitates. "What did he say?"

"He asked me if I was happy."

"And what did you say?"

"I told him I am when I'm with you."

HIS FIRST TWO winters in Florida were spent under Sheila's care. They stayed at a house she rented from an older woman, Mrs. Schwartz, that had a backyard with flowers, and they didn't see the others much. He remembers it now as a time of breezes, the land flat and with more shrubs than trees, a lake behind the house he would go to and sit by, reminding him of the one holding his mother somewhere else. They didn't go out much during those first two winters, eating meals Sheila cooked and visiting some with Mrs. Schwartz, who had an accent and liked to reminisce about things in the old country. She asked, "You're the boy, eh?" when they arrived but said little more to him after.

Sheila brought him lots of books, and one day they bundled up—her tattoos hidden, his wings and hair too—and made a trip to the county library. He had heard of such places but never been to or seen one, and he found that when confronted with thousands of books, he was overwhelmed. The place had a musty smell and a quietness, others studying or reaching or standing, everyone looking at and reading books. When he said something to Sheila, she held a thumb up to her lips, warning him in a whisper that he mustn't raise his voice here. He found books about airplanes and history and creatures, detectives and

Jesus and lots of other things. He could spend days in here, literally, weeks and months if they'd let him, looking and walking and stopping a bit and reading more. She let him pick several books and checked these out for him, later checked out more, and he liked to look at the ink stamps and due dates, imagining the people reading these stories before him. No matter how many times he asked to accompany her again, though, she declined.

One day they went to the beach, a gusty and cloudy day with few people out exploring, the smell of the salt reminding him of long before, the drive to the train station with Mr. Paul and his mother. Was that really his life? It had become hard to reach and touch it. He and Sheila sat bundled in the sand, eating pretzels and drinking colas she'd brought in a paper bag. The sky was as gray as an old hat but moving, little ripples above them like strange and silent waves, and he followed one from the land's edge to the sea until he lost it. An airplane appeared then, and he regarded this in silent awe, listening to the churning motor, the sound that changed with the wind's turns and thrusts. A pelican dove into the gulf like a bomb dropped, emerged lifting and bobbing, tilting back its gleaming neck. Sand blew, the gulls shrieked. When they left he let her take his hand and hold it, and felt neither ashamed nor repelled by her touch. His memories still held, though, like a grave marked inside his head.

This winter he stays with Alfred and Boris, in a boarding house with ten small rooms, one of which is assigned to him. There's a bathroom down the hall with a real shower and toilet, and the nearby rooms house boarders from other shows: an old man named Giles who is a clown and can twist his face; Jimmy, who works with animals and trains them; another man named Phil who never says much. They're polite to Johnny and familiar with his fame, and sometimes he catches one or the other of them staring at his back, which is protected by his shirt and coat. The bathroom has a pull latch, and he's careful not to be caught there or in the hallway or at his door, but no troubling deeds or encounters take place.

Alfred and Boris look out for him as they have before, and on the nights they go out "on the town," he stays in his room and reads. He enjoys hearing the men talk, mornings at breakfast and in the afternoons, the tales of other shows and disasters: the time an elephant stampeded and killed people, the midget who was struck by a knife thrown but wanted the knife left in his leg. The he-she who is truly a he-she. The patrons who die from shock at the shows. There's much talk of the economy too, and the boy reads of this: of Roosevelt and work camps and unions forming and courts. Alfred and Boris don't mind him journeying out during the daytime, and he spends many an afternoon in what passes for woods in this Florida: stands of pines mixed with palms and brush, weeds and smaller trees. The odors remind him some of the side camp—the sweetness of needles and fire ash, the rich punch of rot and decay—and he thinks of Elias and the time they spent there, the things the other boy said when they met those weeks before.

The sun here is bright, the trees farther apart and distinct-looking, the palms with their trunks and aprons like dancers bowed. In between some trees lie thickets black and dense with vines. Possums and deer scamper, snakes lie in the sun, but nothing like the wildlife common at the camp. He sees Tot and Winifred only twice in two months—they're lodged in a home on the far side of the town, a thirty-minute walk from the house where he stays—despite his journeys there and his looking, his asking and calling on them several times. Zorat is apparently residing in another town or place, as Johnny doesn't encounter him at all.

Sometimes he hears others speak of him. "I hear he has powers," says a tall boarding-house man. Another, maybe Phil: "Have you seen them? What are they like?" Even Alfred: "They'll be six feet or longer by the time that he's fully grown." And then, on one of his two visits with Winifred, he overhears Tot talking on a telephone in another room: "He's one of a kind, alright. No, I wouldn't think of a sale—are you nuts? Of course, if the price was right, or there was a merger . . .

No, that's insulting. You're out of your mind! Good luck to you and yours." He gets almost no alone time with Winifred, their only true contact a furtive and hurried, less-than-satisfying kiss.

"We'll be starting again soon, Johnny," she tells him. "First show in Pensacola. A few new acts, I hear. A priest will bless us with water before we open up under canvas."

He wants to be with her. He doesn't care where they go.

Though he thinks often of going to town during the winter, he never does. Is this due to fear—the seed Tot placed so firmly—that this would produce bedlam, that he'd trigger a shameful, wounding, frightful scene? There are so many wintering showpeople that this outcome seems remote. Still, it's not until the day before they're to leave, a morning when the sky clings to the ground like a huge gray cat, that he walks down and enters a store on Tampa Street called Sarah's Toys. He's struck immediately by the coldness of the air inside, a droning sound somewhere and dryness, and he realizes that this must be the "air-conditioning" he has heard so much about. He's not sure that he likes it, bundled even as he is, and when a woman with birdlike eyes appears and asks if she can help, he shakes his head in a flutter and hurries outside again. There he encounters Sheila, umbrella up against the coming rain.

"Johnny!" she calls out, a smile lighting and broadening her face.

"Hi." His heart does . . . what? He can't describe it. He claps his hands once, then twice in his surprise, the uncertainty and total confusion of it all, seeing her again and meeting now in this fashion.

She stops some feet away but leans in toward him. "So nice to see you! Are you doing okay?"

"Yes, just fine." A smile forms on his face. Should he ask her now why she left? He reels sideways and pauses. A car motors down the street. Then: "What are you doing here?"

"Oh, I'm talking with show managers. You know, still in the business!" Her grin recedes. There are circles below her eyes that seem new, the highest tattoos just visible at her neck. "I miss you, Johnny."

"I miss you too." And he does but he wants to leave her, to escape and dart off. Does this make him ungrateful? He shuffles his feet and looks down, his shirt tight on his back, his mouth fumbling at pardons, excuses, answers, old doubts. He sputters some as he speaks. "I've got to go."

"So soon! Well, it's . . . it's so good to see you. Can we see each other again? Here, I'm staying at—"

"Nice to see you, too!" He spins a half circle and begins almost to run.

"Johnny!"

At her scream he turns back to see her pulling her dress down, the tattoos of wings draped from her neck to where she holds her hands. Her arms shake as she twirls, her breasts white and exposed then, as if she wants him to say something, to applaud, grouse, or laugh, even to snort or shriek. Instead, he is mute, her scream in the air like a smell left behind her. He expects others' looks, enquiries in alarm at this uproar and display, but no one emerges from any shop or along the street; no one else is to be seen anywhere. Are they peering from windows in outrage or wonder, or are they, too, disordered, perplexed, afraid? The rain falls much harder, cold on his head and down his face and shirt, and this shift permits him to break from her, to turn his head away and continue home. His shirt whistles and pops against his back as he scoots and trots, the wet fabric chafing, the rain a thudding curtain pulled close. He neither turns again nor hears more until he arrives at the boarding-house porch minutes on.

The guilt sweeps him later. He regrets so his haste, his dread shown and his leaving. What harm would have occurred if he'd stayed? He could have talked to her gently, asked about her new life, shown her that he cares still, wing tattoos or not. Did she look angry or crazy? The inked wings stay on his mind. It's been almost a year since he saw her, since the slap, her professing her love and her exit, and he decides against telling either Alfred or Boris. Better to let this play out and be done.

Grabbing a newspaper, he returns to his room, his mind spinning motor-like, his heart still beating quick. His things are packed now—he still has few belongings. Alfred bought him new clothes with funds Tot provided, but Johnny hasn't looked at these or tried them on. He settles down with the paper, his hands strangely shaky, the paper flapping and rustling before a picture claims his gaze: a man in a bent fedora, speaking before an assembled crowd. Something about his posture, or maybe it's his eyes, the shape of his head, or even the crowd, looks so familiar that it seems almost grotesque. The boy scans and studies it, scouring his brain for some connection or clue: Is it someone who's attended a show and received a photo? Someone he saw in town? The caption says "DOYLE ANDREWS, CANDIDATE FOR FLORIDA GOVERNOR." He slips the page out and tucks it in his bag, among the clothes still in their packages, his mother's bracelet, and his books.

CHAPTER EIGHTEEN

They arrive in Pensacola just before a looming storm. It's not a hurricane, he is told, as it's not the right season, but the wind blows and rain darts and one of the tents collapses, another blown some yards away. The show area afterward is a soupy mess, with water standing in tents, cots stacked upon boxes to dry, props likely ruined and lost. Then it turns cold and most of the crew becomes sick, with coughing and fevers, as they await the delayed opening. The electricity they were promised doesn't work for three days, and by the time the show starts, the normal excitement is missing, replaced by a sullenness and a wish to get on with it, to begin and move quickly to better fortune and somewhere else.

Johnny's illness isn't as bad as some, but by the first of his shows a dull ache remains, and he feels more like sleeping than striding out to show himself. He has devised a routine he's anxious to attempt, though, to relieve what he sees as the staleness in his act. His wings have grown so that if he ducks his shoulders, he can make them wave, and he has practiced before a mirror, walking to and fro like a goose. As the show starts, he reconsiders, given his pain and a sudden fear he'll look silly—an oversized flightless bird—but he takes his cape off and dips and shrugs as he planned. The audience seems impressed, a few words breaking through: ". . . can't believe this." "Did you see that, Luke?" ". . . boy must tuck those things in to sleep."

The line after for photos is longer than ever, and he's so tired from the day that he has trouble focusing, flubbing inscriptions: "No, *Tom*, not John," "It's spelled B-I-L-L . . . ." By the last man in the line, he can barely think, and he looks for Carl or Bud, as sometimes they'll cut things at the end. He smiles at the last man without looking up at him, pen poised above glossy image on a cardboard sheet.

"How would you like it?" His voice sounds worn and thin.

The man at first doesn't speak, but when he does his voice is as if pulled forth from a dream. "Your mother Lena?"

The boy's head lifts but not his eyes. He turns partway, still without looking, far enough to see the sleeve hanging, the missing hand. Spittle clogs his throat.

"Thought so," the man continues. "Thought you were dead. Saw your grave, or where she said it was."

Johnny puts down the pen.

"She still alive?"

He shakes his head. "No." Softly.

The man remains. "Thought that was the case, though I wasn't sure. Everybody lies. She did, so maybe it's your turn now." His laugh is a car's start, short and with clacking.

Johnny straightens to face him, his back shifted away, spine held firm. The man's eyes are so light-colored that they look like tinted glass. He is older, partly gray-headed, but otherwise still the same: nose and chin, lips, ears. For seconds, maybe minutes, they stare at each other in silence as they did before, or as the boy did through the cupboard's crack at the man searching for him then.

"What do you want?" Johnny asks. His voice is strong-sounding. Beyond is the clamor of the show's end and closing: footsteps and talking, a few short and muffled laughs.

The man grins. "A photo signed. You're a star! You see, I saw this here flier, and I knew. I could see the resemblance. It pulls it together—you being called special and all just like that. That's what we'd heard way back then, now, yessiree."

"We?"

The man's brows lift and bunch. He nods without speaking.

"How did you know my ma?"

A half grin. "Now you have all the questions."

"And my pa?" It dawns on the boy that this man could be his father, though he neither sees nor believes this. The fever from before creeps back up his neck, twisting him into a stretched shape, coughs and a shiver following.

"Yeah, your pa. Know 'em both, or knew her. She really dead? I suppose so, or you wouldn't be here."

"Who is he?"

The man grins again, pleased-like. Slowly shakes his head.

Again comes the rage, the boy thinking to rush him, to knock him down fast and bash his one arm till it bleeds, kick his smile inside his mouth. Instead, he turns farther, catching Bud's glance and motioning. He chews his lip, his eyes hot and stinging. His gaze remains on Bud. "Don't let this man in again."

Bud starts toward them. "He being a bother?"

"Yeah. Never again."

The man holds his one arm up, his body hunched then sideways. "I just want my photo."

"No photo." Johnny is up and retreating, heading for the fold on the tent's far side. He neither looks back nor listens for more, his vision blurry, wings scraping on his shirt. He is Kip the monkey, picked and pawed at in his tiny cage.

"We'll see each other, we will." The man laughs. "Welcome back to the living, Johnny!" Coins clink in his pocket as he walks away.

FOR DAYS HE exists in a cloud. The old nightmares return, dating back from his first days at the camp, of the one-armed man peering in as he sleeps, touching his face, his back, his arms and chest and legs, his feet. Kidnapping him from the show and taking him off somewhere else, back to the men in the mean house or farther, to a place perhaps stranger or lower and even worse. Again he considers whether the man could be his father, as why else would he follow him, and how would he know so much? The statement about his mother—that she must be dead if he's on the show—hurts the worst. Soon his mother enters his dreams too, her voice faint and tender, saying, "Johnny, be calm when you wake." Touching him, staring. Asking, "Who is my child now? Are you broken by lights, being shown but not seen?"

He continues to study the Bible with Zorat, their focus now on the Revelation. Zorat provides context, stating that the book is symbolic—written while John was a prisoner on the isle of Patmos—lurid and prophetic, riveting and dense. The boy just finds it strange:

"And he sent and signified it by his angel, unto his servant John: Who bare record of the word of God, and of the testimony of Jesus Christ, and of all things that he saw." What he saw: the seven golden candlesticks and seven lamps of fire burning, **"and the four beasts had each of them six wings about *him*."**

He and Zorat read the verses aloud, alternating except when Johnny stops him to ask: Why was John in prison? Why was the name of the star Wormwood? What are the seven seals? The words float to him during the day like ghosts or the twirls of magic—a new and distant strangeness—and he finds himself rereading things at night, memorizing certain passages:

"And when the dragon saw that he was cast unto the earth, he persecuted the woman which brought forth the man *child*. And to the woman were given two wings of a great eagle, that she might fly into the wilderness, into her place, where she is nourished for a time, and times, and half a time, from the face of the serpent."

What does any of this mean?

Zorat is encouraged by the boy's interest, and matches it. "There's so much to learn here, Johnny. Every time I read it, I see different things." Spittle forms as he says this, his eyes as if lit by lamps, and in his fervor he touches Johnny's arm but pulls back. "Some say that the Revelation is the key to everything. I took a whole course on the book back in college."

"Tell me about college."

Zorat pauses, sniffs. "What do you want to know?"

"What was it like?"

"Lot of students, some of them serious, some not serious at all. You sign up for the classes you're interested in, to move toward your degree. My interest was in religion."

The boy asks him more: How big were the classes? What were the teachers like? Were there lots of lessons, and books? Why religion and not business or medicine, or law? Zorat provides answers but in brief, rapid fashion, as if annoyed that they've ventured onto this tangent. His leg shimmies and wriggles, his voice takes a higher tone. He directs Johnny back to the text with a hairy finger.

"Do you see that it follows a pattern: creation and fall, then judgment, redemption? It's like the whole of the Bible, the message, wrapped in one. It's both a warning and triumph, this show of light over darkness. Something everyone ought to prize and know."

Johnny still doesn't grasp it. Sometimes sleep fails him after these talks and readings, and he prays as he hasn't since he was very small. He and Zorat offer prayers at each session, again taking turns, and the boy strives for his to be as clear and as smart as Zorat's, though they rarely are. The awkwardness of his voice grates, the words stuck or spilled out in a torrent, and should he plead for his wings to fall off or applaud them? It intrigues him that wings are mentioned so often in the Revelation. He considers that there may be others so maimed: freaks with the same flaw whom he just hasn't found yet, and his best means to find them is probably through the show. He can put himself out there, a draw for the others to come and find *him*! His mother's dream words float, though, merged with his weariness, of the viewings and spectacle, of what he has become. The desire to be hidden, to blend with others in a dull, unseen mass, seeps like gum leaked from a new-cut tree. This isn't his family. There is more to see. The world still draws and entices him outward, even the puzzle and menace of the strange one-armed man.

His "teaching" of Winifred has been somewhat less than successful. Tot agreed that he could step in as her tutor, and they have afternoon class in the trailer, Tot sometimes also there. Winifred is an indifferent student, bored with all reading and passive in her math, yet quite smart (he sees that), and on the few subjects that interest her (the different textures of hair, the intricacies of the human body, First Lady Eleanor Roosevelt), she can become quite engaged. Tot says to him once, "See, this is the way of it. She's as contrary with you as with me. It just doesn't work with her one-on-one." But one-on-one he is with her, so close that he can hear her breathe, and occasionally when Tot is gone he will touch her to gain her attention, their mouths wet and close, eyes wide and clear. At other times her obstinance makes him want to flee.

At one of the next stops, somewhere in Alabama, on an off day he sneaks to town. The weather is cool, the sky so deep it seems darkened, the trees spiked with new buds. He wears a cap and a coat to keep from drawing stares. Taking a back road rather than the main route, he tells no one that he's going for fear of his being stopped, his head down and back held arched and firm. The distance to town is unclear, and he worries over getting lost, the trip tiring him more than he expected at its start. Carts pass and cars, but he looks up at none of them, making no wave or contact, the few clouds above him bunched like ashes or ribs. The ground below him is clay, orange and slick, greenish tinged, the land where it's scraped for crops looking wounded. Birds twitch and call and for a moment he's carried back: to the pine woods and honeyed, tarry smell of the side camp, to refuge and closeness, belonging. But this fades. The few trees here are leafless, their branches bonelike and gray.

At last he reaches a small cluster of buildings, people walking and some businesses open: a beauty shop, a grocer, several restaurants, a store that sells seeds. He has entered a wonderland, a place from his books and thoughts, as he's not been in a town since he was very small, except for the few trips at winter. Sights and smells catch him, even the familiar made somehow new. A pile of horse droppings steams idly in the street; the smell of bread drifts; the ruler-straight lines of sidewalks flank the stores. The awnings in front of shops hang like teeth. It's all like a stage or a movie inviting him in. Is it his interest that makes this unlike the town back in Florida, his past, or something else? He *sees* things and notices them here, in and around him, up in the sky and sometimes far ahead.

Keeping an eye out for show members, he spots none as he stops, keeping his back straight and staying in shadows, dipping his cap-covered, hot and sweaty head. Winifred went into town with her mother; where might they be? He must be on guard. He half expects Sheila to come marching up. After a time, he enters a space between buildings, standing and eyeing the townspeople and wondering about their days, enjoying being the watcher instead of being watched. Two people passing speak: a man he didn't notice approaching, who smiles and says hello; a young boy on a bicycle who grunts, "Hi" and waves a hand. Is he noticeable in his watching? He's thinking of things he has never learned to do—swim, ride a bike, cook anything, bounce a ball—when he shifts to stay out of the sun and comes upon a lurid flier plastered on a post, describing his very show.

"Alexander's Traveling Oddities!" "See Amazing Freaks!" There on the front is his own cloudy picture, with great, beastlike wings painted behind him, huge and fake. His hair colored white when it isn't quite that anymore. He stares at this inflated image, caught and stunned by the scale of its falsehood. An oddity—he is odd, the weird and primary oddity! The great and freakish blow-off of the show. How he wants instead to be the biking boy, going to school with other, similar children, preparing to go on to college and out to the greater world. He stares still at the flier and the figures shown: Kenneth, Otto, and the dummy Cletus, back to the oversized wings that stretch and glow. Is it possible to be both injured and honored?

He is a beast like those named in the Revelation, but maybe all men are beasts, some with blue eyes and some left with brown, some fat or thin, and—

"Johnny!"

He looks up. Tot and Winifred hurry crossways toward him, arms thrusting, knees quick. He steps back into the shelter of the opening's depth.

"What are you doing?" Tot is red-faced and breathless, Winifred smiling, amused.

"I decided to come into town, just like you." He sounds defensive.

"Haven't we spoken of this?" Tot's voice squeaks and rises; mindful, she lowers it. Lines on her face spread like ripples in a pond. Others stop and look on: a man, a woman wearing a hat. A boy—the boy on the bike—joins the group quietly.

Tears are hot on his face before he knows that they're falling. He hasn't cried in years, and his hands pluck and pat to try and cover this leakage. Someone, maybe the bike boy, whispers, "Look there. It's *him*!" Fingers point at the flier stretched like a bright, dead thing on the cratered post. People glance at Tot and then back to Johnny, the bike boy jumping and pointing, laughing and whooping, "See there? See!"

"Ladies and gentlemen—yes, it's true!" Tot assumes her bally voice. Heads swivel toward her. More stop across the street. Her head is back, chest out. "Oddities from another planet, right here in your own backyard."

The group's size increases: another woman, an old man.

"Come out to the show this afternoon! Alexander's Traveling Oddities, right down the road at the fairgrounds on Thirty-Four. We have fire-eaters and a talking dummy, knife throwing and a dancing chimp, and some of the strangest things seen in nature, including this young man. The winged boy! Now, on account of women and children being present, we can't show you his back right here and now, but if you come to the show in a few hours, you'll see that and so much more! I promise that you've never seen anything like it before in your life."

Someone—he's not sure who—reaches and takes his cap off, exposing his thatch of whitish, uncombed hair. There's a gasp that's familiar, the sound bringing a thrill despite his wish to deny it, as if he stands now before them nude. Spreading his legs, with his head bowed and back, he watches from eye corners as others wander up to look: a farmer, a clerk of some kind, a young girl, a policeman. Tot nudges Winifred and Johnny with her foot.

"We have to be going now. We'll see you soon!"

There's a groan before the crowd parts and they take their leave. The three proceed slowly down the brick-paved street, Carl waiting beside their parked truck with a stare and frown. The walk seems to occur in half steps, despite Tot's head-down charging, the pavement like a desert spreading out before them. He expects to be chastised after they line up and climb inside, the doors closed, the motor cranked, but instead Tot's voice is soft, her tone measured and kind.

"I know what it's like, Johnny." She's seated in front, turned as when she and Carl first picked him up. "Believe me, I know. You want to be like everyone else, to be ignored. Is that true?"

He can only nod. The tears return, welling and cooling, sniffed back into his head with a honk like a muffled snore. Is it all so obvious?

"We each experience this—ask Kenneth, or even Otto. Sometimes you get tired of the staring, of standing out so in every crowd; I know that I do. You want your freedom! You want to be left alone, to just be you and be *normal*, but there is no normal, Johnny. You want to be everyone else, and yet they're all of them strange and different, unique to each other whether you know it or not. There *is* no normal life. It takes time to accept this, and even then, it can go in spurts. There are days where I want to never leave my bed, to never speak to anyone or be seen. To never again be looked at like an animal in a cage at some zoo. I am what I am, though, and you are what you are. In the end, you'll be alright. It just takes time to see it."

He nods again. He wants to say that he's thankful. Winifred takes his hand.

"I hear Robert and others condemning, saying what we're doing is wrong." Tot leans farther back, one hand with a tiny tremble. "I don't believe that at all—I truly don't. What life would I have if I wasn't here doing this? And Otto? He didn't ask to be the way he is any more than you did, or me. Once you accept that, I think the key is to find the joy in it. Some will make themselves bitter; that's the Kenneth way. Some will follow drink into the grave. I hope you do neither and take your pleasure on the stage instead. I think you do now, maybe more than you know it. You're a star, a performer, no less than a singer at a cabaret in New York. You're there to provide entertainment, and there's so much that's needed and simply human in doing that. For me it's the sell: the crowd's rush arriving, convincing them to buy and pay for what we're offering, to acknowledge us as a prized and different, valued thing. With you, I think it's something more than that."

Her voice has a shake to it. She licks her lips.

"Maybe I've convinced only Winifred and myself, but I've decided I'm grateful that I'm unlike everyone else. The names and titles have never bothered me much: freak and oddity, midget and gnome. I am what God made me. What a boring life otherwise it might be."

It's the most he's heard her say since his first days at the show. Winifred squeezes his hand, his tears dried now to crust. Reaching and smiling, she wipes his face with one hand as he sniffs and tries not to, clearing his throat in a husky, manful harrumph. Cars whine and pass, the sky above vague and watery. He considers the day and its hurdles and finish, and whether his fortune is entirely good or bad.

HE NOTICES THE crowds more and their varied makeups, or maybe they were always forged in certain ways. Some days there are women, more often now children. For a while he counts the sighs and screams. There's a falling ovation at least every other day, until abruptly there isn't, leaving him wondering how and why this has happened, the changes in him or the act that makes this so. Once, during a coloreds-only performance, he hears an old lady sobbing and saying prayers for him. Occasionally there are drunks and he's taunted and heckled, but he's apart from the men and doesn't mind this that much. Carl and Bud generally shut down these jeers, but sometimes the audience tosses things at him: flags and popcorn, coins that can hurt, women's scarves and underthings.

On a rainy Saturday only three people watch his show, and he wants to talk to them, to ask why they are there, to discover what lured or drew them, to find out if they're leaving pleased. Attendance in general is down, some of the bleachers an empty gray that seems sad, and there are times he can tell that few are listening to the bally. He weighs this with his questioning. He adds close-up views to his show.

HE MAKES NO more trips to town, feeling no further call or desire to. One day, though, after Tot and Winifred leave in the morning, only Tot returns. He scours the show for Winifred later, thinking he has missed her somehow in passing, that she waits at the toilet or cook tent or out at the rope line where the horses munch grass. He asks others.

"I heard she's traveling a few days," replies Alfred, or rather Cletus, the dummy on Alfred's lap.

"Where?" The boy's chest heaves up and down.

The dummy's lips pull with a clack sound. "I don't know!" His voice is pitched higher. Sometimes Johnny will stare hard at Alfred's lips, trying to detect movement but seeing nothing there. He notices now only the sagging skin around Alfred's neck, the signs of what was once a rounder, fatter man. He wonders what Alfred's dreams were back then.

"You have no idea?"

"Maybe to visit her father?"

He asks this of others but gets the same shrugging nonresponse. Finally he confronts Tot herself.

"She's visiting a school." The paint on Tot's lips is raised up in the middle. Her eyelashes are thickened, somehow larger and full.

He recalls now this discussion, this chance, but Winifred never told him she was leaving—wouldn't she have told him? How do the others know it? "We were making headway, progress with her schooling." His thoughts dart and tumble. He'll come up with a plan, he'll give it to Tot for her to sign off on, he'll *force* Winifred to work so that she won't be required to leave . . .

Tot smiles without malice. Pulls out a cigarette, lights it, smokes. "Don't fret, now—she'll be back soon. But she will go to school at some point."

"So she can live a normal life."

There's a pause. Tot's head cocks. The smoke curls like a rope. "She is who she is. You are you. I am me."

He nods and with briskness walks away.

CHAPTER NINETEEN

Winifred doesn't return for weeks. He walks and looks, at times almost frantic, searching for her familiar figure each day, trying to refrain from asking about her. Maybe she found her father, and the bond she and Johnny shared is no more. Maybe she doesn't love the winged boy and never did. He can't talk to anyone about it, not even Zorat, and his shows as a result have assumed a hurried and sloppy sameness. One day, frenzied and wretched in the fog of his wait, he sneaks into Tot's trailer during one of her bally talks, rummaging around in it for clues, for a sign or message from Winifred. She must have written her mother, having been gone now so long. Are there train tickets, dates on a calendar? Notes made or receipts? He sees the newspapers Tot reads and often gives him afterward, the boxes of lipstick and makeup, the childlike clothes scattered and strewn.

Examining a desk where she keeps books and ledgers, he rifles through bills and keepsakes, show ads and pens, and is surprised to find not a letter from Winifred but one addressed to Johnny Cruel. The envelope is open, the logo of the Northern Insurance Company on its front; there's a similar one below it addressed to a Kenneth James. He holds his for a moment like a candle before him, having never received a letter from anyone. He pulls out the paper partly stuck inside.

Hand fluttering, he drops this, squats to pick it up. What might Tot do if she finds him in her trailer? The paper is a legal something that doesn't make much sense, and at an uptick in the crowd noise he shoves it back in the envelope and leaves. He wonders if she'll be able to tell he was there, notice something he moved or touched—a footprint or dirt clod remaining, maybe a telltale scent. Did anyone see him enter? What did the Northern Insurance Company have to do with him?

He realizes that Kenneth James of the letter is Kenneth the dog-faced man, and though they've spoken but little, he decides to pay him a visit. Kenneth resides in a trailer on the show's farthest edge that, owing perhaps to his surplusage of hair, gives off a stale odor. The girly girls called it a "stunk," as in "Honey, have you been by that Kenneth's place? There's a stunk." Johnny waits until the other shows finish and his own photo seekers leave—the time when workers are usually gathered at Cookie's tent to eat—to make his call. The dog-faced man growls when he knocks but waves him in when he sees who's outside.

For a moment the man stares without speaking. Then, "What do you want?"

Only his eyes are visible, hair covering the entirety of his head and face, even his nose. His words when he speaks are hard to hear and to understand. The trailer is sparsely furnished compared to Zorat's and to Tot's: a table and chairs, bed and dresser, a picture of what looks like the sun.

Johnny clears his throat, softly. "May I tell you about something?"

A silence. Then, "Of course. What is it?" The pinkness of Kenneth's mouth seems in contrast to the rest of him.

"I saw . . ." the boy says. The words trip coming out.

There's a pause. "Well, what?"

"I saw envelopes in Tot's trailer, addressed to you and to me, from the Northern Insurance Company. Do you know what those might be?"

Kenneth runs his hands down his face. Such a humanlike gesture seems odd and unfitting; a tail swish or barking would match up much better. "Insurance company?"

A breath out. "Yes."

"Could mean that Tot's buying insurance on us. My guess is that it's life insurance, that if we die, she gets paid." The boy realizes that the hair around Kenneth's eyes has been cut so that the dog-faced man can see.

"But why?"

"There's some logic. We're among the most valuable things she controls. If something happens to either of us, she loses money. How would the show then go on?"

Johnny swallows, considering this. "They pay her if we *die*?"

Kenneth shrugs. "That's the way it works." The hair on his jaw moves in what the boy decides is a grin. The palms of his hands are naked-looking and brownish.

"What if we just left? Would they pay her then?"

"No. Why? You thinking of leaving?"

He hasn't been, but the notion lifts. He and Winifred could take off, get married somewhere. Live their life away, and free.

"I've thought about it myself. But what would I do—go on to another show? I'd have no assurance it'd be better than this one. I could shave my face and try to make it at a normal job, but that would be hard, and is it what I really want? I'm treated here fair enough, or at least I am now."

"Do you like it, showing yourself?"

Again his face twists, the beard or hair or fur. "I've learned over the years, Johnny, that life isn't perfect, and it's definitely not sure or fair. I wouldn't say that I like it, showing myself. I'd rather sit by a lake and read a book. I hate being treated like a child or someone's pet. But I'm paid for doing this. There's a lot worse places to be, and I've been in some of 'em." The curve of his mouth lifts, like a dog's behind showing. Kenneth's few teeth emerge. "My father was hairier than me."

Pay—the boy recalls Sheila's talk about this. He is paid nothing that he knows of or has seen, and shouldn't Tot pay him at least something? How will he marry Winifred with no funds to call his own? He tries to envision the future: his and hers, theirs. The show's.

"Have you been in love?" he asks with a wheezing, rushed sound, this odd and rash question left hanging in the air. He doesn't know Kenneth well. They were talking about shows and money. Why would he ask of something personal in between?

The hairy man sighs. "Yeah." His fingers touch his neck and chin, his cheek, and the boy realizes he has no idea how old Kenneth might be. Thirty? Maybe fifty? At first Kenneth offers nothing more, and Johnny fears that he's confused or insulted him. "Love is a strange thing," he finally says. "Sometimes what you think is love isn't, and sometimes it's there whether you know it is or not. I have women who show me interest"—he indicates his downy chest, his matted legs—"but it's hard to have that and do what we do. Usually, it just won't work."

Johnny's face is still hot from his asking. He looks down and swallows. Tries to shift things back. "Does the insurance thing bother you?"

Kenneth turns his shaggy head. Is a scowl shown or frown? His hands are so hairy that they truly look like paws. "I guess not. I don't know what the policy amount is, but I figure I'm worth more to her alive than dead. Maybe I'll ask her about it." Another pause. "Or maybe not."

There's a silence. The trailer rocks and creaks.

"Thanks for talking to me."

"Sure. Glad to."

The boy makes to leave.

"Hey, don't be afraid to take chances, eh?"

He looks back. He's not sure that he heard right. "What's that?"

Again, the pink mouth. "Who am I, to offer advice to anyone? Avoid regrets, though, Johnny. Regrets can stay real a long time."

The boy ponders this as he exits the trailer, encountering Zorat walking just outside. A look of surprise grips the other's face.

"What were you doing in there? I've been looking for you up and down."

"Just talking some."

"I'd stay away from him." Zorat's eyes shift. It's almost dark out, lines and shadows flitting across his bony cheeks. His lips open like scissors. "I mean, you never know what he might say or do. I've heard him tell people that he's the biggest star, bigger than the winged boy. Did he say things like that?" There's no space for any answer. "Did he want to touch you, touch your wings?" He dips close, so close that Johnny smells his sharp breath and sees the sweat painted on his forehead. "Have you eaten?"

"Not yet." He thinks to tell Zorat about the insurance but doesn't. "Let's go eat."

WINIFRED RETURNS THE next day. He watches as the car arrives and she steps white shoes into a summery morning. She looks older but the same, and his heart slams with a force that he fears he might faint from, or be moved as a result to say stupid things. He retreats, pacing about in his tent, not wanting to appear too tense or eager, thinking that she might now come to him. Did she meet someone normal while so long away? He practices what he'll say to her even as he listens for footsteps, but after some time he leaves and wanders the ropes and tents. He circles Tot's trailer several times before stopping, hesitating and faltering, finally stepping up and rapping on its wooden door. Inside he finds Winifred sitting placidly on a couch. It's as it was the first time he came here. Tot is somewhere else.

"Hello." All the words he practiced before fade and leave him.

"Hi." She smiles. The sliver in her eye casts its own special light, in turns dimming and blazing, carving his insides into great blocks of stone.

Silence follows before they both speak at once.

"How was your trip?"

"What've you been doing?"

"Where . . . ?"

"Why, I . . ."

He reaches out and they laugh, embracing and kissing, the smell and feel of her so familiar and strangely soft. Tears form that he blinks back. His wings itch and pull. She steps in slowness away from him.

"You look so good."

"Me? You're an angel."

She glows and laughs.

"You were gone for forever!"

"No, not that long."

"But you didn't tell me you were going! That you'd be gone long."

"I tried to but I couldn't find you! Then I was whisked away."

He won't allow himself anger or doubt. "Shall we take a walk?"

"Yes. Let's do that."

"Let's see our world."

They circle the show three times and then more, talking of everything and anything and nothing much at all. She tells him of the schools she visited—the Monmouth School in Virginia and something called Hartford in Tennessee—and while she found them interesting and stately, she doesn't want to attend either.

"Is she going to make you?"

"I don't know." Her head shakes with a fierceness. "Sometimes I think she resents me. It can be puzzling and weird."

"How long would you stay if you went?"

She shrugs without speaking. Tears form that he kisses, the salt on his lips like a taste of the earth or sky.

"We'll be together, I promise. I won't let us be apart again." He pauses, catching his breath at this. "Did you go all by yourself?"

"Elizabeth accompanied me." Elizabeth is one of the minstrels.

"I didn't know that you knew her."

"I didn't, until this. I suppose Mother paid her."

"Oh." He thinks to mention the insurance and his questions but tells her instead only of meeting Kenneth. "I thought he was okay," he says slowly. "Different, but not so bad just to talk to. He didn't try to eat me or anything."

"Well, that's surely a relief."

"I had all these worries, though, when I couldn't find you. I was afraid that you'd never come back, that you'd found your father or gone on to live your life somewhere else."

"My father?"

"Yeah." He glances off. "I thought maybe she told you who he was. I always asked my mother about that."

They haven't discussed this topic much; it's a subject she veers from, as does he, the bubble around them that neither wants to pierce or touch. Now, she turns to him.

"I know who my father is, or was," she says quietly. "He's dead."

He's not sure what to say. "When did you find out?"

She frowns. "Mother would only make references before. She'd say, 'Oh, he's pond scum' or 'You're better not knowing him.' Just before this trip, though, as I got on the train, she told me he had passed away. I asked her about him, and she told me a little more: that his name was Roy Malcolm. He was also a dwarf."

"He was?" He had assumed her father was normal-sized. "What happened to him?"

"She wouldn't say. Only that he was dead, and that he lived in Roanoke. So I set out to find him—that's why I was so long getting back. It took a while, but I found his grave and learned a little bit more. He'd been in prison in Roanoke, murdered someone in Virginia Beach. Little Roy, they called him."

"Wow."

Her tears pool and flow again, dripping like wax down her cheeks. "Why didn't she tell me? Why'd I have to find this out on my own? I'm so angry with her for keeping it to herself all this time." She draws in breath, a great, raspy sucking sound. "I can barely stand to see her now or hear her speak."

He stares at the ground.

"I don't want to talk about it anymore."

His thoughts flit to his own mother, to her secrets held. She never told him much either, leaving him to resolve and pursue things by himself. Maybe his father had killed men or been to prison, or maybe his mother had committed foul crimes herself. The uncertainty is what plagues him! The sense of unfairness rushes back. "Let's run away, Winifred," he blurts out. "Just you and me." He doesn't bring up marriage as any part of this boldness, as that doesn't seem right yet. He hasn't thought this fully through.

She looks surprised but not fearful. "Run away? Where?"

He frowns. "I don't know. Do you have any money?"

Her head shakes. "Not much."

"Neither do I. Should I be getting money from your ma?"

"For the show?"

"Yes."

She pauses. "I'd think so." Her brows line up. "Why don't I ask her? Maybe there's a fund for you somewhere. Seems like there ought to be. I've never thought about it."

"I can ask her too. I've been here three years, going on four. There should be something, I agree."

"Oh, Johnny!" They embrace again, close behind the minstrel tent in the shadows on the show's far side. They kiss, deeply and at length, and this time when his hand slips between her legs, she neither slaps him nor removes it. He is at once at his dizziest and happiest, and also at his most afraid.

CLETUS SMACKS HIS lips and claps. Behind him, Alfred's neck is pulled tight into knots, but otherwise there's no movement. This still astounds Johnny, no matter how many times he sees it: the technique that transforms the wooden boy into life, making him perky and bright and limber. Normal. Real.

"Oh, Johnny, Johnny," Cletus says. "Ask me a question—any question!" This is a part of his act, his stock routine.

"Why do people only grow to a certain height?" The boy means all people, but it sounds as if he's referring to Tot.

Cletus shakes his head. "Depends on what they were born with! Ha! Ha! It's all from fate."

Johnny turns and smiles. "Here's another: Does Alfred get scared when Boris throws his sharp knives?"

"Oh boy, yes. But Boris doesn't miss. Even when he is mad at Alfred, he will never miss."

The boy turns again, pleased.

"Can I ask you something?" Cletus lifts his big eyes.

"Sure. I guess."

"Do you have any powers?"

He laughs, his head up. "What do you mean?"

"Some say you have powers. I've heard it here." His head twists, his hands up.

Johnny glances from Cletus to Alfred, their faces blank and near the same. "What powers would I have?" A memory from long before circles, of his mother again, explaining. Of him trying to understand.

"Oh, I don't know." The voice is especially singsong. "Maybe the power to do things others can't. To heal people. To fly."

Johnny's jaw clenches. Alfred is teasing him. He's so tired of bearing others' probes. Alfred's face remains empty, his eyes as clear as his dummy's. Johnny sighs and shifts, his head swinging in answer. "My turn now to ask questions, Cletus." He pauses. "What will happen with this show?"

"What do you mean?"

"Does it continue on? For how long? Do you stay here forever?"

Alfred's face grows pink. Cletus clacks his lips once, twice, bats his eyes with a snapping sound. "Only a fool thinks things stay the same, Johnny. Life is a struggle: the world, the show, this country, each of us. There'll be another day, and it may well be different." He makes a slight bow. "That is the future. Good night, now! Good night to all my friends!" This is the way Cletus ends all his shows.

CHAPTER TWENTY

Winifred

Mother brought a new act on, and that sent everything downward. It happened not long after I returned from being gone, my anger still keen and ripe as a reddened peach, and even my quarrels with her failed to dim her thrill.

"I've got something special. You'll be so impressed!" She was hopping and jerking a bit, her wig bent like an animal perched and twirled atop her head.

"What about *me*?"

"What *about* you? You defied me and went to find him. Are you content now? To know that you're descended from a murderer and a thief? Is that any better for you, to know this pleasing fact?"

"You could have told me."

"I could have. And why?"

"So I would know."

"Now you know. Things move on, thank God, or at least I did. What about the schools?"

"Ah, they were okay, but I don't want to go there. I want to stay here with you."

Ordinarily she would have scowled or lectured me in response to this, but such was her frenzy that she couldn't stay on task.

"I'm telling you, Winifred, this puts us at the top! I've worried so about things, about whether we'll endure, even with all this talent, all my hard work and sweat and plans!" She lifted short arms. "This will preserve and save us! This gives us the security that can send you on to school."

"So, what is it?"

She smiled, a Tot smile. I saw my own face in it. I kneeled and she hugged me. We can be so much the same. "Oh, you'll see."

I've seen many things in my life here with the show: human blockheads, people that stretch skin up and away from their chests, an old man named Jim who could bug his eyes out and scare a crowd. A woman—a bender—who could twist herself into knots, a man who sucked his stomach fully into his backbone's shell, a boy who could fit nine golf balls in his mouth. (Not to mention those who tried and failed to get hired—the fake oddities, the tricks that weren't tricks. The man who offered to swallow mule dung on stage. All manner of clowns—Mother won't have them.)

What I saw a day or so later was Laslo. A foreign man, he spoke a strange English, his hair dark and wetted, a neat mustache forming lines. He dressed in a businessman's suit and appeared otherwise normal, except for the extra pair of arms jutting out of his torso. These were smaller than his own arms, childlike in appearance, and he could move them but not much. One of the small hands could grasp and turn things. Laslo was calm and open regarding this.

"It is my twin," he said in his accent, "but he was not fully formed or birthed. A part of him is still in me." He shrugged as if this was normal and common and perhaps we just didn't know about it yet.

Mother was right about the intrigue and reaction, at least at first. The show buzzed like a beehive. Everybody came to see. The responses were generally positive, even from the working acts, who I think sensed something was necessary to keep the show going on. Our attendance had dwindled, a state discussed often when the door to our trailer swung shut. The poring over receipts and bills, the blame given, complaints strewn. "Do you know how much it costs to feed this group? To move it?" She'd chew on a pencil or a stick of gum. "Not to mention the other payments and promises that must be made."

The reaction from the freaks was more hushed. One never knows what Otto thinks, or if he does, as he was the first to touch the small hands. (I thought Laslo would object to this, but he didn't.) Kenneth was Kenneth, looking on briefly but saying nothing else. Only Johnny was truly aloof, the look on his face one of concern or maybe revulsion. Or was it envy? I thought I recognized this and knew of it. As a nonfreak, I felt it too. Why was I so common, so depressingly middling and bland? Placed among people who were truly remarkable and unique.

I talked to him some about it. We went on walks as we had before.

Me: "He seems like a nice fellow."

Him: "Uh-huh."

"I don't see it changing things much now. Do you?"

"I don't know, Winifred. I just don't know. I mean, it makes me more expendable, don't you think? Tot has a new star now. She can cut me out and send me on."

"That's rot, and you know it. Now she has two major stars! She loves you. Why would she send you on? And weren't you talking about leaving, regardless?"

With me. Leaving with me.

"You say that she loves me?"

"Well, not like *I* love you." I touched his neck and face.

"You love the fact of my oddness."

"Wha . . . What?"

He shrugged and his breath puffed. "That much seems true."

"Is that what you think of me?" My blood surged and throbbed. "That I'm just a mark that has fallen? Another innocent babe that the wings have lured in?"

He twitched once, his face splotched red.

"That I don't really love *you*—that without your wings, I'd simply walk on past?" I thought at the time: Why would he want me?

"That's not—"

"It's not?"

"Let's forget it. I'm sorry." He blinked twice and swallowed, a swallow forming a pledge. "Did you talk to your ma about paying me," he continued, "and whether there are funds that are set aside?"

I had, and it hadn't gone well. She insisted that there was no money, that Johnny should be happy to have food and a place to sleep, to bathe in the richness of doing nothing every day. "I'm working twelve, fourteen, sixteen hours, dawn to dark!" she fumed. "What does he have to complain about?" I told Johnny, my voice low: "I will, soon."

"Does she want you to go away?"

I hadn't pressed this either. It wasn't the time, with Laslo coming on and her focus turned to that. Yes, she had mentioned it, but I hoped that with all the hubbub she would soon forget, or that I could convince her otherwise. I didn't want to jump out yet.

My silence seemed to inflame him. His face became redder. "You know others say that she's evil."

"Mother? Who says that?" I turned and stopped. This was unfair, and false. "Robert? That loon? You should stay away from him, Johnny. The others worry about him, and you."

"They do, huh?"

I regretted saying this. We rarely argue. The urge to leave all of this rose like a bird trapped inside my chest. "Let's talk about something else."

"Let's talk about God."

"My goodness. Now?" We've discussed this before, of course, but in general. I've never questioned his conviction or faith or criticized his time with the Bible or Robert. I've never challenged him on anything like this. Until now.

"I believe," he said simply.

"I do too. Is that it?" My belief is a haziness, prone to swoop off and fade, whereas Johnny's seems sharper, a sword that can cut and maim. I'm surprised he doesn't talk of it more, but I'm also cheered and relieved by this. A part of me fears learning what he really thinks, the poison perhaps transferred within the walls of Robert's trailer. I want things to be the way they were, as they are. Just now. *Just with me.*

He smiled in response to my question. "Well, yes, it is. That's important to me, Winifred. I'm so thrilled and pleased."

"What else should we talk about?"

"Let's talk about leaving."

"Oh, Johnny. Let's." I could have wrapped him in my arms and crushed him to a tiny pulp.

BUD PAINTED NEW banners: "Nothing as Shocking as This Has Been Seen!" "He'll Talk to You and Perform—The Only One in the World!" Laslo's picture showed his brother's arms juggling, which of course he couldn't do, but our crowds doubled overnight, a sea of overalls, kerchiefs, suspenders, and flat caps. There were frequent screams. Johnny's show stayed as a blow-off too, and his crowds were solid, but Laslo was the final act. Mother did the talk for Laslo's bally and Alfred did Johnny's, the latter of course being not near as good, and I think it disturbed Johnny: this lessening seen as demotion, as a lowering of his state and place. Mother must have seen it all play out before.

During this time, Johnny and I at first alternated between closeness and an awkward semi-rift. He spent more time with Robert, which vexed and annoyed me, and as I came upon them one day I heard Robert say, **"And men were scorched with great heat, and blasphemed the name of God, which hath power over those plagues: and they repented not."** Didn't this smack of madness? I worried Johnny was becoming barmy or a fool. Some days it felt like I might be touched myself. I saw the hunger in the way Robert watched him, a lust I pegged at first as fleshly (I had seen Robert hanging around the shower area when Johnny was using it, ducking when he saw me and pretending to be doing something else) but came to see more as worshipfulness, if that's a word. Robert wanted to *be* Johnny—that's the best way I can describe it. He saw Johnny as having something neither he nor others had.

Robert's interactions with me were cordial, for the most part. I think he feared me in the way he feared Mother, but he was less guarded in his talks with me. I confronted him once, after Johnny and he had spent days wrapped and huddled, when I ran into him near the cook tent, his head swiveling like a bird's. Zorat was refusing to perform then on Sundays.

"So I hear you say my mother is evil."

"I don't recall saying that." He looked up and snorted. "But is it true?" He thought of himself as so keen and crafty—him with his college degree, and me there with next to nothing.

"No. It's untrue."

"But you're sure?" His laugh had a mock to it.

I hummed and half nodded, my eyes kept on his. "I understand that you're here due to her."

"Did she say that?"

"That and more." She hadn't, not really, but Mother has taught me that being mysterious often works.

"Is that so?" Said as curt statement.

"She said that you had been scarred, and that this made you crazy for God."

She'd never said this, though it seemed to strike home. His lips turned like he'd spit. "I don't know that one can be too 'crazy for God.'" His palms lifted skyward.

"I hope that's not what you're teaching Johnny."

His smile returned. "You should join us sometime and see."

Johnny had offered this too. My head shook and swung toward Robert. "I think you're in love with him, or maybe the idea of him."

"Johnny? Is this jealousy I hear call?"

"No, just my watching. You look like you want to swallow him, wings, legs, and all."

A smile, a near bow. "Well, aren't you the clever one? Brash and presumptuous and uncivil, to boot!" He turned sharply and left, probably to curse me. Maybe to start on some prayer or a conjuring, or to offer up a big old nasty hex.

Johnny spent time with Kenneth as well. I asked him what things they discussed.

"Not a lot. Kenneth doesn't say much."

"What do you do in his trailer?"

"Sit, mostly. Sometimes I read. Sometimes we talk about 'freakdom'—that's what we call it. At other times we don't speak."

"What's Kenneth's take on freakdom?"

"Nothing you haven't heard. We talk about the audience, about the people who stand out, the jerks and the fainters—the people who are there to be shocked."

"Isn't everyone there to be shocked? What does he say?"

"He finds the marks curious, and strange. They're seeking a thrill just like those who leap out from planes, or people who bet on the horses or the running of those greyhound dogs. He said he feels it when he goes up onstage, as do I—there's probably a word for it. It just seems—I don't know, nor does he—it just seems to display *life* in some way."

I sighed, my head back. I almost never speak to Kenneth or even see him much, as he rarely eats at the cook tent when the others assemble. He recently stopped me as I was walking, though, and uttered something strange, his voice laced with gaps of air.

"Did you know your mother has insurance on me and Johnny? I assume that she wants to kill us. Is that so?"

These questions burst forth like gunshots, similar to the way that Robert's dropped and fell. Kenneth was hard to understand. "What?"

He scowled and went on his way. Later, I told Johnny of this.

"Yes, I know. I found letters when you were gone, when I went looking around in your trailer."

"You were looking around in our trailer?"

He sighed. "I was desperate. I didn't know when you'd return, or if you'd return at all. I thought there might be a message, or else—"

"But how lowdown and sneaky! Why didn't you tell me this? Are we to have these little secrets between us?"

He squirmed, his head hanging.

I pulled his chin up, brushing and kissing him, his taste that of roots and trees. We're so alike: tossed here together by fate or, okay, by God. "I want to know all of you, Johnny, and you to know all of me. Tell me everything, the good and the bad, the dark, the unknowable. Every little secret thing." We can't have walls.

He looked at me a long time. "Alright," he said. "Let's start with this: I was buried alive when I was young. It sounds crazy to say it, and sometimes I question whether it really took place, but it did." He was quiet for moments, his eyes shifting back and forth. "I've never told anyone else." He described it: the horror of the crowds formed and his mother's fear, or such as she told him and that he could still recall. The box, though, he remembered well. "It was dark and hot, and it smelled of dirt. I couldn't move, and I screamed until I couldn't scream more. To this day I can't stand to be in a close, confined space."

I struggled to understand this. To believe it. "But why?"

He snorted and jerked a thumb over his shoulder. "People were scared. She was scared."

I shook my head at it, dizzy.

"There's some more." He told me of the one-armed man, both his visit back with his mother and again just weeks before.

"But why didn't you tell me these things?" I lifted my hands up when he finished.

"I don't know." His eyes shone like glass. "It just seems so strange—too strange and off." He laughed with his neck back, his face still held tight. "Or maybe I'm no longer strange enough."

"Johnny. My poor boy." I didn't ask of his time before with the men, and he didn't offer this. The burial, even if in his mind, was enough.

"I don't want pity," he said, interrupting my thinking. His voice was harder. "I've never wanted that."

"But how could your mother do such a thing? To her child?"

"It was love," he insisted. "It was never to hurt me. She felt that she had no choice."

"But you could have died!" Love. Weakness, fear.

"Maybe that was the point. The illusion. The trick of it."

I wanted no argument. I will fight anyone who would do him harm. The thought of him suffering . . . "And what of this one-armed man?"

His shoulders swelled. "I have no idea. It's spooky, though. I've had nightmares about it. He warned me not to leave."

"Leave the show? Why would he want you here?"

"To keep track of me? I can't figure it either. There's a lot that I still don't understand."

He doesn't understand that people love him, that *I* love him. That all I want is for him to accept and believe in me. I had this on my mind when I had it out later, hot-faced, with my mother.

"Why do you have insurance on the performers?" I asked. Johnny's disclosures had made me even wilder. Are children always just pawns?

She stared in the way she does. Even I sometimes see her as childlike. "Are you wanting now to run the show?"

"Are you planning to kill them?"

Her laugh rose high and shrill. "Am I planning to cut off my leg? Please, Winifred. Why would I do that?"

"I don't know." This was confusing. My youth and lack of learning can catch me up at times. She whirled and pounced then, sensing a weakness.

"You really know nothing. Are you fifteen or five? God knows what will become of you if you can't learn to use your head."

Tears rose that I huffed back. My vision wobbled up and down. She's told me more than once that my birth almost killed her. "I know that I'll be in a place that's not here. I won't be in the middle of a cornfield, running some sad-ass freak show."

She shrugged and a smile formed, the smile that means vengeance. Something fell in my stomach. Her eyes were diamond-sharp. "I agree—let's get you out of here. In fact, I've already planned it. You leave next month."

"No!"

"Yes." A pause. "It's for the best," and her voice became softer. "You'll see Johnny again. You'll see me!"

"Then he can come too!"

She barked. Laughed. "Of course not."

"But I love him!"

"Oh, Winifred, please. You really don't understand much at all, do you?"

THAT NIGHT I had my own nightmare, of Robert with his jaws open and throat huge like a feeding snake, wriggling toward Johnny as he lay sleeping, unaware. I awoke in a panic, sweating in my cotton gown, pulled on a robe, and slipped out the door of our trailer in the dark. I made my way on to Johnny's, past the snoring and sleeping men, just to check up on him, to gaze in on his fair and peaceful, blameless face. When my eyes fully adjusted, his white hair just visible through a tent seam's tiny crack, I took my robe off and lay down beside him, careful not to disturb him, not to tip the cot. His heart beat through his sheets as if expanding beyond him, his breath a damp and whistling breeze. To be with him, to be close and safe after thinking I'd lost him—how could I even begin to describe this? I was in a state in which I'd never been. I ran my hand down the length of his sleep shirt, up through his shock of snowy hair, along the white of his eyebrows to his neck's rougher, warmer skin. Might I now die? Waves came on, fever, dreams. When he woke, I kissed him and pulled his body up and over mine, our clothes soon wrenched off and his thing thrust deep inside me, our souls united, our bodies joined and pushed. Effortlessly, lightly. Connected and bound up together, complete in *love*. My hands gripping the length and power of his folded wings.

CHAPTER TWENTY-ONE

Laslo's boost to the show proves short-lived. After a few frantic weeks, the crowds decline again, and the show stops in one place for a week with no jump, a break without shows—a worrisome first for the tour. The tents flap vacantly through breeze and rain, the banners folded and flags down; without patrons, the show is a blank and purposeless place. The men play cards to kill time, smoking even more and drinking in metal cups. Tot is gone several times for days, during which dark talk is rampant and rumor scatters and flows.

"Wonder what she paid for Laslo." Boris snorts. "That may have bankrupted the whole shebang."

"It's the Depression," Lenny says. "The whole country's going down. No one's got money. She let the Negras in as if they have some but they don't. Nobody's got nothing."

"I hear the Michigan Fair this year is half its normal size."

"It's the end of an era. All the shows are dying. People want rides and animals, or movies, or something more."

"I'm writing a letter to Jim Johnson over at Ringling, see if he'll take me on. I worked with him once before. This is going south here, I'm certain. This thing is gonna fold."

Tot when she's present is by turns raging and mute. "Of course we'll go on. We're completely fine. We've got enough cash to make it to winter break, and after that we'll reform and go again at things the way we do. Anybody that don't want a job anymore can leave."

Even Laslo seems downcast. "It is a sad world," he says, his voice just above a whisper. His brother's arms move slowly and crablike, in swirls. "But what can you do?" Both sets of arms wave in a gesture of patience and pleading. This shuts everyone up for a moment, the others staring or swallowing and then looking off. Only Otto makes noises: "It's a charade, isn't it? Ha, ha ha. It's a great charade."

Johnny has little contact with Laslo, but what he does have is friendly. This leaves him a bit surprised.

"I've heard of you," says the little man. His added arms are upturned now and bug-like, swinging somewhat at random, seeming to strike out on their own.

"Oh?"

"Yes. It's a small world: the true freaks. In Europe, there are more. We each know the trials of being the way we are."

"Were you mistreated, growing up?"

Laslo sighs. "I was hidden. My parents were so ashamed. That is, until they realized they could profit from me. Then things changed much. It is one of the reasons I came to America, to escape them. Still, they follow." He raises several arms. "I have gone from being the ugly duckling to the golden goose." He laughs, his teeth yellow. "This is life. And you?"

"People thought I was evil," Johnny says, in time. "Maybe they still do. They wanted to blame me for things, to punish me to shield themselves."

Laslo spreads his main arms. "It is the beauty, John, of being on a show. We are together! And people expect—they want and seek—to be shocked and scared. This is why they come to see us."

"Have you . . ." The boy's voice falters. "Have you seen others, with wings?"

Laslo shakes his head. "I have heard of this, yes, but I have not seen them. It is the same with me." He points to his brother. "The fact I have not seen them does not mean that they are not there."

THEIR CROWDS REMAIN thin and fitful; one night at Johnny's blow-off, no one pays to come inside, sending him shuffling back to his cot. Sounds are enlarged, given the few in attendance: Otto's slow chanting, the lone handclaps like drums, the single scream made at Laslo's blow-off and reveal. Men crowd the rope line like crows, unable to pay to enter, some looking on in envy, others only staring off. A boy combs through refuse. A woman begs Cookie for food. Then word comes that payment to artists will be delayed. Carl delivers this message at the cook tent when Tot is gone, his big hands lifting and falling as if working the levers on a great and violent machine.

"Listen, we're going to be a few days late in getting your money. Tot's off in Little Rock working with a banker, and she'll be back Thursday with the funds and more. Everybody hang tough, now, and it'll all be just fine. Things are improving each day, and we'll be good if we stay united. Nobody has any place to spend cash here, regardless— ain't that right?"

They are out in a pasture somewhere, again without electric lights; they've been there for some days, one of those spent in a relentless, pouring rain. This news spawns more grumbling, the men off in pairs to grouse and whisper and mutter, to rail at Tot and the world or to scheme. Johnny hears Alfred and Boris through his tent.

"Thought it would come to this, just not so soon-like."

"So, what'll we do?"

There's a grunt, a coughing sound. "See what she does. This is my last tour with her, though. Next year, something else."

Boris clears his throat. "If we don't get paid soon, we may be out before that. Can't you feel things a-splintering?"

"But go where, in midseason? I suppose we could run to Chicago, see could we get on with Cole, but that's chancy, and we'd burn cash in going. At least here, we get fed."

"We do now."

"Yeah. We do now."

A crinkling starts and stops, as if the men lift and turn then. "Johnny, you there?"

He knows they don't trust him, his relationship with Winifred siding him in their minds with Tot. "Yes, I'm here."

Alfred peeks in.

"Don't worry. My mouth remains shut."

"Good boy." A quick grin. The flap closes, swings.

The discussion of money highlights that he has none. He wants to discuss this with Winifred, to solidify their plan to leave—do they have a plan now to leave? He won't betray Alfred and Boris. For the moment, he's avoiding Zorat. He recalls his failed runs from the men who once held him.

Then Tot returns, payments are made, and the show makes a midnight jump. Things return to normal or to something near, the grumbling for the moment quelled. The tents are erected, a new show begins. But the crowds remain poor and small in the days following.

HE STUDIES WINGS. He's never taken an interest before, but now he examines every bird that hops near, noting their differences, the ways they flutter and swoop and take flight. Winifred's schoolbooks include part of an encyclopedia, and he reads the bird articles again and again, learning terms: primary flight feathers, secondaries and coverts, diurnals, hind toes, syrinxes, crowns. How wings evolved, the different shapes tied to bird types, how bones are hollow and hearts quite large, the three separate forms of flight. How some birds seem to magically lift, while others launch a running takeoff. He finds such beauty in the way birds rise, the command shown and power in it, the grace and ease. His studying is secret; he wants no one, not even Winifred, to know, as why would he be so occupied and absorbed in this? He no longer looks at his own wings. His new tent includes no mirrors, though he senses their presence always, and must adjust to their breadth and span. One day he notices something on his cot that he can't identify. Thinking it an insect, he carefully picks it up, holding it to the light, studying and examining. Determining. It's a tiny feather.

THINGS ARE ODD with Winifred since she came to him in the night. The event seems a part of an overworked dream, his waking to find her and then her lying atop him, flesh on flesh warming, a lock fit in a key. After, she held him and he told her that he loved her, without embarrassment for his nakedness or the taint of foulness from his life before. When he awoke again, she was gone, like something forged or imagined, hoped for or half recalled. In the day following he feels eyes even more—Alfred's stare as if Cletus knows something, Boris humming and grinning as he slaps his knives. Were they truly asleep? Did they hear things or see them? Tot when she meets him scowls and turns away. Later that day, he sees Winifred near the toilet.

"Hi."

"Hi."

What should he say now? He feels old; they are older. He is bold but unsure, nervous and halting, desiring still, dazed. The suppleness of her body comes springing back, her breath pulling him forward, her hair and sweet smell and skin. Could every awakening be something like this? He would die for her, happily, willingly. He clears his throat. "Are we going to leave?"

"I want to. Don't you?"

"Yes. Of course."

"Mother says I'm to depart for school in two weeks. Should we do it before then or have you join me when I'm gone?"

He hadn't considered the latter. Him, attend school? He doesn't think that would work, though is this even what she's suggesting? He tries to see himself sitting in class, feet tucked beneath a desk. "How should we go?"

"I'm not sure. Let me think a bit on it."

"What about funds?"

"We'll need some. Yes." There's a pause.

"Where does your mother keep hers?"

Winifred sighs. Again: "I'm not sure. Carl has something to do with it. I could look." She grasps his arm, a look of hopefulness or worry spread across her face. For a perilous moment, he seems to not know her at all.

"Then we should go!"

"But we need a plan." She is calm, her lips pressed to lines like a box newly shut. He should lead or propose something; he should be planning and acting, but he can't seem to offer up very much. "Let's set a date that we'll do it. We need to get far enough so that they don't find and bring us back. Maybe I should go on to the school, Johnny, and then run from there, and we could meet!" She repeats this idea. "That might be easier."

But that would leave him alone, and what if he failed to find her? The thought of venturing off by himself, after his one trip into town, stiffens his belly like a punch. "Yes, we could do that. I wish I could drive a car. Then we could take one and be miles away before we're missed, or we could board a train!" This notion lures him, perhaps due to his prior trip, the train ride begun and halted. It would be means to renew that, to go on to Tennessee, to—

"That comes back to money. I'll look and see what I find. When she's out at her bally today, I'll go through her things. I have some funds myself, a small allowance I've saved, but it's not enough for the both of us."

The both of us. She'll leave her mother for him, and he feels himself blushing, the awkwardness from before ripped like a cloth in high wind. "Oh, Winifred." He grasps her hand, interlocking their fingers. "We're going to do this, aren't we? We're going to make it!" The sun is so bright that its reflection transforms things, making spots stars and giving trees wide and shining wings. His voice sounds steady and certain, a new sureness in his tone, at least in his wording and to his own waiting, wishful ears.

IT POPS OUT in a prayer: ". . . and Lord, please protect those who leave this show, as they strive to lead other dutiful and godly lives." He hadn't planned on saying this, didn't mean to imply things, but Zorat picks up on the reference straightaway.

"Why'd you say that? Who's leaving the show?"

"What?"

"What you just said, in your prayer."

"Lots are talking about it, Robert." He uses Zorat's real name. "I'd like to be leaving at some point myself. I think that the show is gonna go bust now. I mean . . ." A pause comes, a heartbeat. "Don't you?" He looks up.

"Of course not." Zorat's lips bend and turn. "Who says that's so? I'm not going anywhere. No one is leaving." He sucks in air. A man shouts beyond them. "Where would you go if you left?"

"I . . . I don't know."

"It's her, isn't it—Winifred? Are you planning on eloping, or something crazy like that? Merciful God up in heaven. Have you learned absolutely nothing from me?"

"I don't understand." But he does: Zorat wants him to stay and doesn't want to be left, and there's a beauty in this but something, too, small and sad. He knows it well: the sense of a failing; the crushing fear of abandonment. **"'No man, having put his hand to the plough, and looking back, is fit for the kingdom of God'**—that's Luke, isn't it?"

"You're quoting me scripture?" Zorat's mouth curls farther down. "The Bible isn't a taffy you bend to your use on a whim. You speak of the kingdom of God when you haven't a clue as to what that means. Your ignorance shows."

Johnny grinds his teeth. "I have the scriptures. I can read them myself. I can also think." The old rage stirs and quickens, coals banked and flaming up, but this melts into something: compassion? He's not sure.

Zorat's face gleams, his eyes spread into slivers. The stubble on his face looks like dots of swarming ants. "I thought our work would have shown you how far yet you have to go. If you have a brain but won't use it, you are a puppet—a vacant fool." He grabs the boy's arm but with a shrug Johnny shakes him off.

"Maybe I was wrong about you, John." Zorat sits, continues. "I thought you weren't like the other freaks: abominations fated to roam the earth, a warning of what harm could likely come." His face looks impassive yet mournful. "I thought you were special." Another pause. "I've had such dreams and hopes."

The boy's heart thumps his face. He thinks of falseness and fury, of Gordon and his beaten chimp. His hands shake and his sight dims, but he offers up nothing else. His stomach reaches his mouth. Finally: "I'll miss you, if I go."

"So you might not be going?"

"When I go." He tries to smile. "I have to go, sometime."

"But again, to where? To do what? Has all your *thinking* focused in on this?"

Johnny's wings twitch. He wants to rub against something, to use pain as a compress and scrape himself pure and clean. His head lifts, his back. "I've learned a lot from you, sir," he says gently. "Of how much is out there—things beyond just myself. Of the things Christ can do and change. For all of this, I'm so grateful."

"You'll end up in a home somewhere, or a gutter. She'll use you—she will, John! She doesn't love you. You don't know what love is."

"How can you say this?" He can't stop his breath's lift. "**'Therefore shall a man leave his father and his mother, and shall cleave unto his wife, and they shall be one flesh.'**"

"Augghh!" Zorat bows his head, the sides of his neck bulging out as in his act. "Don't misconstrue . . ." He pauses. "That isn't license . . ." A final heave, like a bird lifting its feathers. "This isn't that!" His eyes flap and close, his voice growing softer, slower: "Please, Johnny, please. Do not do this to yourself."

"I'm not. I have to—"

"I should have known." Zorat crosses himself left to right, fingers out as if stabbing. "Why didn't I see it? Those obscene wings . . ." Heat issues from him like a flame. His head dips and tilts, his neck muscles hinge-like, clumping and then loosed and stretched into cords and ropes. "**'Ye are of your father the devil, and the lusts of your father ye will do.'** Yes, go on and leave me—leave me now! **'The unrighteous shall not inherit . . .' 'He that justifieth the wicked . . .'**" His knees buckle and quiver, his eyes aglow like twin suns. "The *betrayal* in all of this, the . . ." Tears—are there tears? A breath draws, a shivering. "Get away from me, Lucifer!" He shoves the boy from his trailer, down the steps to land on his backside below.

IT'S A WEEK or so later, somewhere in Georgia (at least he thinks they're in Georgia), the crowds small once more, when the boy sees him standing at the photo line's end. Bud doesn't see him or heed

Johnny's prior demand, but the boy makes no protest. He's more alert now than before, less scared and more forceful, maybe bold, curious. He bites his bottom lip.

"And how should I make it out?" he asks as the man nears, the absent arm giving his walk a slow twist. A smile forms on the face before him, spiteful in its slowness. One of the man's teeth is darkened, a feature unrecalled.

"Oh, just to Warren."

"Warren what?"

"Just Warren."

"But you know so much about me. Shouldn't I know about you?"

The man laughs, low and familiar, the sound bringing a rush of chills. "Nah. Just doing some checking. Wanted to make sure you're okay."

"I'm okay."

The man looks around, gesturing with his single arm, a hat held in his hand. "Crowds look smaller. You sure everything is fine?"

"Far as I know." He holds the pen aloft, waiting. A sound comes like wind or rain. "What do you want from me, Warren?"

Again, the slow smile. "Just to see you. It makes me nervous if I don't know where you are. You're not thinking of leaving, are you?"

The chills climb his back. How could the man know this? The boy's face must be revealing. The man leans in close.

"Don't go nowhere, Johnny."

"Why? What do you care?"

"I'm concerned for your safety. I'll find you, if you leave." He pauses. "You really go in that grave?"

The boy makes no response.

Bud, noticing the length of the conversation, ambles over.

"Just enjoyed the show, sir." Warren's tone is made friendly. He swings his one arm. "Just wanted this thing signed."

Johnny hands the photograph over. The man glances toward it, his lips drooped at the corners. There's a moment of silence, of stillness.

"Ready?" asks Bud.

"Sure." The man places his fedora on his head. "They ought to burn this place down."

"What?"

Warren turns and strides off without looking, without pausing or waiting for Bud to catch up. Bud follows, then stops, peering out from the tent to ensure the man's leaving. He steps back to Johnny.

"That was weird. Do you know him or something?"

"He's been here before."

"What'd you write to him?"

"'To a bigger freak. With love, Johnny.'"

Bud laughs and the boy joins in this. Claps come as Laslo's show concludes the night.

IT ALL HAPPENS together on a Tuesday in Georgia where haze shimmers the distance a blotchy gray and blue. First, there's no sign of the minstrels.

"Where are they?" asks Tot. It's the morning of a first show, with their tent needing to be put up, straw laid and sawdust, but their wagons haven't arrived yet.

"Maybe they broke down," someone says.

"Who?"

"The jig show."

"They been late before. If you're coming in a horse and buggy . . ."

"Wonder if Tot paid them."

Tot shrugs it all off. "They'll be here or they won't. If they're not, we go without 'em."

Back in the tent with Alfred and Boris, the two men shake their heads. "It's like this show is cursed now, don't you think? There's all these signs." Alfred is fiddling with Cletus, but it's Alfred's voice that flows through.

"And we put our tent up over a hole—look at this!" There's a depression in the middle of their tent area. They've placed their cots around it, as if circling a campfire or a cave. "Too late to move." Boris shrugs. Cletus's mouth shuts with a clapping.

No one says more, the silence stretched then in waves. Do the men still consider him loyal to Tot? Eyes shift, heads lower. A shaking noise comes from Cletus; the tent sighs and sways. Johnny returns to his side space, lying down to stretch his back.

Maybe he sleeps, as he's roused then by shouting, the three exiting the tent to find Gordon holding his monkey, yelling over and over in an echoing, cutting voice: "I've been robbed! There's been a plunder, I tell you! I've been robbed! There's a fucking thief!"

Others circle around, questioning. Listening. It's only hours till showtime, the acts in mid-prep: costumes at half dress; some makeup on; props being serviced, readied, and arranged. Gordon is breathless and almost sobbing in his rage.

"I keep my cash rolled in a sock buried in a sack of clothes. No one could know it was there, and now it's gone! All my money is gone. I've got nothing but this cursed chimp, and someone among us is a thief! A thief is among us!"

The boy's thoughts go to Winifred. She failed to find Tot's cash, but did she somehow grab Gordon's? This seems so unlike her, so corrupt and fantastic, and yet she is not with those grouped around the frenzied man. Johnny—who has stayed far from Gordon since their prior clash—remains silent, clad in the sequined pants he wears now for his show, his cape pulled around him. His eyes shut. His jaw aches.

"When did you last have it?" Tot is asking Gordon.

"Last night, before the jump. I rode in the truck with Lenny and Alfred." This hangs in the air as a near accusation. Necks stiffen. Heads lower.

"Maybe the minstrels took it," someone said.

"Could be why they're missin'."

"How much was there, Gordon?"

He doesn't say.

The men look one to the other and back. Johnny assumes that they all hide cash somewhere—everyone on the show, that is, except him. He slips by the others to go look for Winifred. "I'll bet it was that fucking monkey," someone grumbles, shifting as he edges past.

"Did you hear?" he asks when he finds her in her trailer.

"Hear what?"

"Someone stole money from Gordon."

"Oh." She doesn't seem surprised. "I wish it was us."

He half smiles and looks off. A silence forms. A low scratching. "I wonder if they'll call the police."

Tot bursts through the door then, Carl trailing just behind her. "Can you two leave?" Her lips curl to half-moons. The youths pause and stand. There's a silence again, gazes raised and then lowered. Johnny and Winifred shuffle to the wooden steps.

Exiting the trailer, a new mayhem awaits. The cops have indeed come, three crowded carloads of clean-shaven, grim-faced men, uniformed and with guns held, and how was such quick contact made? Gordon only just yelled of the stealing. The squad strides through the show, fanning out like gray soldiers, followed by a man in a collar and several black-clad nuns. The sameness strikes chords: Is this the group from before that cast the girly girls out? He can't quite be sure—that could have been elsewhere, maybe Indiana or Alabam. The head policeman looks different. Plus, the girly girl act is gone. This seems too large a force, though, to investigate a single robbery.

Tot plunges forward, followed by Bud and Carl. The others cluster behind them, the two groups gathered like armies.

"What is it you want?" Tot calls out.

"We hear you're a freak show," says the head policeman, stepping out in between the two groups. The cap on his head makes him thin-necked and birdlike. He turns as if looking to peck things, his beak up. "We don't allow nothing like that around here."

"We're a variety act," Tot replies. "We've got a permit—don't we, Bud?"

"We do. We got a permit."

"Your permit is for a variety show. Not for this." The man gestures toward Otto and Kenneth and the others. "Not for these monsters."

Groans. A new shifting. "This is nature!" someone yells.

"Science. The real world!"

The nuns begin muttering. One starts to shake as in some affliction, the others giving way, nodding, expectant. Admiring.

"Can we discuss this in private?" Tot looks up at the policeman, up at them all.

"There's nothing more to discuss. There'll be no show. I'm leaving some of my men here now to make sure. I want you gone by tomorrow morning. And I don't want you going into town, neither—none of you. Not a single one." He waves an arm as if casting his own spell upon them.

The performers say nothing, though there's a sourness in their stance. The policemen withdraw even as Bud brings forth his paper. Tot moves to join him, but the head cop now retreats, and no other steps forward or appears to want to speak. The preacher holds out a Bible as the nuns surround him to sing, their voices dismal and piercing, heads jerking down and up. Within minutes, they've turned and vanished the way they came. The policemen withdraw too, climbing back into cars, boots thumping, doors slamming. The grumbling from the performers reaches an angrier, higher pitch.

"She can't buy her way out of this. Ain't no more money! We're plumb out of luck."

"Have to move on, and sure won't get paid now for this one. How many more we got left?"

"We're almost done."

That evening the drinking is open. Bottles appear and men

sharply flip cards, plumes of smoke a blue mist looping above their bent heads. Insects dance in the lights and float in clouds around them. Johnny and Winifred walk the rope line in silence, taking in the cops beyond and their watching, the smoke rising from cars, the sounds of their sneezing and coughing and splashing piss.

"I say we go, Johnny."

"With the cops out there waiting? And go where? Do we know even where we are?"

"I just feel like if we don't go now, we don't make it."

"And the money?" Again, the fear hovers, of her involvement in the theft.

"I have my allowance. We can do it now, tonight." She pauses, one finger tapping her wrist, up and down. "We can leave."

His mind turns and slips, gone then to Elias, their failed flight from the side camp like a dream lost and returned. "I don't know."

"So, it's all just been talk?"

"No, no. It's . . ." He remembers before when he went to town, the discomfort and strangeness, the pain. The times he'd run from the men. "I just need to think."

"Oh. To think." The words spurt with edges, little spikes like tiny pins. Her eyes dance up and away from him, her jaw flat.

He breathes out through his nose. Again, "Just some time to think."

THE MEAL AT the cook tent is sullen. No one has much at all to say. Gordon isn't there, nor Kenneth or Zorat or Tot, though this isn't uncommon. The men drink even more, some of them—Lenny and Walter, Bud—appearing watery-eyed now and drunken. Johnny goes to his cot after the meal and thinks to gather his things up, but what things does he have? Little more than when he arrived here. He looks around, scanning the tent sides, breathing the sawdust and mildew and popcorn smell. Is it foolish to leave now? If they even make it to Jacksonville, what will they say and do there? At least here is structure, some form of shelter and movement, food given and a plan. He pulls out his Bible, given him a year back by Zorat, and reads from Isaiah:

"Remember ye not the former things, neither consider the things of old."

From Ecclesiastes:

"Sorrow *is* better than laughter; for by the sadness of the countenance the heart is made better."

From I Corinthians:

"Behold, I shew you a mystery; We shall not all sleep, but we shall all be changed."

He thinks to go and see Zorat but knows he cannot. Should he discuss things more with Winifred? He falls asleep with the Bible on his chest, knowing this only because he rolls on it in his slumber, and when he awakens it is by and under him, caught in the sweep of an arm and one wing. He was dreaming of horses, four of them fast and pulling him onward, first on a wagon and then a black cart, then somehow sliding along the dark ground. He is relieved not to be injured. He is not quite sure where he is. Noises intrude: people running, someone yelling and screeching, and this jerks him upward from the depths of his haze and sleep.

He cannot see much, cannot breathe, and he realizes that his tent and that of Alfred and Boris are filled with smoke and heat. Black waves roll toward him, puffs of smoke as from Zorat's torch, a hundred such flaming torches. His eyes water, and he coughs in rapid bursts. Stumbling and falling, he crawls to the adjoining tent, shouting but he cannot shout, hearing heartbeats and nothing, a blast coming from somewhere that stops all other sound. Near the ground he can breathe but still the smell chokes him—an oily and toxic, curdled stench—flames now visible at the tent's peak and up its sides, exposing the bones of its structure and framework. It's as if he's surrounded by a fire ring like the gum still, sputtering and hissing and glowing an angry red.

A roar comes of explosion, a great and whooshing collapse, things falling around him fiery, heavy, and fast, something hot landing on his arm. When he ducks, he sees Winifred, creeping through the flames with her mouth open and hands out, and as he watches arms pull her beneath an upturned cot, the men huddled below it in the depression he observed before. When she joins them, they beckon, her voice now heard calling, his name ringing over and over: "Johnny! Johnny! Johnny, please!" Alfred's voice higher: "Hurry, get under! Get under here! Hurry! Quick!"

She came to retrieve him; his mind clears to this, the flames at a roar, but he can't pull himself under, his fear so rooted and dating back for so long, to dirt and the box and confinement, to certain death. He chokes and screams: long, painful blasts for which breath fails him after; he tries to move legs, arms, and wings. The smoke is so thick that he can no longer hear or see, his eyes burning, tears spent—the heat like nothing he's ever felt or known. His last memory before darkness is of Tot's high-pitched shriek, shouting for Winifred, her voice over other sound. Then a wind and a burning, a lift. Nothing beyond this. Nothing more.

PART III: 1936

CHAPTER TWENTY-TWO

The Windsor Hotel dates from 1875, part of a boom at that time in Florida, the railroad bringing Northerners down and the state still with spare, cheap land. By 1936 it is fading, newer hotels having opened—the Carling, the George Washington—and with its biggest allure (a subterranean room full of liquor and pourings) gone now since Prohibition's end. Still, it employs seventy-five, including cooks, busboys, bellhops, housekeepers, and yardmen, including as of November 14 one John C. Crews.

He went to find Elias as he said he would, although it took him some years. His memory of that time—between the fire and arriving in Jacksonville—he tamps back, as with his time chained in Georgia, pieces surfacing in odd and sudden spikes: sleeping on park benches; working a dock in New York; traveling in buses or riding the rails; being on his feet. He binds his wings now with tape, like the pictures of women's feet someone once showed him, walking stiffly and slowly upright due to this. His arms still show burn marks, the skin massed in folds and scars, and people assume that his back is scorched too. He doesn't correct this. No one has seen his wings since he last bared them at the show; his hope is that no one ever will.

He arrived one day at the clipped grounds of the Windsor, a square, fortresslike manor painted yellow with a red-tiled roof, striped awnings out front and a little flag waving at its top. On the grounds stood a statue, a pillar. He didn't get close enough to read of whom. The St. Johns River flowed slowly nearby. He asked one of the gardeners, "Do you know Elias?" but the man only stared, slow shakes of his head made, a downward turn of lips. By then Johnny was dyeing his eyebrows and cutting his hair short, though he knew he was still strange-looking, his green eyes drawing stares.

The black man called another, and they both pointed to the hotel door. "Ask the front."

He trudged on. The reception there was no better, a similar silence maintained, the heavy black man in a uniform asking finally, "What you want?"

"I'm . . . I'm a friend."

"Friend."

"I'm looking for a job."

"Ain't no jobs here." The words were quick.

He had heard this, many times. "Could you tell him Johnny came by?"

There was no response. He turned and left.

He'd reached the midpoint of the driveway when the man called back. "Hey!"

He turned again.

"Go wait by that fence over there and I'll see if he wants to talk to you. He's working now, though. He can't take no break."

It was hours before a lanky black man strode over. Elias looked much the same as he had outside the show, maybe a little thicker, the mustache more grown in. He wore the uniform of a bellhop, cap smart on his head, his vest frayed at the bottom, stains on his pants but his shoes shiny black.

"Johnny Cruel."

"It's me. You said to come find you, and I did."

"So I see. You not with the show now?"

"Nah." He didn't go into it.

"Seems like I heard something 'bout a fire. Bunch of people killed. Few years ago now—that was y'all?"

He looked off. The smell came of water, dark. "Yeah. That was us."

"But you're alive."

"I'm alive." He coughed and looked up again. "I need a job, Elias. Can you help?" It sounded sad as he said it, so pathetic and needy. He thought to take it back and deny things. To turn around and simply leave.

Elias grimaced. "I don't know, Johnny. They're firin' people, not hirin'. I'm lucky to have what I got. People are scared that they'll be up and gone."

"I understand. Anything. Anything at all." The day was hot for November, his binding and clothing damp with sweat. He wiped his face with one hand, rubbed this down his trousers.

Elias waved at his torso. "You all wrapped up, I see."

"Yeah. I am."

Elias was silent, looking away and then back, back and away again. Johnny recalled that when they last met, he'd wanted to show Elias his wings. Now he stood straighter. Despite the moisture and heat, he began almost shivering.

"Where you staying?"

Johnny shrugged.

Elias shook his head. "You eaten today?"

"Yeah."

Teeth on lips. "Meet me back here at six when I get off."

"Okay." A pause. He searched for something to say. "Thank you."

He followed Elias to his apartment that evening, a sour-smelling building fronted by laundry and curls of smoke. The smells were of cooking and the sounds of crying children, footsteps echoing above them and from beyond, an argument sputtering somewhere. He could never have slept or stayed here long amid that. A pot banged, a door slammed. Stares came from the residents, wide-eyed and wondering, reminding him of the side camp, the watchfulness also at the show.

"Rita, this here's Johnny. I knew him when I was a boy."

The woman looked up from a stove, unsmiling, confusion knotting her dark and glistening face. She said nothing, made no other move. A small boy peered from behind her full skirts. The apartment was one room, maybe two.

"This here's Arthur. Arthur, say hello to Mr. John."

The boy hid his face and then said quietly, "Hi-ho."

Johnny knelt and smiled. "Hi." Children seemed so strange now that he was not one himself. He caught Rita's glance, figured Elias had likely mentioned him to her—the show, the boy with the wings, the oddness. He looked up. "I won't be staying. Just stopping by to say hello."

Elias eyed him. "Where you gon' stay?"

"I got some money, Elias. I worked a while."

"But you need a job."

"Yeah. I do."

"I talked to one of the boss men today, Mr. Ford. He said they're gon' fire one of the busboys. You might could get on next week."

"That would be great. Thank you." It sounded so formal. Rita turned back to the stove, and he imagined what she saw: a white man with his hair shorn, stiff and so odd-looking, clear flaws to his body. He coughed into his hand and fist. The worst pain, he decided, was to have had something and lost it.

"You can stay for dinner if you'd like," she said softly, her head up but still turned. "There's not much but we'll share."

"Thank you but no. I'd better be going." A pause. "It was a pleasure to meet you."

She turned back then and nodded, unsmiling still, reminding him somehow—though he fought this—of Hester. What became of her after Sam died? He'd never thought of her again before this, never asked.

Elias saw him out the door. A toy clown tilted sideways in a chair. "Check back with me before Friday, Johnny."

"I will. Thanks again."

Days on, he wears a uniform, black shirt and black pants he is forced to buy—the shirt large to hide his binding. He's the only white among the five busboys: Stanley, Otis, Nat, JT, and him. At first the others ignore him, the only comment JT's: "How'd you get this job, boy?" His boss is Mr. Sims, a red-faced white man who runs the kitchen. With the exception of one waitress, Evelyn, all the cooks and waitresses are black. The shunning by the busboys extends to the other workers, even Evelyn, and the traps and tricks he expects soon follow: the water too scalding to wash with; the assigning to him of the dirtiest of tasks; the criticisms of him to Mr. Sims; the laughter or yelling when he makes mistakes. He has never fit in before—not at the side camp or even the show—so why would he expect to now? He has difficulty reaching anything that is placed beyond him.

"Whitey, can't you walk straight?"

"Come on, White, clear these plates."

"That ain't mopping. Who taught you how to mop?"

"Boy got something wrong with him, can't you see?"

"How do you know Elias? What you got now on him?"

He manages to avoid dropping dishes, despite the attempts made to nudge or trip him, but he does fall several times, once on his back so that he must lift himself up with caution. He finds Evelyn staring, but she shows no mercy either. "Jesus," she mutters. And, as if knowing something: "This is a damned freak show."

The patrons treat all the workers, including him, as if they don't exist. For him this is welcome, but in the others he sees resentment: the lowering of eyelids, the bending always toward the floor. He watches Mr. Sims berate Otis for looking a white woman in the eye. The waitress Mattie is fired due to a guest's offhand complaint. His blood rises in sympathy, in his own guarded ire and spite, but what can he do but watch and feel their shame? He notes the way they take it, ignore it, swallow it, and endure things. Bend and work harder, grimace and soldier on.

He rents a room on the north side and rides the streetcar to work. Most of his meals he takes at a small diner, keeping to himself with care, bringing bread to his room he can eat later in the evenings. He never eats the discarded food from the plates at the Windsor, though the other busboys and even the waitresses often do. Sleep is on his side or stomach. He sees Elias but they don't speak that much, as fraternizing among the employees is discouraged by his boss. He comes to know the city a little, sometimes taking walks on the waterfront, but mostly he simply works. On his days off he goes to the library, taking books from the shelves to read but checking nothing out, and he can't say why he does this; perhaps the worry of exposing himself remains too deep. He still has dreams of the one-armed man coming to find him, to shoot or retrieve or to blame him, to erase him and do him harm.

After a time, the other staff become used to his presence, or seem to. He learns the names of the cooks, Joe and Jim, and the waitresses; he learns how the hotel works. The winter is the busy season, with tourists arriving by train to escape the cold up north. The guests arrive and are fed, housed, cleaned, fed again, and then depart. There are stories and myths: deaths that occur, hookers slipped in or swept out. Booze flows; the air smells of tobacco smoke, stale and still burning. Occasionally he thinks he sees people he has seen before. He keeps his head down, his hands busy, his mind fixed on his job. They call him "Whitey" or "White" still, or "Stoop." He rarely says anything at all.

On his library visits he begins reading newspapers rolled up on spindles: the *Florida Times-Union and Citizen*, the *Jacksonville Journal*, the *Tallahassee Democrat*, the *Palm Beach Post*. He spends hours perusing the stories of the election and Roosevelt's victory, of the national economy, the opening of the San Francisco-Oakland Bay Bridge, the Florida governor removing a rival from office, as well as overseas news: the war between Japan and China, the alliance between Germany, Japan, and Italy's Mussolini. It's while reading these that he stumbles upon the story of trapped miners in England: how the authorities tried to rescue them over the course of several days, how their oxygen became depleted until, one by one, they passed away. The last alive scrawled a note on a slip of paper: "They are gone, all. Give my love to Anne and the little one."

When he places the paper back, he is numb and shaking, his appetite lost, and he cannot later rest or sleep. When he does sleep, he dreams of the box again, of the dirt smell he hates so and of being bound and held, the air squeezed into bullets he is unable to stop or breathe. In the dreams he is trying to write something, to say something more, but can't move or speak. Winifred is there and calling, then Tot and Alfred, then Winifred calling again, her voice lilting like a song. He wakes from these thrashing and moaning, his bed wet and mouth dry, his eyes sore, his tongue thick. His wings up behind him like billowing, full-on sails.

The dreams plague him for weeks, affecting his alertness and causing mistakes at work, where others begin to jeer again, to complain and protest. Even Evelyn asks, "Johnny, you okay?" He says yes and gives excuses, continues his cleaning and mopping and setting up. The sight of the food makes him sick to his stomach. One day during lunch he smells smoke back in the kitchen, and again memories claim him: flames leaping and the sour scent of burning flesh; the sight of the giant Myron's body and a smaller one with blond curls; coming face-to-face with Kip the freed monkey, wild-eyed and running loose out in the woods. He blanks out for minutes or seconds, rocking back against a wall, until someone—maybe Otis or JT—snaps him out of it: "Hey, man, why you cryin'?" He flexes his back and manages to stop himself in his sniffling. He wonders if he has now gone entirely mad.

Once after work he accompanies Elias and two of the other men, Otis and a man they call Bones, to the Rooster, a tavern. It's not far from Elias's apartment, past the newsboys and shoeshine and smell of cooked sausage, with a band playing in the corner of a room filled with people, smoke, and jazz. Black people, all of them, and they eye Johnny but then ignore him, returning to their talking and drinking and claps of bright laughter. A man and old woman dance slowly by themselves.

"What you want?" asks Elias. It's a Friday and payday, his hands full of paper cash.

Johnny shakes his head. He's remembering when he met Elias outside the show, the paper sack at his feet and sweet smell on his breath then.

"Aw, come on. I'll buy you one."

"Buy me one too." Bones's voice is like a siren. It's hard to hear much in the tiny, crowded room.

"Don't waste your dough," Johnny calls, but they buy him one anyway, a rum drink that's sugary and burns going down his throat. After a few gulps, his mind swells and loosens, running to places he doesn't want it to go. Guilt follows, sorrow. His first drink with Winifred. He pulls himself back.

"How much of this stuff do you drink?" he asks Elias.

There's a stiffening, a frown. "Not that much. Why?"

"I dunno." Bones has begun speaking to a woman nearby.

"You don't know much about me, Johnny, or not as much as you might think."

"I didn't say I did."

"And me not that much about you." Elias is swinging into his second drink. "Like, why are you never with a woman? You're always by yourself."

Johnny shrugs. He's been with only a few women since the show, awkward encounters where he wouldn't fully undress. He thinks of women sometimes in bursts of desire followed by clouds of shame. The women are faceless or backless. He takes a long draw at his drink.

Elias is ordering another. "Yeah, I like my drink, Johnny. I don't hide or deny it. It helps me get through things, you know? Get through the pain of this life that we have, make things look good for a moment, maybe two or three."

"Where does that leave you?" The drink frees him further, and he knows that he shouldn't keep talking. He's remembering Elias behind the tree when he left the side camp, his look like something was being taken from him then, and is his own look the same to Elias—one of doubt and aloneness, of anguish, even now?

"In a gutter, is that what you're sayin'?" The other's tone is sharp. "Here I get you a job, bring your white ass here with folks eyeing and asking, and you scorning and shaming me?"

"I wasn't—"

"Fuck you, Johnny Cruel." His voice is low and then higher. "Should I shout it out—come look and see! The winged boy, straight from the circus! Check out his *back*, y'all!"

Johnny stands but Elias puts his arm out. Bones is looking back their way.

"Hey," says Elias, his voice soft once again. "I don't mean nothing by it." He grins, the old grin, but it's gone soon. "Relax. We need to get you a friendly girl."

The evening goes on, the band stops and plays again. Elias begins talking to a tall, sharp-faced woman, and Johnny thinks to leave, his head spinning and the smoke dark in his throat, when one of the waitresses from the Windsor, Lou, brings a chair over to sit with them.

"Johnny C."

"Hello."

"Good to see you out. You gon' buy me a drink?"

He nods. "Sure."

She has a whiskey, and they talk. She asks him about his back, and he tells her he hurt it. Later he won't recall much about what they said, only that at some point memory flashed—voices from the ruined show, policemen calling for an investigation, his heart thumping the mud in a nearby bog. Again, he knocks and shakes, as if he's having a seizure, Lou having gone to the restroom, and by the time she returns he is gulping his drink, wiping his face and the scars raised on his arms. He finds himself out in the street, in an alley and kissing her, and soon they're in a small apartment, up some stairs and in a bed.

Fumbling with her clothes, with his clothes, the drink in his eyes and memory still a lit spark, he tries to think about nothing, to remember almost nothing else. Still the scenes follow, the fire and dirt and hands reached and calling, and when he climbs atop her and thrusts at her his wings unfold, flapping up and about him like great propellers or surging sheets. He won't remember much of this either, other than a baby crying somewhere, a smell in the room like pine gum or syrup, and Lou's harsh and terrified, panicked screams.

CHAPTER TWENTY-THREE

Elias

I catch Johnny Monday morning on his way coming into work. I wanted to find him on the weekend to talk, but I don't know where he stays. I've never known what he does when not at work, how he gets food or spends his time or washes things, or how he lives.

"Hey." We're halfway across the hotel's front lawn, near where we met when he first showed up. It's one of those days that start cold and turn nice, the air with an edge and a sweetness you can almost taste. The flowers make the place look tidy-bright. Waving him to me, I pull him off to one side.

"Hey." He looks only half surprised.

"Lou's been running her mouth some," I tell him. The words spurt out, squished-up and tumbling, hose-like in their flow. "Says you're a devil, that you got these big wings, that they're hidden up under your shirt like something dead."

He straightens but says nothing.

"I think . . ." My voice stops. A mockingbird swoops down and up. "I think you best leave now, Johnny. I don't think you can go back in." I make a look sideways and behind me, a pull with my neck and head.

He's gazing off at the river, brown today more than blue, away from the hotel and its people and bustling. The trees are a light green with the burst made of springtime, the pollen coating things in a golden dust below. In time, he turns back, all bony and stiff-like, his eyes dull and head up. "Yeah," he says. There's more silence. "That's probably so." A crunching sound follows this, maybe his jaw or teeth.

"I mean, they'll be talking there. She'll be . . ." Another pause. "It won't work."

His lips pull up and down. With his hair short, his face looks thin and paler, and I want to tell him to let it all go, to be his own self, but I can't. "I . . . I got some connections. Some friends in Miami, a cousin in Alabam. You could go there, start over."

A breath. "I was starting over here."

We don't speak again for another minute or longer. I'm thinking on his wings, on the brief glimpse I had of them only a few days before. Thinking on what Lou saw. The boss made Johnny change after a kitchen spill, and I happened to be in the storeroom next to the colored bathroom, which he has to use. Things were visible through a mirror—he didn't know I was there—and I saw his full back then, those things stretching down past his waistline, swelled up but restrained with tape. They aren't like you see in the pictures, neither attached to his shoulders nor fluffed up with curves, but instead are long and firm-looking, like muscles, making you think he could bust those straps off with a breath. They are covered in feathers; it could be hair, but it's feathers, I think, their color a bit grayish, darker than his hair color, and they look neither stiff nor soft.

I watched as he put the shirt on, amazed that this doesn't stand out more, that it doesn't look like some kind of parcel or rucksack on his back, but it doesn't. It's just Johnny. We're still friends, standing by a broad river in sunny Jacksonville, Florida. It's getting on time for me to go but I don't, not just yet.

"I saw someone, when I worked in New York," he says finally, "someone who was on the show. I hadn't seen anyone since the fire, never knew for sure what happened—didn't want to know what happened, near-tricking my mind into thinking it never occurred. His name is Bud: he was a rigger, a helper. I wasn't expecting to see him when he showed up on the docks one day, his hair gray and arms bulging, his smile with a missing tooth. He turned sweaty and pale when he saw me.

"'Johnny? Johnny Cruel?' he called out. 'I thought you were dead.'

"'No,' I told him. 'I made it out. I'm not quite sure how. I guess you did too, Bud.'

"'Yeah. It was crazy—everybody that survived blaming everybody else. I think there are still some lawsuits going on. All those dead . . .' His voice faded and hollowed a bit as he said this.

"'Tot? Did Tot survive?' I asked him. She was the one who ran the show—the little lady. Her daughter was the girl . . . The girl I . . ." He coughs into a clenched fist. "She was my girlfriend."

We stare out across the lawn.

"Bud wouldn't look at me in response," he continues. "'Yeah,' he said. 'Some said she did it, to collect on the insurance. She paid a large price, though.'

"His saying this cut me, made me sick to my stomach. I couldn't listen to him anymore after that."

"And the girl?" I ask Johnny. I wonder what he did in those several years before he came here.

His face twitches. Sweat blooms. "Bud asked me before we parted, 'Johnny, is this what you're doing? Making it in the real world at the bottom, when you're a star?' A star." He frowns and spits, his teeth bright for a moment. I stare at the wet spot left glistening on the ground. "Her screaming brought it back—Lou's screaming did. That night of the fire and all the noise, the smoke and falling things." His head shakes; there's a shivering. "I shouldn't have had anything to drink."

"When, Friday night?"

He nods. "Maybe you shouldn't have either."

I hold my tongue. "We talked on that, didn't we? I do what I do. There ain't no more to it."

He looks back then at the river. "It's hard, ain't it, trying to keep the past screened and blocked? Sometimes I can do it—for days and weeks and months strung on end—but then it's on me like a speeding train."

"I guess so." I shift my weight.

"I see how it goes here." He jerks his head. "How you're treated as coloreds. All the looking down and the cuts made, the constant reminders that you're *different*, that you're not as good as and unlike *them*. Throwing your past in your face so that you don't forget what's behind you. I've felt it and know it; I know it all so well."

I wipe at my nose. My voice when it comes is a whip's lash, a dagger. "You don't know nothin'." I sniff and snort. The river cheeps brightly behind us. It has a freshness this morning, as on some days it pools and stinks. "You might think you do but you don't. Not one bit. You were a star or could be; I never was and won't. You hide yourself or do a pretty good job of it. Hell, you could go see a doctor and have him cut your damn wings! This skin, though"—and I show him, rubbing myself on my arm—"is with me every day. With my wife and son, and his son then too, a target for every white man in this state. Your story ain't mine, John. You may think that you have a taste of it, a feel for the pain, but you don't know *nothin'*." I pinch my leg just to calm things, stare back; my voice is low. "Not a goddamned thing."

He looks up. A new silence comes on. "I didn't mean no harm." He starts to speak and then stops, pauses, starts again. "Does it get you down then, or make you jumpy or crazy? For me, each time I feel like my head's above water, I'm pulled back down. The fire and the death, all the way back to my mother, to even before the side camp. I can't say why or where." He bites his lip. "I just don't know."

"I found my father's body. Did I tell you?" I'd not planned to speak of it. "It was after we left the camp. Everything had shut down, and he didn't have no work, all of us begging to get food off of someone, hitting up our friends and kin. He woke one morning and said he couldn't take it anymore. Hester had run off then; it was just him and me and Rebecca. He robbed a store that afternoon and gave me the money, told me to take care of her, told me not to follow, then took off down the rail tracks. I did follow, though. I heard the gun. He was still bleeding when I got there. But he was gone."

"My God." His mouth is open. "What happened to Rebecca?"

I sigh. "She's here in town. It ain't worked out so well for her neither."

He doesn't ask more. There's a low shuffling sound. Air passes his lips. "But you've done okay. You've got a job, and a wife and son."

"I got that." Birds peep above and beside us. "It ain't what we thought it'd be, though, is it, Johnny? What we hoped and dreamed."

He's looking off again, down. "You wouldn't do that, would you?"

"What's that?"

He gestures. "Shoot yourself."

I look at him level. In fact, I think on it near all the time. I don't say this now; I don't admit it to nobody. Each day I plan to be better, and strong. "Nah, I don't think so. Would you?"

His nose does a twitch. He breathes and sighs. "I hope not. I'm more worried I'll puff up like a balloon and then explode. Sometimes I feel I'm a bottle, the insides all shook and fizzed. Eventually I'll just spew and blow, ruining everything and everyone that's around me."

I push a breath out and can see it. I know just what Johnny means.

"What happened to the gun?"

This jolts me. "I got it."

The sound of the men at the bell stand carries, their talk and laughs. A door slams shut. A flag curls and slaps. "Remember when I left the side camp, Elias? The last thing I remember is you looking from behind a tree. I didn't think we'd meet again, and now here we are talking, together, rejoined. Maybe it's a gift from above, or maybe not. Maybe it's all something else." He shifts his feet. "Do you believe?"

"Believe . . . in God?"

"Yeah."

I rub my chin. "Sort of. We don't go to church much like some do, or carry on a bunch of praying and praising and such. Do I believe that there's another, better life? Well, I hope there's one better than this, so yeah. But maybe that's me being bitter." I shift my jaw. "How 'bout you?"

"I don't know." The green eyes shine like gems. "Not like I once did, I guess. There's so much grief and pain." Another pause. Again, the men, the birds, the slushing sound of the river. "It doesn't explain much, does it?" The grind of Johnny's teeth.

More silence.

"I got to go."

"We gonna see each other?"

"Again?" I finish the question. "Course we are. We still got our business to get up—right, Johnny?"

He nods, his eyes down. "Thank you for everything you've done, Elias."

I turn, my throat choked-like. For a minute I think I might cry. I don't want to speak or do something awkward, something foolish or weak. Or weird. Embarrassing.

He smiles when I turn back, that old Whitey, Johnny smile, and I lean in and kiss him, my lips hard on his, our noses placed side to side. I know the men see this, but I don't look or care—I don't care about nothing just then, except us. I grab his shoulders but not his back or wings, his body shaking in something, maybe laughter or hidden tears. We stay locked there a long time. I know that we have something special, that by fate or God's hand we've been blessed, that we can't ever go backwards. That this is the last I will see of him, our paths forked and split. Johnny. Johnny Cruel.

CHAPTER TWENTY-FOUR

He takes the bus to Tallahassee. He's traveled on buses only twice before: once on his way to New York and again on the way back down, though he recalls little about either trip. It's hot for a March morning in Florida, some windows down while some remain up, and what breeze there is doesn't cool the bus much. People fan with papers or other objects near at hand, the motion like the swish and cross-saw of feeding flies.

The bus is near full, though no one sits beside him, a fact for which he is thankful, albeit hurt too. Everything crimps, despite the blank space adjacent, and he finds he must stare out the window to keep his stomach in place—to clear his mind and to blot things, to taste the warm air that fans his cheeks. Fields shine as the bus rolls, trees with vines strung between them and limbs like combed hair. Clouds shift and bunch to reveal a hole in the sky, dark and then lightened, a beam flashed and hidden, covered again quickly in shades of white film. In the bus, heads bob, elbows and arms peeking from cracked seats and sleeves, an odor of sweat mixing with perfume, smoke, and grease.

When he entered the bus, he made his way first to the back. He thought little of doing so, worrying more over his posture and the hiding of his wings, and when he sat next to a black woman who scowled, he figured she'd heard—that Lou's savage frenzy had spread its way across the town. Others turned and looked, white men and women seated before him, coloreds beside and behind, and after a time the driver made his way slowly down the aisle.

"They're seats up front," he said to Johnny, his voice a thin bleat, his face red and perspiring. Extra-long lashes made his face look girl-like, soft.

"It's okay."

"I'd *prefer* that you sit up front. I don't want no trouble, now."

Johnny didn't respond. The woman seated next to him rose and changed seats. A man behind said, "Go on, now. We don't want trouble neither."

He coughed and stood, wishing to avoid the attention, desiring as always to blend in unseen, following the driver to an open seat midway back. The driver turned as he passed this, his look one of annoyance or perhaps of concern, the other riders duly or politely staring off. Johnny's wings caught as he sat, an awkward wavering that he assumed exposed his back's defect, so that he slammed into the seat when released with a jolting. Face burning, neck up, he tapped on the window to feel of its hardness, staring until the motor roared and the bus shuddered and groaned, spouted smoke, and left.

He has no idea what he will do in Tallahassee, or even why he travels there. It is closer to where he once lived, and maybe he'll go on farther to the coast, try to locate what's left of the side camp, find the still where they fired the gum. He considers going south instead, to see who might remain near Bradenton after the shows left, but this offers little appeal. Thought of the bus seat fiasco still plagues him, and he thinks to return to the spot he intended, to take his seat in the back with stubborn pride or grit, to challenge the driver and the other unjust whites. Elias's words filter back: "You don't know nothin'," and it's true: he knows so little of men or of the world, of rules and ways or even of himself. He is a failure and a fool—a great weirdness, a simple freak.

Up in front of him on the bus, a man snaps a fart out like a gunshot. "Sorry," he offers. A woman's voice, behind: "Sue, he jerked himself from Milton to Quincy. Got down on his knees in the aisle, I tell you. Said he'd had himself a right long, trying day." Another, beside him: "Then he soiled those doilies. Christ, it was horrible." "Her tapeworm was big as a possum." Another fart, louder. "Sorry!" Johnny shifts and his wings itch. The bus sways and motors on.

At a stop in Lake City, he gets out to walk around, looking at no one, a part then of nothing. A chicken waddles up the pavement like it's leaving to go somewhere else. A man says, "No, I didn't." A child squeals; a dog barks. When the bus leaves moments later in another cloud of smoke, Johnny remains on the roadway behind it, watching the wheels turn as it disappears.

He can't say why he's done this. His mind plays new tricks: Roots become snakes that spin and wave as he passes; a tree loses its leaves from within—a ghost tree—as he looks. He's only a block or so from the station when he sees it: a flier pushing a fair and show, garish in yellow and bright dabs of orange paint. "BE THRILLED AND ASTOUNDED! SEE AMAZING FEATS!" It's for something called Johnson's Circus, and he makes his way to it as if pulled on strings, trudging on sunbaked roads coated in reddish dust. The yellow of pollen inks puddles in loops; a late fog with the sun paints things egg-like shades. A crow rattles in warning, unseen from the nearby trees. He sees the tents from near a mile off, their stripes and shapes instantly welcoming and familiar, but as he draws closer, changes show: trailers with bars that house some type of animal; a wire that may be a trapeze part or a swing; an oval that looks like a path for a game or ride. Several police cars are parked at angles out in front.

Standing at the perimeter, he watches the movement and setup, telling himself he has no need or desire to go in. He certainly doesn't want to speak to or see people, or for them to see him, or to be a rube or job seeker or pest of any kind. The police seem friendly with the workers passing by, and he concludes after a time that they are not there to shut the show down. A big cat—tiger?—is walked on a chain by two men. The large ears and feet of a clown suit stretch and turn. Perhaps there are freaks too, though he can't detect them. No banners are up yet; no one lures or calls. He can't name what he feels: Is it longing or envy, desperation or a sudden thirst? The light that can burn or shine. He's near-on to leaving when something grabs his eye: a certain furry and scruffy profile, marked and distinctive. He squints at the shape to be certain, though he's sure even as he does. Edging around the rope line, he stops a hundred yards away.

A guard with a felt hat approaches, halting in the sun some feet off. "Sir, the show doesn't start until seven. I have to ask you to leave now."

He doesn't say anything at first, the weight of it crashing down, the roles reversed with him standing outside, alone. Remembering that Elias had waited for hours to see him. Sweat drips to the end of his nose. "Tell Kenneth that it's Johnny, Johnny Cruel. I'd like to talk to him, if I could. Please."

THEY'RE SITTING IN Kenneth's trailer—not the same trailer, but so similar as to keep the prickle moving up his back. Few furnishings grace it, and there's little on the walls, the place with the same cramped, moldy odor. Kenneth is much the same too, and yet different: the burn streaks striping the hair on his arms and neck, making him look even more strange and different, exposing the pinkness and softness underneath.

"I wondered what happened to you. We all did, the survivors." Kenneth's mouth puckers and folds. It's still hard to understand him.

Johnny sighs. He'd not wanted to talk of the fire deaths or survivors, or had he? His heart thumps fast, his lips chapped and gone dry now, the memory of Winifred so quick upon him that he finds he can't breathe. His mind is aswirl; just the day after mention of Bud, now here is Kenneth, bristly and puzzling, scarred but still very much intact. It's as if aimless ghosts have stirred and now wakened, stalking and following him around the brutal earth.

The dog-faced man blinks, maybe smiles or frowns. "I was in a hospital for weeks with some others: Lenny and Gordon. I've never known such fierce pain. We talked: Some said it was Robert that did it, others claimed it was Tot, or that the church folks and cops were the ones set the fire—remember them swarming out? There weren't no funerals for the dead, as no one had money, and the townsfolk just wanted us up and gone quick. I was afraid I'd be finished right there on the gurney! I couldn't move, couldn't sleep or eat. The day they discharged me, I boarded a bus for Cleveland to seek out my family, but that was the mistake I should have known it would be. Came back down to Florida, signed on for another show." He lifts his arms, the hair beneath thicker than on his neck. "Nature's tricky, though—ain't I right? It's like a dream you can't quite escape from."

Johnny gestures about. A fly dips and buzzes. "You like it here?"

The pink mouth opens and shuts. "I like it fine." He shrugs, the motion rippling his hair. He touches fingers to his face as if to comb it. "You want to get on with us?"

Johnny shakes his head. "Nah." This thought has spun since he saw the flier, somewhere before that perhaps as well. Does he want to, really? He considers himself older and sadder and past all this now. No more shows or entertaining. No more midway great reveals.

"Why are you here, then?"

"Just passing through. I saw the sign."

Kenneth wrinkles his nose. "Where you going?"

"Tallahassee."

"I see. Out in the real world." He draws a curl with one finger. "I see you're bound up."

"Yeah. I guess so."

"What happened, Johnny?"

"When?"

"That night. The night of the fire."

His breath pulls, his head shaking back and forth like a swing released. He knows this is the price of his speaking to Kenneth, the exchange due in their meeting. He pauses, though, wavering. "I'm still not sure. One moment I was there, the fire raging all around me, and the next I'm in the mud in the woods."

"That's it?"

"That's it."

Kenneth nods slowly. "I saw Tot over the winter."

"Oh?"

"Ran into her on the street in Palmetto. She's not doing well."

"No?"

"I think she's sick—I don't know. We didn't talk a lot. She's been through so much. She asked about you, though."

"About me?" His voice squeaks and bends.

"Yeah. Some of the others she wasn't sure made it. Said the only one she stays in touch with is Carl."

A man walks by the trailer whistling. Blond, with curly hair—arms outstretched, coming to gather him, calling his name out in rapid bursts. A sheet pulled over and trapping her, pinning her down to the gurney, covering her face. He shakes his head. "The insurance. They paid her?"

Kenneth shrugs. "I have no idea. You and I are alive, right? She didn't get money there, I don't think. Nothing surprises me, though, at this point, Johnny—nothing very much at all. In a way, she was still defiant when I saw her." He shrugs more, then stretches, doglike with extended arms. Johnny can envision a hunch, a tail wagging. A pink tongue lapping rain. "You coming to the show tonight?"

"Nah. I guess I'll move on."

"You change your mind and want a place, you come and find us. Okay?"

They stand and stare, the room made smaller, and should he offer Kenneth his hand? Not to may insult him. Still, he wants neither to touch nor be touched, by Kenneth or by anyone.

"Hey." Kenneth is pointing.

"Hey."

"The world don't understand different. We both know how true that is. People come to our shows because we display what unnerves them. We put ourselves out there." He coughs. Laughs. "So much is fear." His torso seems to lengthen; his nose looks more dark and wet. "No regrets, eh, now?" The pink mouth, the few teeth lined and set, the hair pushed in different directions. "Good to see you, Johnny."

"You too." He smiles. "No regrets."

HE DECIDES TO walk on to Tallahassee, figuring it will take three more days. The rigor and time lost do not trouble him. He can't see getting on a bus again. He's unsure on trains. He's heard of hitchhiking but never done it, so he walks, along the main highway or in ditches and fields, his shoes and clothes dusty, his odor sharp even to him. His feet hurt, his knees; sunburn stings his nose and neck. Stubble roughens his face, making it itch, and sores form there. His wings he keeps bound, the motion and rubbing when he walks jerking him side to side, front to back. His clothes are wet through and stained with his sweating.

He obtains food and drink at small stores. He carries some cash in his pockets. People stare and avoid him, this stiff man with a strange back who smells and is empty-handed, as he left his belongings on the bus. They were nothing he cares about—his mother's bracelet lost in the deadly fire—and he has trouble remembering anything else he had. At night he sleeps in fields or under sprawling oaks, and the rain that threatens under eyebrow clouds holds off. He scans the sky: the light dimmed like a lamp with its shade worn and patched; a flock of bunched birds that forms a quicker, darker cloud. A puff of smoke stretches, a giant's long hair, and again come the memories: the cindery and oily smell; the knifed sound of Tot's screams; Alfred yelling and beckoning, "Hurry, get under!"; the fire as things fell. His body sways in his daydream, his guilt so heavy that he could touch it like a flame.

Tot is sick now and the others dead—or at least some are—and he should have died too. Why did he escape? The thought of killing himself swells up in a wave, and he considers how he would do it and who would find him, or maybe no one would find him, his bones simply left to rot. He could enter a lake and drown himself or step before a speeding train, and in each case silence would follow his action, the muteness and comfort of a calmed, spent, and stilling mind. The images from before return, bright with new clearness: the snakes hung like rope in trees; the branches waving and dancing; the clouds shifting; darting birds. He wishes he hadn't seen Bud or Kenneth, hadn't been to New York or even stopped by the circus. What good was done then, what peace brought or sown?

He squats by the road and talks softly to no one, inspecting a winged insect, noting a moss clump that dangles like a wispy beard. The ground is hot enough to burn his feet. The smell of dried grass wraps around him like a belt, the wind in the trees the sound of a dragging chain. Eleven steps with the chain, its pull and heaviness, the sores left on his leg, the restrictions on turning. The bucket, the shame. His bowels start to move in thinking on it, remembering.

He must dream or sleep, for he wakes in the sun with a man standing over him. A hint of a beard sprouts on a sweating, youthful face, reddened eyes that are wet-looking.

"Hey," the man says, toeing Johnny with a weathered boot.

He sits up. His face is moist with his sweat pooled, the sun beating on his skin. He turns without thinking, straightening and shielding his back from this stranger. He coughs and squints.

"What are you doin'? I thought you was dead."

"Nothing. Sleeping. I'm traveling."

"Travelin' where?"

"Tallahassee."

"That's a ways. You ain't got bags?"

"No." Johnny stands, slow in his rising, the bindings with a twist and pull. At night he lets his wings fall loose, like a woman removing her bodice, he assumes, or letting down pinned-up hair. The tape leaves marks and raw spots on his sides and back.

"Well, this is my land here, and you're trespassin'." The man looks near Johnny's age, maybe a year or two either direction.

"I'm sorry. I'll move on."

The man produces a knife, shiny-sharp in the sunlight, as if offering up a slender hand. No cars are passing, no people anywhere about. They stand only a few feet off the road. "I think you need pay me."

"Pay for what?" The old rage ramps like a flame caught, climbing his legs and spreading to his arms and chest. He eyes the knife: fluttering above his beltline, sparkling with the sun.

"Crossin' my land." Spittle on the man's lips hangs cocoon-like, clear.

Johnny nods. Insects buzz them, unseen. "If I asked you to cut me, would you do it? Would you kill me?" He sits down again, glances up. "Kill me," he repeats.

"Come on, now, don't be like that." The knife shakes in his face, as if the man writes things in the air. "I don't wanna cut nobody. I just gotta do what I gotta do. No killin' is needed." He blows a long breath. "Why you making this hard?"

He sees how it could happen, how with one move he could wrest the knife away, one upward, brutal thrust. The knife on the ground then or in his own hand, a weapon gathered and wielded. The pulsing blood. He watches as the spittle ball expands and shrinks, expands and shrinks, the young man's eyes cut. "Come on, now!"

Johnny stands again slowly, dips in a pocket, and hands forth some cash. The man steps back and counts it, steps back some more. The knife dips and wavers, his hand to his side then and shoved back out of sight.

"You gonna cut me?" Johnny asks.

No response.

"I want you to cut me. Come cut me here . . ."

The man wheels and runs, his boots turning dust swirls that fade and tumble behind him. The clacking of his feet and breath are like the sounds of a retreating horse. One of the bills flies from his grip, but he doesn't stop, the paper fluttering to the ground to lay almost on its side. Johnny stares at and considers this but veers around it, the bill flapping once in the breeze. He doesn't bother to pick it up.

THE VISIONS RETURN. In one there's the ghost of his mother, hazy and shimmering, urging him on in her soft, even voice.

"You're on your way, aren't you?"

"On my way . . . where?"

"Why, to home, sir! It's but a few miles more." She pulls her hair back in the way he recalls, and has she aged much? He can't be sure.

"Why didn't you tell me," he asks, "about our past and what I might know?"

She slumps and sighs. Her face is slack. "I tried to protect you, Johnny—I really did. That's the fight and the great gamble of love."

"Protect me from what?"

"Why, from the world! From the thrust of people's delusions, their madness and anger. It can be so sad."

He keeps walking. "Who is he, my father? You never told me that."

"No one to know. Not then and not now: a mistake that's mine, and it dies with me, Johnny, buried deep. Evil prowls—do you not know this, and believe it? If you don't, then you should. You can. You must."

"If he was so evil, how—"

"You'll know what you need to. I didn't plan to leave. But you've learned now, haven't you, John? You've seen the miracles. Why, you've—"

"No!" His shout falls, birds shooting out and past him from the ground and trees. A car passes, slows, then speeds up again. He walks on.

HE CAN'T RECALL when he ate or drank last or what he had or from where it came. His mouth is as dry as last year's stored hay. He spies a book on the side of the road—a Bible, a sign!—and hurries to it, finding it instead titled *The Trial of Sandy Slim*. A picture of palm trees spreads across its front, an ocean or water beyond this, and his eyes blur so that he sees only the first few words: "In the quiet of a purple morning, the sailor looked upon the sea . . ." Closing the book, he carries it with him, swinging it in his hand like a flattened club or shield. Every few minutes he tries to read more but can't. He smells the binding, touches the pages, even shakes it once to hear what might be said.

Biblical verses float above and about him:

"Now king David was old and stricken in years; and they covered him with clothes, but he gat no heat."

"There is an evil which I have seen under the sun, and it is common among men . . ."

"Though we walk in the flesh, we do not war after the flesh . . ."

But these are random, without pattern or meaning that he can find or judge. Isn't it all, as dead Otto claimed, a charade? A great charade? He stares at the book again, its cover wet from his sweating. Poor Sandy, he thinks, and places the book down in a grassy field.

When he stands he sees men gathered before him in the distance, grouped beneath a giant tree. At first, he assumes he has conjured this, but as he nears them he hears and sees with more focus, the shapes and circumstance becoming plainer and clear. Two trucks have been pulled nose-to-nose, with two men in one truck bed, one dark-skinned, one white, a rope draped around the dark man's neck. The tree's branches and leaves twist, mimicking veins in a human arm, something he knows from his youth or maybe felt before this. Words are spoken, too soft and low to be understood, though again they're familiar, something near to song. Men exit the other truck, one white-haired, another large and holding a gun in one hand. Johnny continues toward them, swaying in his rigid and twisting, clumsy gait, his feet making dull splat-sounds in the grass and dead leaves. With a start they take sight of him, heads lifting, mouths turned. Things are tightened, hurried, switched. The white-haired man holds a long arm up like a staff.

"Whoa, son. It's best you continue on outta here. This ain't nothing to do with you."

Johnny shuffles before them, trying to confirm things and to understand. "What is it that's happening?" he asks. The Negro's eyes are white and wide. Insects make the grass wavy, flickering under the tree in soft schemes and glimmers.

"Go on, now—you heard him!" The man with the gun's voice is low.

"Are you . . . hanging him?" he asks softly. "What has he done to each of you?"

There's a silence, brief. The gunman responds. "He said it weren't no cause of yourn! Now git on! Git!"

The older man's hand remains high. "It's a matter of honor, and virtue, and what must be done must be done. People have got to do right, and when they don't, well, there's consequence."

Consequence. Judgment. Johnny steps even closer. His vision blurs more, so that the men sway in the heat. "This can't be right." His voice sounds, his throat vibrating, twitching. There's a rumble he knows in his stomach, his neck, his feet.

"One more step and I shoot!" The man with the gun has turned, raising his arms and the weapon.

Johnny lifts his foot high. When the shotgun roars, things swing to new motion—his body writhing and twisting, his shirt falling to the ground. The pellets whistle and sting, his face hit and side ripped, and a scream falls that could be the gunman's or the black man's or his own. He is conscious of moving, of lifting, of seeing it all now from a different perch: mouths and eyes wide, the road in the distance, the growths on the limbs stretched above like green scabs. Swooping and changing, the odor of piss strong and dung stretched behind it, the smell of the gun and the heat and spilled blood. The sun streams white oil, snaking in long cords through the trees.

When he takes the rope there's a blubbering, the shotgun pumped fast and loud for another round. He closes his eyes.

Voices:

"Goddamn."

"Jarrod, git your . . . !"

"Christ, if I ever . . ."

His own voice, the words: "Late. Before it."

CHAPTER TWENTY-FIVE

Warren

The report came from the sheriff's office in Union County. We get these all the time—things they want state help to deal with, problems too big for an office patrolling a hundred miles. This one, though, caught my eye: ". . . said a man with wings grabbed the Negro and took him off."

I called Sheriff Wilson. "What you got there?"

"Craziness, I'd say, but I know these boys told this. They're not given to lyin'."

"So, what were they doing?" We both knew the answer.

"Escorting a prisoner, one accused of Bob King's daughter's rape. Said this thing just swooped down from the sky."

"Uh-huh. Anything else?"

"Nah, that's it." The line cracked. "You gon' get the Army?"

I snorted. "Don't think so. No. Goodbye."

I knew it was him. He must be headed this way or maybe already here (the report was days back), come home to papa now that he's all grown up, and with his wings a-flapping! I didn't know that could be. He shoulda stayed there on the freak show, though I guess the one he was on done burned up. I thought he was dead then, but I've thought that before about Johnny Cruel. I think now on telling the governor and showing him these things, explaining. The angles need to be covered. This won't go down well.

The governor and me have a long and complex relationship. We've known each other for years, since the time following my accident and the amputation. That was back in '05, when I was twenty-one. I lost my left arm at the place I grew up on, a wagon rolling and pinning me, cutting, and I lost so much blood they didn't think I would make it. I did but my arm didn't. Old Doc Banks hacked it off at the farm, not some sterile ward. I remember the men huddled and being told to bite rope, the sensation of being sawed on and pain, a passel of horrid dreams, but that's it. The pain, though, would follow me, or lead like a horse pulled on a bridle. I told people afterward that I'd been wounded in the war, but they knew this was lying, and who wants to see or hire a one-armed man? What girl wants to be with one? I up and moved to Tallahassee, striking out then on my own, trying to figure out what to do next or who to be, how to make for myself some sort of working life. I met Doyle Andrews the first day I arrived, in an eight-stool little oyster bar due south of the capitol. It was true chance, strange luck, and my glorious destiny then to find him—also danger, confusion, and warped, full-on crazy shit.

Doyle was one of those guys who had everything but couldn't grasp it, or at least he couldn't then. He was a good-looking young man—women followed and pressed him—with hair that fell to his face, a strong neck and white teeth, and those bright-green eyes. He was an athlete: He'd played baseball but given that up after high school, and he could bowl and golf. Clearly, he was smart; he told me he was going to law school, though he ended up training with a lawyer instead, learning the way to talk and to pitch things to get at the various treasures he sought. He liked to drink, too, and he drank a lot. The day we met he was flushed and bleary drunk, seated at a table at a place now called Rick's, just the other side of the train tracks. It smelled of fried things, stale beer, and fish.

He was carrying on when I saw him, a couple of men gathered around, including a big guy in overalls who looked like he'd just given up the plow. Since I didn't know any of 'em, I crept off to the farthest stool, but the place was so tiny I couldn't help hearing what he said.

"You just wait, Sy. One day I'll be governor, and I'll be handing out tickets to farm hicks like you, or having the sheriff work you on a chain. You see, one of us is going one way and the other, the other."

"Oh, is that so?" the fat farmer responded. His arms and neck were cow-tongue pink. This type I knew. "Your daddy gon' make that happen?"

"Well, *he* ain't in prison, like the rest of your Watkins clan. Hell, y'all 'bout got a reunion—"

The big man swung and knocked Doyle off his chair. The other man joined him, kicking and punching as Doyle lay on the ground, and I feared they would kill him. I don't know why I stepped in.

"Leave him be." I flashed my knife, as I'd started carrying one with me, a sharp and sturdy blade with a black, polished grip. I could cut one of these two—maybe both.

They turned on me like a chicken on a June bug, surprise stamped on faces. "What's it to you, Pete? You and your one piddlin' arm." The fat one gave a sneer. Without much thought, I stuck his upper thigh, blood spurting like a fountain and him squealing like a pig in pain. The owner of the place had arrived by that point, trying to get set between us, sending his son out to drum up the local law. I managed to get Doyle up, and the two of us stumbled out of there into the roasting summer heat.

He took me to his father's place, this big manor house up on a hill north of town. The old man wasn't there, but a servant tended to Doyle like he was used to doing so, wiping his face down and asking him who I was.

"This fellow just saved me," he told the stooped old black man. There was a clock there taller than he was. Doyle turned with a puzzled look. "What'd you say your name was?"

"Warren."

"Warren." He waved an arm as if whirling a lasso. "He's my friend for life."

I WOULDN'T SAY we became friends, truly—more like commander and worker, teacher and pupil, maybe destroyer and cleaning man. Doyle had a long run of wildness, plowing through jobs and women and liquor, with me and his father blocking jail and other things. He married Beth Smith, but that didn't stop matters; he was a bit more discreet with his drinking after that, a lot more discreet with his women, but otherwise things kept on. He worked for his father, then at H. Milne & Co., an outfit that built wagons and crates and had a good business, and they took me on too, to do whatever things they might need. I learned to drive with one hand, tallied accounts when they told me, provided a knife here and there when somebody crossed a clear-drawn line.

I became quite proficient with my "little lady," as I call her, skilled at cutting before someone knew they'd been hit. The secret is to always strike hard and first, fast. I only killed a few then: one being a man who threatened Doyle over a girlfriend, and his killing was even an accident, his vein cut and him bleeding out on the floor. Mr. Zeke, Doyle's father, got that one hushed up. The second one was a nigger, and nobody cared about that. Killing is like a woman giving up pussy, I decided, and I still think this is mostly true. After the battle that first time, that chase and capture, resistance, thrust, and release, it ain't really that big a fucking deal.

As Doyle moved up in the company, he talked about running for office. Mr. Zeke boosted this thought, wanting his boy to be something brighter and bigger, to move the family farther up the power line. Doyle wasn't ambitious, but he sure liked the limelight, liked everyone asking things and taking his picture, and so he was always carrying on. There were more girls: Cindy at the diner and

Donna that worked the store, and Mary Lou who ran the front desk at the company and had to be forty-five. Doyle said she sang "Rock of Ages" as he fucked her in her kitchen. He said another woman, Harriet, spread her legs in a car on Call Street as ladies with children strolled past outside. Sometimes I picked up his castoffs, and there were others hanging about far and near, but I've never liked women who are caught up in my maiming—wanting to rub on my stump some, or worse—and I've kept myself single all these many years. Just doing my job and putting the fires out, making things right (which takes time now, and effort), and keeping all quiet. Worse could have happened to a one-armed farm boy from Clermont.

He didn't tell me about the girl Lena till later, till she had borne his bastard child. I'd heard there was another offspring dating from before I met him, a female Mr. Zeke paid to go somewhere far away. But by the time of Lena, Mr. Zeke was dead, felled by a heart attack at the plant on a Sunday, and so when Doyle heard a few things about this child, he sent me around to take a look.

"What was it you heard, exactly?" I asked.

"Weirdness," he replied. He was readying to run for state rep; he'd already had his announcement. Hair hung over his face like it does, making him look like he's serious, like he's thinking hard or deep. "Said he got powers or something. Course, as my boy, having power is natural, but this sounds a bit strange. I didn't think she was still pregnant, that lying and scheming tart. I'm not sure he's even mine. She's a sweet one, that Lena, but mean as a bobcat if you cross her, prone to spit flames and show claws. No tellin' what troubles and nuttiness she's cooked up down there."

"So, what do you want me to do?" I asked.

"Handle it."

"Handle it?" He'd told me of some official's retard kid who hadn't received the right care, how it got all in the papers and caused this man's defeat. Such is the fear, the paranoia of politicians. It's all how it *looks*. I just shook my head.

"Do what needs doin'. We'll get you money or something more if you need it. I don't want to see or hear of this kid again."

It became a kind of code for us afterward: "Do what needs doin'." My job as the cleaner, doing this man's dirty work, being the sap and the muscle behind him, the arms and back, broom and pan. He never said a thing about killing, but Doyle ain't a bit innocent. I was to find a path, a way forward. And so I did.

I traveled to Carrabelle, where Doyle said she'd be. Asked around a bit when I got there—this fish camp big as a gnat's ass, sand everywhere and the sun hot as fire—had people heard of a Lena Cruel. Nobody wanted to say nothing, shying away when I brought her name up, and I thought it might be my arm, which can spook folks sometimes. I'm used to people acting strange. Finally this old boy on a horse told the tale: about this kid they said was unnatural and how people were afraid and hid, how children had died and they claimed he was to blame for it, how he himself had passed on just some weeks before. If this was all true, it solved all our problems, though I needed to check things out to be sure, and so I got directions out to where he said she lived, a shack on a swamp that smelled of salt and old outhouse.

She let me in, sort of. I looked around but saw nothing there. She was a pretty thing, and I could see why Doyle grabbed her, but when thought came of taking advantage, I didn't, following her directions out to the grave where she said he was. There weren't no headstone, only a little cross with "JOHN CRUEL" scratched upon it, the ground there still soft, so I figured we were done and I came on back to Tally. Something nagged at me, though—something that didn't feel right after, and it'd be days before it came to me one night in a dream: that there'd been someone else in that shack besides the two of us, something lodged there and hidden. I made my way back to Carrabelle just a few weeks later on, thinking to go 'round and see her and maybe try my luck or at least scratch this itch, but I found her gone, the house open and empty. When I asked folks about it, they claimed to not know where she went. I thought this all seemed very suspicious.

But there weren't nothing more to do.

I kept going around there, kept on asking. Nothing turned up, but I went back every few months. I looked in the papers, even hired a man just to find her, but he came up with nothing much. By this time Doyle had forgotten her, but for some reason I never did. She just up and vanished. I hired another man, had him check the papers and death records, looking for anything or anyone he might could track, as surely there were some relatives. They couldn't be this hard to find. I told him to hunt down everyone in the South by the name of Cruel. One day years on he came in, sweating and cheap-looking, said he still hadn't seen nothing on her but he'd found out something about a boy named Johnny Cruel.

He handed me a circus flier, or at least that's what the thing looked like. It peddled a freak show, something called Alexander's Traveling Oddities. A winged boy, a dog-faced man, a lady dwarf—a bunch of real weirdness. Likely fake.

"What is this?" Patience isn't my virtue.

"That there's him."

"Who?"

"The winged boy."

"What?"

"Name is Johnny Cruel."

"How do you know that?"

"See this here." He handed me something else, a news article from the *Montgomery Advertiser*, describing this same queer show:

> "People have flocked to the fairgrounds to see the wonders presented by Alexander's Traveling Oddities, featuring what they claim is the strangest group of such specimens in the world: a woman with a full beard; a midget lady; a pinhead who rides a tricycle, and a boy with honest-to-goodness wings. We caught up with the dwarf owner, Esmerelda Hopkins, and she introduced us around to the pinhead Otto, to Kenneth the Dog-Faced Man, and to the boy with wings, whose real name is Johnny Cruel . . ."

I looked up at the man, name of Horace Jones. It'd been some six years since I first went to Carrabelle, maybe one or two more than that. "Good work," I told him. I tipped him too, and I never tip, but I knew all along that I was gut-right on this one. By now Doyle was a senator and getting ready for his governor run, but I didn't say nothing yet. I wanted to be sure of my facts. I told him instead that I needed a few days off, to do some traveling.

"Where you going?" he asked. "You don't never go nowhere, at least not without me."

This was true, or it was then. Now that he's governor, things have changed a bit. We operate in our separate channels, him roaming and speechmaking (and how he loves this! puffed up on the crowd like a drink), me home and getting things done. I remember considering once whether I hated or loved him but decided it was neither: I respect him and his way with people, his strategizing and thinking and prompting folks and smarts. Something about him makes folks do things just for him, but there's a resentment that tags along with that. I've saved Doyle's ass many times, but there's rarely been a thanks given or acknowledgment, only a tacit acceptance and pact: *You do what I need, and for that things come to you.* These things include money, but also power and spoils; my title is "governor's special assistant." If I want something, I get it—even if it means a man's firing or the changing of a long-held law. In return, I take care of problems or head them off before they get bad, just like I will this one. That in itself provides pleasure, if no credit, glory, or praise from him.

"I'll be back; don't you worry," I told him.

Some issue had his attention—an election, I think. He was in his grand mood. "Most people don't get it, Warren. There's babies and flowers, yes, but also shit and death, and you have to have one for the other, as they're all of them joined and paired. Voters are like children, see: You give 'em their candy and tell 'em what they want to hear. It's all a big magic show! People see what they want to, and the trick is for them to see themselves—or what they think of themselves—in something bigger, which is me. It just ain't that hard. They all want to be led and want strength, and with strength comes an ugliness, though we keep that out of sight. Evolution ain't pretty. It's just the way it is." He shakes his head with his glass lifting, that lion's mane tilted back. "You understand it, Warren. You've seen both them sides."

I snorted and hiccupped, didn't offer up nothing else.

"Are you happy, Warren? I think you need you a woman. You want a woman?" He waved a stubby finger once in the air.

"I'm fine, Senator."

"Maybe you need a boy?"

"Stop it." He does this some. I have women when I want them, but he likes to gig me.

"Tell me what you want."

I want to cut the boy's wings off and leave them on his pillow. I want to get in a car and leave and not come back. I want to drive a knife deep into the now governor's manful throat. I've dreamed of these acts, shaped and patterned each one of them, and the thought of it all leaves me shaking, the same now as back then. "I'm good, Senator," I told him. "I've got pretty much what I need."

"Nobody has what they need, Warren. If they did, they'd be dead."

I caught a train the next day up to somewhere mid-Georgia, a place just past Columbus. Entering the show, this Alexander's Oddities, I found it vile and strange—a display of deformities that people pay money to see. Some folks stared at me like I was part of the entertainment, though I stayed on the fringes, assessing and watchful and taking note. I paid to see Johnny's show, and I knew from the moment I saw him that it was true; his eyes were his father's, more clear green than Doyle's, his hair (though odd-colored) the same too. Fingering my little lady, I watched his odd strip routine, him teasing and taunting, then disrobing in a rush, exposing the weirdness of his back to this hectoring crowd of men. And it *was* weird: the raised ridges on each side of his spine he fluffed and pushed out, covered in hair or feathers or something, and damn if they didn't look like wings.

I'd never seen anything like it in my life. The men oohed and aahed, and some of them called things out, but I stayed in the back, figuring on what I should do. It occurred to me that I knew something vital to Doyle that he didn't, and I pondered whether this wasn't somehow to my profit, but in the end I spoke to Johnny. I got in the line to get a picture after his show ended for the night.

"Your mother Lena?"

It was if he knew me but didn't—his expression all knotted as I watched his tender face. I came away concluding that he didn't know all that much, maybe not even who his father might be or where he lives, and I thought about this on the train ride back home. Doing away with him, given the crowds, would be tricky but not impossible. By the time I returned to Tally, I'd decided we didn't need to. Yet.

"Well, I found him," I told Doyle.

"Who?"

"Your boy by Lena." I showed him the flier and news story.

"What? What is this? You're joking, right? I thought he was dead!" It's not so often that you see our Doyle flustered. I couldn't help smiling back, watching him pitch and turn like a skittish bobcat, his face clenching up tight as he pranced about, howled and squirmed.

"Thought he was but he's not. I've seen him myself—talked to him, even."

"And? What is this winged stuff? This . . . this . . . traveling show?" His face was all red-tinged and splotched. With his eyes, it looked like Christmas.

"Weirdest damn thing I ever saw. He's some kind of freak." I shook my head with a slow sigh of sadness.

"Jesus in heaven." He seemed stumped for words. "Is it real?"

"Seems so."

"What did he say?"

"Nothing much. Admitted to me who his mother was, said she's dead. Didn't seem to know about you."

He relaxed a bit. A glance sailed to the booze cabinet. "Still, this can't be. You know that."

"Yeah, I know. But I think for now we just let things lie, till I can get up a good way to deal with the situation."

"You need to do your job. I thought you had."

I had expected this, but my breath still climbed a ladder. "Don't worry now, Senator." I rubbed my knife through my pants. Ain't it always the fathers? "I almost didn't tell you 'cause I didn't want you to be worryin'. It'll be taken care of. I got it covered. Old Warren's gonna make things good and right, again."

I MONITORED THIS for the next few years, went to see Johnny again when the show was in Pensacola. He didn't seem to know more than he did before this, but he was older and less afraid of me. I saw this as worrying, that and the state of the show, as Alexander's Oddities seemed on the verge of collapse. The crowds were a quarter of what I'd seen before, and the place had the feel of something near-on to shuttering. I gauged making a quick slash and run, envisioning a slice to his neck and the blood spurting and flowing, but a guard was nearby, and I'd have been seen in the act. I don't hide well, regardless, as you might expect. I thought about this on my way back to the capitol, devising scheme after scheme for it, and I actually considered a fire before someone did that for me. I saw the clip later: "CIRCUS GOES UP IN FLAMES," though it wasn't a circus—even I knew that much. Was he alive still, again? The article said that some survived. I went back to Tennessee, even toured the hospital and checked with the coroner, but I found no sign of him or his death. I had to assume he'd escaped. I didn't say nothing about this to Doyle.

For the last years I've looked, I've hired new men to seek and find him, men who are skillful, but no one turned up a thing. We've stalked the freak shows, been to Carrabelle and the coast, watched all the papers without sign of anything at all, not until this little report filtered in. I feel for him, almost, coming home to his slaughter. It seems in a way like the whole thing was doomed to spin this way. The strange thought comes—from what deep and crazy place?—that he could have been my child and offspring, my deformed mongrel son. I consider again whether to speak to Doyle about it but don't.

He asked me about Johnny a year or more ago, on a cold evening with a fire glowing and several tumblers of bourbon gone.

"What happened to the winged boy?" It came out of nowhere.

I pulled my drink. "I don't know." I've learned not to lie to the governor. He has a hound's nose for fibs. "Freak show he was in burned down some months back. He seems to have disappeared."

"Dead?"

"I tend to doubt it."

"So do I." He smiled—the wolf smile. I know all his humors. "You need to take care of this, and you haven't."

I set my jaw. "He'll turn up."

"Make sure that he doesn't."

And now he has. I call in Stevens, my assistant. "Get some extra protection around the governor. There's been a threat."

"What kind of threat?"

"Do as I say. An extra man on it; go with him everywhere. Shower, toilet, bed. Got it?"

"He won't like that."

I only stare.

I call in Monroe, another of my agents. Young and mean as a nude nun but smart. He reminds me of myself. "Go around to the hotels and rooming houses here in town. You're looking for a young man just arrived, white hair—no, check that, maybe dyed. Green eyes. Walks strange, that's the main thing. Ask around. Let me know what you find out there."

I think of where Johnny would have gone when he arrived. The report mentioned him saving a coon from lynching—maybe he's one of those restore zealots now. I call in McDonald, my nigger-man, fat with a head big as a cow's front, nostrils the size of gun chambers. He knows his clan and will do what needs to be done when I tell him. "Ask around among the coloreds. Young white man in town, walks strange, maybe dyed hair, green eyes. Let me know if you hear something."

McDonald doesn't say nothing, only grunts and nods. He has these gray eyes that look somehow like open graves.

I can feel myself closing in.

IT TAKES A few days, but I find him. McDonald is the one does it, coming into my office late one afternoon. His hair is all tufted out, his eyes smooth like stones, and he stinks like a polecat or yesterday's left-out garbage.

"We found your man."

"Who?"

"White man you said you looking for. Stiff, strange hair."

"Where?" My pulse jumps.

"Staying at a house down on the southside. Been there 'bout a week." McDonald's dead eyes sometimes give me the shivers. "You want me to do it?"

"Nah. I'll do this. Just tell me where he is."

CHAPTER TWENTY-SIX

"Are you a god?"
"No, not a god."
The man's name is Charlie Jones. Raw and puffy streaks mark his neck like a kerchief. His eyes are red, white splotches below them showing the tracks of his leaking tears. "I can't believe nothing about it. I keep thinkin' I'm in heaven or somewhere, but I'm still right down here. I ain't sleeping and dreamin' this, am I? Am I now, mister? I ain't right in my head."

"Could you lend me your shirt?" Johnny seeks a shield, intent on hiding again his bared and hanging wings. His own shirt was left on the ground by the tree, his bindings broken, gone. Blood trickles down his side like a spring.

"Whatever you want." The man shrugs his shirt off, extends out one arm. "I . . . I need to clean up." He points down to his pants.

Johnny lifts his head. He has trouble getting the shirt on, ripping it under one arm as he lifts. Twisting his back, he pulls and stretches the fabric, wishing he could tape down his wings. He is standing in a wooded glade, different from the area where he encountered the men and trucks, and he has no idea how he got here or where they might be. He has no other thoughts, no scheme formed or plan. His side aches, his face, his hands. He's so tired.

Charlie returns from the trees, his brown torso glistening. He's younger than Johnny thought, maybe his own age or near.

"What'd you do to deserve this?" Johnny asks. He picks a pellet out from deep within his arm.

"Nothing," the man responds. "They say I raped a white girl but I didn't—I promise! We just talked and kissed. I wanted to get with her, sure, and she said she wanted to but then changed her mind, 'cause next thing I know the sheriff's saying she claims a rape. Then these men come . . ." His body jerks and shakes, like a dog shedding water. "And you, keepin' and savin'—"

"We need to leave."

"Yeah. They'll be lookin'."

"You know where we are?"

Charlie nods.

"I say we stick deep in the woods until dark, then move at night. Somebody sees us . . ." He motions to Charlie, his own bulging shirt. Its side is stained now a dirty red.

"There'll be dogs."

He'd not considered this. He looks up. "When?"

"Soon as they get 'em. Maybe not afore dark." Charlie glances at the sky. "And go where?"

"Tallahassee?"

"Yeah. My kin are there."

"How far is it?"

A shrug, a stare. "Maybe two days' walk."

They set off. The woods are thick with vines and new growth, and they backtrack and detour in and around the low spots, beneath giant, twisted, spreading trees. For a time they walk among pines that are like at the side camp, and he imagines the workers and the smell of cut gum, the catfaces and swinging of the hogal, hack, and axe. Dead limbs mark a tree trunk like hooked and crossing thumbs; stripped bark shows the scars of old lightning. Curtains of moss drape the oaks in gray tears. They skirt rolling farmland, though in time this extends in almost every direction, and they decide to wait until dark to avoid exposure in the fields. Johnny listens for dogs. Charlie draws patterns in the dirt with his feet.

"Where you from?" Charlie asks.

"Jacksonville."

"What'd you do there?"

"Work at a hotel." He doesn't want to talk of it, think of it. To remember very much at all.

"Are you in pain?" Charlie eyes his shirt.

"Not too much."

"How . . . how'd you get those—"

"Just did."

"And you . . . you go around savin' folks?"

He shakes his head. "I can't even save myself." He smiles as to take the sting out. "I'd rather not talk on it now, if that's okay. Let's just get you to safety. Then we'll figure things out best we can." It hurts if he breathes deep, if he twists much to his right or left. "What will you do in town?"

Charlie sighs. "Move on from there, I suppose—somewhere far away. They'll come for me otherwise; I'm right certain on that. It's what happened to my friend Sam. He made it to Macon and they found him, brought him back. I got to start now with nothing, with nobody." He grins, teeth bright with one tooth brown. "Better than hangin' from a rope and a tree."

They move at dark, thirsty and hungry, stopping at a creek to drink in great, noisy gulps, noses to the water like bending dogs. The trail for a time cuts through old crop rows made ridgelike, trees now sprouted through them. Occasionally they see lights and make great loops to avoid these. Things scurry before them in the dark like ghosts. Sometimes eyes flash, white or red or pink. More than once they hear dogs, the sound freezing them in the starlight, stepping their pace up, but nothing more follows. Smells come of cinders, of leaves and sweet burning wood. Thunder cracks and wind, rain, a fog-like steam.

They don't speak much as they walk, listening to their steps and the crackle of things beneath them; Johnny asks once, pointing in the direction they're heading, "Are you sure?" to which Charlie nods.

Their bodies stink. Maybe it's the hunger or weakness, but Johnny's mind plays new tricks: A tree's branches form talons; clouds swirl into downspouts; Charlie's back is a bear's or a giant's, a great and quiet cat's. For a moment he *is* Charlie, picking his way through the darkness, tight-muscled and hounded, held by a chain tugged and dragged like a heavy weight. Bats dart and his wings twitch, rustling in his shirt as if in a wish to rise and join them. Spiderwebs catch and cling. For seconds he thinks he sees Tot, her gun raised, and Alfred, even Zorat, but they fade and sink, dulled and winking. Gone. The moon is an eyelash stretched far above them, the stars bright and scattered like thrown sparks.

They sleep in the day beneath an oak's sweeping cover, his dreams again of the side camp and the food they ate there, the hay and the loft that first night with his mother, her body then grown stiff and cold. The fire warms him later, the smell of flesh burning and smoke caught in his throat, his coughing and turning, the confines of the box. Always the box: the smell of dirt that embraces and chokes him; his arms thrashing as he wakes to a weight and touch, the light of the sun suddenly warm on his forehead. He leaps up as a shape falls back, a brownness sweating and gleaming, and they each stare in silence, fighters poised before renewed assault.

"What are you doing?"

"Nothing!"

"You touched . . . my back."

"I just wanted to see it, try to get things figured out." He offers up light-skinned palms. "You're an angel, ain't that right?"

"I am not."

"But then how—"

"I don't know. Do you understand? I don't know what else I can say or do. I was born this way and I'll die the same, as you'll die the way you are." He hears himself say it. "I was in a show before, with lots of malformed people . . . freaks. People came to watch and stare. We were *entertainment*. I was used, as were others, maybe all, but I'm not . . ." He gulps and pauses. A hawk passes overhead. "Folks have to make their way. I lived, and others didn't." He stops, straightening himself out of habit, making his back small or smaller, tilting his head upward to the sky. It's the most he's said since Elias, but Charlie isn't Elias—he has to remind himself that. His side feels like he's been beaten with boards, though the bleeding has stopped. He won't look down at it. "And you?"

"Nothin' much to tell. I thought I was dead but I'm not. I'm alive still, I guess, since I'm here hot and hungry. And I have you to thank for it, for giving me this second run. I'm not sure I deserve it. I've done things before that ain't good." He looks around at the greenery. A dragonfly alights, multiwinged, on his arm. "I want to pay you back for what you done, for my life. How can I repay you?"

There's a pause. "Just get me to Tallahassee. Save yourself. Hide us both." He picks up a grass blade and chews it, its taste sharp, then bitter, the blade split into mush and pulp. His head throbs like a motor. "I'll hide the rest of my life."

Charlie doesn't respond at first. Then, "You can try."

THEY ARRIVE IN the city in darkness. They saw the lights from a distance, a glow on the horizon dull and strange like a western sun. Fences loom and long streets, dogs barking and people that they veer from and avoid; they keep to the shadows and the calming, shielding dark. Charlie knows the way, down through clay alleys and past trash piles and sheds, through parks and by buildings large and small, new and old. Only a few cars are seen, their headlights searching and turning, alert. A voice sounds or voices, a note plucked and trilled, but for the most part things are deadened and quiet, asleep. Climbing a hill, they see the structures below it, lamps here and there and a few spiked, flickering fires. The smell of smoke follows, and something catches in Johnny, a coldness along his back and spreading down his side and wings. When they stop before a house in the darkness, his heart pounds a rhythm he feels in his legs and feet. His hands grip a post, guarding against falling, his mind dulled and eyes woolly-dry and dimmed. Charlie's whispers snake back, rising and hissing, though Johnny can't make out anything asked or said.

They follow a figure to a barn behind the house, the first wisps of a fog rising, so that it seems they trail a phantom more than a woman or man. The door creaks in opening, the smells and sounds following of insects and beasts. He won't look at the hay loft. "We gon' be fine here," whispers Charlie. "She says we can't stay long, maybe leave tomorrow or the next. We gotta keep going. Can you go on?"

"Yeah."

They sleep. In the morning a boy comes and the animals are led out one by one: a horse and three cows, their tails twitching. The horse huffs once. The boy eyes the men with surprise but doesn't speak. An old dog noses inside the barn and out again before the door shuts. From their glimpses outside they seem to be in a field in the midst of town, the tops of buildings in blocks and rows past the meadow, trees blocking and bending against the morning sun. It grows hot soon in the barn, dust making the light twist, several stalls and a stack of hay mounted but little else to be seen. Rustles come, again sparking memory: of insects, mice. Wretchedness. Something else. After a time, the door opens again and a girl enters, bringing a box of food and a pail of water, a cup on a string looped around her neck. Maybe seven or eight, she likewise says nothing, stares, bows low and retreats. Squatting, they devour sweet cakes of some kind, bacon, and cold corn, washing it down with the water. Afterward they sit on the hay where they slept. Charlie peers through cracks between the boards sheltering and housing them.

"Maybe we go tonight, eh?" He turns to Johnny.

"Where we going?"

"My aunt Tilda lives off in the swamp, near the coast. It might be safer there. Less people about. Nothing much around her."

"Would the dogs have followed us?"

"No, I think we escaped that. People will be looking, though. I can't imagine what it must be like back home."

Johnny clicks his teeth. Neither speaks for minutes or maybe hours. Sounds come from afar: hoof clops, a lead clinking, motors of tractors or trucks or of cars. Suddenly the door opens in a flash of light, but it's the girl, toting a metal tub heavy with water. She must have filled it nearby, as it bows her in carrying it, water sloshing from either side and escaping, wetting her, prompting a soft laugh and gasp. She goes back outside and returns with a package.

"Clothes," she says, in a high, girlish voice.

They bathe when she leaves, Charlie crouched in the tub, his body firm and symmetrical as he rubs, stands, and swivels, dries himself off with a bend and a little shimmy. Johnny wipes down his body with a cloth, his back held from Charlie, care taken with his wounds, and they change into the clothes that smell of soap and the bag they were carried in. Johnny's pants are too short, fluting up at his ankles, but the shirt is large enough to fit his wings within. Without tape they hang strangely, as if he is hunchbacked or deformed in some new way, and he looks for something to tie them but finds nothing of use. Charlie stuffs their old clothes back into the bag with a twist and pop.

"Let's try to sleep."

But he can't, thinking of Cletus and Hester and a hundred lush and varied things, until he does without waking or turning, without bright and astonishing, frightful dreams.

The girl returns with dinner, rousing them. It is almost dark. Charlie speaks to her in looping half whispers, questioning and explaining. The horse and cows are back in their stalls in the barn.

"What's your name?"

"Lillian." She twists her neck shyly.

"The boy your brother?"

"Ethan. That's him."

"Your mother Sarah?"

She nods. "She says you in trouble."

Charlie sighs. "We might be."

IN THE NIGHT comes a whisper: "I'm gon' go check on things. Be right back."

It's quiet after Charlie leaves, even the animals stilled and listening, a wind rocking the barn that likely means coming rain. His mind roams as he waits, envisioning different scenes that play out in long sequence, none of them happy, hopeful, or good. If they're caught, is he chained again? Is Charlie hung? These thoughts came before but leap out now toward him, pushing him up to a cliff's sharpened edge, a drop that shows the tops of trees. Fire roars there too, his great blame of himself still, his guilt so strong that for a time he sees his having lit the fateful match. A weight then and now—Charlie is safer without a freak dragged behind him—his mind again turns to closings, to hoisting himself as they meant for Charlie, to ridding the world of this strange, futile, dreadful woe. Aren't they a step away: heaven and hell; good and bad; forward and backward; life and death? Maybe there is a Devil. He is standing and looking, feeling for rope or something else in the gloom when the door opens and Charlie slips in, stealthy and shadowlike, wetted by the tilting rain.

Water beads in the man's stiff, coarse hair, caught in the light before the door swings shut again. "Can't leave in this stuff," he says, resuming a more normal volume. The rain makes it hard to hear even this. "I think we might stay one more day, regardless." He pauses, shifting about. His eyes stray from Johnny. "There's someone I'd like to see."

"Oh?"

"A girl I just want to say bye to, as we ain't gon' see each other much again." He stares off. A train moans in the distance, washed in through the downpour's rush. "You could go on, though, if you're worried. Go on to Aunt Tilda's—I'll meet you there. Here, I'll draw you a map." He scratches something onto a cleared space on the ground, pointing out landmarks and roads, directions. None of it makes much sense.

"Charlie, I can wait. But I'm thinking I'm slowing you down, putting you at risk. Maybe you should go on now on your own."

The barn remains dark in the rain. Johnny can just make out Charlie's lips, rounded like bullets, moving up and down. "You saved my life. I owe you at least to get you outta here."

IN THE NIGHT he dreams of Winifred, the brightest of his glowing dreams. Her curls touch and tickle him, the thrill sharp from her laugh, the beauty and torment of her face crimped in fear. She moves and her voice sounds, asking him of what happened, wanting him to speak and explain things, to stay and defend her. "I can't," he says, but she doesn't hear or see him. "I love you!" he shouts, though she is gone now to bigger things: an education, a life, a plan, her own death. He tells her that he wants it all to start over, but she smiles and shakes her head. Her voice sounds again, catching and echoing. "Johnny, love. Show me your wings."

WHEN THE BOY comes for the animals the next morning, Charlie isn't there. Johnny must have dozed or slept, as he didn't hear or see him leave, and he studies the barn for a moment, thinking Charlie is hidden or bedded down in a stall. The boy says nothing as on the day before, guiding the animals out into daylight, closing the door behind him with care. Outside it is fresh and cooler, the rain gone and sun up, and Johnny fights the urge to follow him and not return, to walk and keep walking, whistling a freedom tune. The girl Lillian comes later with their box of food, plates for both him and Charlie, but Charlie is still off somewhere. Johnny thinks to speak out but then doesn't, only bows to her once and smiles.

He settles down in a corner after eating but doesn't sleep, thinking odd thoughts and remembering things Zorat said, Winifred too, even Elias, and what has he done with his life? Fear mounts and climbs that Charlie has left him like the others, and he tells himself he deserves this, has always deserved it—has always known he'd be thus: alone. After some time, he stretches, walking the dim barn from one end to the other, and his back is to the door when it opens once again, bringing the light and freshness and a man. He turns, expecting to see Charlie, but it is someone else—tall, the sun behind him, a hat on his head, an empty hanging sleeve.

For a long time the man stands in the doorway. Light bends as he twists his long neck. "Hello, Johnny."

Johnny doesn't respond.

"You been missin', ain't ya? Told you I needed to know where you are." Warren takes a step forward, pulling the door back to close it. Things are quiet again. "Got a report over from Union County, said a man with wings interfered with a prisoner. I figured that had to be you." He looks around, creases his face up. "Where is he now?"

Johnny shakes his head.

"Left you behind, huh? Probably a smart thing to do." He breathes out. "It's been a difficult life, ain't it? Sometimes that's just how it is. Your mother, the freak show, the fire, the deaths, and this."

"What of my mother?"

"Well, she tried once to kill you, at least 'fore she changed her mind. I figure she was embarrassed, ashamed of you and likely scared. Lonely, maybe crazy. Haunted." He squints and shrugs, the motion lopsided with just the one arm. "Does that make you sad?" He lifts his shoulder again, the one above his missing arm. "I know, I know. I know what it feels like, being stared at because you're odd. *Unique*." He spits this out, sucking air back through his teeth. "It ain't a barrel of fun, now, is it?"

"And my father?"

"Your father. You don't know nothing?"

A head shake. "Nothing."

"I find that hard to believe. Why else would you be here?"

"So he's here?"

There's a silence.

"Is it you?"

Warren laughs. "No, not me. You really don't know, do you?"

"No, I don't."

The door opens wide to allow Charlie's entrance, and it all happens fast: the one-armed man's turning, a knife gripped in his hand, plunging it into Charlie's stomach with a swerve and a single thrust, a broken grunt following. Charlie's pant after and gurgling sounds, a step or two taken. The look on his face one of wonder. He sits.

"Johnny," he calls, his voice clear but weak.

Johnny can't move; it's as if something holds him, leaving him to watch as Warren's knife pulls across Charlie's throat, like ripping through burlap, the blood splashing as if poured. Turning toward Johnny then as Charlie falls, hand blackened, the knife wet, the odor of blood sharp and ironlike around them. Warren's face is calm, his eyes ashen. His gaze settles in on Johnny like a ball rolling to a hole.

"I'm sorry it has to be this way; I really am. But it does." He walks slowly forward, the knife held loosely in his hand. "He told me. Yep, he did."

Johnny still doesn't budge. Memory flickers: of the house in Georgia when men came to call; as a boy quiet, submissive; his heart pressed and bumpy; teeth chewing on his tongue. Waiting and knowing what was soon to come. His wings, yes! His cursed and wretched, slack and needless wings. He watches. Warren stops a foot away.

"You're smart not to run, or to fly—can you fly?" His head shakes and teeth shine. "Who would have thought, Governor? What things can be overcome." He shoves the knife into Johnny's belly, the pain and release known returned, driving him to the ground with his back up, knees down. His body feels split in half. The knife rips his shirt then, exposing his naked wings, and it's as if he's back at the show that first night, revealed, tears running and breath held and eyes pointed to his feet. Blood seeps through his hands.

At the cut to his wing his body shakes as with fever, the old rage or something inside him unleashed, its strength such that he bucks the man off his back, the knife landing somewhere between them. Each is left on bent knee, staring eye to eye from inches apart and now gasping, close enough to strike again, or bite or kiss. Later he will ponder what happens next, remembering and disremembering: the knife grabbed and plunged into Warren's chest like a swinging hack; the sweetness in connecting and entering; the heat of the man's blood mixed with his own; the stench. The eyes wide and staring, the single word—"weak" (or is it "freak"?)—at Warren's lips. The boost to his own heart. The fire. The certain thrill.

Then he is up and leaving the barn in the blinding sun, stuffing a rag up against his middle, his back hunched and burning, blood trickling down his wings and rump. He doesn't remember much more, doesn't see the black man as he exits, the tufted hair and gray eyes near a gum tree and watching, neither surprise nor unease nor anything more than reflection spread across his face.

CHAPTER TWENTY-SEVEN

He wakes to her bathing his side and his back, working with care past his wounds and the pain there, dabbing with gentle swabs of a cloth. She hums as she does this in the way that she has, his memory sharp or dimmed by his sleep, his recall of the years now long rushed past. The sense comes—dream-fueled—that she'd left and he missed her, but she is back now, and he rests and can stretch himself more, reclaiming sweet slumber, letting things go again. His stomach hurts so, and if he moves pain stabs through him, but she shushes his mutterings and bids him lie still. A minty smell cloaks them, cool on his back and rolled up on his belly, and when his eyes open briefly he sees bottles above him, plants with their tongues out. Hearts and fuzzy flowers. Ashes heaped. Wings.

"It's okay." The whisper he knows well, and where has it hidden? Where has she? There's a tug like a draining, but as he stills it goes away. "You're gonna make it. You're just fine, now."

She'd said this before and had heartened him, saved him, and what was the message? In which realm or plan? There were trees and a chain, fire. An old shack, cold in the winter and with the trees he used to stand and watch. The train that he played with, and one day the dark . . .

He opens his eyes but can't sit or focus, the plants above him and bottles all mixed. The words come, the motion, the smell, and yet things are different, peculiar and jarring, crazy and slanted off. It is not as it was or would have been in his mind-space. He focuses enough to see her shoulder, her neck and skin.

"Who are you?" he asks, though the words may not have left him, as she makes no noise or response to his asking. The rubbing continues, the mint smell. The humming. The pain and the whispers. The oddness. His wonder.

MUSIC AGAIN. A fire burns near or far, its fumes bitter, cutting. He can't sit or move much on account of his stomach, his back hurting when he turns, though he can shift some now. His eyes open hinge-like, slowly and heavily, training on the woman beside him: small and springy, her age neither old nor young. Thin and dark-eyed. He has never seen her.

"I thought . . ." His mouth dry. "I thought you . . ."

"I know," she says quietly. She doesn't smile, only hums again. "My name is Tilda."

"Tilda." He tongues it. Memory catches, a train jerked and pulled. "Charlie's aunt."

A slow nod.

"And Charlie?" But he knows.

She sighs. "I thought you gon' die too, but you ain't. At least not now."

"How . . ." It's so hard. "How did I get here?"

She gives a shrug. "You just did. Bled all over my floor, what blood you had left. Infected, too. Pellets."

"How long ago?"

She shrugs again. "Days. Weeks."

He shifts and the pain reels. He gasps and groans. "What will happen?"

"Well, I hope you'll get better. Then you'll need to figure some things out."

"Figure them out." Birds chirp beyond him. Crickets squall, perhaps screaming in his head. A frog croaks. "What do you think, Aunt Tilda?"

A pause. A slow breath. "I think you a fighter-man."

DAYS PASS. SHE wipes his bottom, carts his piss off in a bucket. Feeds him and tends to his wounds, humming things as she does so, putting on salves and creams that can sting. Strength returns, some force or new punch. His arms look like withered sticks. He sees the hole in his stomach, red still and raw-looking, an opening bored as in a rotten tree. His hands burn and tingle; he has fevers and often sleeps. He can't eat much, can't stand. The sight of his blood makes his heart jerk and scurry.

They talk, though she speaks little. Her words are in the mornings only. He learns about her in pieces, in scraps like scattered seeds.

"Came down here in twenty-nine. I lived in Greenville afore. Wanted to get out of there—needed to. Said I killed someone." Her grin is all spoke-toothed, her eyes slanted away from him. She doesn't smile much. Her nose is flat against her face.

"Did you?"

"Maybe not. People call me this or that, think they know what I am but they don't." A hand lifts. "Who really knows anyone? I give people some strength. I try to help." She waves at the bottles, the crawling plants. He's discovered that the plants occupy the entirety of the darkened shack, extending around its walls and out and into the sandy yard, or as much as he sees of it. There's a salty, crumbly smell.

"Where are we, exactly?"

"We're somewhere safe."

She turns away most of his questions, replies made in shifts and grunts. He guesses her age at near fifty, her wild hair patched with gray, the lines of age evident on her face and neck. She wears no brassiere and sometimes no clothes at all, to which he says nothing, watching and not watching, drained, detached. Thinking that he is alive still, somewhere out in these trees and somehow. He offers her thanks, which she bats back at him. "I do what I do," she says without looking. She scratches a thumb on her arm, leaving a long, grayish mark. "This is who I am."

"Do you have any books?" he asks one long day, a bright sun painting branches. Usually, the haze and trees make it murky, rain coming in the afternoons.

"Nah." She lifts her arms up and around. "I got this. You get well enough, we'll explore things. We'll learn some. You'll see."

Her shack is near water, the wet shown by mold on the outside planks. A palm looms past the window—the only window—near his bed, and beyond this are pines and a cypress, vines that are arm-thick. The light plays green and gray, and occasionally he hears sounds that make him think of a lake or sea. Tilda leaves the house some days, absent for hours and coming back with roots and leaves, and the food she makes him is a mix of the odd and familiar: corn cakes and a bitter powder, long eggs of some kind and a meat tasting of dirt and blood. During her absences he is prone to panic, convinced then that she won't return, leaving him short-breathed and sleepless until, measured and laden, her face wet, she finally does.

Her shack is one room in which he occupies the only bed; she sleeps on the floor just beside him, nearly touching. When he protests this, she is scornful. "I sleep on the floor. Always have. You get your rest." The only light in the evenings is the flicker of a single candle. The room is crammed with cracked and broken objects, beyond the bottles and plants crowding the warped shelves: old bits of metal; half-built chairs; a crib with a doll in it; a sign warning of curves. At the back is a chimney thing where she cooks; he can't see this well. Things are so close, the stuff so packed in, that sometimes when he wakes he feels surrounded by armies, by swarms of soldiers and weapons, rivals, men. In their sleep her body is so close that he smells her, nearly feels her, hearing the draw and slow call of her breath. The shack is bewildering and different when she's not there.

On the day he sits up, she pulls his face close and hugs him, rocking and saying nothing, her body wrapped and pressed on his. She doesn't smile or speak as she does this; nor does he. The rising dizzies him, to where she must lay him down after, but soon he is able to sit some each day. After a few days more he can move a bit around the room. The first time he stands and makes his way outside the shack, she says to him in a singsong voice, "I have something for you."

He turns, dizzy again, sweaty and breathless from the strain. The leaves flicker and shine like eyes or suns. He swallows, long. "What's that?"

She hands him something silver, gleaming, hard. He turns it over in his hands, fingering its tip, its edge. Holds it up to the light. Warren's knife.

THEY ROAM THE area around and behind her shack. It's as swampy as he imagined it, a stand of black water yards away but the land high in spots, with trees as at the side camp and oaks with muscled limbs. The ground is sandy and soft rather than dirt or smooth clay. She points out plants and trees: swamp cabbage, hickory, azalea, cedar, cattails, beautyberry, firebush, beech. She tells him of times the sky rained frogs and fire crept from the ground, the water whipped wild and air made harsh and feral. The wind blowing salt from the ocean miles away. He shows her his interest and asks lots of things, as he wants to know and discover, to probe and to learn then of more. Much, though, remains mystery: the shack and her work; how he came to find her; when he must go and why, and to where.

One day on their walk he sees a dead rat and possum, strung by their tails like stockings stretched from a tree. Another time she stops him, hand across his chest, refusing to let him go farther down a shady trail. Once they see hundreds of white birds sitting. Watching. Tilda puzzles him, this silent, odd woman who neither fears him nor is awed, and who seeks nothing from him, at least not that he's found. Knocks come at the shack and she leaves, retrieving herbs or things first in the darkness, and how can she mark things or gauge them, or even see? Usually, a woman or child waits beyond—sick, he supposes, the door closed behind her—and she warns him to make no motion or noise during these appeals. In the afternoons she makes her visits, gone for long periods with a sack slung on her back, weeds and stems poking out as if she's a roaming gardener, a frayed and quiet, leafy knight.

He can't say what he feels for her beyond duty and obligation. Shouldn't he offer her more and give more, at least show a thankful something? Her care and respect he mimics, the calmness of her bearing, drive. He doesn't want her, man to woman, though the thought sometimes rakes his mind; he trusts that she doesn't want him either, at least not in a fleshly way. His wings are exposed, the cut on the left still sore but near healed now, and he can tell that the wing flops, perhaps with no further function. He can't see this, of course, hasn't tested it and doesn't plan to, but he feels the difference as he would a strain or pull. He goes shirtless as she does, appendages flapping without hitch or restraint, cooler this way and unbridled, free. He spends days beside her, exploring and walking, staring and wondering, except for those restless times when she leaves. He uses the same outhouse now as she, home to ants and a roach she calls a palmetto bug, located behind the shack on the edge of the silent swamp. Their refuse falls to the water and splashes, spatters, floats. He studies the grandeur of the roach's sets of wings.

He only wishes she'd talk more, as she knows things of and about him, things perhaps told in his sleep: that he is an orphan; that he stabbed the man who cut Charlie's throat. Other things buried well. She says to him one day, "Your father did this?" pointing a thumb at his sore, ruined stomach, and he's unsure how to respond to this.

"My father?"

"Warren worked for your father, right?"

"He did?"

"What don't you see?" But she says no more. He asks her of this and herself, of Charlie and their family, whether she has children of her own or ever wed, but she scowls and turns her back. The one time he gets much reaction is when, almost asleep, he quotes a verse from the Bible: **"Since by man came death, by man came also the resurrection of the—"**

"Stop it!" she hisses beside him on the floor. She still prefers the ground. "Go to sleep," she says softly, more warmly. "Sleep then, Johnny Cruel."

He gulps and half coughs; she's not before spoken harshly, and has he ever heard her say his name? He repeats the verse slowly and methodically in his mind, unsure of just why he does so, pausing on the different words. Sleep prods his memory and turns it: dreams of Alfred and Boris, of being pinned to the bed by thrown knives, of plunging the blade deep into Warren's chest. The knife pulled back slow through the muscle, as if to reverse or complete things. The unfairness of all like a film layered on his tongue. In the dream he stabs again and again, and again.

The next morning appears to have jumped from his dreamworld, the sky hazy and distant, the air wispy, a decayed smell. He sits at a table in front of the weathered shack, an area where she dries her roots and herbs. It's the only treeless place near, the light through limbs forming streaks and making halos, black-and-white chickens scuttling near his feet; she keeps a flock that runs about wild and brutish, penning them up only at night for protection. Is it their strange eggs he eats? One flaps her wings and lifts a few feet before dropping, leading him to ponder their structure and attempts at flight, to consider whether this hop shows success or marks a bust. Their wings are so tucked and fanlike, so flat and feathery and small! He lifts his arms and feels his own wings flexed and spreading, the knife held in one hand. Could he lift himself up again? The knife has a weight, and he pauses to study it, touching its edge, its spine and face. Pincers and talons, lances and blades: everything piercing, tearing, and pulling back.

"Can you toss it?"

He starts. He'd not heard her behind him. A chill prickles his arms and neck. Has she read his dreams? "What's that?"

"Toss the knife. Like at the show."

What does she know of the show? Sweat sprouts. "I'm not sure." He turns and hurls it at a tree some yards away, the knife missing and landing with a thud in the brush. He must hunt among thorns and weeds to find it.

"Practice," she says.

He does without doubting, without thinking about this very much. He recalls watching Boris, how he gripped and held things still, how the knife twirled and spun as it flew. Boris's arm remained straight as he aimed and heaved it, ending stretched out rather than at his side, and what strength and poise he showed then! What focus and concentration. Johnny's mind plays it through—one foot forward, the position of back and body, the thud as each knife hit its mark and dug in. His next toss hits the tree but glances off it, and the throw pulls his stomach, a pain felt and tearing, but something else too: pride and thrill. The next toss pierces the tree's trunk.

"Now you must clean it," she says, "the knife. It should stay sharp, too. Do you want another, to use for your practice?"

"Another knife? No." Her words rock him, the motion and action, the *exchange* made and held. "Just this one. I'll need help to clean and sharpen it. Will you help?"

She nods in a slow, close-mouthed assent.

HE PRACTICES WITH the knife every day, sometimes at dusk or at night beneath the moon and stars. His arm becomes sore with it, his hand flat and calloused, his stomach firm and healing, stretched. The thump of a hit is like an echo, a heartbeat, the cleanness of a hammer swung through air and striking home. Sometimes she watches him but mostly she doesn't, leaving him to test and to try things, to alter his form and make adjustments, mistakes. He imagines himself Boris, Alfred standing before him, and could he make himself do this? At what risk and cost? He sees Alfred unflinching as the knives stick all around. "Balance and follow-through," he tells himself always. "See the knife fly in your mind. See it as part of yourself."

His shoulder burns and stings, his elbow, wrist, and hand. He fingers the blade's tip through the new thickness of his skin. "Follow-through, balance. Hear it. Feel it." At night he sharpens the blade on a stone she has given him. He dreams of the knife, the toss, the strike made, the air. Weeks on, he hits a target from different angles and distances every time. He tries throwing with his eyes closed. He makes a pattern of notches on a long, dead limb. He spins and hurls as if firing a short gun. His thoughts fill with hangings, with injustice to anyone made or seen different, but he thinks about nothing at all when he throws. The motion, the power. She speaks after one such toss, surprising him, interrupting.

"Will you throw it at me?"

He pulls back, his chin down. They stare for some seconds, her eyes black in the shade. His feet make scratching and scuffling sounds. "Why would I do that?"

She shrugs. "Test yourself."

He exhales. Shakes his head. "That's crazy."

"Crazy?" Her snort sends a spray. "I passed myself off as a man at A&M. For weeks, maybe a month."

He looks up. He's not sure what to say. "What do you want from me, Tilda?" His voice rises at her name.

"Not a thing. What do you want from yourself?"

It's the most he's heard her say in what seems like weeks. Months? "I don't know."

"Does it feel good, the throwing? The marks hit and release?"

"Yes." He pauses. He waits in silence for more.

"The man Warren, was he was wicked?"

His mouth shifts with the subject. "I suppose."

"And the one who sent him?"

Catching her arm, he pulls her in closer, feeling the heat of her, the knife in his other hand. Her face bends near his, her eyes and hair, teeth, her breath surging warm and wet. How long since he's held someone, since he's reached to touch another's flesh? Instead of ardor's lift, though, his belly throbs and twitches, the need to take action like a bone caught in his throat. He finds he can't look at her. He doesn't want to do her harm. "How do you know things about me?"

She laughs with her head back. It's so unlike her, it stuns him; he nearly drops her in his surprise, permitting her to sidestep and glide some length away, face up and eyes bright. Something gurgles in her throat. "Knowledge is strength, Johnny, even if it's buried like a vault inside." She points to his forehead. "You killed a man and flail now in a guilty sea, though you know too the joy in it, the justice gained and held. Think some on that, John. What came first was evil: the men to hang Charlie and the one who struck him dead and you, the blood of it staining the governor's fat, white hands. You think now he quits? It all circles and burns a bit—stings some yet, don't it? Your faith but a wall then, a mask stretched on your head."

She strokes a chicken pecking by her feet. "See it and right something, Johnny—stand and expose yourself. What's the point of healing if you can't stop what makes you sick?" She lifts the chicken and breaks its neck with a cracking, blood flung about then like rain, the chicken's feet moving, then slowing, achieving with a thrust a shaky, final halt. "That's just life, now. Life, or what's past it." Her words sound of dare or sneer. She places the chicken carcass on the ground with a slap. "If you're not ready to die, there ain't no such thing as freedom." Eyes curled, her few teeth shine. Her gums are the black of night. "Everything is stolen: wealth, life, joy, even death. Go on and *do something*, Johnny." A long whoosh comes like wind blown. "Be a fighter-man."

IT STORMS IN the night, great billows of air pushed and rain. The shack sways from the onslaught, water dripping through eaves and reaching the floor in great plops. A splat hits his forehead. A screech owl clacks and barks.

"Man came up to me in the store yesterday," Tilda says. Their candle has been extinguished. He was not expecting words or speech. She touches his arm—something not done since his first days in the shack. "Asked about you, about Charlie."

He says nothing, waiting. The wind howls as if massed, venomous and made alive. He was thinking of his father, about the clipping of the governor that he saved so long ago. He had known it—she was right—without grasping things somehow, or maybe he had recognized it all along. His mother forsaken, saddled with his birth and oddness, the root of his suffering, his fury and his hopeless pain. He traces his anger from desertion and darkness to the stinking box, through guilt laid and his shaming to the breath whistled now past clenched teeth. He is his rage; there's no denying it, no other choices or paths to march down. Unable to turn this, he can spar and can act still, and isn't conflict a curing, and action really change?

"I didn't say nothin'," she continues. "But I think you best go."

He frowns through the darkness. Blood pounds his eyes and ears. He smells his own juices, tastes them and swallows, something before him that he's long sought and craved. Dreamed of. Feared. "Where would you suggest?"

There's a pause. The storm has calmed, drips now soft from trees, from the roof of the twisted shack to the ground. The first call of birds stirring, the wet, sweet smell. "Why, to the capitol, Johnny. That's where you need to be."

CHAPTER TWENTY-EIGHT

Doyle

"Where is Warren?"

The man, Monroe, shakes his head. "Don't know. No one's seen him since Friday."

Silence falls, an odd air in the room. Warren never strays far without telling me, like a dog that slinks home after his rutting and scouting, often showing up hungry, spiteful, and mean.

"He working on something?"

"The usual. Monitoring. That murder down in Arcadia. Sheriff dirty in Osceola. Mayor in Jacksonville has some lady issues. I don't think Warren was travelin'." He pauses, chewing a lip. "Oh, he asked me to look at hotels here for a strange bird: green eyes and a weird walk. But that's it."

Waves roll in my gut. Green eyes and a weird walk? Warren hasn't spoken to me of this at all, at least lately. Is he running some watch without sharing—luring or baiting or boosting, *right here in town*? I don't like things withheld. He should have told me what was happening, even his doubts or hunches, odd concerns. We've got enough surprises. When I find him, I'll jump him and wring his red, stubborn, stringy neck.

"Hell, in this state, everyone has a weird walk and is crazy." I wave Monroe off. I close my door to chew on this news some, to think and brood about things just a bit.

Warren and me go back a long ways, which explains (in part) why I keep him—this relic with one arm and bad skin and teeth, prone in addition to say vile or stupid things. There've been some embarrassments. Warren, though, is wholly loyal to me, and if I ask him to do something—no matter how foul or distasteful—he mostly gets it done. That's why this whole deformed-child thing is puzzling. Warren should have taken care of this years ago, told me he *had* taken care of it. A part of me thinks he's using it now in some blackmail. It could be; he could turn. I've seen things stranger. In this seat there are knives waving and poking from just about every hole. I prize loyalty over virtue, over brains or strength or anything else in addition, even the closeness of family, aides and colleagues, public pals and other kin.

I've always wondered if Warren had a thing for Lena. Lena Cruel—that was her name, or such is what she told me. I don't recall now how we met, only that she was a pretty, young country mare with an upturned nose and a syrup-thick Southern twang. This was at a time I ran on like a chased bandit, my stress seeking out release with money and autos, cheap booze, and cute girls. I can't claim today that I'm pleased or proud of it, but such is the drive God gives man: to live by eating and drinking, talking and laughing, fighting and lying and fucking and going home. The sap can get up in your brain some.

I remember Lena saying things like "I've never eaten in a restaurant" and "You mean you drive your own car?" She was fresh-faced and sweet-smelling, with a smile like a moon sliver and a body that made me ache. I remember her anger, hissing and snakelike when she found out I was married, a father as well to several little kids. I never hid this from my girlfriends, at least not that I recall, but I didn't broadcast it either; again, I don't count myself proud or glad. I assumed they all knew or would learn things soon enough, but Lena was so naive and country that she just didn't. The last time I saw her, there in my car outside the doorway of the F&T, she told me that she was pregnant, sweat bathing our faces like a dripping, cheerless rain. I tried to kiss her but she pulled away, got her finally to drink some killing stuff—this had worked in some cases but I guess didn't take with her. Did she believe we were getting married, that I was planning on dumping my family for her? The foolishness of people, the towers and fancies made. That's when Warren rolled into this wholesome and sanctified, Sunday-go-to-meeting mess.

Maybe he was there before with her, around her; my memory can sometimes fail. He was involved, though, for certain, in trying to run her down some years on, to find her once the child came, to pay her off or push her more. He told me at first she was missing, then that he'd found her and it was boxed up and handled, then that she was dead and it wasn't. The crazy story of a boy with wings made me think he was trying to get my goat up, having a laugh at old Doyle's expense—but Warren doesn't mess around much. That's what makes this thing all the stranger.

He told me he had an eye on it, that it was too hard to do much with the boy in this circus, that it wouldn't become a problem and the boy had no clue, at least about his father: me. He even gave me a show photo, and damn if there weren't a likeness, except of course for those strange and awful wings. I kept that picture awhile and then burned the thing. Why would I hold on to something nutty like that? I wondered if Lena hadn't tossed a hex out, and I prayed on it when I went to church, asking the Lord to forgive me, as I'm sure this was a godly scolding and payback for all my sins. I wanted Warren to make the whole thing go away.

It's later that afternoon when Connors, my chief of staff, enters. "Sir, Monroe needs to see you."

The old biddies I'm bumping gums with turn, heads bent like flowers—they're pushing more shrubbery along the roads in St. Pete. One of them smells like dead blooms herself; another keeps calling me "General." They have money, lots of it. "Now?" I ask Connors.

"Yes, sir. Indeed."

"Ladies, I'm sorry, but I'm going to have to break away. We'll look into this shortly—you heard them, Jim? I think we'll do something. We'll just have to see. It'll be nice down there, charming. You ladies have a pleasant day!" I exit to the anteroom to allow them time to leave, reenter when they've trundled out. Monroe is there when I'm back, along with Stevens and the Negro McDonald, the one with gray eyes. McDonald shuts the door with a click.

"We found Warren's body."

I lift my head.

"Stabbed to death."

The only noise is a whirring fan. Chatter from the street beyond us.

"Where?"

"Trash pile south of town."

"Who knows?"

They look one to the other. "Kid who found her. Police that were called."

"Press?" I clear my throat.

"Don't think so."

"Make sure, then. Go back to the police, tell the chief I'll have his balls if a word leaks. Nobody knows nothing on it, okay? Make sure even the kid that found it don't talk, the kid's family, brothers and sisters—shut them all up. Threaten 'em if you need to." I wave them out. "Stevens, stay."

The others turn and depart. Stevens is a tall man with an Adam's apple like a rock, his mouth a cut line, the faint trace of a mustache. The radio echoes from the adjoining room, a piano's thump and clink, sax and drums. "Any more to this?" I spread my hands. A strip shines on his jaw that he missed in his shaving.

"Not that I know of."

I turn to Connors at the side door. "He ain't got family to speak of, so nothing there. A woman? Jealous husband?" I turn back to Stevens. I know this isn't it.

He shrugs. "We can ask around."

"Don't. Any idea on what happened?"

"No more than what Monroe said the other day. Monitoring as usual. Told us to look for this weird guy. That's all I know."

"Keep looking for the weird guy. I want you around me like a glove, around my family. When we piss, you're splashed. Got it?"

Nodding.

"Where are we with the buzzer?" We had talked about getting a buzzer for my desk—something I could trigger if a problem cropped up, though the guards are but two doors down.

"They're putting it in tomorrow, Governor."

"Good. Don't let anyone in Warren's office or house. Connors will go through that. You get Warren's billfold, and knife?"

"Got his billfold—nothing missing that I could see. Money still there. His knife was gone, though."

I turn away.

I GO THROUGH Warren's office myself. Can't have some diary or notes or such found, though I doubt the man kept anything damning or detailed like that. Warren wasn't a writer or even much of a talker. Still, he might have kept files that could prove troublesome.

I don't find much of anything, which is odd in and of itself. The office is as clean as a convent. A calendar with a few marks on it but nothing noted on the day he died, pens and pencils and a spittoon he didn't use but no circus photos of a boy with spreading wings. Nothing much personal. I think about Warren as I sit quiet in his chair, wondering if I should go to his house or send someone there, trying to remember where he lived. Were we friends? Not quite friends—something more and less than that closeness. Most of my "friends" tend to want things from my office, but Warren never did. He only wished to be busy and needed, to be bound and kept close. To be taken care of, I suppose, though I've never thought of it that way. I can live without Warren—I pay for safety and guards—but there's something to having a history, and Warren could sometimes surprise me. I remember the one time I entered his office and found his eyes wet with tears, his face an odd clay color. I'd never seen Warren cry.

"What the hell's going on?" I asked him.

He just shook his head.

"You're crying for no reason in the middle of the day? You gotten soft?"

"Fuck you, Doyle. *Governor.*" Spit flew in streams.

"Come on, now, Warren." I tried to be softer. He'd worked for me twenty years by that point, and we'd picked each other off bar planks and seen our share of blood and whores. Saving and being saved, courting and dodging, finding our next beer and shot. Stumbling and correcting and explaining, moving on. "What is it?"

"Kid I know from back home. Lost his arm just like I did." He touched his desk and frog-gulped, his fingers out like he'd been stung. "He don't know what's in store now. God, Doyle, he don't know . . ." He near choked in saying this, the hate in his eyes—for me and my office, for everyone else—making me look away. His face had turned dim and ashy, like a long-dead wire and bulb. I thought to say more, as there ain't no use in moping, or so said my daddy. I left him instead and headed back out the door.

He didn't talk much on the arm, as I don't talk on things that don't need it neither. Warren could keep his mouth shut—a virtue in any man, or woman, for that matter—and he'd seen the low side of quite a number of spats, performed some dark and twisted deeds himself. Had he said anything of these to others? I end up having Stevens search his house; he finds nothing there—says the place was so clean looked like nobody ever lived a day in it. Sad, and a bit creepy. I had him comb the yard, also, but no lumps or buried things were unearthed, no clue or treasure. Just nothing much. I think on how skilled Warren was with that knife, of how it must have gone down at the end. On what I should have said to him, or maybe did say, or he said to me:

Stay on offense. Round the bases. Do what needs doing. Hit the fucking ball.

WELDON COMES BY that evening. My son is twenty-two and big like me, same nose, jaw, and hair. His mother's blue eyes rather than my green. Women crawl around him like flies, seeking his attention, and yet most of the time he seems not to care. He's plenty smart—the brain part of my family carried on down—but uninterested in hunting, gambling or sports, or even cars or games. I don't claim to understand it. His destiny and aim shine, though, better than mine did back then, so less crippled by flaw and booze, dolls and shame. He's the way and the light, the future, the fortune. The course and the certain plan to push us onward.

"Hey. What you doin'?"

Weldon is in college in Gainesville, all professors and books. Working new theories, stretching his mind. Sometimes he brings a passel of folks home, maybe for show or to build his base higher, but today it's just Weldon, which is fine with me. I can't hardly see or hear him without my heart bursting out with pride: I want to touch him, to weigh and to judge things, to listen to the sound of his voice that's near mine. It's not the same with his mother or sister, though I love and care for them very much—it's just him; him and me. Something passed straight on down. Life, I guess. I can't name or explain it.

"Thought I'd come home. What you doin'?"

I spread my hands. "Same as always. Dealing with dopes. How is school?"

"Good." He smiles slowly. His face is older in a pleasing way. "I'm taking this religion class I really love. Dr. Edwards. Makes you think a lot."

"Oh? What you thinkin'?" I lean myself back. The radio plays "One O'Clock Jump" in the other room. There's the smell of baking bread. "You want a drink?"

"No thanks." He doesn't drink like I did or do. I watch for signs of it. Another thing that makes me pleased and proud.

"I . . . I wanna talk with you about something."

I feel the smile freeze on my face. "Sure!" Here it comes: pregnancy, maybe death. Madness. Money needs. I'm a goddamn veteran.

"This class has made me think about whether I have a callin', a callin' to go into the ministry. I think I might."

"The ministry?" Music continues from the side room, the horns, the beat and swing—"Goodnight, My Love." I should turn it all off.

"Yeah. I wanna help people find the light. I wanna help 'em think, and see."

He's so pure, so young! Again, my heart floats, my mind seized in the largeness of my love and trust. Things are what they are and not what we might wish them, but he doesn't yet know this, his virtue fresh and rare. Everyone wants to believe, I've discovered; everyone wants to claim that they're free. There is plenty of time still for him to learn and to know things, for the snag of reality to rear its slimy head. Whatever most folks want is what we do in this country—it's really quite simple. There are winners and losers, commerce. It's the only way.

I think to say this and steer things back to the warped, rough world, but I won't be my father; I'll give ground and listen and let bubbles burst themselves. He shouldn't bear my grand mistakes. "Well, if that's what you truly want," I tell him. "Take your time to think it all through, and make sure you're certain. Things can change fast—you'll see this as you're older—but if that's what you end up doing, then be the very best." I think of the old man with his cane, riding me always to measure up, perform and fight, to climb hills and rule things. Hissing into my ear once, "There's no pride in weakness." Summoning me into his office, his face white and cold, the rage at my wrongs pushed him-to-me like a summer storm. The women I claimed then. The battles. The ministry.

"I see myself preaching."

He goes on to explain this, but my mind has run afield, to the grace of this child and his half sibling the freak—the one so right and normal, the other marred and cursed. I think on Anna as well, Weldon's sister, so pure, and even Elizabeth, my lovely wife. Such good stock there and lineage! Would I let a monster destroy this? I envision the press corps, their tongues out like dogs, the news and hurt to my family, the harm then and damage done. Shielding; isn't shielding love? I ponder what this Johnny—is that even his name?—must now want: money, no doubt, but also exposure and care, acceptance and payback. My crash and destruction on top of that. He is without doubt a madman, a murderer. The thought sends a chill crawling up my back, spine to crown.

"I think God is leading me to this," Weldon continues, "just like He led me here. I really believe so, Pop. It's like a message and vision. I think I can really do something good."

I'm damp from my sweating, my hand running through my hair. "I love you," I blurt out, something my pop never told me. "Follow the star that leads you, then lead folks yourself. Goodness can come in different ways, different places. See that you make it happen! Do what needs doin'. Don't stall."

He stands and we hug, me gripping his shoulders. "The wonderful thing about Christ," I say, my patter returned now, my voice deepening and rich, "is that he died for all sinners. That's what's got us down here yet." I lift my head. "That's how we've gone this far."

DAYS PASS, WEEKS, a month with nothing happening—nothing with the winged boy, that is. There's plenty going on, what with the coloreds and the press and the growers and bad economy, and some say Europe will be at war soon. Long-faced men and dirty kids still clog our streets. The do-gooders push their dreams. There's brief talk of me and the presidency, a story of my taking on Roosevelt when he fails, and of course I deny interest, as I'm focused only on the state. (Did Weldon see this? I should call or wire him. A lie is a lie is a lie, until it's not.) If the old man were alive and his business still flush, he'd fund this run for glory, or maybe he wouldn't; who can say for sure?

I relax the guards. Maybe Warren was killed by a vagrant or something otherwise random or removed occurred. I've been minding my manners, staying off booze and away from other temptations, though I stumbled once when a woman insisted I screw her atop the state seal. I ended up bending her over my desk instead. I don't apologize for being male; I am what God made me. At least my door still double-locks.

When Weldon asks me to accompany him to church, I go praying for mercy, for God to see the good I've done and the great freedoms kept, to hear my promises that if saved I won't fail Him. I smile at Elizabeth and the kids after my petition, reminding the Lord that there's a noble side to me too. I renewed the contract with the Division of the Blind at the capitol, for example—something I could have revoked, but I feel for the poor and unlucky; I won't be outflanked by my noble and selfless son.

I saw a hunchbacked girl mopping last week, ugly as sin and purblind as a newborn, and thought the angels in heaven should be dancing and pleased. No one can say that Governor Doyle lacks compassion or kindness, or feels no mercy or pity. I've never intentionally been mean. The Lord's light can certainly shine straight through me.

CHAPTER TWENTY-NINE

He's never been inside a church. He's seen photos and movies and imagined himself attending, even planned to go once with Zorat—a country church in a country town—but never did. He's wondered what he would feel if he did go, whether something would strike and mark him for good or bad, but as he crosses the threshold into the First Baptist Church, he feels neither awe nor any great reverence, nothing transforming, no broad shift or change. He wears a gray suit coat, bulked to hide his bound wings, a tie knotted the best he can. His head is near shaved, with glasses clamped on his face, though not the dark ones he wears at work, the pretense made there. Not the wig or the heavy, shapeless dress.

He can't say quite how he got here or how the job at the capitol came to be. Tilda took him to Crawfordville to meet a man, and in the back of a dingy stable he was given clothes and told to see a Mr. Finn at an address in Tallahassee. There he found a large house with a black man in the doorway, directing him down a hallway to what seemed a secret room: a hidden door down to a cellar, damp-smelling but clean, with electric lights, a shower and toilet. Thoughts sprang up quick of a box buried underground, but he kept his head up and his neck moving, his thoughts steered afar. He tossed the knife at a board propped against the farthest wall: thunk and click, pull. Step. Thunk and click. Clothes were provided and food and drink brought, and the man told him to see a woman, Millie, at Blind Services. Johnny failed to understand.

"What am I to do?" he asked.

"Whatever they tell you." Finn was neither young nor old, his head almost completely bald, only a hint of eyebrows. His ears hung like feathers. "Edna will help you get dressed."

He didn't grasp this either. Edna was the young woman, the girl, who brought him food. One afternoon—or was it night? he's unsure—she brought in a box and asked him to take his shirt off. Hesitant and shaking somewhat, he did so, keeping his back from her, his wings hanging loose and free. She bid him turn and he did this, quivering as she began to bind him, slowly and better than he could have done himself. When she finished, she turned him again and pulled a large cloth from the box, something else with it: a brassiere. She half smiled.

"Put it on."

"Why?" He took steps back. He would not be pulled into some silly dress-up. The object in her hands looked like a bridle, or handcuffs.

Head back, her teeth showed. She looked eighteen or near it, her frame small and deerlike. She handed him dark glasses too. "Your disguise."

He did as she asked. The brassiere felt odd, and he was awkward with it and clumsy. She ended up strapping it underneath his wings. The dress was hung on top of him like a blanket.

"Take your pants off."

He did, fumbling beneath the great tent-dress. She pulled something else from the box, bunched up and stringy; it looked like the end of a mop. She shook it out with one hand, viewing it.

"What is this?"

"This your wig."

"What?" He gulped and went mutely along, thinking it all mad and foolish, that he could never pass as a blind person, a *woman* of all crazy things, but it worked. No one regarded him more than they would a blank wall, ignoring or stepping around him as he found his way to the office that this Millie ran. Millie wore dark glasses like his, holding things at odd angles with her head tipped in different ways, speaking as if looking somewhere to his left. He was assigned to another woman, Frida, short and plump and of uncertain age, who moved in a waddle and spoke with a hiccupping accent.

"We clean," she said, handing him rags as they pushed a cart down the hallways in their dresses made to deflect any mark or stare. He felt on edge and self-conscious, but hadn't he known fraud and hoaxes for the whole of his freakish life? A performer again now, an actor and trickster, he waited for men to see through his deceit, to clamor and call him out with a laugh, but no one did. No one looked. He saw himself performing, like Zorat and Boris, Sheila, Alfred, and Tot. He was Cletus, and Wilma; he was even glum and spiteful Kip. The wig made him sweat, and he kept wanting to scratch with or rub it or doff it like a hat. Men gave him the widest of wide hallways berths.

Today, though, he is bareheaded, his face cool as he scans the church. He expected to be challenged on entering, to be stopped and questioned and held, but no one pays him attention here either; he's a ghost stooped and entering the hall. An older man greets him and hands him a paper program; another escorts him, turning and gesturing to suggest a filling row. Here there are benches—pews—with odd buttoned cushions, shelves built in seat backs holding hardbound books. He assumes these are Bibles, touching one as he moves sideways past, feeling the binding, the pages.

Down front is a platform, people in robes seated on it, and above this, on the wall, a giant golden cross. An organ plays softly and speech is in whispers, a laugh muffled here and there, quiet motions, smiles. He follows a man and his wife down the row, women behind him and each settling in with care, hands crossed and heads up. He meets no one's eyes. Velvet ropes reserve several open pews before him, and he knows that these must be for the governor and his group. Separating them, marking. A child cries and is shushed. The organ stops and starts with a rumble, a dark and whistling hiss.

He bows and waits, fingering the knife's crease and outline in the pocket of his suit. His wings brush the seat back so that he sits straight as he watches; halos formed by the glasses bring a sharp and steady glare. Counting the rows, he's some ten in back, easily close enough to do what he must, to confront and connect things, to strike now and start anew. The church smells of old paper, tobacco, and stale perfume; women's hats are like gumdrops bobbing before him and to his sides.

With a turn he scans escape routes, knowing that flight is doubtful, with legs to trip over and a sprint needed to the door. He finds that he cares little about this, regardless. He no longer cares about himself at all. The murdered Charlie keeps coming back, blood foaming and death-sprayed, standing again on the truck beneath the dreadful tree. The put-downs of the hotel guests; the words of the man who picked him up from the side camp. "You with a bunch of niggers, boy." Taken, from Elias and from Mama Lo, traded and sentenced, tossed and sent from the show now to . . . here. He's an outcast, a stranger. His hate is so clean and pure. No Negroes are to be seen anywhere in the church, only shuffling white people, upright in their sureness, worshipful masks stretched across old, hollowed bones. Under a cross and belief in forgiveness, that blanket of license given to a button-downed, silent sea.

A rustling in the crowd alerts him, an usher leading a group up front: a young man and girl with a middle-aged woman behind them, followed by a burly man. Johnny's heart jumps at sight of this, his hand scrabbling to the knife, and he notes things and studies them: the men and their common build; the balanced and trim female shapes; the clothes that look new and fitting; the hair neatly combed and trimmed. The response and acceptance of the group by the crowd— the turning and nodding, repositioning. Admitting in. The son sits next to his father, the daughter opposite, and the woman—slow and more regal—to her side. His relations, Johnny thinks: His half family. His blood and kin. His father at last, real and near touchable, present and seated before him after all these years.

The organ stops and people shuffle, then stand. A robed man enters from the platform's side, followed by others who take seats behind him. As the one man bows in prayer, other heads drop in rhythm, though Johnny's gaze remains fixed and up, eyeing the spot where he'll lodge the blade, seeing the knife flung, twirling, shiny and swift. He examines each detail: the ears so like his own, the dense hair with waves to it, the sameness of movements, the jaw at a turn of head. Would his body thicken in this way, like his father's? The blood through his veins is its own beast in its raging, but his hands and his breathing remain steady and calm. He is certain of his aim and skill. After the prayer, a hymn starts with the organ, the choir up and singing and his mind on his goal and plan: He is muscle and impulse, reflex and pattern; intent filed and hardened, all doubt long since quelled. The choir sits and a man stands, reading words from the Bible, one of the Psalms, the word "joy" launched and sticking—Johnny's thoughts on the camp and Elias, the men and the chain, the fire and what followed, Warren's arm. Winifred calling and calling. The Windsor and Charlie's death.

He switches grips on the knife, picking it up with his fingers, but before he can stand and hurl it, the son reaches an arm across his father's large shoulder, obstructing the target. This halts him mid-crouch and returns him to sitting, those around him now looking, his heart beating in his teeth. The son pulls his arm away, but by then folks are standing, heads blocking the knife's path, and when they sit the son's arm again thwarts his plan. Johnny's mind, his skin, even his bones thump and spasm; his body is one big, bloody pulse. The promise—the old promise!—of everything beyond ekes and trickles out, even as luck deals its hand and spews fresh unfairness, foiling him, blocking. The rapture lost, the knife's plunge before and the blood . . . He breathes quieting words ("You are unseen still. Remain patient, calmed!"), repeating these to accept them, the belief that his time will yet come, that there will be other chances; closure and wholeness and endings still loom.

Leaving the church, his hand aches from the tight grip, his wrist trembling and weak. Liquid drips that he knows is his bleeding, proof of loss and frustration, his only cut being of himself. The sting of his ruin and failure near blinds him, the drain of waiting and folly, of rout, defeat. He bites down till new blood flows. He tilts his head.

There will be no turning back.

HE LEARNS THE capitol's spaces, its corners, ins and outs: the senate chambers and house, the basement with its greasy lunchroom, the upstairs with the governor's rooms. The clanking doors of the elevator the cleaners are told they may not use. A little man named Herbert operates this with a duck and pull: "Hello, Senator!" "Good day!" He knows all their names. Johnny knows no one save for the few women he works with: Frida and Harriet, sometimes a girl, Sally Rose. They call him Claire Louise. No coloreds are seen in the capitol, not even to clean or to serve, and he finds himself in a familiar position, different and the same as at the Windsor Hotel: separate, alone. This time as a woman, one of the few inside the dome, and he hears the jeers and the scorn flung their way, the complaints that they've taken what should have been the jobs of men. Erased now as a person, he is ignored and newly masked, and is it better, this being unseen? People can be smug and blind.

He sees the governor only twice, and then from a distance, men gathered about him like clouds circling the sun, the fog and smell of cigar smoke made thick. Johnny empties the ashtrays and takes out the cups and garbage, sweeps and mops the old floors, even wipes the sinks and commodes, none of which he minds much. He cleans the governor's rooms too, noting the assorted contents: the desk with its leather top and large chair; the portrait (of whom?) behind this; the doors to the toilet and side room, all of them with locks that work. There's a smell to the place of old smoke and coffee, and despite the color of pictures, its appearance is stale and grim. Was it all just a dream—Tilda and Tot and the whole of it? He wipes the desk, checking the garbage and toilet, behind the drapes and in the cubbyholes on the shelves, and what does he seek or expect to find there? He scans the photos of children and the same glowing woman—his stepmother, smiling—his vision blurring so that he must focus in on her again.

These are mere strangers, grouped in a show and on another world and stage, living their lives, busy and normal and pleased-looking, comely. He tries imagining himself in the photos, his mother too, but he can't, as even the attempt brings a jolt to his chest: to call a life forth then, to insert, replace; to wipe away pain, time, and death in a cleansing eyeblink.

One evening as he and Frida are cleaning, several men burst into the governor's rooms. One holds a cigar, its black odor biting, another a glass with liquid near its brim. A third peers inside, then ducks out again in a flourish, Frida lifting her head up, as she sees so little. "I am so sorry," she says in her accent. She turns to Johnny. "We leave now, yes?"

"Stay!" the fatter of the two roars, loosening his tie as if unhitching a horse. The other, younger and balder, jerks his head in a rhythm. "The governor will be along in a minute. We got us a party coming on strong!" The fat one's face is the color of beefsteak, his neck swollen like a ham. The other one laughs with his head tilted backward, his row of teeth shortened, ears a fevered red.

Frida turns, unsure of the fat man's direction, bumping him crossways with her side as she moves. In a quickness he grabs her, swinging her about in a slow, swirling dance, spinning her out even on his arm in the swaying. The sack dress she wears is barely rippled by this.

"Hey, here we go!"

Frida gasps without protest, her face with neither shock nor fear; maybe she's used to such excess and freedoms. The other man grabs Johnny's rump as he waits, prompting a whirl and strike at the hand,

Johnny's fear more for his wings than for his pride or bottom. His breath, though, skips and rises, his face growing hot and wet, one hand to the knife strapped in a sheath against his leg. The man reels away from him, his breath like an open sewer.

"Damn, now. Don't get all haughty!"

"Kind of an ugly one, eh?" The cigar paints the air. "Frida, where'd you find her at?"

Frida half giggles, her glasses slipped low, her eyes beneath small and blinking and pinkish. She's sitting astride the fat man, held but not straining, her face caught in a look somewhere between sanction and dismay. Johnny scowls and says nothing, as he speaks in whispers when at work, knowing his voice would quickly unveil him. Frida assumes he's mute. Sometimes she points, as though he can't hear what she's saying.

"Leave her alone, now," Frida tells them. "She's new and doesn't know of your madness. She's still so young."

The door opens again, admitting the governor into this speech and now-stilled room. He scans them in sequence, his satchel placed slowly down, a grin pushing lips and cheeks. Up close and frontal, again Johnny sees their likeness, and at this glimpse he ducks, concerned that his eyes—though mostly shielded—will betray him yet. For long seconds no one speaks. Footsteps echo far back down the hall. There's the sound of ice shifting, a clock's ticking, wheezing. Johnny glances from eye corners, his breath sharp and quick, his face tilted slightly, his head still angled down.

"What we got on?" asks the governor, hands up and tongue tip out. "The old hanky-panky? Or maybe it's the hokey pokey. We don't allow that stuff here."

The two men snort and chuckle. Frida offers a head-turned grin.

The governor stretches, his eyes dark and bottle green. "Come on, boys, let's get back to work for a minute. You can visit with these two later, I'm sure. We got to act fast 'fore wigs are blown off down the hallway."

"Sure do, Gov. You've pegged it just right." The fat one turns to Frida. "Y'all come back and carouse a bit, hear? Give us an hour to get the state all worked up! We'll need a release then, a reversal. I'll be out there and lookin'!"

Johnny turns and walks out, careful to slow himself, keeping his back lifted and true. He passes his father but feels the other's gaze, and when he turns, the governor is rooted, staring straight at him as if at something known but strange. Is this it? He'll be caught now for certain, the men stripping and thrashing him like a dog, but Frida blocks his view and pulls the door shut as she leaves. His hands flap and shake, his pulse still jumped and quickened, and he waits for the door to open and an assault to burst forth. Instead, Frida follows him down the hallway pushing her noisy cart, one wheel catching and sticking so that it skids and thumps. When they're yards away and around a corner, he stops.

"Is it like this all the time?" he whispers, his mind running as he asks, a train carrying his thoughts fast. Only madness could grind his hate to this fine point. Nothing would please him more than a knife run through that sturdy neck.

She looks up in surprise. "Yes." She dips her head as though afraid to admit to it. "We put up with so much. I want to kill them—I do. All the time, yes. Almost every one."

IT'S A FEW days later that he finds himself working alone, Frida having taken sick. He sweeps the hallway near the governor's rooms, preparing to mop when the others have gone, and is it fate that draws him or courage, curiosity or merely chance? He knows that if he doesn't act soon, he won't. Heart thundering and back bent, he turns the doorknob, expecting to find it locked but it's not, expecting to be challenged—but no one waits beyond; the office is empty and dark. He leaves his broom propped outside it.

He stands in the larger room, spinning about in a circle, taking it in again, breathing the cool, stale air. The photos ensnare him, the letters and trophies placed in order on shelves, and he locks the side door and sits in the governor's large chair, listening and thinking and sighing and looking on. How did this happen? He feels no pride, sees in the photos of his siblings little that he wants to share. The knife binds his leg as he sits, and he touches it, gently, listening for footsteps, but he is caught up in another world. For an instant he is Boris, preparing his knives, or Alfred, trusting in life and aim, or even Tot, barking her summons to everyone to come inside. The odor of an oily spittoon lifts his head. When the door opens and a man enters, Johnny has only just risen from behind the great desk, no fear clouding his vision, no tremor now in his hands. What will happen will happen. His heart has returned, on its own, to his chest.

The governor's head tilts partway down, so that at first he sees no one, locking the door firmly behind him with a click. When he turns there's a widening of his eyes but that's all; he stands straight with his hand open, his frame bearishly large and still. "Hello," he says, in a voice neither warm nor cold, his face only questioning, as if asking directions or the hour of the afternoon.

Johnny doesn't respond, only blinks, and stares. Slowly he removes the glasses, pulls away, too, the clownish wig. He places them both on the desktop, still without speaking, without motion made or other act. His hand rubs through his hair. His father advances but slows to a stop now before him, his jowls with a flush to them, his green eyes calm and clear. Music from somewhere dips and ends, a brief trilling.

"So," says the governor. "After all this time. Or maybe during all this time." He points to the wig and the glasses. "You needn't have hid."

"Is that so?" His voice is steady, soft. He glances downward. "I've never been much good at hiding." He gives a shrug, and a pause follows. "Here I am." The knife remains on his leg; he must bend to retrieve it. The governor eyes his movement, the wig, his dress, the desk.

"What do you want from me?" asks his father. "Before this whole thing falls to dust. Before you're removed and taken away from here. You were with your own people. Why couldn't you stay where you were?" He lifts his hands. "Live your life, just as I live my own?"

"Live my life." Johnny unhooks the dress, pulling it over his head so that he stands in his underclothes, wings bound behind him. Sweat cools on his legs. His blood isn't throbbing like it was at the church; he's not heated or ruffled. The governor, meanwhile, creeps a step or two closer, near enough now for scars to line up on his forehead, his cologne and tobacco scent to roll forth in a wave.

The big man smiles. "Let's talk this through, shall we? I'm sure we can work something worthy out. We can make up for things—for time, so much time—and our lack of contact, our distance that's been so great. We can find things to be done. It's just so strange and all, now: you in your world and me here in mine, each of us moving down our separate paths. But that's the way life can be. That's the way things simply are."

He cranes to take in Johnny's back, a bird lifting its neck or a horse dipped in drinking, curious despite everything. "Good lord above." His head turns as if shaken. "We . . ." He pauses, his voice deep. "We'll have you studied, and assessed—why, you can be a boon to science! Like the dead bodies probed, or a weapon—a great weapon! There will be conflict, war. Your country will need you, require you, the government and the Army, the state."

He bends and swallows, his eyes gone big and soft. His face is awash in a shimmer of tenderness, in what could only be wonder, or maybe sweet regret. "Look, I made mistakes. I did some things I shouldn't have. I was young, and it's the way I grew up, the way my father shaped me, the way the South fashioned us one and all. I'm a sinner, I am—a man. I admit it. I was deceitful, pigheaded, and just plain damn wrong." He turns, brashly and doglike, near friendly, kind. "Now, though, things are different. Why, you can join us and be part and a key to things! We'll be one big . . . outfit and family. A wonderful grouping! A special team." His nose is up, preparing, resolving. "There's a spare room in my house. We'll get you help and a car, a real job, a profession. Is that what you want, John? We'll get you a servant, some funds, and a pretty girl . . ."

Johnny says nothing. The knife is pressing and fiery, burning his leg so that he must turn and shift his weight. He can almost *believe*, almost persuade himself. Acceptance—isn't it all he wants? The light in the room changes from plum to golden pink.

"Here, let me touch . . ." His father grasps Johnny's arm but at the same time bears down on it with all of his weight, his son's wrist snapped as cleanly as a bough broken from a tree. The noise is a rifle shot, the hurt fierce and immediate. The governor twists and holds on then, teeth bared as if biting, as if defending his castle by the strength of his massive jaws, his grip that of one drowning or dangling out on the steepest ledge. Johnny bends in his torment, his own teeth clenched, his free hand in his father's hair. His arm—his throwing arm—feels unhooked and severed, his mind clouding and spinning from the ferocity of the pain and shock.

"Did you think you would walk in and ruin me, take my family? After all this time, all my work and achievement? What did you expect would happen, huh? Tell me this! What did you plan you would do?" His face hangs pink over Johnny's, his mouth a line curling up to his ear. His breath and skin feel seared, aflame. "If you want me to tell you I love you, I don't. It's simple, really: I don't know you or want you or wish to know of you at all. That harlot of a mother . . ." He tosses his head at the photos, his eyes wide and marble green. "It's about them, see. It's not you and me; it was never about you—that would have been impossible." He laughs, the sound bright and thunderous. "Just *absurd!*" His face twists and straightens, his chest up and back as he takes in new air. "Those ridiculous wings," he begins, before a shiver sweeps him to a stop in his speech. "I could make myself sick."

He presses a button alongside the big desk, and in the move Johnny wrenches his arm away, freed but flooded in even more crippling pain. His wrist forlorn in its wilting, the hurt dimming his vision as the fake glasses had, he retrieves the knife, but the desk is again between them. The governor is yelling, his voice like a ringing bell, his neck taut and face red: "Help! There's an intruder! Guards! I need my guards! Now, you fucking bastards! Get in here now, quick!"

Working the knife with his good hand, Johnny cuts the brassiere and his bindings, his wings swinging down free, unrestrained. Knocks sound at the door, frantic twists of the door latch, the distant shouts of hoarse men: "Open up! Hey, come on!" Now at the side door, pounding and thumping along with his heartbeat, the aching and throbbing of his mangled wrist. He springs but his father ducks, the desk kept between them, the older man's eyes wide and white now more than green, froth pushed out and filmy along his ample lips. Switching hands with the knife, Johnny no longer feels it, his right hand so numbed, his mind searching out paths: his once-clear intentions, his unfinished plan. His life and his wrath, that steady companion, bound and held in a box for so long, belonging to nothing, to no one, chained to him.

His throat has gone dry, his face warm and moistened, the pain like a beating drum, but he sees. The governor has quit all his shouting, though his mouth still fills with words, snarled now and near senseless: "Help, Warren, you sandman. Don't. Cross and cruel, fuck. The lies. Robbery, I tell you! My thieving God . . ."

An axe slams, the door splintering wood and latch like a bomb burst. From dulled fingers Johnny throws the knife, the pain so sharp that it buckles him, but the blade sails, shining and catching his father in a meaty forearm, pinning him to the back wall. Johnny's vision falls to pounding, sickening, thick grayish shades. The governor whirls and wails, trying to pull the knife or his arm away, but he can't, flapping and twisting, bent before turning back. Mouth open and wordless, his eyes blink like the dummy Cletus: up and then down; down and then up; held for long, slow, heavy beats.

Johnny plucks a letter opener off the desk and advances, blurred eyes blinking fast, pointing the opener at his father's sweating, heaving chest. There's silence and breathing, flutters and swinging of the unpinned arm and fist, a moan bespeaking pain or anger or relief. Sounds of the men still bunched and pushing at the shattered door. In a rush the governor's bladder and bowels release, the sound and smell of this thrust drawing memory: Charlie on the truck bed; the smell of burned flesh; the stink as the knife pierced Warren's heart and chest. His own foulness in the box. "Coward," he cries or half thinks he says this, the filth of life on him, the core of pitiable and helpless man.

For a long time—so it seems—he waits, eye to eye, breath on breath, but the rage from before can't be reclaimed or brought forth, the warmth and aid gone of Warren's bracing, spurting blood. He drops the thin blade and pries open a window. The door is now broken and others rush in, shouting and pointing, the sounds lost in the air. Blood drips and falls, his father flailing and screaming. Johnny tastes salt and dirt. To one side a black man with gray eyes stares, his look strangely of resignation, as if he'd expected this always or seen it all posed and staged before.

EPILOGUE: 1939

The train stops on the way into the city, a platform outside with people standing about, and he realizes after a time that they're watching a performance: a priest or magician conjuring or making something disappear. The man, clad in a dark suit and neither young nor old, bearded and stooped some, motions and directs the focus of his viewers, pulling ribbons from sleeves, a bouquet of flowers, and finally, just as the train shifts, a small white dove. Those gathered applaud, a few on the train clapping too, heads turned before the engine fires and the car creaks and lurches. The man gives the smallest of bows. Quickly he is out of view.

Johnny leans sideways in his seat, careful of his wrist that still aches when a storm blows, of his wings held firm beneath his coat. Their heaviness is harder to shield and to hide now, bunching his shoulders and pinching his neck and back. He wears a businessman's outfit: a suit and tie and sturdy shoes, though he keeps on his overcoat, using its weight and bulk as a cover. It all makes him sweat, so that he prefers wind and coldness, keeping the window open when others would desire it closed; he will close it if asked, if things get too loud or smoky, and today with a rain coming, he pulls it shut. The car is soon cramped, airless. Confined. He always takes the window seat.

The man to his side is about his age, well dressed and inquisitive-looking, no paper or book apparently brought with him to read. Johnny tries to ignore him, twisting his body in an attempt to deter speech, but something in the man's posture says that he likes to chat.

The pomade on his hair smells like fruit, and Johnny eyes him without seeming to, noting the polished shoes, the Windsor knot, the neat, pinkish-white nails. Perhaps he should pretend to fall asleep, feign illness, scowl or offer up a snide or harsh complaint. It isn't that he dislikes people, or that he hates any conversation, but he talks so much each day—questions and answers and defenses and statements—that by the end he wants silence. Today, he won't get this.

"Say, that's a fine coat." The young man leans forward.

Johnny half turns. He won't permit himself rudeness. "Thank you."

"Are you in business?"

"Sort of. You?"

"Oh, yes. I'm in sales. Well, that and manufacturing. I'm with Kingsley Munitions." A card is produced in a dramatic thrust, held between middle fingers.

Johnny takes and studies it. "I see."

"What do you do?" The man's eyes are bright, birdlike.

"I work with people trying to get on their feet. I try to help them find jobs."

"Oh. Are you with the church?"

"No." A pause. "The government."

The man coughs and shifts. The train passes another, a furious clacking sound made and gone. "Is it a success, what you do? I mean, are you able to help them?"

Johnny smiles, his neck back on his collar. "Sometimes."

"Are they grateful? I mean, when you help them."

Grateful. Not often. People want so much. "At times, I guess."

A beat lifts and falls. The box of their seating pulls them closer and tighter. "It looks bad now in Europe," the man says, as if he planned this statement, his voice loud and rushed. "Don't you think so? Hitler's in Austria now, and they say he may well go on. I say I'm glad we're over here!" He barks a brief laugh. Sends another cough. "I hope we stay out of it. Let them carve themselves up if they want; it doesn't involve us." He bends his legs and recrosses them, scissorlike, seemingly wanting to fight or to argue, or for Johnny to speak up now and agree. The man would take yes as a prize for his effort, or take no as a challenge. Veins in his neck stretch and tense, pulled like strings.

"Maybe you're right; I guess I don't know. But the world is so full of hardship and strangeness. It's hard to run far from things; I suppose I've learned that much. Maybe it's why I do what I do."

"And what is it you do again?"

The talk persists. By the time the train hits Penn Station, Johnny's face and neck have grown sore from his listening, his expressions of interest, his respect shown and tact. His wings cramp against the seat. The young man offers his hand as the train stops, the brakes like screams.

"Great talking to you. I'm Stan Waldrop. Good luck with your men!"

His men. "Nice talking to you too, Stan." He stands with care. He starts to add his own name, but Stan has waved and now left him. The brown bottoms of shoes flap in short, rapid steps. He is alone, again.

Johnny queues and waits, trudging into the bustle of the crowded terminal, its sounds and echoes, features and familiar smells. Even underground, his anonymity is pleasing, the hundreds or thousands who care nothing about his back or what his troubles might be, and he has rounded a turn for his next train when a figure begging blocks his path. He strides closer without plan or desire, as he always gives if requested: He figures it's the least he can grant or do. This woman—he assumes it's a woman—is hideously deformed, her head under a scarf and scars or growths welting her face and neck, so that her mouth is hard to determine. A cup moves below her like a snake. He places coins in and she speaks, a moan of thanks or perhaps a nod to her suffering, and he is standing again to move on when something stalls him—he can't say what. She keeps trying to say something he doesn't understand, her disease or disfigurement affecting her mouth and her speech, and she digs in a bag at her side as he watches, signaling him somehow that she wishes him not to leave. Pigeons nearby flap, disturbed in their shelter;

people shuffle, incurious, herdlike, at ease. Turning and producing a paper, the woman holds it fluttering before him, to where he perceives it and knows it: his own photo from the show.

He starts in acknowledgment, a churn in his gut at being found now, a defensive smile formed as he stares at the image. He was so small then, so young! It was another life or state or world. He realizes that she is speaking again or trying to, and rather than deny it, he sighs, his wings strained against the leather bindings behind him. Never to escape, even after all this time. Still sought out and searched for. All these fateful years.

"Honey!" she says, or another thing like this, and again there's awareness, an echoing something drifting from the past. Something warped, perhaps, changed, and a chill sweeps up through him, down his wings to his neck and out to his arms and legs. He recognizes now what she's saying: "Johnny."

The photo waves more, his wings waggling in time with it. Sweat coats his back. Who is this person who knows him, knows his name? Someone more than a watcher, he thinks—more than an obsessed, freak-haunted, simply nostalgic fan. Someone wanting a job, maybe, but he can offer no job to her. Maybe someone from the governor . . .? He keeps expecting to be tracked or captured, detained.

She tries to say more, but he still can't understand her. He thinks to smile and move past, as what can he do or say to ease her pain? To acknowledge her, or him, or the truth of an exploitation? This is America, darling. This is the wise and blessed world. She shifts and clucks as if in dry agreement. A single dulled curl pokes from beneath her scarf, escaped.

Breath sounds and leaves him. His lips won't form shapes or words. He takes in the air's moistness, grinds his teeth front to back to front. Finally: "Winifred?"

She nods with a shaking.

"My dear God. I thought . . . I thought you died in the fire, at the show! I-I saw you on a gurney. Your hair . . ." His voice won't continue. "I can't believe . . ." He shivers and staggers, his arm out, legs braced. "This can't be."

She shakes her head with her mouth open, one or two teeth hung like bats inside a cave. Her face is the texture of clay poked with a stick, lines running through it and edges wrapped and laced. She dips again in her bag, pulling out pad and pencil, writing out something on this with a clawlike, scaly hand.

"I survived."

"But how? Where have you been all this time?"

She writes more. "It's been hard. Mother died two years back, and I've been on my own ever since." She shrugs and turns, something of the way she did back before, back in the show days. Her voice squeaks and caws, a bit more understandable: "I'm a fighter, Johnny. I'm still here."

His head tilts to the ceiling. He kneels and takes her in his arms. Dimly he's aware of passersby staring, people observing and stopping, holding up others. Moving on. His face rubs on skin that is hard and misshapen, his lips pressed on the contours of her creased and ravaged cheek. One of her eyes is twisted down and nearly shut. He tastes salt that he assumes must be her tears.

She writes more: "I didn't think I'd ever see you."

He responds: "I never dreamed . . ."

Then they say nothing, only holding and rocking, releasing and re-embracing. Her arms that are scars on scars. Her scabby face.

Writing, understanding: "I'm sure that I now repulse you."

Memory catches and gleams: her curls and smile before and her body, the guilt and pain he pulls on like a pair of pants. He looks away, his gaze back on the photo—his smooth child-face, the oversized, phony wings—and he laughs, long and loud and without curb or shame to it. Again, people stop, staring and crowding. Skirting, avoiding.

She writes once more. "You need to catch your train."

He takes his coat off and his shirt, dropping these in clumps below him. With his fingers he loosens the bindings, shaking himself once, arching his neck and back like a bow. A murmur comes slowly, a doubt or a judgment, a few gasps and calls as there'd been once before. "Is this a show of some kind?" someone asks. A response: "It's New York." There's a handclap. A muttering. Bodies turned and pressed, to know, to see.

He glances around at the throng, the eyes shifting, bent faces. Through a gap the sky gleams blue past the terminal, its stripes like wet paint shining dark through rough clouds. A breeze swirls and stirs. Doors clank, slap and fold. He pulls himself up and strides about like he used to, thrusting his wings like feathered swords or great scepters, swirling them, swinging them, a dancer unveiling a giant, living, flapping fan. People give way, figures shift and twist, duck. A woman shouts, "They're not real!" A man groans, a child shrieks. "Oh, my God!" someone yells. Hands stroke and grab him. Something sharp pricks his back.

Coins fall into Winifred's cup like warm rain.

THE END

ACKNOWLEDGMENTS

I've thought about, begun to write, stopped, and restarted this novel over many years. Along the way, I've been influenced by a number of works, including the 1932 Tod Browning film *Freaks*, the 1947 (Edmond Goulding) and 2021 (Guillermo del Toro) versions of *Nightmare Alley*, the documentary *Side Show: Alive on the Inside* (Lynn Dougherty, 1996), the books *Freak Babylon* by Jack Hunter, *American Sideshow* by Marc Hartzman, *Truevine* by Beth Macy, *Ward Hall – King of the Sideshow* by Tim O'Brien, and the brilliant novel *Geek Love* by Katherine Dunn. The Showmen's Museum in Riverview, Florida, is definitely worth a visit.

I owe debts to many, but particularly to my agent, Claire Roberts; to Hannah Woodlan, Suzanne Bradshaw, and the good folks at Koehler Books; to the team at Books Forward, including Marissa DeCuir and Jackie Karneth; to the writers Jeff VanderMeer, Kristen Arnett, Chris Bohjalian, Michael Farris Smith, and Katy Simpson Smith; to Sally Bradshaw and my friends at Midtown Reader; to Sara Marchessault and all the Word of South folks; and, of course, my wife Greta and family, without whom I could do none of this. Thank you, all. I am so very grateful.

www.ingramcontent.com/pod-product-compliance
Ingram Content Group UK Ltd.
Pitfield, Milton Keynes, MK11 3LW, UK
UKHW031107170325
456354UK00005B/374